The Harp of Kings

"This big-hearted novel completely transported me to the wonder and enchantment of ancient Ireland—and its resonance lingered long after the final page."

—Callie Bates, author of *The Soul of Power*

"Breathtaking, often heartbreaking. . . . This lush fantasy is sure to win Marillier many new fans."

—*Publishers Weekly* (starred review)

"A cast of characters that will not be forgotten. . . . A must-read for any fan of fairy-tale lore and historical fantasy." —*Booklist*

"Lush world-building and well-rounded characters."

—*Library Journal*

"Marillier's enchanting characters, immersive details, and truly stunning prose have all helped crown her an undisputed queen of the fantasy genre. *The Harp of Kings* is no different; readers new and returning will be undoubtedly captivated by Marillier's newest tale." —*BookPage*

"Juliet Marillier is a master storyteller." —Books of My Heart

Praise for Juliet Marillier and Her Fantasy Novels

"An enchanting tale."
—Jacqueline Carey, *New York Times* bestselling author
of *Starless*

"A fabulous read, a rich tale that resonates of deepest myth."
—Kristen Britain, *New York Times* bestselling author
of the Green Rider series

"A simply gorgeous story with wonderful, intriguing, and complex characters."
—Karen Brooks, author of *The Chocolate Maker's Wife*

"Utter perfection." —The BiblioSanctum

"Enchanting and haunting. . . . Rich and incredible. Marillier has the world-building down to a science!" —The Eater of Books!

Also by Juliet Marillier

The Warrior Bards Novels

THE HARP OF KINGS

The Blackthorn & Grim Novels

DREAMER'S POOL
TOWER OF THORNS
DEN OF WOLVES

The Sevenwaters Novels

DAUGHTER OF THE FOREST
SON OF THE SHADOWS
CHILD OF THE PROPHECY
HEIR TO SEVENWATERS
SEER OF SEVENWATERS
FLAME OF SEVENWATERS

The Light Isles Novels

WOLFSKIN
FOXMASK

The Bridei Chronicles

THE DARK MIRROR
BLADE OF FORTRIU
THE WELL OF SHADES

HEART'S BLOOD

PRICKLE MOON

For Young Adults
The Wildwood Novels

WILDWOOD DANCING
CYBELE'S SECRET

The Shadowfell Novels

SHADOWFELL
RAVEN FLIGHT
THE CALLER

BEAUTIFUL

A
DANCE
with FATE

———◇◇◇◇———

Juliet Marillier

ACE
New York

ACE
Published by Berkley
An imprint of Penguin Random House LLC
penguinrandomhouse.com

Copyright © 2020 by Juliet Marillier
Penguin Random House supports copyright. Copyright fuels creativity,
encourages diverse voices, promotes free speech, and creates a vibrant culture.
Thank you for buying an authorized edition of this book and for complying with
copyright laws by not reproducing, scanning, or distributing any part of it in any
form without permission. You are supporting writers and allowing Penguin
Random House to continue to publish books for every reader.

ACE is a registered trademark and the A colophon is a trademark of
Penguin Random House LLC.

Library of Congress Cataloging-in-Publication Data

Names: Marillier, Juliet, author.
Title: A dance with fate / Juliet Marillier.
Description: First Edition. | New York: Ace, 2020. | Series: Warrior bards
Identifiers: LCCN 2020011381 (print) | LCCN 2020011382 (ebook) |
ISBN 9780451492807 (trade paperback) | ISBN 9780451492814 (ebook)
Subjects: GSAFD: Fantasy fiction.
Classification: LCC PR9619.3.M26755 D35 2020 (print) |
LCC PR9619.3.M26755 (ebook) | DDC 823/.914—dc23
LC record available at https://lccn.loc.gov/2020011381
LC ebook record available at https://lccn.loc.gov/2020011382

First Edition: September 2020

Printed in the United States of America
1   3   5   7   9   10   8   6   4   2

Cover illustration by Mélanie Delon
Cover design by Adam Auerbach

To the dogs I've loved and lost,
especially Harry, Zen, and Fergal

CHARACTER LIST

Pronunciations are provided for the more difficult names.
Note: *kh* is a soft guttural sound, as in the Scottish *loch*.

SWAN ISLAND

Liobhan (*lee*-von)

Brocc

Dau (rhymes with *now*)

Archu (*ar*-khoo)

Cionnaola (kin-*eh*-la)

Brigid (breed)

Illann

Cuan

Haki

Eabha (*eh*-va)

Fergus: resident healer

Criodan: island druid

Guss

Hrothgar

Yann

Garbh (gorv)

Eimear (*ee*-mer)

Deirdre: herbalist in mainland settlement
Jabir: Moorish healer
Saran: lawman from the court of Dalriada
Gáeth: steward at a house on the way to Oakhill

OAKHILL

Lord Scannal: Dau's father, chieftain
Seanan: Dau's eldest brother
Ruarc: Dau's second brother
Beanón (ban-*ohn*): Lord Scannal's lawman
Naithí (no-hi): Lord Scannal's councilor
Ardgan: Seanan's body servant
Gobán: Lord Scannal's body servant
Ultán: Seanan's henchman
Donn: man-at-arms
Canagan: man-at-arms
Morann: man-at-arms
Fergal: master-at-arms
Iarla: steward
Torna: former steward, now deceased
Berrach: one of Seanan's men
Padraig: stable hand
Caol (kehl): stable hand
Torcan: stable hand
Fionn: head farrier
Íonait (*ee*-nit): Fionn's wife, assistant cook
Mongan: stable master
Corb: kitchen hand
Niall: in charge of wall-mending crew
Miach (*mee*-akh): household herbalist
Lughan: groom
Tomas: groom

Davan: crippled man in Liobhan's story
Flannat: beautiful girl in Liobhan's story
Cian: a musician
Master Fiachna: scribe

ST. PADRAIG'S

Brother Íobhar (*ee*-var)
Brother Petrán: infirmarian
Brother Pól: assistant infirmarian
Brother Martán: apothecary/herbalist
Father Eláir: prior
Brother Máedóc: formerly a lawman

FAIRWOOD

Lord Ross: chieftain
Cormac: his son
Sárnait (*sar*-nit): his daughter

OTHERWORLD

Brocc
Eirne (*ehr*-nyeh)
Rowan
Nightshade
Gentle-Foot
Moth-Weed
Thistle-Coat
True (Elouan)
Nimble-Swift
Moon-Fleet
Conmael

OTHER CHARACTERS MENTIONED BY NAME

Blackthorn: a wisewoman, mother of Liobhan, Brocc, and Galen

Grim: father of Liobhan, Brocc, and Galen

Galen: their elder son, body servant and minder to Prince Aolu

Aolu (*eh*-loo): crown prince of Dalriada

Oran: king of Dalriada, father of Aolu

Faelan: king of Breifne

Juniper: a wisewoman

1

LIOBHAN

It's a glorious day. The sun is warm, the clouds are high puffs of white, the sea is as calm as it ever gets around Swan Island. We're sitting on the bench seats at the combat area, tingling with anticipation, knowing today's celebration marks the end of many months of grueling work. Work that we've loved and hated. Work that has tried us to the edge of our endurance and stretched us to the furthest bounds of our ability—though, as Archu has told us, in a crisis you can always find a bit more to give. Work that has forged not only four warriors fit to join the island's permanent force, but also four true friends.

They don't choose many. When we started training there were twenty in our group. Fifteen went home. My brother Brocc was lost on our first mission. Not dead; gone to the Otherworld, in a strange and baffling series of events. I miss him every day. I think of him every time I sing. I'm afraid he will never come back.

"All right?" murmurs Dau, who's sitting beside me.

"Fine." I sound sharp, but I can't help it. I so wish Brocc was here with us, enjoying this day, sharing our success. "Look, there they are!"

We jump to our feet, shouting encouragement as our fellow trainees walk out onto the combat ground, staves in hand.

They have the next display bout, then it's Dau and me. We're well warmed up, ready to go, but we're not going to miss watching Hrothgar and Yann show their talents. A great noise goes up, the voices of every resident of Swan Island cheering the combatants. There's nobody off on a mission at present, so there's a crowd of nearly sixty watching: fighters, trainers, the folk who support the work of the island, and the elders: Cionnaola, our leader; Archu, our chief combat trainer; Brigid and Eabha and Haki and the others. They're the best of the best. Those lucky enough—and talented enough—to be trained here are highly sought after when kings and chieftains need a task completed that's beyond the ability of their own men-at-arms. Or their own spies, if they have them. Sometimes our missions fall somewhat outside the rules of law. We do covert work. Secret work. That's why we live and train in such an isolated place. It's why few outsiders come here. And it's why the training period is so long. They've not only been testing our physical skills, they've been making sure we're trustworthy. Making sure we won't crack under torture. And making sure we can think for ourselves. It's unusual for them to take four new fighters at once. We know how lucky we are. And we know we've earned it.

Hrothgar and Yann enter the combat space. The field edge is marked by a circle of rope laid on the ground. The combatants halt, facing the elders, and with staves held upright they bow. Cionnaola gives a grave nod of acknowledgment. The crowd is quiet now.

"Three coppers on Hrothgar," whispers Dau in my ear.

"Done." Hrothgar, a Norseman, is taller and broader than Yann. But the Armorican has a talent for deception. That makes him dangerous. Yann's beaten me once or twice, using that skill, and I know it's a mistake to underestimate him.

The two turn to face each other and bow again. They assume

a fighting pose, staff gripped in both hands, one near the end, one partway up the shaft. They move about, backward and forward, jabbing in turn, each looking for an opening. Both men wear protective leather helms—those things get hot as an oven and you end up with sweat obscuring your vision, but for this sort of fight you need them—and padded jerkins over their trousers and tunics.

"Wait for it, wait for it," murmurs Dau. "Ah!" as Yann loses patience and rushes forward. His intention is clear: to knock aside Hrothgar's staff, then jab his own toward the other man's midriff. But he's not quick enough; the end of Hrothgar's weapon strikes Yann's arm hard. I know what that does: your fingers go numb for long, precious moments. Yann skips back out of reach, winces, shaking his hand, flexing his fingers.

"Playactor," mutters Dau.

I can't argue. When Yann grips his staff again, he's moved his hands; now they're a handspan further along. This will place the staff slightly further away from Hrothgar than before. Yann's used his own error to his advantage. And now, under cover of a momentary hesitation, he puts one foot forward but leans his upper body back. "Clever," I murmur.

Hrothgar thrusts high to low, aiming for his opponent's chest. If Yann hadn't tricked him, this would be a bout-ending move. But Yann is closer than Hrothgar expected. The Armorican shifts his weight to the front foot and slides his staff through his front hand straight into Hrothgar's chest, between the lower ribs. Hrothgar folds. He can't breathe. His hand goes up in the gesture, *I yield*.

The crowd roars. Yann steps back, waits for his opponent to catch his breath—it takes a while—then stands beside Hrothgar again as they acknowledge the applause.

Dau and I don't wait to see them walk off. It's our bout now. The last of the day; an unarmed combat, best of three rounds.

"Can't bet on this one," says Dau with a crooked smile as we make our way down to the combat area, where someone is raking the ground, getting it ready for us. Folk do have a habit of throwing things when they get excited. Dust rises around the rake.

"But if you could, you'd bet on yourself to win, no doubt."

"No doubt. I'd wish you good luck, but I want Bran's Blade, so I won't."

"Skill beats luck," I tell him, pausing to put on my helm. Gods, I hate these things! They get even hotter when you have a lot of hair to squash in, as I do. I've been tempted to cut my hair short, but when I'm not fighting I'm a musician, and the long hair feels right when I dress up to perform. And useful when I'm working under cover and needing to look more like an ordinary woman and less like a Swan Island warrior.

At a gesture from Archu, Dau and I walk together into the combat space, where all is now in readiness. Folk cheer and shout as we go; this is a joyful day not only for us but for the whole community. A special day. Bran's Blade is displayed on a cushion, next to Cionnaola. It will be awarded to the most outstanding fighter, not only of today but of the whole training period. It's an old, well-kept dagger, beautifully balanced, of plain design apart from the tiny image of a bee in flight carved on the oak hilt. This weapon is said to have belonged to the man who founded Swan Island long ago, a man who was called an outlaw but who showed great heart, spirit, and generosity to his fighting team. His son and his grandson were in their turn part of the island community, and there are descendants of that original crew still among us. Nobody gets to keep Bran's Blade forever. One of us will be given it today, to look after and to use until a new custodian earns the privilege through some act of outstanding valor or skill. A training and testing period such as the one that saw me and my three comrades win places on the island happens only rarely. It's more usual for fighters to join the community one at a time, each coming here by his or her own path. You have to be capable. You have to be skilled. And you need the right attitude. I thought Dau lacked that when I first met him. His manner was arrogant, scornful, aloof, as you might expect from a chieftain's son. The mission changed my opinion. It changed both of us. But the old rivalry still remains. We both want Bran's Blade. We both want to be the best.

We salute the elders, bow to Cionnaola, position ourselves within the rope guideline.

"Three rounds," calls out Archu, informing the crowd of what we already know. "Win two and you're the victor. Set foot outside the boundary and you lose that round immediately. No eye gouging. No groin strikes. Remember it's a display bout, not a fight to the death. Break those rules and you'll not only forfeit the fight, you'll be emptying privies and hauling goods up from the ferry for a good long while. Understood?"

This is probably meant for me. I do have a reputation for using dirty tricks to win if the situation requires it. But I know better than to try that today of all days. Dau and I both nod and murmur, "Understood."

"Begin," calls Archu.

I have a plan. As we dance around, I edge toward the rope. Close enough? Yes! I dive for Dau's knees, aiming to send him toppling back. But as he falls he twists, managing to land inside the field. I grab at his leg. He slips from my grasp, and almost before I know it we're both on the ground. He's got me in a hold we call the crab, with him underneath me on his back, his legs hooked over my hips and his arm around my throat. Shit! It's yield or pass out within a count of five. I lift my hand and make the yield sign to show I'm forfeiting the bout. Dau relaxes his grip. I suck in air. I'm shaking with fury as we disentangle

ourselves and rise to our feet. Not angry with Dau. Furious
with myself for not seeing that coming. For being too slow. A
pox on it! Now I have to win both remaining bouts. I stand. I
make myself breathe. This wretched helm is driving me crazy;
it's so hot and I'm sweating like a pig. I unbuckle the strap and
take the thing off, throwing it beyond the field edge. It's not
compulsory to wear them for unarmed bouts; we're supposed
to use our own judgment. After a moment, Dau takes his own
helm off and discards it. Gives me a little smile, or more of a
smirk. In that expression I see the old Dau, the one I didn't like
much, and I grit my teeth. I'll win this one and the next. I want
Bran's Blade. If I win it, I'll be the first woman to do so; even
Brigid, a seasoned fighter and a combat trainer, has never had
custody of the weapon.

"Go, Liobhan!" yells someone from the crowd, and a chorus
of shouting follows, some for me, some for Dau, some for both
of us. I steady myself. Bout two and I need to get the advantage
quickly.

"Begin!" calls Archu.

Dau closes straightaway for a grapple, but I'm expecting that
after the last bout. I duck under his grab and drive my elbow
into his liver. Cruel. But effective. He groans and collapses,
curled up on himself in agony. When he can make himself
move, he stretches out a hand and signals *yield*.

I help him to his feet. Part of me wants to say sorry. He's
my friend and I've hurt him. But you don't let friendship get in
the way of a good fight. One more round and I've got it. Dau's
weakened by that blow. I can do this. I look across and meet
his eye. He's a bit pale and he's breathing hard, as I am. Sweat
sheens his face and darkens his fair hair. His eyes are narrowed;
his jaw is set tight. I glare right back at him.

"Begin!" comes the call.

We circle. No sound from the crowd now; a deathly silence lies over all. Then, lightning quick, Dau feints a straight punch at my stomach. I grab his arm and pull him further off balance, then hook his foot out from under him. He stumbles, rolls, recovers, is back on his feet.

Keep moving, Liobhan. I go for his waist. I'm a better fighter on the ground than he is. If I can tackle him down . . .

He slides free and ankle-taps me. I stumble, fall, roll to my feet, and put a few steps between us to buy time. He grins. Too cocky by half. I'll win this. I have to.

I grab for Dau's leg. He skips back out of reach, catches his foot on something, and falls heavily. His head hits the ground so hard I hear the thud. I move to leap on him and get him in a leg lock, but suddenly I'm still. The crowd falls silent.

Dau is lying faceup on the hard-packed earth, with his arms flung out wide like those of a sleeping child. His eyes are closed. His face is a ghost's, sickly pale, and he's very, very still. My heart skips a beat as I kneel down beside him. There was a time not so long ago when I thought I'd killed a man simply by pushing him away a bit too hard. That man lived, and so will Dau; he's breathing.

"Step back, Liobhan." Archu is beside me, and others are striding toward us: Cionnaola and Swan Island's resident healer, Fergus. I move out of their way, but I'm not going anywhere until I know Dau's all right. People do get knocked out from time to time during our practice bouts; you can't run a school of warcraft without people sometimes injuring each other or themselves, though all our training is carried out under strict rules to keep us safe.

Dau still hasn't moved. Fergus performs various checks, then shakes his head and murmurs to Archu, who calls out, "Stretcher!" Two men bring the stretcher; four men, under the healer's direction, lift Dau extremely carefully onto it, keeping his body as still as they can. I want to help, but Archu motions me away.

They carry the stretcher out at a snail's pace, as if the slightest jolt might do the occupant damage. Archu and Cionnaola stay behind. They're examining the spot where Dau fell. As I watch, Archu lifts something out of the earth. It looks like a leather cord with something strung on it, maybe a good-luck charm. The sort of thing that folk throw, sometimes, when they get excited. Too small to be dangerous. Or so one would think.

"He may have tripped on this," says Cionnaola. "Easy enough to miss it with the rake." He glances toward the onlookers, who are talking together in hushed voices. "Sheer bad luck." He turns to look at me. "You didn't see this?" He shows me briefly, then slips the little item in his pocket. It's a token in the form of a bird, and I know who it belongs to, as Cionnaola likely does—the daughter of one of our cooks. A child of five, so excited by the fighting that she threw her lucky charm into the ring. I didn't see that, but I heard her screaming, *Come on, Liobhan!*

"No. It must have been partly buried. There was a lot of dust blowing around." I glance over toward the gate, where the stretcher is at this moment being carried out of view. "Will he be all right?"

"I can't answer that." Archu sounds grim. "You'd best go back to your quarters, Liobhan." Perhaps seeing something on my face, he softens a little. "I'll make sure you're kept informed."

I go to my quarters and fetch clean clothing. Then it's the bathhouse, where I strip off what I'm wearing. I scrub every inch of my body. I undo my hair from its tightly plaited combat style and wash it. I dry myself and get into the gown and overdress

I've brought with me, slipping my feet into soft shoes. I bundle up the shirt and trousers to wash later. I go to the armory and clean my leather jerkin, my belt, and my boots until they're spotless. One or two people are about, but I don't look at them and they don't speak to me. By the time I get back to the women's quarters—much smaller than the men's, since most of the island's population is male—I have my fears under better control. But I can't get the image out of my mind. Someone once described Dau as a handsome prince from a tale. That was how he looked: a dead prince, fallen on the battlefield in the flower of his youth, golden hair dusty and bloodied, lids closed over the sky-blue eyes, skin shadowy pale. How long will it be before Archu has news for me? Dau must be conscious by now, surely?

I hang around outside the women's quarters for a while. Everyone's left the combat area. People have returned to their work, and outwardly this looks like any clear spring day on the island. The breeze has got up. It's turning the sea to whitecaps. Gulls circle and wheel overhead, crying out. Everyone will be busy. Some will be preparing the evening meal, tending to sheep or chickens, repairing drains or buildings or drystone walls. Some will be practicing with weapons or maintaining their fitness by climbing or running or doing exercises. Some will be doing other forms of training. Swan Island must always have people ready to be sent on a mission. Calls for our expert services can come at short notice. That's what happened last summer, when we went under cover as traveling minstrels—Brocc and I were chosen because of our experience singing and playing back home. Oh, I so wish he was here with me now. Why hasn't anyone brought news of Dau?

I pace up and down awhile, asking myself questions with no answers. In the end I go to the infirmary to find out what's happening, even though Archu told me to stay in the quarters. The door to the stone building is ajar, but there's no sound from inside. I don't know if that's good or bad. I stand outside waiting until Archu spots me and comes out, closing the door behind him.

"Liobhan. Best if you are not here right now."

His carefully controlled tone makes me sick with worry. His expression is somber. A flood of words is ready to burst from me, but I hold it back. Instead I say quietly, "I just want to know how he is."

Archu sighs. "That was a severe knock to the head, and Fergus tells me it was in a particularly delicate spot. Dau has regained consciousness, but he's not well. He's in pain and confused, as you might expect. And . . . it seems his sight may be affected."

A chill breath of dread passes through me. "You mean—how bad—may I see him?" I put a hand up to my mouth, press the back of it against my lips to shut myself up. Otherwise I'll wail or curse or do something stupid.

"Fergus says no visitors. He requested the assistance of another healer, and we've sent for that man. Until he arrives, Criodan's helping." Archu folds his arms and gives me a direct sort of look. "I see you're upset, and I understand why. But you're not needed here at present."

"But—" *But Dau's my friend. I want to know he's all right. I want to know that he'll be able to stay here and fight and have a future.*

"Liobhan. Go. And stay away this time. Make yourself useful elsewhere."

Yann and Hrothgar find me as I'm washing my clothes with such violence that they threaten to come apart at the seams. One of the good things about living on Swan Island, and there are many, is that you're surrounded by comrades, and those comrades understand how it feels when you get things wrong. Hrothgar, the tall Norseman, hauls himself up to sit on the workbench with his legs dangling, and Yann asks in his soft

Armorican accent if I'm all right. I shut my eyes for a moment, my hands still in the washtub.

"Want to talk about it?" asks Hrothgar.

I lift the trousers out of the trough and wring them out hard. Yann reaches past me without a word and does the same with the shirt. "Have you heard anything?" I make myself ask. "Any news on how he's doing?"

"Nothing yet. I heard him shouting, earlier. Sore head, I suppose. He went down hard."

"Shouting what?"

"Not words. Just angry noises."

I'm silent as I go out the back to hang the garments on a line, where the wind will dry them quickly. The two men follow. We stand there awhile looking out toward the mainland. There's a small settlement over there, part of the Swan Island community. It houses a secretive training establishment known as the Barn, a stable block and exercise area for horses, and accommodation for the folk who work there. Dau and I trained for our mission in the Barn, with my brother. Gods, was that only three seasons ago? The mission, losing Brocc, having to go home and explain to my parents, then coming back here and working myself to the breaking point to win a permanent place—all of that between one summer and the next spring? Today's display should have been a celebration of our achievement. It still can be. Dau may appear at suppertime, a little pale and unsteady but managing a wry comment or two and a bite to eat. He may be back to his old self by tomorrow or the next day. "I heard they were getting a healer from the mainland," I say, wondering if what I see out there is one of our boats or a fishing vessel from elsewhere.

The men don't comment.

"He tripped on something so small. Just a strip of cord and a tiny amulet. I don't know how it could do so much damage."

"He struck his head hard." Yann's voice is grave. "These things happen, even when you are careful. Simple bad luck."

"It was my fault." I make myself say it. "If he'd been wearing his helm he wouldn't have been so badly injured. He took it off because I took mine off. To make the bout fair. And look what happened."

"You can't blame yourself," says Hrothgar. "This was pure accident. And removing the helm was Dau's choice."

There's a long silence then. I suspect the two of them are thinking what I'm thinking. Eventually I say it; better to get it out now, to my friends, than have to ask Archu or, worse still, Cionnaola, who is the highest figure of authority on Swan Island. "What if he's really badly hurt? So badly that he can't stay on here? What would happen?"

"That's a question for the elders, not us," says Hrothgar.

"Folk do sometimes stay on after injuries," says Yann. "If there is other work they can do, something that is needed." That's true, as far as it goes. A person with a lame leg could still maintain weaponry, draw maps, devise strategy, teach others. A damaged arm would mean no more combat, but that person could still keep night watch or help look after the sheep. A head injury is more challenging, but the codes of Swan Island, the ones we all live by, mean the community stands by its wounded and broken. There's a warrior named Guss on the island, a man of around forty who has bouts of dizziness and confusion from a blow to the head. He's big and strong, but he can't fight anymore. They could have sent Guss home. But Swan Island had been his life since he was a young man of our age, and he had no other home, so they found a job for him. He lives in a lean-to at the back of the druid's hut. He fetches Criodan's meals, helps tend his little garden, and does other useful things such as mixing ink and gathering quills for pens. He and Criodan watch over each other, and the whole community watches over the two of them. Swan Island may be full of fierce fighters, but tolerance and compassion rank high on its list of codes. And there's work for everyone. Or there should be. I can't think of any job on the island that would be safe for a blind person, and from the looks on my companions' faces, I deduce they've reached the same conclusion. Nobody's asking the hardest question: *What if he dies?*

"He'll get better," Hrothgar says. "This is Dau we're talking about. He's unbreakable."

"Unstoppable," says Yann. "Before you know it, he will be fully recovered. Meanwhile enjoy the reprieve from his biting wit."

Suppertime comes and there's still no news. The mood in the dining hall is subdued. On most nights we have music after the meal, and sometimes dancing—we work long, hard days and that's a good way to end them. Generally the band consists of Archu on the bodhrán, me singing and playing the whistle, a woman named Eimear on a second whistle, and whoever else feels like joining in. My brother Brocc is a skilled harpist whose singing voice could melt the stoniest of hearts. Every time we play without him, I feel his absence as an ache in my chest.

There will be no music tonight. I don't even bother taking my whistle with me to the hall. There's a chill in me that runs deep. I can't keep my thoughts in order. *If he's going to die, they would have told us.* That's no comfort at all. *Maybe they just can't work out what's wrong.* Very possible, since they sent for the second healer. And if that man is not yet here, we may have to wait until morning for news. The healer might have been in the middle of setting a broken leg or delivering a child. He might live some distance away.

"Liobhan?"

Hrothgar digs me in the ribs, jolting me back to the here and now. How long have I been sitting over my untouched meal staring at nothing? Archu is in the doorway of the dining hall. He looks tired and sad. The whole place has gone silent.

"We'll be moving Dau across to the mainland in the morning," Archu says. He's working on sounding calm and confident, with some success. "Fergus will go over with him, and the other healer, when he arrives, will meet with them there. We can look after Dau more effectively at the Barn, at least until we have further insight into his condition." A pause. I glance at my companions—Yann on my left, Hrothgar on my right—and hope someone will ask the question I can't ask.

It comes from Brigid, who is seated at a different table. "How is Dau faring, Archu? Has his condition improved at all?"

A murmur goes around the hall; everyone is concerned. Dau may have a habit of rubbing folk the wrong way, but he's one of us.

"I wish I had better news for you," says Archu. "He's drifting in and out of consciousness. In pain and not making much sense. He still has no vision. We must hope that condition is temporary."

Before anyone else can get a word in—it's clear people want to speak—Brigid says, "No more questions now. You can see Archu's tired. Someone fetch him food and drink. And let us eat in peace. We're all concerned. And we all know Dau will receive the best care that can possibly be provided. In the morning you get up as usual, you eat your breakfast, and you get on with your work."

Archu leaves most of his supper. He drinks his ale, has a quiet word with Cionnaola and Brigid and some of the other elders, then leaves the hall. Since he's given no sign of wanting to talk to me, I don't follow him out with my own questions. I'd like to go to the infirmary and offer my services. My mother is a healer and I couldn't have grown up in her household without learning useful skills. I could sit up with Dau overnight so Fergus could catch some sleep. I can make poultices and administer drafts, and I know when to call in someone with more expertise. But it feels like I'm the last person who should offer.

The night is endless. Either I'm lying wide awake on my bed trying not to disturb the other women or I'm having nightmares so black I wake drenched in sweat and shaking. Before dawn I get up, dress, and walk all the way to the other end of the island and back, so fast that if Brigid could see me she would reprimand me for taking unnecessary risks on the cliff paths. Which would be funny if I could find the least scrap of fun in me anywhere, because when Dau was asked to assess my performance in our shared mission—Archu does that kind of thing—he identified my tendency toward risk-taking as both an asset and a liability.

When the community buildings come into view I slow my pace to a brisk stride. I'm not a great believer in gods or their capacity to respond to our prayers. But I pray now, a childish sort of prayer to anyone who might be listening. *Let him be better today. Let him speak properly, even if it's only to curse his misfortune. Let him open his eyes and see.*

Archu is up early, too. He's coming along the path toward me, wearing his big fur cloak as if ready for travel. We meet and halt.

"Liobhan." His tone is grave and kind and deadly serious. "We're taking him over on the boat after breakfast. He had a restless night and is much the same this morning. I want you to come with us. Go and pack a bag. The healers need an assistant who knows what she's doing."

"Of course. I'm glad I can be of some help."

Archu folds his arms and looks down at the ground. "There's something further you need to know. We've sent a message to Dau's family, telling them he's been seriously injured and asking what they want to do. If they send someone here it's possible, even likely, that the person may want to speak to you. You understand why we would not want their representative on the island."

I do understand. The code of secrecy is long established in the Swan Island community. The more folk learn about what we do, the harder it becomes to keep missions covert and the less likely it is that we'll be hired. That's not all. Many of our folk have secrets they don't want known, dark events of the past that are best set behind them. The island code forgives the time before a person joins us; all that is asked is that the new arrival treads a different path from that moment on, a better, wiser, braver path. So yes, I understand what he's saying, and in Dau's case it's horribly ironic. His kinsfolk possibly coming here? That can't happen.

Around us dawn is breaking; the sea is turning from lead to sparkling gold. Birds wing their way out from the ledges, calling to one another. How do I frame the next question? When Dau told me about his past, it was in strictest confidence. "Did you consult Dau about sending his family a message? I know he wouldn't want that. You may not be aware that they are . . . estranged. Worse than that. Much worse." It took a long while for Dau to start confiding in me. Growing up, he suffered terribly at the hands of his brothers, and it scarred him deep. His father did nothing to stop it. Dau ran away from home at thirteen. He once told me he hoped he would never see his brothers again. "What if his father decides to take him home? That is the last thing Dau would want. The very last thing."

Archu sighs. "We tried to ask him, of course," he says, "but he's in no fit state to give us a coherent response; when he's conscious, he's not lucid. The elders discussed it at length, I promise you. Dau came to us from a place other than his family home; we did understand he had lived elsewhere for some

time, young as he is. We wouldn't have accepted him for training without knowing his origins. He gave us his father's name,
the place, no more. He's very badly hurt, Liobhan. We don't
know if the healers will be able to help him. And . . . to be blunt,
there's a possibility he won't survive this. His father is a chieftain, a man of means and influence. We came to a decision that
we should advise the family. Just as we advised your family
when your brother left us so abruptly."

"That was different," I say, knowing I shouldn't argue the
point, but unable to forget the look on Dau's face when he
spoke of his brothers. "My family is not like Dau's."

"We are obliged to tell them, whatever they are like. Fergus
thought he might die during the night. If he survives he may
be blind. His mind may be affected." Archu hesitates.

I wait. Whatever's coming, it's not good.

"The situation is complicated by our own need for secrecy.
We don't want Swan Island under public scrutiny; the less this
tale is spread abroad the better. So, we've advised them early.
We've made it clear the injury was accidental. We've let them
know we have two expert healers on the job and that we will
cover the cost of treatment."

"Did they even know Dau was on Swan Island? He wouldn't
want—"

"We felt it necessary to advise them, Liobhan. As I've explained."

I mutter a coarse oath, then an apology. "Sorry. But he'll
hate this. He'll hate it so much. What if they decide to come
here? To confront us face-to-face?"

"To the extent we can, we must go along with the family's
wishes in the matter. If you're to be useful you must exercise
self-control, even if you don't like the way this is being handled."

"I understand." What I understand is that this is going to be
a real test, and a hard one.

"We have time to prepare. Their family holding is quite far away; closer to the scene of our mission in Breifne than to Swan Island, but further to the east. And I imagine that even if they do come here, we'll have due notice."

"You'll come over to the settlement, too?"

The ghost of a smile crosses Archu's broad face. "I'll be there. I carry my own share of the responsibility for this."

"I should go and pack," I say. "Shall I ask Hrothgar to pack a bag for Dau?"

"Thank you. Just a change of clothing and his small personal items. For now, at least."

As I return to the women's quarters, where the others are just starting to stir, I consider those last words. They sound ominous. Still, the other healer hasn't seen Dau yet. Someone did say he's an expert on head injuries. Perhaps all will be well. By the time an answer comes to the message, Dau's vision may be fully restored and his head clear. If that happens, the first thing he'll want is to have that final bout again. I think of him beating me and claiming Bran's Blade, then trying to keep the grin of triumph from his face as he pays me the three coppers he owes me from our wager on Hrothgar and Yann's fight. I want to see that. I want to see my friend smile again. Winning a fight, claiming a prize, making the elders proud—right now, none of that seems to matter.

2
DAU

Sounds screech and clash and assault my ears. My head shivers like a bell struck by a heavy hammer. My eyes hurt. My neck hurts.

Some of the sounds come from my own mouth. I can't stop them. Groans, moans, grunts, shouts. But not words. The words are in my head, but they won't come out right. I'm hot, then cold, then hot again, throwing off the blankets and shouting at Fergus as if this were his fault. Archu is close by, I hear him talking though he's keeping it to a murmur, and I shout at him, too, I curse and swear and rage, and it's the garbled ravings of a crazy man. If this is how things are going to be from now on, I'll be out of this hut the first chance I get and I'll run for the cliffs and hurl myself off. At least that way it will be over quickly.

They put me on a boat. The sea goes up and down and I am sick. Someone wipes my mouth and I push them away, hard. Then there's someone holding me, someone strong, and I sit there in the dark as the ferry bounces over the waves and my face is damp with sea spray and I hear the birds screaming farewell. If I could pray, I would pray to be as I was before. But I do not believe in gods. Men are cruel. Fate is cruel.

I can see almost nothing. One eye looks out on utter darkness.

The other opens to a shadowy world, all grays, in which shapes move but cannot be identified.

I cannot fight. I cannot ride. I cannot be the warrior I have worked so hard to become. I cannot be strong. I am as I was before: the helpless child, the boy without answers, the one who lived with fear.

I wish I believed in gods.

3

LIOBHAN

Dau won't talk to me. He hardly talks to anyone, though at least now he can make himself understood. For a while I wondered if his wits were damaged along with his eyes, and although Fergus and the other healer, a soft-voiced, dark-skinned man named Jabir, never spoke about this in my hearing, I know they did, too.

I hate what's happening to Dau. When we were on the mission he had to pretend he couldn't speak; that was part of his cover. And he was good at it. The handsome prince, the proudest of the trainee warriors, put in a convincing performance as a mute stable hand. I see that voiceless lad in him now, on the rare occasions when he comes out from the isolated part of the Barn where he's being tended. He can understand us. His responses make that clear. But he's all closed in on himself, like a beaten animal hiding away in a dark corner. The healers are doing their best. They're making sure he eats, and getting him up and walking around with one or both of them to help. They're trying different things with his eyes.

Jabir has told me quietly that Dau prefers I do not tend to him. That's like a slap in the face, though there are plenty of other tasks to keep me busy. I gather herbs for the healers; I prepare soothing eyewashes and various tonics. When Fergus and Jabir don't need me, I help muck out stables, I fetch water, I sweep floors and chop wood. I help prepare meals. I run through the exercises that keep me strong. There are other Swan Island fighters training at the Barn, but they stay out of our way most of the time, and I don't ask them about their upcoming mission—if they're over here that will be what they're preparing for. I see them at mealtimes and I sleep in the same communal quarters, where a screen separates men and women. Right now I'm the only woman at the Barn. In the settlement around it there are eight separate houses, and families live in them, but they're all part of the Swan Island community. One husband-and-wife team builds and maintains fishing boats. Others look after the horses that are stabled here for the purpose of training us in mounted combat and to provide transport when required. A former fighter, injured on duty and now reliant on the aid of a stick for walking, looks after the pigeons that carry messages between Swan Island and various strategically situated friendly households—these are dotted all over Erin. There's an herbalist, and she has her own stillroom attached to her cottage. That gives me an idea.

"Have you tried a wash with parsley and calamint?" I ask Jabir when I encounter him outside the Barn, taking a break from his duties. "My mother finds that effective to reduce inflammation of the eyes. And there's a tea that can be brewed from dried holly leaves; I don't suppose we'll have time for that, but I could gather the leaves and start the drying, just in case." When Jabir does not reply immediately, I add, "I know that kind of remedy won't restore his sight, but the wash will help with the pain, and the tea will provide some ease of mind."

"By all means gather the herbs and prepare the wash," Jabir says. "Ease of mind . . . I wish we could provide that for him now. He is greatly troubled. In despair, I think. Unable or unwilling to help himself. That makes our task harder. We have few answers."

It's good to get away from the Barn for a while. Because this place is, in effect, an outpost of Swan Island, I have to get Archu's permission, then speak to the guards on duty as I walk out of the settlement—they need to know where I'm going and for how long. They advise me to keep an eye out for trouble. I have my big knife at my belt and a little one hidden in my boot, as well as the implement I use for cutting herbs. As I set out toward the woodland with a willow basket over my arm and my trousers on under my skirt, I must look like a curious mixture of herbalist and fighter. But I'm still within the domain of Swan Island, a place quite unlike the outside world. I love life on the island. I love combat, I love testing myself and becoming stronger and facing new challenges. I love living among comrades with the same zest for this unusual existence. And I love the cliffs and crashing waves and wild skies of the island itself, so different from the quiet forest where I grew up. But I hate what's happening now. My friend had a wretched childhood. Now he faces an uncertain future. If anyone deserves to stay on Swan Island and be a warrior, the best of the best, it's Dau.

I harvest the herbs I need, finding them in a sunny clearing to the south. There's holly in the woods. I cut some of that as well, in case we're here long enough for me to dry out the leaves. Those tasks done, I take off my boots and sit beside the stream for a while, letting the cool water run over my feet and thinking of the time when I had to go home and tell my parents that Brocc was gone. Dau came as my escort, and our household was a shock to him, I could see that from the first. He couldn't quite believe we were so kind to one another. He seemed astonished that my father was so patient, always ready to listen if someone needed to spill out their woes, always offering a word of comfort or advice or plain common sense. My father is a man of quite intimidating appearance; folk who don't know him often expect him to be slow-witted and belligerent. In fact he's the opposite. It's my mother who is short-tempered, though she works hard to keep it under control. I wish she were here now. I can see her marching into the sickroom and giving the patient a sharp talking-to. *What's happened has happened,* she would say. *It's hard, I know. But you're strong, you're brave, you've got folk who care about you. Shouting and throwing things is the response of an unruly child, Dau. You are a grown man.* I wish I could do that. But he doesn't want me.

I walk back to the settlement and head for the herbalist's cottage, where Deirdre, a youngish woman with her dark hair tied back in a kerchief, finds me a corner in her stillroom and leaves me to prepare my wash while she completes a decoction. Three cats weave around her ankles while she works, one ginger, one black, one tabby striped. Deirdre has heard about Dau. Both Fergus and Jabir have asked her for advice.

"Do you think he'll get his sight back eventually?" I don't want to hear the answer, but I ask the question anyway. "Have you seen anything like this before?"

She takes her time to reply. I concentrate on chopping the leaves and try not to think too hard. "Like this, no," Deirdre says eventually. "I've seen a man blind from a sickness, who got his sight back, partly at least."

A glimmer of hope. "What was done to treat that man?"

"A long period of rest. Leeches. Poultices. But it was different from your friend's condition. Not caused by a blow, but by ill humors of some kind. Those ill humors left his body with time, and his eyes recovered quite well."

"Quite well?"

"He was a shepherd. He didn't regain full vision, but he could see well enough to do the job safely."

I don't reply. To do what we do on Swan Island, Dau needs to be able to see keenly, sharply. *Quite well* won't be good enough. And he's not the kind of man who'll be content to feed the chickens and turn the compost heap.

"Try your eyewash and your holly tea," says Deirdre. "We do what we can. We have to make our peace with that."

I feel an unreasonable anger rising and I squash it down. None of this is Deirdre's fault or Jabir's or Fergus's. It's not mine either, though guilt hangs over me anyway, a personal dark cloud. It's chance, it's fate, it's horrible ill luck. And when I've got everything ready, when I've said farewell to Deirdre and walked back to the Barn, I find out just how ill that luck really is for Dau. Because a pigeon has come in with a message from Lord Scannal. His representative is on his way here, and he's bringing a lawman with him.

4

DAU

Fergus makes me walk. Up and down, up and down. Around the Barn, so I can hear the sounds of people training, the clash of blades, the knock of staves, the shouts of encouragement or challenge. At first I walk with my arm through his, a degree of intimacy I find humiliating. Then I put my hand on his shoulder, which means I either trip or bump into things. He doesn't always warn me. When I challenge this, he says I will learn to sense objects close at hand and to avoid them. What utter bollocks.

It is quite clear they do not expect me to regain my sight, though nobody is prepared to tell me this. They think, perhaps, that I would shout, throw things, run mad. They wish to be kind to the crippled man, the man who was ruined at the very moment of achieving his goal. What is supposed to be my goal now? To walk twenty feet without falling over? To eat my breakfast porridge without spilling it down my shirt? A pox on that!

Jabir is kind. So kind, I want to hit the man.

Then, one afternoon, things change. Jabir is washing my eyes with a cool, sweet-smelling mixture. It feels good; I am forced to admit that. There's a knock on the door and it's Archu.

"I'll come in, if I may," he says. "Dau, how are you feeling today?"

I want to deliver the withering response this platitude deserves, but I shrug and grunt instead.

"Liobhan's eyewash is effective, simple as it is," observes Jabir, telling me something I didn't know. "I will ask her to gather more of the herbs and to show me how she makes it up. The inflammation has reduced further."

There's a silence, then Archu says, "I have some news. A message came earlier today. From your family, Dau, in response to our notification of your injury."

I stand up so violently that there's a crash and a splash and an exclamation from Jabir. Before I can move further, strong hands restrain me.

"Calm yourself," says Archu. "Use what you've been taught. You may not be on a mission now, but you are still one of us. Now sit down. No matter how badly hurt you are, you exercise self-discipline at all times. Yes?"

What complete rot. I'm blind, I'm useless, and he expects me to go on acting like a warrior? What am I supposed to be fighting, dreams and shadows?

I sit. Archu moves his hands to my shoulders. He keeps holding on until my breathing calms. The man has patience. I can't slow my heart. It's drumming hard. The monster of the past is on the hunt and it's closing in on me. "News," I make myself say. It comes out as a strangled squeak. "What news?" Inside me the trapped child is muttering to himself, *Don't let them come here, don't let them find me, don't let them take me . . .*

"To say your father is displeased would be an understatement." Archu moves to seat himself a little further away. I hear the scrape of wood on slate as he shifts the bench, and beside me the soft sounds of Jabir mopping up the spillage and retrieving the pieces of his broken bowl. "He assumes that if your condition doesn't improve soon you'll need to return home—no, Dau, sit easy—and that you'll require an escort to Oakhill. He makes it clear that he wants some answers."

I'm so full of fear and rage and darkness that I hardly know what will come out of my mouth. I can't be the warrior Archu still wants me to be. That man's gone, vanished in an instant on the training ground. There's only this man, this helpless apology for a man whose eyes are brimming with tears. My teeth are clenched so tight my whole jaw aches. "I'm not going back," I say. "I'm not going. They can't make me."

Archu doesn't tell me I sound like a child. He waits awhile, and Jabir returns to bathing my eyes; there is a second bowl, I suppose, and a generous supply of whatever it is Liobhan made. Why is she over here anyway? She should be back on the island doing her work. There was no reason for her to come here.

"We need to talk," Archu says. "Or rather, I need to explain some things to you, and you need to sit quietly and listen. I understand your fury, Dau. I understand how frustrating this must be for you. But you are still a member of our Swan Island community and I need you to put the community's needs ahead of your own. Will you listen while I explain?"

I don't nod, because I know it will hurt, but I grunt a yes. Who'd have thought those skills I exercised on our mission in Breifne, where I played the part of a mute man, would come in useful now?

Archu explains the need to avoid all eyes turning to Swan Island if there's a fuss about what's happened to me. He reads part of the message from my father, sent by pigeon to the court of Dalriada and carried on here by one of King Oran's riders.

*You supply scant detail of this incident. That leads me to
ponder exactly what the true circumstances may have been.*

*How is it possible that a man could suffer such a serious
injury outside a situation of real conflict? Quite clearly the
incident requires further investigation. My representative
will be accompanied by a lawman, since it may be necessary
for this matter to proceed to a formal hearing. You tell me my
son may be blind. He is not yet twenty years old. You might
consider—*

"Well, never mind that." Archu falls silent. I hear a crackle;
perhaps he has set the parchment down on the table.

"Read the rest." I want to hear all of it. The false compassion,
the sudden interest in my welfare, the tone of lofty superiority—
six years have passed since I ran away from home, but it's plain
my father has not changed at all. When Archu does not reply,
I growl, "Read it!"

Archu clears his throat. Jabir is using a soft cloth to dry my
face gently. The eyewash has run down my cheeks like fragrant
tears.

*You might consider what compensation could possibly be
adequate for snatching away a young man's future prospects;
for robbing him of the best part of his lifetime. You might
weigh up the cost to a family of supporting a kinsman who
will be completely dependent on others for many years. My
representative and his party are traveling to your location as I
write this. All being well, they should reach you in less than
twelve days. I will expect you to receive them and to ensure
appropriate discussions take place promptly. If my son is well
enough to travel, and if it is established that his condition
cannot improve sufficiently for him to remain with you, the
party has the means to convey him back to Oakhill.*

I don't shout this time. I don't try to leap up and blunder out the door. Here at the Barn there are no cliffs close by, only watchful guards. But what I feel must show plainly on my face, because Jabir puts his hand on my shoulder and Archu says quietly, "I would have spared you that. But the fact is, this representative is already on the way, he will want answers, and it's in your best interest that we prepare ourselves as well as possible. We'll need our own lawman."

I find my voice. "I'm not going. I'm not going home. I'm a grown man and I'm not answerable to my father."

Another silence. "Jabir," Archu says, "you might take a walk in the garden, perhaps find yourself some refreshments. I'll stay with Dau until you return."

Jabir retreats. I can barely hear his footsteps.

"I explained to Liobhan and I'll explain to you why it's so important that we keep this contained," Archu says. "The less information spreads to folk outside the Swan Island community the better." He tells me what I can guess already: that if there's a legal hearing, too much attention will fall on Swan Island. Our activities, most of which are secret, may be exposed in a way that threatens the island community's future. The local folk have an idea of what we do. Further afield we are either a mystery or unknown, and that's the way the elders want it to stay. None of them wants a formal hearing. If my father demands compensation in silver it will be paid, though the amount will be negotiable. If he wants something else, they'll try to provide it.

"Whatever he wants," I say, trying to still the shivering that has taken over my body, "you can be sure it doesn't include welcoming me back home. That part is lies. I was never wanted there. They despised me even when I had all my faculties."

Archu doesn't try to contradict this. "Nonetheless, he sent the letter. And when his representative and the lawman arrive, we must deal with them. Dau, understand that when we made the decision to notify your father, we feared you might not last the night. You're seriously ill. Yes, you are not a child but a man, and a man makes his own choices. We must hope this injury does not limit those choices. Fergus is capable. Jabir is highly qualified. But your father, with his resources, may well be able to find someone more expert, someone with a deeper understanding of your condition. And his household will surely accommodate you in more comfort than we can do on the island or here at the Barn. You say they don't want you back. But years have passed since you fell out with them. Is it not possible the situation has changed? Or might you yourself not take steps to change it?"

Hah! Change the household at Oakhill? Not in a thousand years. Is Archu telling me there's no future for me on Swan Island, or even here at the Barn? No work I could possibly set my hand to? The answer must be yes, or he would offer, surely. I can't bring myself to ask. I can't bear to hear him say it.

My mind goes down a devious pathway. They could lie. The elders could tell this representative that my eyes are slowly improving and that if I stay under the care of Jabir and Fergus for long enough, I will fully regain my sight and resume my place in the warrior band. They could point out that they are paying for my care. The representative could report all that back to my father, whose annoyance at not receiving a bag of silver in compensation would be outweighed by his relief that I am not, after all, coming home to be a burden to him for the rest of my life. I consider telling Archu that if he insists on sending me back I will kill myself before it can happen. I know where the weapon store is, here at the Barn. I wonder how it feels to slit your own throat.

"Liobhan told us you were estranged from your family," Archu says quietly.

"Estranged. You could put it that way. What else did Liobhan say?" If she's betrayed any confidences I'll kill her. Only I won't, because now that I'm blind she'll win any fight hands down.

"About your family circumstances, very little. She was upset to hear that we had contacted them without consulting you first. We did try to do that, Dau. At that point you were not capable of understanding." He goes quiet for a little, then adds, "I thought you and Liobhan were friends. It might do you good to talk to her."

I've told them a thousand times that I don't want to talk to Liobhan. The moment I hear her voice I'll be reminded all over again that I'm not the fit and healthy person I was. That I'm not the man who once heard himself described as a handsome prince. That I can't be a Swan Island warrior after all. I can't be any sort of warrior. I can't even be the man who cleans the weapons and mends the boots, or the one who mops the floor, or the one who keeps the sheep from wandering where they shouldn't. "There's no point," I growl.

There's a silence. I hear Archu move. He's leaving. Good riddance. I don't want him and his bad news. I don't want Jabir and his gentle voice. I don't want anyone.

"Dau," says Archu, and his tone has changed. This is the voice he uses on Swan Island when someone makes a mistake, and I don't mean fumbling a combat move. He speaks like this when someone breaks the rules for daily life, the ones that keep our community orderly. Yes, it's a place devoted to the art of fighting. But that makes it all the more important, the elders told us when we were new to the place, that we practice courtesy toward others and learn to listen. I've just broken that rule. Not that it matters, since I no longer belong here. "I remind you, again, that you are still part of our community," Archu goes on, as if he can guess what I'm thinking. "I am your senior on Swan Island. However furious you are at what fate has delivered, I still deserve your respect. You will address me and whoever else comes your way with that same respect. Without those codes, Dau, Swan Island could never have grown and developed into what it is."

All right, I'm a seething mass of resentment right now, underlain with sheer terror, but I haven't forgotten how much I learned from this man, or how much freedom he allowed me and Liobhan on our mission, freedom that could have led to disaster but ended up making the whole thing a brilliant success. Apart from the loss of Brocc, of course. Some part of me knows I'm being unfair to Liobhan. If I try to explain to Archu, I'll sound selfish. She's fit and strong, I'm not. She's still a Swan Island warrior, and whatever Archu may say, I'm not. Hearing her voice will bring back a lot of memories. Memories that tell me, now, what the future might have been.

"Dau?" He's waiting for a response.

"I'm sorry."

"Good. Now I have one more thing to say to you. As your elder and as your trainer, I want you to talk to Liobhan. You will do so today. I'm not asking, I'm telling. If you want someone else to be present, we can arrange that."

"Why must I talk to her?"

"Because," Archu says, "I suspect she's the only one who can talk some sense into you. So please conduct the meeting in a civil fashion. Keep your temper. Use the opportunity to talk about what happens next."

"She—" I stop myself before I can say, *She knows nothing.* Because, of all the people I've met since I came to Swan Island, not counting a certain old woman in Breifne, Liobhan is the only one who knows how bad things were at home before I ran away. I haven't told her everything; some of it, I can't make myself say aloud. But she knows a fair bit. Which means she will understand why I can't go back there, couldn't go back even as a fit, strong fighting man, and most certainly can't go as a crippled burden on my father's resources. It would be like walking willingly into a torture chamber. If anyone's likely to help me, it will be Liobhan.

"All right, I'll do it. And I don't want anyone else there. I promise not to attack her."

Archu does not speak.

"Not even with words," I add.

5

BROCC

B rocc!" Rowan motions me over to where he stands beneath an old oak. There, among its tangle of roots, a dark form is splayed out in a drift of feathers. There's blood. The thing's claws are curled tight, but there's nothing in them. Its eyes are open but unseeing.

"Don't touch!" I warn as he crouches down beside it. "Make sure it's dead."

"It's dead." Rowan's tone is flat as he picks up a stick and pokes it at the corpse, which rocks eerily to and fro against the tree roots. The leaves above us rustle in the wind; out in the forest the birds are quiet. We look down at the creature. This is the first time we have been so close to one of the Crow Folk, the strange beings that have established themselves in both Eirne's realm and the human world, creatures neither bird nor animal but something else entirely. I have fought them with song and with fire. I have seen them killed with knives. I have seen what remained of one of Eirne's small folk after they had ripped it apart. I still do not know what they are, only that they attack without warning and without any discernible pattern.

Since I came to live here among the Fair Folk, Rowan and I have set up regular patrols to keep watch on our strange enemy. Although I am now Eirne's husband, he is still her protector, her

right-hand man. I am content with that. The last thing I want
to do is displace or offend any of her people. It must be strange
enough for them that their queen has chosen a man of humankind to rule alongside her. Though I am not entirely that. I
have both fey and human blood, and so does Eirne. I was raised
in one world, she in the other from the time she was five years
old. Her folk love her. Me, they tolerate. They like my music; I
am the first bard to live here in many years.

"It's still warm," I say, examining the dead thing more closely.
It smells vile, like rotting fish. I use a stick to lift one wing, to
investigate the dark-feathered body, so much bigger than that
of an ordinary crow. I peer more closely at the fearsome beak,
which gapes slightly open, and the glazed, staring eye.

Rowan looks up into the oak, then scans the forest all
around us. "I see no more of them," he says. "Unusual for one
to be out alone. How did it die, I wonder."

The creature has wounds; beneath the tree roots on which
it lies, the ground is stained with its blood. "Look here," I say,
lifting the other wing and wishing I could bring myself to
touch the thing with my bare hands. "This is no attack by wolf
or eagle. These cuts were not made by a desperate man or
woman fighting to survive. They look . . ." What I see is hard
to believe; hard to make sense of. In the tender area under the
wing, the creature's skin has been burned away in narrow
strips, exposing the raw flesh beneath. The strips are in a pattern, though the swelling makes it hard to see the exact shape.
But it looks almost like an Ogham sign or a rune of some kind.
A brand of ownership? A mark of magic?

"And there, on the beak." Rowan points. "Perhaps the same
symbol. Not burned, but carved with a small, sharp knife.
Who could have got close enough to do that? We know how
ferocious these things are."

"I want to turn it over. Will you help me?"

Rowan looks somewhat like a fox, and somewhat like a young man. I have no trouble reading the reluctance on his face; he, too, does not want to touch. But we take one wing each and turn the creature awkwardly onto its front. "Some claws damaged," Rowan says. "See here? And some cut right off."

"It's lost a lot of feathers." And there's something else: a collar of raw flesh right around the neck, swollen and festering. "Died of wounds," I murmur. "But such strange wounds."

We look at each other.

"Torture," says Rowan. "Here, in Eirne's realm. None of our folk would do this. Nor could they; the Crow Folk are too strong."

"It may not have been done here. The Crow Folk move freely between worlds, as birds and animals do. Sorry as I am to admit it, Rowan, I suspect the hand of humankind. But I don't understand why. There's a degree of cruelty here that troubles me greatly. We'd best head back and report this to Eirne."

But we hesitate, the two of us, standing over the broken body of an enemy.

"We can't leave it like this," I say, though my mind pictures our encounter with the Crow Folk last summer and the way they destroyed one of our little ones and hurt another. "We should lay it to rest." We're far out in the forest, a long walk from the area where Eirne's folk gather. Rowan has his knife of bone and I have a staff. The ground here must be full of tree roots; we won't be digging a grave.

"You possess far greater compassion than I, Brocc," Rowan says. "Perhaps that comes of being a bard. I hate these stinking things. If I could burn it, I would. But there is a shallow cave not far from here. We could lay it there. Perhaps cover it with what we find nearby. You might sing a song over it, if you're feeling particularly tenderhearted."

He's teasing me, of course. We are friends. But when the creature is placed in its final resting place, hardly a cave, more a small hollow under a rocky overhang, and when we have laid a blanket of leaves and twigs over its damaged body, with fallen branches to shield it, I stand quiet, considering. A death is a death, whether it be of friend or foe, one's own kind or an alien kind. The Crow Folk are cruel, destructive, and willful. Their attacks make no sense. They do not eat their kill but leave it lying. They do not defend territory; some travelers they let pass unmolested, others they swoop upon with talons at the ready, to rip and slash and ruin. But there must be a reason for their madness. I have wondered if some malign spell was cast over them, if they were driven from their home, if perhaps they watched the unfolding of events so terrible their minds were forever blighted. This one has been killed in a particularly vile manner. No battle set those scars on its body. Rowan was right; it has been tortured to death. So I sing, not in the way I did when I drove them to the borders of Eirne's realm, using my voice as a weapon to strike fear into them, but gently, as to a sleeping child.

> Be at peace, your flight is o'er
> Fold your wings on peaceful shore
> May love and goodness wrap you close
> Farewell to pain and grief and loss.

Rowan steps forward to lay a small flower on the creature's final resting place. It's only when we are making our way back home that he asks me, "Is that a human thing, that you sing fair words over such a foul being? You know what they are. You have seen what they do."

"Unless it died at the hand of one of its fellows, and the

nature of the injuries did not suggest that, it seems the Crow Folk do not have a monopoly on evil deeds. And . . . I wonder why they are the way they are. If we could know that, if we could talk to them, that might give us the key."

Rowan makes a noise that tells me just what he thinks of that idea. It is indeed impractical. They see us coming, they attack. And if they don't attack, they stay high in the trees, watching. They are wild. Unpredictable. Violent. How would a man go about communicating with such a creature? How could I do such a thing without risking not only my own life but those of all Eirne's folk? I must be mad. A mad minstrel.

I wish Liobhan was here. My sister is the voice of common sense, the voice of practical solutions. She is brave and decisive. I miss her so much. Eirne is my beloved, and I am fond of the strange beings that make up her clan. Along with Rowan, several others have become close friends to me. But Liobhan is my sister. We are almost of an age; I was left on her parents' doorstep less than a season before she was born. We grew up doing everything together: playing and singing, running and climbing and learning to fight. When I went with her to Swan Island to join the warrior band I thought we would both stay there. Together forever. But it was not to be, and now here I am, wed to an Otherworld queen and, I suspect, about to displease her greatly.

We find Eirne in consultation with Nightshade, her sage. Nightshade has something of the owl about her looks, but in form she is a woman. As for my wife, she might pass for fully human, as I did for so long. Eirne's hair is brown and glossy; today she has it plaited and pinned up high. Her eyes are a limpid gray, her complexion is like the petals of a wild rose, her expression is sweetly inquiring as she rises from the fallen tree on which she and Nightshade were sitting and steps forward to greet me and my companion. "You were away a long time," she says, going up on tiptoes to give me a chaste peck on the cheek. "We were concerned."

I love my wife. For her I gave up my life in the human world, the precious gifts of family and home. I gave up much that was dear to me. But here in the Otherworld I am still finding my place. When it gets hard I think of Eirne's story—reclaimed by her fey father at the age of five, brought here and left among the unusual folk who make up her clan. At that tender age she discovered she was a queen. Rowan and Nightshade and the others taught her how to rule, how to keep the peace, how to protect her folk as best she could. I am here to help them all; that is my life now.

Sometimes I am a little afraid of Eirne. She is the sweet young woman who sings with me and walks through the woods with me and shares her bed with me at night. But she can turn in an instant to the fey queen who rules over this realm, the one whose anger is like a knife to the heart. I believe Eirne truly loves me. But she does not always listen.

"We found one of the Crow Folk, dead." I come straight out with it. I know that if I don't tell the full story, Rowan will, so I go on, "Killed most terribly, perhaps by torture. We laid it to rest as best we could. There were no others of its kind in sight."

"The bard sang over its resting place," says Rowan. "Not the kind of fell song he uses to drive them off, but a song such as one might sing over a comrade fallen in battle. Or a dead child."

Eirne turns her lovely light-filled eyes on me. She says not a word.

"It was a cruel death," I say. "The wounds had not been made by beak and claws, but by other weapons, and by burning. I did not want to leave the creature lying where it was, out in the open."

"The Crow Folk are our enemies. They are malign. You say

this was a cruel death. What, then, were the many deaths these evil things have inflicted on our own people? Are they not cruel? What of our defenseless little ones, ripped bodily apart and left to die in their blood? You think the Crow Folk worthy of dignity in death? You think them worthy of compassion? You are a warrior, not a priest, Brocc. You are becoming too soft."

Eirne's words hang in the air for a little; the rest of us are silent. Rowan looks down at the ground. Nightshade has turned her big eyes on me. I cannot tell what she is thinking, but she is a sage and will have weighed the matter up in her mind. Eirne's cheeks are flushed; her lips are set tight.

"I am no priest," I say, holding on to calm. "Only a bard. And sometimes a warrior, yes. The Crow Folk have performed terrible acts of violence. They have killed and maimed. They do not discriminate between good and bad, strong and weak, humankind or animals or Fair Folk. But . . ." I glance at Nightshade. "But do you never consider *why* they behave as they do? Might not discovering that be the key to ending their attacks? I find it hard to believe they act thus for no reason at all."

"And yet that is exactly how it is," says Eirne. She gets up and paces to and fro, her arms wrapped around herself. "We've seen it over and over. They will be the death of us; they will be the end of our people. Why would you waste your music over such a creature? Why would you waste your tears?"

She cannot understand this. At such times I am reminded that she has spent far more of her life in the Otherworld than I have of mine; it is less than a year since I came here. In ten years' time, in fifteen, will I be like her in my thinking? Will the fey part of me outweigh the human? That troubles me. The Fair Folk often seem lacking in compassion; they find it hard to put themselves in other folk's shoes. "The song was not wasted, Eirne," I say quietly. "It was a recognition of suffering; it was an acknowledgment of pain and loss; it was a wish that all creatures could rest easy. Perhaps it was only for the singer, who knows? An attempt to make sense of the senseless."

"You speak wisely." Nightshade gives me a grave nod of recognition. "My lady, when we face the darkness, when we face a battle whose odds seem impossible, is it not good to explore every pathway that might lead us into the light?"

"You side with the bard." Eirne is sharp. She has her back turned to us. I know how the long struggle against the Crow Folk has wearied her. I wonder if she hoped her bard and warrior, her new husband, would find a way to banish them forever within a season or two of his arrival in the Otherworld. Alas, I am not so remarkable a man.

"A sage does not take sides," Nightshade says. "She listens; she muses; sometimes she offers suggestions."

"And a bard sings and plays. Sometimes a song will come when he does not expect it; sometimes a moment calls for music." I should stop talking before I say something I regret. Before Eirne tells me a queen decides how things will be done and others obey. Her husband included.

"Your voice is our most powerful weapon, Brocc. Your singing is the only thing that has halted their advance. We have used fire, of course; their fear of it holds them back briefly, until our brands die down or our bonfires are quenched by the rain. But since you came here, since you sang your song of death and flight, they have retreated to the very margins of my realm. At least . . ." Eirne lifts her brows in question.

Rowan has been very quiet. Now he speaks. "The creature we found dead was within the boundaries of our forest, yes. Far to the east but not yet beyond Breifne's borders."

"In my realm? Or in the human world?"

Rowan is uncomfortable. He drops his gaze, not meeting Eirne's eye. Officially, our patrols go only as far as the edges of Eirne's realm. Our duties do not extend to pursuing the Crow

Folk into what was my own world. To do so would put Rowan in particular at great risk; most people out there think the Fair Folk a thing of ancient story, long gone. Perhaps never real. He would be viewed as a freak, an oddity, something to be poked and prodded and kept for show. But as the Crow Folk move easily between worlds we cannot track their movements without sometimes crossing over. We have not spoken of this to Eirne. Not yet.

"Close to the place where the human kingdom of Breifne, King Faelan's land, meets that of the neighboring territory," I say. "On the very eastern edge of the forest."

Eirne simply looks at me.

"I cannot tell you if the creature was killed within this realm or in the human world." I will not make this a confession. I refuse to be a child caught out in an act of naughtiness. I am her husband. Her equal. "We laid it to rest close to where we found it. There was no way to tell what had befallen the creature, save what I have already told you of its wounds."

Still she does not speak. The silence draws out until I feel deep unease. This response is too much. Neither stepping over the border between worlds nor singing kindly over an enemy's corpse justifies it, in my book. Is something else awry? What have I missed?

"Come," says Eirne, her voice tight. She holds out her hand to me—this seems a good sign—and at the same time dismisses both Nightshade and Rowan with a jerk of her head. Her mouth is set grim and when I take her hand I feel the tension in her body. She leads me in the direction of the gathering place, but before we reach it Eirne takes a side path into a different part of the woods. Here the trees grow close and the ground is always shaded. A streamlet flows between banks blanketed by water-loving herbs, cresses and the like. Before us a narrow bridge crosses this small waterway, a thing made from a single willow pole. It is a bridge for folk no bigger than the tiny birds that go between Eirne's realm and the house of Mistress Juniper the wisewoman, carrying messages. A mouse could traverse this bridge warily; a marten could sprint across.

"Over here," Eirne says, leading me toward this delicate construction.

I will not step on the willow pole and crack it. Even her slighter weight could not be supported there. "Let me," I say, and lift her in my arms as if she were a child. I take one careful stride across the stream, then set her down on the opposite bank. For a moment she lays her palm against my chest and looks at me with warmer eyes.

"I need to show you something, Brocc. Up here. Come quietly, we don't want to scare them."

Scare whom? I walk with her, treading as softly as I can. There's a rocky outcrop not far off, surrounded by thickly clustering bushes. Eirne leads the way around this until an opening comes into sight, half-concealed by that dense growth. She motions, finger to lips: *Shh.* Do I hear movement from within that secret shelter?

Eirne opens her mouth and calls softly. She does not use words; her cry is like that of a bird at the earliest moment of dawn, melodious, gentle, almost tentative. I could write a song about that.

There's a response: a tiny echo of the same sound.

"I have the bard with me," Eirne says, still keeping her voice down. "May we come closer?"

"Come."

We move to the opening, a low arch into a shallow cave. Too low for a person of my height to crawl through. The little shelter is well concealed from curious eyes, not only those of humankind but also those of predatory birds, though I imagine a fox or badger might find the place easily enough. Within is one of Eirne's smaller folk, Gentle-Foot, a being of human shape, but clearly no human, for she comes barely as high as my knee and her body is covered with soft brown fur. I remember that I have not seen Gentle-Foot at our evening gatherings for some time, and when I see what she is cradling in her arms I realize why. I make a small involuntary sound of surprise and wonder, and Eirne glances at me, smiling.

Gentle-Foot has a baby. It is the first young one I have seen in all the time I have lived among Eirne's folk. I do not need to be told how wonderful this is, and how frightening.

Eirne drops gracefully to sit cross-legged on the ground outside the little cave. I kneel beside her. "How is he faring, Gentle-Foot?" Eirne asks.

"Well, thank you, my lady. He has a good appetite, and so do I. Moth-Weed has gone to fetch food; he will be back soon."

I'm thinking hard. Thinking of beaks and claws and how far it is to the gathering place from here. The young one would be a single mouthful for a hungry owl. Gentle-Foot herself would be no match for a fox. She and Moth-Weed and the little one need guarding. Or they need bringing in to the area where more of Eirne's folk live, so we can all watch over them. But I hesitate to say so. Eirne's face is tender as she regards mother and child; Gentle-Foot looks on her infant with glowing pride. The tight unease in my belly is at war with the delight in my heart; already my thoughts are on the song I will make for this day.

"We will wait with you until Moth-Weed returns," Eirne says. "Your child is remarkable, Gentle-Foot. Precious beyond any jewel." No doubt she, too, is thinking how vulnerable they are out here, even in such a well-hidden shelter. Perhaps she is thinking that if Rowan and I were not taking risks out on the borders, we could stand guard over them. And there is a bigger, longer game in play. This child is a sign of hope. Its birth brings the possibility of renewal in Eirne's realm. Her people may grow and flourish and become stronger, especially now Faelan has come to the throne of Breifne in the human world, a king who respects and understands the old things. More children may come. But the Crow Folk linger; my presence here is not enough to keep them away altogether. And they still wreak havoc in the outside world. By bringing me to see mother and infant, Eirne is telling me I cannot afford a moment's weakness. I imagine her thoughts now, as she chats with Gentle-Foot in the quiet of the forest. *One day you lay a creature to rest with respect and with music. The next day one of its fellows seizes this most tender of small ones and rips it apart before its mother's eyes. If you would deal with the Crow Folk, you cannot afford softness, Brocc. You must be as hard as iron, and as cruel.*

6

LIOBHAN

It's a testament to Dau's abilities, I suppose, that even now he's blind he manages to creep up on me and make me start in fright. I'm doing something I haven't done for a long while: playing my whistle. Archu said to pack only essential items, but to me this is essential. It'll stop me from going crazy waiting for Dau to get better, or for this deputation to arrive from Lord Scannal, and let me say my piece before I turn into a snarling monster who couldn't watch her words if you offered her a bag of silver and a fine riding horse for her trouble.

I'm in the area where horses are exercised now, and because it's a fair way from the Barn and there's nobody around, I'm taking the opportunity to run through a new jig I've been creating, checking whether what I hear in my mind translates well to the instrument. If the tune is a little too hearty for the situation, too bad. I suppose someday, who knows when, I'll return to the old routine of being a warrior by day and a bard by night.

So I'm working through the last part of the jig, adding embellishments and cross-rhythms, which takes some concentration, especially when the player's a little rusty, and a voice says right behind me, "Liobhan." Then, when I nearly jump out of my skin, he adds in something resembling the supercilious tones of old: "You're slipping. What happened to being watchful?"

I stick the whistle through my belt, get to my feet, and turn, all in a moment. There he is, apparently all by himself, with a stick in one hand, which I assume is to feel for obstacles before he crashes into them, and an expression on his face that makes me want to cry, because it's the ghost of the old one from our first training days, when he used that superior manner to make a wall around himself. He sounds every bit what he doesn't want to be: a chieftain's son and a man of privilege. I could say something cruel. I could say, *Keep that up and you'll fit right in back at home.* But instead I say, "This seemed a safe enough spot. There's a bench here, about two paces ahead and to your right. Let's sit down and talk." I don't offer to guide him. I wait for him to find it. He leans the stick against the bench and seats himself beside me. He's lost weight; his face is bones and shadows. He was so strong before. A comrade to be relied on in battle, a fighter who would test me to my limit even in the bouts he lost. I hate to see that strength draining from him. It shouldn't happen. I want to ask if he's feeling better, but he'll slap me down for that, so I hold my tongue.

We sit there for a while. Long enough to hear the whickering of horses in the nearby stable and sounds of activity from elsewhere in the Barn, where people are still preparing for a mission, and the creak of cart wheels as someone from the settlement goes by on the road that links our outpost to the wider world.

"Why are you here?" Dau asks suddenly. He has his arms folded and his blind gaze straight ahead.

"You mean here playing the whistle in this particular spot, or here on the mainland?"

"Both, if you feel like talking."

He's going to make this difficult. That's no surprise. "I'm

supposed to be helping the healers. But since I've been told you don't want me in there, I've been making myself useful any way I can." When Dau says nothing, I go on. "Archu's been drilling me. He thinks that when this deputation comes from your father, they'll want to talk to me. He wants to be sure I won't lose my temper and make things worse." There, I've given him an opportunity to accuse me of poor judgment in choosing to fight without a helm. I've given him the chance to curse and shout at me all he wants. I almost wish he would, but he sits there quiet as a mouse. His jaw is tight and his hands are balled into fists. When he still doesn't speak, I decide to take a different approach. "And I'm here on this bench at this moment not so much because I wanted to work on a new tune in a place where I wouldn't disturb people as because Archu said I could talk to you at last, and I needed time to think what to say."

"If that's the best you can come up with," Dau says with some bitterness, "the time was insufficient. You want to know why I'm here, Liobhan? I'm here because Archu said I had to talk to you whether I liked it or not. And it seemed best to do so privately."

"If you want to shout and swear at me, go right ahead."

It's quiet again for a while. Perhaps he's got all his shouting and swearing done; I've been overhearing quite a lot of it. Then Dau says, "Can we walk around the stables? You might have to help me."

Oddly enough, it's this perfectly ordinary-sounding request that puts tears in my eyes. "Of course. What's easiest for you, a hand on my shoulder or arm in arm?"

"Shoulder," he says, getting up. "Warn me about steps or narrow places. Morrigan's curse, this is like being suddenly sixty years old and frail with it."

Dau and I are close to the same height. He is tall for a man; I am very tall for a woman. We go side by side, his hand on my left shoulder. While I'm there he doesn't need the stick, so I carry it. I can't broach the subject of his future or what happens when his father's representative gets here. That has to come from Dau. He must have been told what I've been told, though perhaps in different words. For now, I'm pleased that he's prepared to talk about anything at all. Even more pleased that he trusts me enough to walk about with me.

Once in the stables, Dau brightens a little. A dog comes over to him. He knows it's there without my needing to tell him. He reaches down, offers his hand for it to sniff, then strokes its neck and scratches it behind the ears. A groom walks over to talk to us. We go around the stalls with him and admire the horses, fine riding animals, some trained for mounted combat. I pause beside each horse, and Dau, his hand on my shoulder, pauses with me. He asks the groom each horse's name in turn and takes time to touch them and speak to them quietly. He asks questions about their care. They're the sort of questions that come only from a person who has done the job himself. When we're finished he thanks the groom, and the two of us go out to sit at the far end of the stables, on a seat near the tower-like structure where messenger pigeons are housed. It's a quiet spot; there's nobody around. I note it as a good place for future whistle practice or even singing, then wonder if that would unsettle the birds.

Dau leans forward, elbows on knees. He's calmer, I think. He loves animals. He's a lot better with them than he is with people.

"Liobhan?"

"Mm?"

"Would you agree that you owe me a favor?"

I didn't see that coming. "Because of what happened, you mean? You can't think—" I shut my mouth before I say the wrong thing. Not that I'm sure what the right thing is.

"Not that. You owe me a favor because I helped you over the wall, when you went searching for Brocc. I helped you break the rules."

This is true. When I needed to go and bring my brother home, when I needed to do exactly what Archu, as our mission leader, had told me not to do, Dau helped me perform an extremely risky exit from the royal fortress of Breifne—risky not only for me but for him as well, since that maneuver could have seen both of us lose our places on Swan Island. I'm not sure I want to hear whatever it is he wants me to do now. But I have no choice. "Is Archu going to regret telling us to talk to each other?" I ask.

"I don't care what he thinks. Liobhan, they've told me I'll stay blind. Not in so many words, but I know what they mean. Unless a miracle cure comes my way, I'm never going to be any use to anyone again. Don't interrupt!" He must have heard me draw a sharp breath, about to contradict him. "Do me the basic courtesy of waiting until I'm finished, will you? You know my father's sending someone here."

"Yes."

"I can't wait for that. They should never have sent word to him. He didn't care then, he doesn't care now. All he wants is a fat payment for what's happened to me. I'm not going back home. Not ever, Liobhan. When I left, I left for good. I can't stay on Swan Island. I understand that." Dau's trying to put a calm argument to me, but with every word his voice is getting rougher and angrier. What is it he wants from me? "And Garalt is dead. I can't go back to him."

Garalt was Dau's mentor, a man with the courage and foresight to befriend the troubled youth and teach him how to be strong. He was Dau's only friend in those dark times. "What is this favor?" I ask.

Dau is silent for a while. "If we'd still been on the island," he says eventually, "I'd have asked you to take me to the edge of the cliff, then turn your back and walk away."

I swallow a curse half-spoken. Make myself breathe.

"But that can't work here," he goes on. "Will you lend me your knife? Or make me up a potion, you know the kind of thing I mean?"

I'm so angry I could hit him. "You can't just give up! Morrigan's curse, Dau! It's early days yet; you might get your vision back, or enough of it to do useful work on the island. Or here at the Barn for that matter, tending to horses. You know how good you are with animals. There must be other healers, other folk they could consult . . ."

His shoulders are set rigidly. "I have nowhere else to go. I have no future. What you suggest is false comfort. False hope. I can't be here when my father's representative arrives. You're the only person I can ask, Liobhan. The only person with the guts to help me."

"To help you kill yourself. Next thing you'll be asking me to do it for you."

"Liobhan. Please."

A pox on the whole thing! I've got tears streaming down my face now, and my heart's going like a galloping horse. Can he actually imagine I would say yes?

"Dau. You're a strong, fit, healthy man of nineteen. Except for your eyes, every part of you is still working perfectly well. There might be a cure. Fergus and Jabir don't know everything. You have to give this a chance. You have to hold on to hope."

"That's a no, then."

"It's a no to that particular question. If you were dying in agony on the battlefield and there was no hope of saving you, I'd consider using my knife to put you out of your misery. But this? I wouldn't dream of it. Has it occurred to you that if I helped you I'd be up on charges of unlawful killing? You may feel bitter toward me after what happened, but I think that would be quite out of proportion to the offense."

There's a long silence, during which I try to work out how I can get a message to Dau's carers about keeping sharp objects out of his reach while not divulging something so deeply private.

"I want to go back in now."

In Dau's voice I hear the child he was, the child beaten and tormented and terrified by his brothers right under his father's eye. I want to wrap my arms around him in a hug of reassurance, but I don't. I wish I could make promises of a better future, but I can't. I think of a wager, the sort Dau and I have a habit of making when we're in tight corners. I'd wager that he would regain his vision within, say, a year. He'd be quick to bet against me. The odds would be clear. A win for me would put everything right. A win for him would mean I had to do what I just refused to do: end his life as a farmer might that of a crippled sheep, with one strong, sure slash of the knife.

As I guide his hand to my shoulder, ready for the walk back, I'm shivering hard, and Dau must feel it. But he says nothing at all, not until we reach the place where we met and he takes back his stick. "I can find my way from here. Archu said you'd talk some sense into me. I'm not sure what he meant."

"Seems I failed. I want to make an agreement, Dau."

"I'm listening."

"I won't tell Archu, or anyone else, about the conversation we just had. In return, you won't take any action to harm yourself."

"If I break the agreement, you'll have no comeback." Dau's tone is flat.

"We're friends, aren't we? Even after this? Friends trust each other."

"How long am I supposed to comply with this agreement?"

I swallow, wondering if I've reduced a matter of life and death to a macabre bargain, and what sort of person that makes me. "Until after this representative has come here and we find out what your father intends. Dau, why don't you tell Archu the full story about what happened when you were a boy? He would speak up for you. He would make sure you were safe. He could probably find you somewhere else to go. One of the safe houses, like Oschu and Maen's, for instance. Swan Island looks after its people."

"You're talking bollocks. Archu may be an elder here, but he's hardly going to call out a chieftain over his past behavior. You haven't met my family. They're expert liars, the lot of them. Besides, you're forgetting something vital."

"What?"

"This is all about hushing up Swan Island's involvement, isn't it? Making sure my father's people are so kindly treated and so generously compensated that they've no reason to spread stories about how and where I was injured. Archu may be a good man, but he's not going to risk the continuing existence of Swan Island for the sake of one individual."

I can find nothing to say. As Dau heads back toward his quarters, feeling his way with the stick, I find myself without a single word of hope.

7

DAU

They're one day's ride away," Archu says, meaning the party from my father's stronghold in Oakhill. He's had observers out. Reports have come back in. He's gathered us in the long room at the Barn, tactfully telling me who's present so I don't need to ask. Apart from him and me, there's Fergus, Brigid, Liobhan, and a lawman named Master Saran, who's arrived from the court of Dalriada to assist us. Cionnaola is also present. I feel like I'm teetering on the edge of that cliff I spoke of to Liobhan, only at the bottom there won't be a short, sharp end to this wretched business, but a suffering that goes on for however long my family decides to extend it. Archu has told me to stay calm when they come. To answer questions courteously when they're put to me. Not to fall silent. He has reminded me, yet again, that I'm still a Swan Island warrior, and that he expects me to act like one.

This meeting, now, should be easy. I am among friends. But it is not easy. I'm clammy with cold sweat. My heart is racing.

If I could see, I would look at Liobhan. I would look in her eyes and take heart from her strength. I would look at her fiery red-gold hair and think of a flame of courage, lighting up even the darkest times. But if I could see, we would be back on Swan Island and not in this nightmare.

"I have a description of the party," Archu goes on. "Seven of them in all. There is a lawman, as we expected. Four men-at-arms. One older fellow who looks like a councilor or similar. And they're led by a youngish man who resembles you, Dau. Your brother, perhaps?"

My head fills with an evil buzzing. My stomach churns. I'm going to faint. Or be sick. Fergus says, "Dau? Are you all right?" He's beside me now, putting a cool hand on my brow. His robe smells of herbs.

"Fair-haired or red?" I manage to ask. Then, before I can hear the answer, I blunder away from the table and bring up my breakfast in a corner. I retch and retch until there's nothing left in my stomach. Around me are the sounds of folk moving quickly, and Fergus is there, steadying me, but the things in my head are screaming now, and I'm shaking, I can't stop.

"You need to lie down," Fergus says. And to someone else, "Find Jabir, will you?"

I drag myself up from whatever foul pit I've fallen into. Try to straighten my back, try to lift my chin. Someone puts a cup of water in my hand. Liobhan. Her hand wraps around mine for a few moments. She's making sure I have a steady hold on the thing. I drink. I breathe. "Which brother?" I ask. With an effort, I make my voice steady. "Seanan or Ruarc?"

"Fair," says Archu. "Could almost be your twin, that's what the informant told us. But older."

Seanan. Of course Ruarc wouldn't come on his own, not with a decision like this to make. He always followed Seanan's lead. Followed it in every act of cruelty; followed it like an obedient servant. "I need to sit down," I say. Dagda's bollocks, no wonder the two of them made sport of tormenting me. After all these years, I'm still weak as piss.

"You're unwell. You should rest—"

"No." I cut Fergus off. "I can do this." We move to the table and sit again. "Archu, how many horses do they have?"

"Eight," says Archu.

So they've brought a mount for me. Unless it's a packhorse. I know deep down it isn't. Seanan plans to take me home with him. My brother wants his old toy back, to tease and torment and oh so methodically reduce to a heap of worthless rubbish.

"We won't be accommodating them here at the Barn," Brigid says. "We have some trusted people at a suitable place, an establishment that can pass for a wayside inn, a discreet distance away. Stabling for horses, good amenities, and a private chamber that will do for a meeting. I think their lawman will understand the advantages of discussing such a sensitive matter at a neutral venue."

"Could Master Saran explain what his role will be?" That's Liobhan. It's a good question, since we know the Swan Island elders don't want this to become a formal hearing. Not officially, anyway. With two lawmen present it's going to be pretty close.

"Will you do that now, Master Saran?" This voice is Cionnaola's. I see him in my mind: his long twists of gray hair, his face that shows the passage of years, his keen-eyed gaze. A strong man in all the ways that count. A leader.

"Firstly, let me say that I have many years' experience in the law and that I will be perfectly discreet on this matter." Master Saran has an old man's voice, but he sounds crisp and confident all the same. "Apart from the king and his senior councilor, nobody at court was told exactly where I was going, only that my services were required by a household a certain distance away. It happens often enough; my absence will not spark questions. Part of my role will be to ensure Lord Scannal's lawman does not deviate from accepted practice in his questioning. The same will apply to Dau's brother. I assume he's here to look after Lord Scannal's interests."

Make Seanan abide by the law? The man's dreaming.

"I've been provided with a detailed account of what occurred on the day Dau was injured, and I have also spoken to the healers about that injury, his treatment, and what is likely for the future. It's important that all the relevant information is heard. I will make sure that happens. If Lord Scannal's party does not call Fergus and Jabir to speak, I will do so—they have agreed to ride with us to the meeting place. That way we can not only hear their expert opinions but also ensure that Dau has appropriate care and support for the day. I trust it will be only one day, though these things do have a tendency to drag on. I'll be wanting to talk to you later, Dau. And also to you, Liobhan." There's a pause; I imagine him looking around the room, assessing each of us in turn. I can smell my own vomit. Perhaps my shirt is stained with it. From that corner come discreet sounds of someone cleaning up.

Can I sink any lower than this? Oh, yes. Tomorrow I most likely will. My shadows are only a hair's breadth away: a boy dropped headfirst down a dark narrow hole; a boy lying in his own excrement behind a locked door; a boy with his arms around a dying dog, and his brothers' laughter ringing in his ears. The blood soaking into my clothing; the little sounds Snow made as she tried so hard to stay with me. I dash a hand across my cheek and hope nobody sees.

"Any further questions?" asks Brigid. "If not, we'll leave this room to Master Saran. He'll send someone to fetch each of you when he's ready. Liobhan, you can make yourself useful by speaking to Illann in the stables—he's come over to do some shoeing for us. Explain to him who's riding to Hawthorn House, and let him know we'll need our horses quite early tomorrow. I want us settled in there with everything ready before these folk arrive. Ask Illann if he'd be free to come with us. It's always handy to have an extra guard, especially one who is good with horses."

I know Illann well. Last summer Liobhan and I were on a mission with him. We went under cover, Illann as a court farrier, I as his mute assistant. Liobhan, her brother, and Archu were traveling minstrels. Illann's a good man. Quiet, capable. A friend. If I leave this place, I'll go back to being the boy with no friends. I should have trusted my own judgment when I first came to Swan Island. I shouldn't have lowered my guard, let people in. If you never make friends, you're spared the pain of losing them. A question comes to me. I don't need to ask it, because Liobhan gets in first.

"Is it safe for Dau to ride? Won't the movement be bad for his eyes?"

Another charged silence. *Don't suggest a litter,* I will them. *Don't say the word* cart. I imagine Fergus telling us the damage is done now so a bit more shaking up won't matter.

"It's an easy ride, flat all the way with good tracks," says Archu. "We'll put your horse on a leading rein if necessary, Dau. I did ask Illann about this. He confirmed that you're a very capable rider. Provided you have someone riding alongside, and the right horse, he believes you can do it easily."

I send a silent thank-you to Illann. I'm not sure if what I feel is terror or excitement at the thought of such a challenge. Both, perhaps. I imagine a wager: Liobhan bets that I keep my seat the whole time without a leading rein; I bet that I fall off and make a fool of myself in front of everyone. The stake: one copper each way.

"I believe that if Dau takes the ride carefully no further damage will be done," says Fergus. "We'll prepare an herbal draft for you to take before we leave, Dau, to dull any pain. We do have to be careful. The leading rein would be an excellent idea."

That's the moment I decide there's no way I'm going on a leading rein. What if Seanan got there before us and saw me coming in like a beast of burden? Saw me before I knew he was there, watched me with that expression on his face, the one that makes my flesh crawl?

Brigid clears us all out of the long room, apart from Master Saran, Cionnaola, and the two healers—Jabir has come in now, his deep, soft voice unmistakable. Someone's clanking a bucket in the corner where I was sick. I remember our training at the Barn—how hard it often was, even cruel. We learned to hold our own under intense forms of pressure. I already knew how to do that. I learned when I was very young. How to endure pain. How to keep going when you are so frightened you wet yourself. How to keep your mind sharp even at the worst times. I performed well in that part of Swan Island training. I wish I could do the same now.

"Dau?" Liobhan's next to me, touching my arm—it's a gentle offer to help me find my way out of the building. I'm close to cursing and dashing her hand away, because what is the point? Why even try? But she says, "Come out to the stables with me. I want your advice." So I go, with my hand through her arm. Providing something useful, even if it's only advice, is better than sitting on a pallet alone and thinking about tomorrow.

When we're outside and walking to the stable block, Liobhan says, "Does Illann know? About what happened when you were growing up, I mean? Did you and he talk?"

"Forgotten that the stable boy was mute, have you?" I know this is unfair. There were plenty of times, in the stall where we slept on hay while we were in Breifne, when Illann and I exchanged information in whispers. And there were some times when I came close to telling him. But we were on a mission, and I held my tongue. Liobhan hasn't said anything, so I go on,

"No, I didn't tell him. And I don't plan to now, if that was your next helpful suggestion." I feel Liobhan's arm tense, then relax. She's made herself count to five. That's what she does to stop herself from cursing, shouting, or otherwise losing her temper. "It would serve no purpose," I go on. "Wait until you meet my brother. He is the smoothest, most expert liar in all Erin. Who'd believe the blind man who vomits in a corner over the future chieftain of Oakhill?"

"Speaking of that," Liobhan says quite calmly, "you need to change your shirt. How about you wait with Illann—I see him coming now—and I'll go and find you a clean one. And while you're out here, ask him about horses for tomorrow. Choose one for yourself."

Despite everything, my lips curve in a smile. "I already have. The obvious choice is the gray mare, Dusk. The most placid of the lot, and sturdy. All I need to ask is whether she's available. For you, I suggest the long-legged chestnut mare, Fleetfoot. Livelier than the gray, but steady when it's required, and strong. The two are good companions; that should make it easier when you have to ride alongside me and make sure I don't fall and do myself further damage."

Liobhan stops walking, which means I stop, too. We stand there arm in arm, and I feel the sun on my face and the warmth of her body touching mine. I think of her maybe counting to twenty this time.

"Dau," she says, "answer this question honestly. Will you keep to that agreement we made? I'd hate to think you'd use a good horse in a way that would end up with . . . with somebody getting hurt. Or an animal getting injured." Then, in a different tone, she says, "Shit, why must this be so hard?" She releases her hold on me. "Let me rephrase that. No falling off on purpose. No jumping off in dangerous places. No making your horse shy and throw you. No doing anything that might endanger anyone in our party, yourself included. Do I make myself clear?" I stand there saying nothing, and after a bit she says, "You think there's something funny about this?"

Was I smiling? I shake my head and instantly regret it; my neck feels as if someone's stuck a skewer through it. "I'll stick to the agreement unless a perfect opportunity presents itself. You must know I wouldn't risk a good horse."

We walk on. Someone's training in the open area near the stables; I hear hoofbeats, voices calling instructions. Liobhan says, "What's funny is that you've already decided who gets which horse. That you remember every single thing the groom told us. I bet you could tell me which horses are right for Archu and Fergus and Master Scannal. And you tell me there's no useful work a blind man can do."

I shrug. It hurts less than shaking my head. "A trick, that's all. I remember things." Even the ones I want so much to forget.

8

LIOBHAN

A good thing about the team on Swan Island: if something needs to happen, they make it happen. By the time the party from Oakhill arrives at Hawthorn House, which is a sturdy wattle-and-mud building with a couple of gnarled old hawthorns guarding its front door, their boughs heavy with blossom, Brigid has us deployed inside while Illann and another man tend to the horses in a stable block at the rear. A wayside inn needs working stables. The house, or inn, was all set up when we got here, early as we were: fires laid, food prepared and set on covered dishes in the kitchen, beds made up for whoever needed to stay overnight—it's unlikely the discussions will be so brief that our visitors will turn around and head homeward without at least one night's sleep. The building has a big room for dining, with a broad hearth and several long tables with benches. We won't be using that room for the meeting, even though Brigid says there will be no other visitors until we're gone. There's a more modest chamber adjoining the dining hall, with some chairs and benches, and a writing desk in a corner. I help to move a round table in there. Master Saran will preside over the meeting, since he is lawman to the king of this region. I wish I could warn him about Dau's family, and how truly terrible Dau's childhood was, but there's no opportunity, and besides, I can't do that without Dau's agreement and I'm quite sure he'd say no. He can be his own worst enemy sometimes.

The round table, Brigid says, will allow Master Saran to be separated from the parties in dispute, while also being informal enough to avoid the appearance of a legal hearing. A pair of Swan Island men will act as both door guards and messengers. There's a room set aside for Dau and the healers, who won't be expected to attend the entire meeting. The same goes for me; I'll wait in an anteroom to the one Dau's in. I want to be there for all of it. I want to hear every single thing Dau's brother says. He sounds vile, just the sort of man who'll try to twist people's words to suit his own interests. But I don't demand to be present; I can't. I'm a Swan Island warrior now, a proper one. I've been trained for today's encounter, and I'm going to do what's been asked of me, even if I feel like giving Seanan of Oakhill a smack in the head and a kick in the backside.

They arrive before the sun is at its peak. I don't have a window, but I hear the horses coming in and then a conversation at the door—Cionnaola's voice, and Brigid's, and others I don't recognize. They move away to the dining room. They'll want refreshments after the long ride, I suppose, and they'll have bags to bring in and unpack. Maybe Dau's brother will expect the attention of servants. Too bad. Let him sort out his own belongings.

In the chamber next to this anteroom it's very quiet. Dau looked like a ghost after the ride here. If he's resting, that's a good thing. But I bet he isn't. His insides must be even more churned up than mine. I sit alone for an interminable waiting period. At one point Brigid brings a tray with food and drink and tells me to take it in for Dau and the healers and to have some myself. I ask in a whisper how long it will be before they start, and she whispers back, "Not long now."

Nobody has any appetite, though Fergus and Jabir eat some of the bread and soup that's been provided. Dau and I both refuse the food and don't touch the mead, though it might lift our spirits a little. Clear heads are going to be essential. It feels odd that Dau's brother didn't come to see him straightaway, though maybe that's just as well. When the healers have finished eating, I get up to go back to the anteroom, but Fergus says, "Stay here, Liobhan, unless you want to be on your own."

I stay, though I wonder if it's quite correct to do so. If Seanan's lawman knew I was with the others, he might accuse us of colluding over our accounts of what happened that day. He might suggest we've put pressure on Dau to answer questions in a certain way; for instance, to say his injury was accidental when maybe it wasn't.

I don't like the way my thoughts are headed. Dau looks bad enough already, wound up tight before we even start. He keeps clenching and unclenching his hands, then pacing up and down the room, until Jabir politely tells him to sit down. Some time later there's a tap on the door, and one of our own men is there. "Liobhan, they want you now."

I'd been sure Dau would be called first, and I'm not ready, despite everything. The two healers stand as I leave the room; after a moment Dau does the same. It's a sign of respect, of fellowship, and it helps.

I walk into the meeting room. The first thing I notice is that Dau's brother is so like him I'd have trouble telling them apart at a distance. This shocks me. The Seanan of Dau's tales is a foul creature, a monster, and even though Archu has told us he looks like Dau, I've been expecting his cruelty to show. He scrutinizes me closely as I go to stand in the spot indicated, a gap between the seats that encircle the round table. I'm directly opposite Master Saran. On one side of me are Cionnaola, Brigid, and Archu. On the other are Seanan, his councilor, and his own lawman, who's been placed next to Master Saran. There's someone at the small corner desk taking notes. And there are two guards in the room, one of ours and one of theirs. Apart from the lawman, who's clad in the standard brown robe, Seanan's party are all wearing dark blue tunics. He has some kind of silver emblem embroidered on his, perhaps a sword. Everyone's very quiet. Then Master Saran speaks.

"Master Cionnaola, will you please introduce this young woman?"

Cionnaola stands. "This is Liobhan of Dalriada. She is a member of the community I lead, and by profession a fighter. Liobhan is nineteen years old and of excellent character. She and Dau came to our community at the same time, about a year ago."

"A fighter." The tone is flat. It gives nothing away. Seanan's eyes are on me, but I can't read his expression. "A woman."

"As you see." Cionnaola's tone shuts off further discussion on this point.

"Thank you," says Master Saran. "Liobhan, we have with us Master Seanan of Oakhill, representing his father, Lord Scannal." I dip my head in a minimal show of respect, aiming in Seanan's general direction but avoiding his eye. "With him are Lord Scannal's lawman, Master Beanón, and his councilor, Master Naithí." I nod again, twice. Neither man responds, though their attention is certainly on me. Waiting for me to blunder, perhaps. Waiting for me to incriminate myself. "Now," Saran goes on, "please set out for us what happened in the combat area when Master Dau received his injury. Anything you can remember may be useful. Take it step by step. When you are finished I will probably have some questions, and so will Master Beanón here." His steady gaze is reassuring. I decide I will keep my eyes on him. I recall some good advice Dau gave me once, when I had to face a room full of powerful, hostile men. *Hold yourself tall. Tell the truth. Don't let them see you're angry.* I'm not angry yet. But I suspect I soon will be.

"Shall I begin, Master Saran?" I hold my hands loosely clasped in front of me. I'm wearing a gown, borrowed from Deirdre. My hair is in a simple plait. That was Brigid's idea. She said I looked less fierce in female garb.

"Please do."

With Dau's words in mind, I straighten my back and begin. "On that day, Dau and I were engaging in an unarmed combat before an audience. We'd done that sort of thing quite frequently as part of our training." I don't want to tell this story again. It hurts. I grit my teeth and get on with it. "The usual fight is three rounds, with whoever takes two the winner. Bouts take place in the training area. The surface is hard-packed earth . . ."

"Go on," says Saran.

"Dau won the first bout, I took the second. We were well into the third when Dau lost his footing and fell heavily, striking his head on the ground." Curse it, my voice is starting to shake. *Hold yourself tall.* "I reached down to help him up and saw that he was unconscious. I checked whether he was breathing, and he was, and then several people came over to help." I make myself take a breath. Archu has told me we won't mention the amulet; for a small child to be implicated would be appalling. But there's a detail I know I should provide, even if it makes things worse for me. "We usually wear leather helms in fights of that kind. But they're hot and uncomfortable. I took mine off after the first round. I didn't ask Dau to remove his, but he did, to keep things fair. That meant his head was not protected."

There's a shocked sound from Seanan, who half rises.

"Be seated, please." Saran keeps his cool head. "Have you any more to tell us, Liobhan?"

"About the fight, no. After that, Archu sent me back to my

quarters. I kept myself occupied with domestic tasks until supper-time, when Archu told us all that Dau was very badly hurt and would be taken to the mainland."

"Did you go to visit your injured comrade? Did you make a formal apology?" Clearly Master Beanón has no intention of waiting to ask his questions.

"Dau was being tended to by Master Fergus. Archu said he couldn't have visitors, so I stayed away. I wanted to see him. We are friends."

"Not anymore, I suspect," says Seanan not quite under his breath. I pretend to ignore it, but I feel my cheeks flush.

I address Master Beanón again. He doesn't actually look hostile, just very intent. "As for an apology, what happened was quite clearly an accident. But if I had been able to see Dau, I would have told him how sad and shocked I was to see him so badly hurt. I would have wished him a full and speedy recovery." Gods, that sounds insincere. It sounds rehearsed. I could kick myself. Especially as it's nothing but the truth.

"Thank you, Liobhan. Anything further to add?"

"No, Master Saran."

"Very well, you may be seated." Saran makes a gesture, and one of the guards—ours—comes over to walk me to a bench at the back, as if I might otherwise bolt or attack someone. I murmur thanks and sit. Seems like I'll be here when Dau gives his statement. I'm glad about that. At the same time I feel sick on his behalf and furious with myself. If I'd kept my helm on, Dau would have done the same. He'd still have his vision and we'd be back on the island settling in to proper work with the team. I may not be guilty. But I'm responsible.

Archu gives his version of events, which is consistent with mine. He's a fine example of composure under pressure, which is just what I would expect of the man.

Master Saran calls Fergus and Jabir. Have they left Dau on his own? They wouldn't, surely, overwrought as he was. Maybe Illann's there. Illann would steady him.

Fergus talks about his first impressions when he saw Dau lying unconscious on the ground. He runs through the steps he took, the checks he performed, the gradual changes in his patient's condition. The realization that Dau couldn't see. The wild behavior on that first day, the shouting, the incoherence. The need to dose the patient with a powerful mixture that would calm him before he hurt himself or someone else. He speaks of the decision to call in Jabir, whom he knew to have greater expertise in treating head injuries. As Jabir stands up to speak, it's plain Seanan wants to interject. He murmurs to his lawman and Master Beanón puts up a hand to attract Master Saran's attention.

"What is it, Master Beanón?"

"We believe it would be more appropriate for the healers to answer questions immediately after their own statements, Master Saran, rather than to wait until all those concerned have been heard. The specialized nature of these statements means that would be easier for all."

"I'm inclined to agree," Saran says. "Master Cionnaola, do you have any objection?"

"If questions are to be asked," says Cionnaola, "surely Dau should also be present."

There's another flurry of consultation, Seanan with Beanón and the councilor, Brigid and Archu with Cionnaola. Then it's agreed that Dau should come in. In my opinion he should have been here from the start. But I keep my mouth shut. I've got through the first part of this all right. The real test is still to come.

Dau comes in with his hand on Illann's shoulder. He doesn't have his stick. If anything, he looks even whiter than before, his blind eyes deeply shadowed. He's standing very upright with his head high. He doesn't look angry. He looks distant. He looks as if he's in a different place from the rest of us. Which, in a way, is true.

Seanan springs to his feet. "Brother!" he exclaims in what sounds like genuine concern, and strides around the table toward Dau. Before Seanan can reach him, before he can touch, embrace, do whatever he intends, Dau raises his hand, palm turned toward his brother. "No," he says. The gesture is imperious. The voice is quiet, clear, and cold as winter frost. Illann's hand lingers near the weapon at his belt.

"Please resume your seat, Master Seanan." Saran is courteous but firm. "This will proceed more smoothly if we adhere to the rules I set out at the beginning." Seanan obeys. If anything he looks surprised, bemused. Hurt, even. Can he have mellowed over those years since Dau left home? Seen the error of his ways?

Brigid vacates her seat and comes to sit beside me. Dau takes her place between Cionnaola and Archu. Illann stands at the back with the guards. It's like a dance, and it leaves Dau facing his brother across the round table.

"Master Jabir," Saran says, "we will hear your statement. When you are finished, questions may be addressed to you and to Master Fergus. Is that acceptable?"

Both healers murmur assent, and Jabir begins. "I serve as senior physician to Lord Coman, a chieftain of Ulaid. I have worked in that household for the last five years. I am also called upon quite frequently to assist other healers in particular cases, so I travel a good deal. I happened to be close to the court of Dalriada when this incident occurred, and I responded to a request for help sent by Master Fergus. In my home country I was trained by a physician with a particular expertise in the treatment of head injuries. I arrived in these parts a few days after Master Dau sustained this damage. At that time he was still in severe pain and greatly distressed, though no longer subject to the violent outbursts I was told had been occurring earlier. He was able to communicate with us clearly. His vision is all but gone. He can see moving shadows with one eye, nothing with the other.

"In consultation, Master Fergus and I drew up a plan for treatment: compresses, drafts, bed rest, and so on. I examined Master Dau's eyes several times daily. I can see no obvious wound to either eye. I believe the damage is internal. For that, we have no answers."

Beanón raises a hand. "Master Jabir, can you state whether this condition is permanent, or whether it might respond to other treatment, perhaps by someone more expert than yourself?"

If he's insulted, Jabir gives no sign of it. "All I can tell you is that there has been no improvement in Master Dau's vision since the injury occurred, although there has been a reduction in the swelling around the eyes and his headaches are no longer constant. As I said, we have no remedy for this sort of injury. I do not know of any physician with the expertise to offer another opinion, Master Beanón. I wish I did. But perhaps Lord Scannal has the resources to search more widely. Beyond the shores of Erin, if necessary."

Seanan folds his arms. "Is my brother likely to have other problems in the future? Is his mind impaired? His judgment? His temper?"

There's a silence. I'm glad I can't see Dau's face; I'm sitting behind him. He's holding himself as straight as a young birch.

"When Master Dau speaks, you will have the opportunity to assess the capacity of his mind," Jabir says quietly.

Seanan and his lawman consult again, in lowered voices. Then Master Beanón speaks. "In your expert opinion, Master Jabir, what effect will this injury have on Master Dau's future?"

I'm still watching Dau. I see him take a deep breath and let it out slowly. *Count to ten*, I will him. *Then do it again. You'll get your turn to speak.*

Jabir takes his time to answer. I suppose it's a reasonable question, one that would be asked in a formal hearing, but it's a cruel one to respond to when Dau is present. "A man of good family, with folk to assist and sustain him, could lead a satisfactory life despite being blind. In all other respects Master Dau is a fit, healthy young man, strong and able. Those who love him could find opportunities for him." He hesitates. "Such a man might do well if he had a personal servant to assist with day-to-day challenges. Or a dog. A well-trained dog as helper and companion, acting as a blind man's protector—his eyes, one might say—can be extremely effective."

A burst of sound comes from Seanan, like muffled laughter. Dau flinches.

"My apologies," Seanan says, recovering his composure. "This is so deeply distressing that I hardly know how to respond. A dog, yes, that is an excellent idea. My brother has always been good with animals."

Morrigan's britches! I want to stride over there and slap the man in the face. I see exactly what he's doing—unsettling Dau before he has to get up and speak, trying to distress him, or frighten him, so he can't be the strong and able young man of Jabir's statement. I can read those eyes like an open book. This is the brother who killed Dau's childhood dog and made him watch. This is the man who took away the only thing Dau loved and scarred him forever. How dare he!

Brigid lays a steadying hand on my arm. I realize I've had my fists clenched hard and my jaw tight; her touch is a reminder of how important it is to stay in control. I give her a little nod and start silently counting.

"If there are no further questions for the healers," says Saran, "we'll move on." He glances around the room, as cool and calm as if the odd little episode had not happened. "Master Dau, we'll hear from you now. You may remain seated."

"I believe my legs are still working." Dau gets to his feet. Now he's looking down at his brother, across the round table. Probably just as well that he can't actually see Seanan. "I'll stand, thank you, Master Saran."

"As you wish. Please let me know if you feel unwell at any point. Go ahead when you're ready, Master Dau. Take us through what happened on the day you were injured. Step by step."

"An unarmed combat display, myself against Liobhan. Three rounds, so whoever prevailed twice would be the winner. We are quite evenly matched; for that reason, we fight frequently and know each other's strengths and weaknesses, and each other's particular tricks. I won the first, she the second round. In the third and deciding round there was a point where Liobhan came forward in attack, aiming for my leg. I skipped back, tripped, and fell. I remember nothing after that, until I woke much later to a splitting headache and . . . darkness."

Everyone's captured by this account. They're seeing the fight in a way they probably didn't when I gave my version. Seanan's councilor, Naithí, puts up a polite hand.

"Questions when Master Dau is finished, Master Naithí," says Saran, but Dau says, "Ask now, if you will."

"Master Jabir described you as a strong and able young man," the councilor says, "and I see this is so. How was it that you could be brought to the ground by a female?"

"Liobhan is a strong and able young woman," says Dau. "Tall. Broad in the shoulders. Quick thinking. You were perhaps not attending when I told you we were evenly matched."

"But—"

"May I respond to the question, Master Saran?"

"Yes, Master Archu. Keep it brief, please."

"We selected our most recent group of new fighters by a lengthy process of training and evaluation, including bouts of the kind both Liobhan and Dau have described to us. If an aspiring trainee shows the right combination of physical and mental strength, along with good judgment, that person is a strong contender for a place among us. Whether that individual is male or female makes no difference to the choice. True, our team is predominantly male. But not exclusively."

"Thank you, Master Archu," says Saran. "A comprehensive answer. Master Dau, please continue your statement. You returned to consciousness to find that you had lost your vision. What then?"

"I was in pain. Confused. Drifting in and out of reality. I failed to act with due respect for the healers. Folk were trying to help me. But it seems that for this condition, there is no help."

Another hand goes up. "Master Dau, I am Master Beanón, your father's lawman. I understand you were not wearing your protective helm during this bout. Why not?"

My gut tightens in apprehension.

"Those things are hot," Dau says. "Uncomfortable. When you're fighting with weapons, staves especially, you keep them on regardless. But for a display fight, unarmed, they're optional. We both took them off after the first round."

"Who was first to do so?" Master Beanón's tone is sharper now.

A moment's silence. "Liobhan was first. A practical decision."

"And you followed, thinking that otherwise she would be at a disadvantage."

Another pause, as if Dau is counting again. "Thinking the helms were uncomfortable."

"You're defending her." Seanan is incredulous. "You're defending the woman who did this to you!"

Saran opens his mouth, no doubt to remind all parties to stick to the facts, but Dau speaks over him. "I'm responding to the question that was put to me. I'm speaking simple truth. What happened was an accident."

After a moment's charged silence, Saran speaks as if the interchange had not happened. "Thank you for your clear account of the events of that day, Master Dau. You may be seated now." Dau sits, and Saran goes on, "I understand Master Seanan wishes to present a statement on his father's behalf. Before we move on to that, are there any further questions? Please raise a hand if you wish to speak."

Nobody does. The question of Dau's future hangs in the silence of the room. My heart is drumming. If I'm wound up as tight as this, how must he be feeling? He's still sitting very straight. Seanan, opposite, is staring at him with a strange look, almost hungry. If I didn't know their story, I'd think that was the face of a man longing to look after his youngest brother, to take him home and care for him in his time of need. If Seanan is anything, he's an expert dissembler.

"I have a suggestion, Master Saran," says Beanón. "I believe we'll need to move into a discussion of the law as it applies to this situation. It might be useful if you and I can speak informally on that subject before we continue. And I wish to have a word with Master Seanan and Master Naithí in private."

Saran glances at Dau, probably thinking a break would be good for him at this point. "That is acceptable, Master Beanón. Your party may remain in this room—I expect the household can send in some refreshments—and Master Cionnaola's people can retire until we're ready to resume." He stands, and so do we. "Thank you, all, for keeping these proceedings orderly. Let us continue as we began."

* * *

Dau doesn't want to rest. He doesn't want to sit down. He doesn't want to talk. It's only after Brigid has a few stern words with him that he settles on a bench, arms folded tightly, jaw clenched, eyes furious. Fergus and Jabir sit on either side of him. I go to the kitchen with one of our guards and find fresh food and drink all ready; whoever is in charge of this place is doing a fine job of being both efficient and invisible. But then, it seems to be a Swan Island safe house, so that shouldn't surprise me. The guard takes a supply to Seanan's people and I do the same for ours. A little later the two lawmen emerge from the smaller chamber and make their way outside, where I assume they'll go through the provisions of the relevant law and perhaps try to reach agreement over whatever it is Dau's father is demanding in compensation. I hope the figure is not impossible. I wish I could go outside myself, not to listen but to run, scream, climb, do anything to still my thoughts. I wish I could take Dau out there for a while. He looked and sounded calm and confident in the hearing. The cost of that is showing now.

"You could go and rest, Dau," Fergus says. "Who knows how long they will be? We could call you when they're ready."

"No!" Dau snarls. Then adds, in calmer tones, "I would prefer to remain here. To stay with you all, for as long as I can."

Nobody speaks. Archu looks stricken. Brigid, who's as tough as boot leather, puts a hand up to shield her face. Cionnaola doesn't move, but I see the pain in his eyes.

"Archu? May I have a word with you privately?"

We go outside, just far enough from the door to be sure nobody can hear.

"What is it, Liobhan?"

"I don't know what Seanan's planning to say. But the payment to Lord Scannal—that would be calculated as sick-maintenance, wouldn't it? The cost to his family of a physician, attendants, and so on?"

"I believe so. We'll have to wait until Dau's brother sets out Lord Scannal's terms." He gives me a very direct look. "Don't trouble yourself about the payment. Provided it's not an unreasonable amount, we can meet it. We keep funds for this kind of thing."

"Archu, I can't betray a confidence. But Dau shouldn't go back to Oakhill. The situation there is . . . If he's forced to go back, he'll be alone in a household of people who don't care about him. Worse than that. They'll be cruel to him. And however physically strong he may be, now that he's blind he'll be vulnerable. I think—" I choke over the words, clear my throat, try again. "I don't think he'll last long. I can't say more without— I'm just saying, I fear for him."

Archu is silent. I've as good as told him Dau will kill himself rather than stay at his father's house. Archu probably doesn't believe it will come to that. He doesn't know Dau as well as I do.

"We should wait to hear what Lord Scannal is demanding," Archu says eventually.

"Couldn't you offer Dau a place somewhere else? At one of the safe houses, maybe? Anywhere away from his brothers?"

"We should wait," he says again. "Wait to hear what Lord Scannal wants from us, and what he's able to offer Dau. Our resources won't stretch to searching for an expert physician beyond the borders of Erin. His may well do so. The situation may not be as dire as you suggest, Liobhan. Both Master Beanón and Master Naithí seem to be reasonable men."

He hasn't understood me. He doesn't realize that rather than accompany his brother to Oakhill, Dau will make an end of himself. "Dau hasn't a single friend in that place," I tell him. "Going back would finish him."

Archu gives me a strange look. I have no idea what he's thinking. "If I could provide him with that friend I would, believe me. Now come, we'd best return indoors. Is it not possible that Dau has learned enough since he left home to cope even with the dire situation you suggest is waiting for him? I think you underestimate him, Liobhan."

9

DAU

Hold yourself together, Dau. This day will end sometime, the words will all be spoken, the sun will go down and night will fall. And there will be an opportunity to make an end to the pain. The moment we hear what outrageous price my father has put on my future, my promise to Liobhan is void. I will not get on a horse and ride home with my brother. I will be gone before he can step forward and, sneering, offer to help me mount. I will find a way. A knife would be best. No chance of taking one off Illann or any of the Swan Island team. Seanan's guards might be less expert. Ask for a shoulder in support, snatch the weapon from his belt? Possible. It'd need to be quick. Or wait until suppertime. If a knife can cut roast meat it can cut a man's throat.

We're called back in. Seems Illann's been given the job of watching over me, since he's the one ushering me around now. We sit on a bench against a wall. Liobhan's on my other side. When everybody is in, the doors are shut and Master Saran recommences the proceedings with an explanation of how Brehon law deals with sick-maintenance, that is, fees to be paid according to the rank of the injured person by whoever is deemed responsible for their hurt, to cover food, drink, and the services of a healer for as long as required. Where appropriate, the fees should also pay for someone to take over the injured individual's work. There are a few murmurs around the room when this part is read out.

"A separate fee covers specific crippling injuries," Saran continues, "such as the loss of a limb. The loss of one's eyesight would come under this provision. I remind you all that this is not a formal hearing, but a discussion from which we hope to reach an agreement acceptable to all parties. Master Beanón, you have a document in which Lord Scannal's requirements for compensation are set out. Will you read that to us now, please?"

"I will read it on my father's behalf, Master Saran." My brother's voice. He sounds calm and courteous. Confident of getting what he wants. Unchanged in all these years. He never achieved his victories by hard work or courage or spirit. Always by playing games, by artful pretense, by devious plotting. His voice makes my flesh crawl. Never mind; I will be gone soon. None of this will matter. This time I will rob him of his triumph.

> I am advised that my youngest son, Dau, has sustained a grievous injury during a fight, while under the authority of the establishment known as Swan Island, which lies within the kingdom of Dalriada. I understand that this injury has left my son blind, a condition likely to be permanent. In reference to this matter, I require the following financial compensation, to be made without delay. For sustenance in my household for the remainder of his life, along with the services of a healer or physician as required, the sum of eight hundred silver pieces.

I hear a few gasps, a few indrawn breaths. The figure is ridiculous. My father has ample resources. The cost of my upkeep would be a drop in the bucket for him. Eight hundred silver pieces would see me fed from gold platters. Provided with a whole crew of personal attendants, each of them a trained physician. Sleeping on sheets of finest silk. It's laughable.

Seanan goes on—yes, astonishing as it seems, my father's demands don't end there.

> *Further, as compensation specifically for the gross physical injury which Dau has sustained, an injury that robbed him in an instant of his opportunity to lead a full life as a man, I require payment of an additional sum of four hundred silver pieces.*

There's a stirring in the room; people want to speak. But Seanan continues.

> *Further to the payment, I require that the individual who inflicted this injury on my son should complete a period of unpaid service in my household. The term of that period is negotiable, but it should be a minimum of one year.*

Beside me, Liobhan makes a wordless sound of shock, then stifles it. I'm on my feet, I can't stop myself. "That's ludicrous!" I shout. "You can't ask for that! Everyone knows it was an accident!"

"I am reading our father's words, brother," Seanan says, silky smooth. "Should the perpetrator of your injury receive no punishment at all? I think you'll find the law provides for this."

There's a buzz of talk in the chamber now, and sounds of movement. "Quiet, please!" calls Master Saran. "Resume your seats. I remind you all to raise a hand if you wish to be heard." The noise dies down. "Master Seanan, I believe the letter sent to your father did include the fact that this was an accidental injury. Today that point has been discussed further, and the statements received have confirmed it. It is not only inappropriate to request that Liobhan provide a period of service in your father's household, it is outside the meaning of the relevant law. This was a fair bout, performed under supervision, with many witnesses. Master Dau slipped while trying to evade a move by his opponent. He fell awkwardly and struck his head. Neither combatant wore a helm. That was unfortunate, but it does not alter the accidental nature of what occurred. Lord Scannal is within his rights to request compensation in the form of a payment, since Master Dau was hurt while working at Master Cionnaola's establishment. The issue of the protective helm may play a part in our determination of the amount."

I make myself breathe. I'm so furious I could scream. But none of it matters. Let them agree to whatever they like. I'll soon be gone and they can set me and my sorry existence behind them.

"Before I left home," Seanan says, "my father gave me precise instructions. All three provisions are to be included in the final settlement: a payment to cover the significant expense of keeping my brother as a household dependent for the rest of his life, a fee as compensation for the specific injury, and a period of service for the person responsible for that injury. Under no circumstances was I to sign an agreement that did not include all three components." A pause. "Perhaps you would like time to discuss this among yourselves, in private? I imagine you won't be keen to see this matter go to a formal hearing before a higher authority."

Oh, so courteous; oh, so considerate. Blind as I am, I can see the look on his face; the eyes of my memory are sharp as knives. My head starts to buzz. I put my elbows on my knees and rest my brow on my hands. I will not be sick. I will not faint. I am strong. For just a little longer, I am a Swan Island warrior.

Beside me, Liobhan rises to her feet. "There's no need to

discuss it." Her voice rings out, strong and confident. It's the voice of a fighter, full of courage. "I'll serve a period of one year, no more, with some agreed provisions for my personal safety while in Lord Scannal's household. However, I will not do so unless the total to be paid is reduced by an amount to be agreed between Master Saran and Master Beanón. Lord Scannal demands twelve hundred silver pieces. I think anyone with a modicum of common sense would agree that this amount is excessive."

She sits abruptly. Under cover of the babble of voices, I hiss, "You're crazy! What in the name of the gods—"

"Shh," Liobhan whispers. "It's all right. We can do this." Her hand clasps mine for a moment. Her body's tight as a bowstring. Now I've got tears in my eyes. Let Seanan not be watching. Let him not see as I scrub them away.

"Danu's mercy, Liobhan," murmurs Illann. "I hope you know what you're doing."

They argue about the payment. They discuss, in excruciating detail, what the requirements will be to keep me alive until I am an old man. They calculate the cost in silver pieces. They don't look at the real cost: a gradual, or not so gradual, descent into madness for the injured man; and for Liobhan, a year of utter hell, while the goal for which she has worked so hard moves further and further away. Who's going to give her time to keep body and mind fit, to practice with her weapons, to ride and run and rehearse her combat moves? They're not hiring her as a guard. She'll be scrubbing floors, cleaning out privies, doing the jobs nobody else wants. We shouldn't have said we were friends. Seanan has seized on that. He'll make her life unbearable. And I'll have to stand by while it happens. Because if Liobhan goes through with this, my plan is impossible. If I make an end of myself, I'll be abandoning my comrade. I'll be leaving her to a year in that household, with my father furious over what's happened and my brothers just waiting to break her as they broke me.

They agree to a total payment of seven hundred and fifty silver pieces, to be paid before Seanan's party leaves for home. Cionnaola, sounding very tired, explains that he will not be able to provide such a sum before tomorrow, especially as it will need to be securely packed for travel. The silver will be weighty. Archu comments that in addition to the eight horses my brother's party brought with them, they will need two packhorses and an additional mount for Liobhan. If these animals are to travel all the way to Oakhill, they will come at a cost. The total payment is reduced to seven hundred and forty-one silver pieces. I want to scream. I can't believe my life has been reduced to this. I can't believe Liobhan's act of—of—I don't know if it was heroism or folly or if she has some mad plan of her own, but whatever it was, her act has snatched away my last scrap of free choice.

The thing is over. When Fergus and Jabir come to escort me to the private room we were in before, I go willingly. Liobhan does not come with us. But a little later Archu knocks on the door and enters.

"Illann's riding back to the settlement with Brigid," he says. "They'll go over on a boat to fetch the rest of your belongings, and Liobhan's."

"She'd want to say good-bye," I say. "To explain to her friends. To—to be there, on the island, if only for long enough to walk around and . . ." I see it in my mind, Liobhan bidding them farewell each in turn, Hrothgar and Yann, her fellow musician Eimear, Haki and Eabha and the rest of the tutors, Brother Criodan and Guss . . . I see her on the clifftop gazing out westward over the whitecapped ocean, with her bright hair streaming in the wind and her shoulders set square. I see her in her russet gown, playing the whistle one last time, taking requests, making jokes, and the crowd stamping and clapping. I hear her singing that song, "The Farewell," the one that makes hardened warriors cry.

"I wish I could allow that for both of you, Dau," says Archu with a sigh. "But the feeling out there is less than conciliatory, despite the agreement we've reached. Best if we do nothing to inflame the situation. If I allowed either you or Liobhan to travel back to the island, certain parties would ask questions about whether you might seize the opportunity to vanish. They might not be prepared to wait and see. We'll stay here until your possessions are delivered to you, and in the morning you will ride on with your brother's party."

"Did she know?" I drop my voice to a murmur. "Did Liobhan know that was coming? Did you know? And if so, why didn't you tell me? How can you let her do this?" The murmur has quickly turned to a shout.

"Dau. Hush." Jabir lays a hand on my arm.

"She did not know, and nor did we, though we were aware that such a provision existed within the law," Archu says. "Her decision took us all by surprise. Perhaps it should not have done. Such a gallant and risky act is entirely in keeping with what we know of our comrade."

"Gallant?" I echo. And then I see it. She's doing this not out of duty to Swan Island or to enact some secret plan of her own. She's sacrificing a year of freedom, a year of friendship, a year of fulfillment, because of me. She's coming to Oakhill not only as a bond servant, but also as a protector. She's doing it to keep me safe. She's doing it to keep me alive.

10

BROCC

I sing a song of new beginnings, even as my heart fills with doubt. I sing a lullaby for Gentle-Foot's infant, yet my mind turns to the Crow Folk and the terror they can bring. They are not far away. They cannot be trusted to remain beyond our boundaries forever. Besides, if my voice is the only thing that keeps them at bay, what would happen if I fell sick? What if I died? Part fey though I am, I am not immortal. And what of the human folk, the folk of Faelan's kingdom? They have their own babes in arms, their own toddling infants, their own husbands and wives and aged parents. Their loved ones, too, are in danger. When we drive the Crow Folk beyond our own borders, we send them into the human world to wreak their havoc.

Eirne is out of sorts. As the spring advances and the air warms, as the new shoots rise from the earth and the sun visits us earlier each day, she is not at all her usual self. She is often short with me; nothing I can do or say is quite right. When I ask her what is wrong, she snaps that it's nothing and tells me not to fuss. She knows, perhaps, that when we perform our patrols, Rowan and I continue to step over that perilous line between worlds.

Thinking she might believe the clan inadequately guarded when both Rowan and I are away from the gathering place, I have sought a safeguard. True, the largest of Eirne's folk, re-sembles a man hewn from stone. Indeed, he has moss growing on many of his surfaces, like soft green hair; the tiniest of Eirne's folk, those we seldom see, like to hide in the cracks and dips and natural hollows of his body. A close look at True will generally reveal a crew of such miniature passengers. They sleep nestled in his mossy pelt.

I have asked True to join us on the patrols, though walking quietly is a challenge for him—he is heavy and solid rather than agile. Now two of us go out every day, while one stays behind and guards the home area. When I told Eirne about this new arrangement, she lifted her brows and shrugged. I do try to please her. In the matters of the bedchamber, the sweet in-terchanges between husband and wife, I believe I acquit myself quite well. But as a warrior, as a safekeeper, even as a confidant, I am starting to fall short of my wife's standards, or so it seems. I do not understand what she wants of me. Not fully. And when she is sad, when she is distant, the small folk feel it, too.

There is one way I can cheer them. Music never fails. So, even when I am homesick, heartsick, even when the future weighs heavily on my thoughts, I play my harp and sing for Eirne's folk every evening after supper. At those times I feel the loss of my sister keenly. Her voice would bring me strength and courage. Her deft fingers on the whistle would have the small folk dancing and leaping and laughing with delight. I imagine her on Swan Island, where she and Dau must surely have won permanent places. I am happy that she has achieved the goal she worked so hard for. And Dau, difficult as he can be at times, will be a good friend to her. I wish them well. I wish them the life of adventure and comradeship and challenge both of them want so badly.

Today Rowan and True are out on patrol and I have the job of keeping the gathering place and its surrounding dwellings safe. Like Gentle-Foot and Moth-Weed and their infant, a number of Eirne's folk have chosen to live in spots at quite a distance from the gathering place. It is not for me to change that. I am a newcomer; they have been part of this clan all their lives. I have asked Rowan to make it known to them, subtly, that with Eirne so concerned about the Crow Folk, it might be a good idea to stay within the area that can be guarded effectively. But if you were born and raised in a certain tree hollow, like your parents and your grandparents before you, it would be hard indeed to move away. I understand that as well as anyone can. When I yearn for home, it is not for the human world itself, nor for Swan Island and the journey I abandoned when it had scarcely begun. I long for my childhood home at Winterfalls, the cottage on the edge of Dreamer's Wood, the safe hands of my father and the wry smile of my mother. If I told Eirne this, she might point out quite correctly that my true roots do not lie in that homely cottage but somewhere in the Otherworld. But I came to Winterfalls as an infant only days old. What would I know of a time before?

The forest is dimming to the gray-blue of the spring dusk, and Rowan and True have not returned from their patrol. I should have made a plan for this. I can't go out to look for them and leave the rest of Eirne's folk alone and unguarded with night coming on. They are busy around the gathering place, preparing for the evening meal and the entertainment to follow. They are lighting lanterns, chopping mushrooms and herbs, conversing in squeaks, hoots, and murmurs. I don't see Eirne there, or Nightshade. I can't leave this until after dark.

I go to Eirne's retreat, hoping she may be resting there or talking to Nightshade. Although Eirne is my wife, we do not always share the same house. I spend much of my time in what has become known as the bard's hut: the dwelling I was given when I first entered the Otherworld and had the job of writing a song with a grand purpose. The bard's hut is perfect for one man to use, with its writing table, its narrow bed, its odd little stove in the corner, and its shelf for food and drink. It is set somewhat apart from the gathering place, so the sound of the harp and of my voice will not disturb folk. But although Eirne visits me there, and although we have on occasion shared that narrow bed with great pleasure, the hut is no habitation for a queen.

Eirne's retreat is both living quarters and council room, an airy spot to eat or make love or sing, a private place to discuss grave or sensitive matters. Nightshade lives nearby, her dwelling high in an oak and reached by a rope ladder which the sage draws up at night. I believe she can fly, but I have never seen her do so. Her body seems to be that of a woman beneath the flowing robes she favors. But who is to say that under those concealing garments she may not also have neatly folded wings to match her bird-like features?

I climb the three steps that lead to Eirne's retreat. The door is carved from oak in a pattern of leaves and acorns. The knocker is formed in the shape of an owl. I raise my hand, but before I can knock, the door opens on the interior of Eirne's home. The corner posts are tree trunks, the walls screens of dangling creepers. There is a little stove that warms the place despite its openness. The stove is shaped like a squatting hare with its ears laid back. The glow of hot coals through its open mouth is unsettling.

"Come in, Brocc," says Eirne. She is sitting on the bed; it's Nightshade who has opened the door to me. "You look worried. Is something wrong?"

"True and Rowan are not back yet. I'm concerned, yes. I walked a little way into the forest and called to them, but there was no response." I hesitate. Eirne has the power to see things ordinary folk cannot. She can scry by means of water or smoke or flame. But it's possible our two friends will walk into the gathering place soon, and scrying leaves a person exhausted. With Eirne so dispirited at present, I am reluctant to ask.

"The light is not good enough for a search," Eirne says. "Don't think of going after them." She turns her lovely eyes on me as if assessing me; as if, after three seasons together, she still does not quite know what I am made of. "I'm tired, Brocc. My mind will not be open to visions. Besides, the scrying bowl does not often show me what is happening now, nor are its insights quickly revealed. We must wait."

I go to sit beside my wife. I take her hand. "I hope your spirits will lift soon," I say, feeling somewhat helpless. "We should perhaps send a messenger to Mistress Juniper in the morning, asking for one of her tonics." Mistress Juniper is the local wisewoman and healer; she lives in the human world, at the edge of this forest. Although she does not cross into the Otherworld, she knows where the portal lies, and she has been known to nurse Eirne's folk back to health in her cottage. Tiny birds act as messengers between worlds, and the smaller of Eirne's folk also cross over when the need arises.

"There are healers among our own folk, Brocc. Moon-Fleet provides me with tonics."

I don't respond to this. Yes, Moon-Fleet has healing skills; I have seen many a sprained foot or burned finger salved and wrapped and muttered over since I came here. But Eirne is different. Not only is she the queen, she is also half-human. For her, I think Mistress Juniper may be a better answer.

"The queen will be well again soon," says Nightshade with a confidence I do not share. "Rest, quiet, good food, good companionship—that is all she needs."

Eirne makes a little sound that might mean yes or no.

"All the same, please give my suggestion some thought. I—"

My speech is cut short by an outcry from the gathering place, many voices raised at once. Among them I hear a deep rumbling tone. True, at least, has returned home. "I should go," I say, releasing Eirne's hand and rising. "It sounds as if they're back. Excuse me."

In the gathering place, where tree-hung lanterns now cast a many-colored light around the clearing, True is surrounded by smaller folk, and it's impossible to tell what has happened because all of them are talking at once. I don't see Rowan.

"Hush!" I walk forward, making a quieting gesture. "Let True be heard."

True looks relieved to see me. He gestures with his big stony hands, and the tiny folk pop their heads up out of the moss to listen.

"We found a bird. Hurt. A mark on its flesh, like this." True holds out one massive arm toward me, and I see a sign scratched there. He gestures to show me that he has done this himself, as a record of what he saw. I think it is the same sign I saw on the bird Rowan and I laid to rest, an upright crossed by another line on an angle. It could be the Ogham sign for hawthorn. But perhaps it means something else entirely. Ogham is a language of the druids, and to use it so cruelly would be an offense against the very core of their beliefs.

"Did the bird die?" I ask. "Where is Rowan now?"

"Rowan is coming. The bird is dead. Someone cut off its wings."

All around the clearing there is a deathly hush. Folk look at one another in shock. Perhaps they do not realize that the bird True speaks of was almost certainly one of the Crow Folk.

"Rowan is bringing the bird here. To show you, Brocc. To show the queen."

At that, the beings around me murmur and shuffle, nervous. "Thank you." I lay a hand on True's arm. "You have done well. You should rest now. Be seated; it is almost suppertime. Nimble-

Swift, will you go to the queen's house and tell her what has happened, please?"

Nimble-Swift, a squirrel-like being, darts off at speed, using not only the pathway on the forest floor but also the trunks and limbs of nearby trees as shortcuts. True speaks again, his deep voice weary. "You should go to meet Rowan, Brocc. He will need your help."

This is a task I cannot delegate. It is odd enough that Rowan has decided to bring the body of this bird back here, where it's likely to be an object of disgust and loathing, and it's even odder that he is the one carrying it, when True is so much bigger and stronger. "I will go now."

True points me in the right direction, then sways, almost toppling, before lowering his bulky form to sit on one of the large flat stones that have been placed around the gathering area for this purpose. "You're hurt," I say. "What is it? Show me."

But True waves me away, gesturing, *It's nothing. I'm fine. Go.*

It's nearly dark, so I leave him with the others and head off into the woods. One of the beings has passed me a small lantern, and I am glad of its glow here, deep under the trees where finding a way is tricky even by daylight. Rowan won't have a lamp; we usually make sure we are back from our patrols well before dusk. The moon won't be visible for a while, and it is so dim that a person could get lost within a few strides of the path.

"Rowan!" I call. "Rowan, are you there?"

Nothing but the murmuring exchanges of birds settling for the night and the faint rustling of leaves. I walk on. From time to time I call. Why didn't he and True come back together? This makes no sense to me. I dismiss several troubling possibilities and keep going, concentrating my thoughts on the task ahead as I learned to do on Swan Island, back in the time when I expected to spend my life as a warrior. But the bard will not be suppressed. In my mind a song starts to write itself. I won't be singing this one for Eirne. It's a piece about the Crow Folk and it's full of darkness and confusion. The melody is based on the pattern the druids call yew mode, with halftones in awkward places, and the overall effect is unsettling. I make sure I don't hum aloud. The song tells of a clan that has lost its way and is condemned forever to wander far from home; of folk cut adrift so harshly that they can no longer tell right from wrong, war from peace, cruelty from kindness. I plan to end it with two strangers laying this clan's slain to rest with a prayer and beginning a path toward healing, but before I can form the final verses I hear Rowan's voice.

"Brocc! Over here!"

He's not far off, standing in the shadow of the trees, an awkward burden in his arms. Not one of the Crow Folk, surely, even shorn of its wings as True suggested; Rowan is holding a bundle of cloth, a small bundle, and whatever is in it is moving.

As I come closer I see that he has something on his back as well. It's knotted into his short cloak, from which he has fashioned a makeshift sling. But it's the thing in his arms that is bothering me most.

"What—?" I begin, but I fall silent when he draws back the cloth that covers the wriggling contents. I raise the lantern, and warm light illuminates Rowan's exhausted face and the creature he has carried here. It's one of them, one of the Crow Folk, it's alive, and it's only the size of a half-grown chicken. But it's not a chicken, and it's not a young crow. It has a look of wildness and desperation I know well. It has, in miniature, the lethal beak, the crazy eyes, the fearsome claws. It looks strong for its size; Rowan's having trouble restraining it. Now that I've seen it, he wraps it up again, tightly, then passes it to me. I set the lantern on the ground and take it. It's vibrating within the cloth, which I recognize as Rowan's tunic; under the cloak he's in shirt and trousers. "A young one?" I ask. "Where did you find it?"

"I found the two of them," Rowan says, turning and crouching down so the light shines on the sling and its burden. What I see makes my gorge rise. The creature within the sling is dead, no doubt of that. Its wings have been hacked off crudely, and its body is marked with that sign. It has other wounds, to its eyes, to its skin, to its feet.

I murmur a curse. We thought the Crow Folk were evil; we thought their mindless acts of cruelty the worst danger Breifne faced. But this, surely, is a deeper evil. "Where?" I ask again as we turn toward home.

"Within this realm, but close to the border. The adult lying dead, maimed as you see. The small one crouched beside its body. When it saw us it shrieked defiance. I would have left it there. True said no, you would not want it abandoned. He was hurt trying to pick it up, but we gathered it and wrapped it. I told him to go back first and I would follow; True was in pain. He would have carried one or the other of them, but I ordered him to return without a load. He doesn't tell you when he's injured. It's not in his nature."

"He was right," I say. "About my not wanting it left to die in the forest with the body of its parent. But what are we to do with it? You know what Eirne will say."

Rowan glances sideways at me; the lantern he carries casts light on his bright-eyed fox's face. "She is the queen, yes, and makes the decisions. But you are her husband, Brocc. You are our bard. You are our war leader."

"Hardly." I think of Swan Island, and how different it is from this place with its motley clan of assorted beings, a few of them capable of fighting, a couple of them able to strategize, and some of them with surprising magic at their disposal, but only Rowan—and perhaps True—worthy of the title *warrior*. War leader, me? I'm a floundering mixture of hope and disappointment and wild ideas, with a song or two thrown in.

"You must stand up to her," Rowan says. "If she does not like one idea, give her another, and another." We walk on in silence, then he adds, "With a new babe born to Gentle-Foot, perhaps the queen will be kindly disposed to this young one, enemy though it is."

"And perhaps she will demand that I wring its neck. She feels our losses keenly. She feels responsible."

"I will support you." This statement, and what he said before it, shows me just how much Rowan has changed since I first met him less than a year ago. He was Eirne's protector and champion. It seemed to me then that he would die for her; that may still be so. I thought he would always take her part. Back then he was slow to trust me. But my trust in him and True to share responsibility for the patrols, to make their own decisions, to play a real part in keeping the community safe, has wrought a change in his thinking. I wonder, now, how Eirne feels about that. She has never spoken of it, but she must see it.

"Thank you, Rowan." I pause in my steps, moving my squirming cargo to a more secure position. "Perhaps I should leave you to return to the gathering place on your own. I could take this creature straight to Mistress Juniper. I think she would help without judgment."

Rowan gives me a penetrating look. If he had eyebrows, he would lift them. "Imagine the ripples it would make if the creature harmed her. It's strong and wild, even if it is an infant. Ripples that would soon reach King Faelan and the human court. Besides . . ."

"Besides, my wife would not be well pleased if I took myself

out of the Otherworld without her permission, yes, I do know
that. Even if Mistress Juniper's house is within walking distance."

"A very long walk. In the dark. Carrying *that*. And . . ."

"And what? Come, we'd better move on."

"If anyone needs the attentions of Mistress Juniper, it's True.
He may seem as strong as stone, but he is not impervious. The
creature's claw marked him on the chest as he was lifting it,
dead and cold as it was. I saw the wound swell and turn red
quite quickly. If the queen will not let him go to the human
world for help, then he must travel the Long Path."

The first time I heard one of Eirne's folk speak of the Long
Path, I thought they meant the passage to death. The Fair Folk
are long-lived; their span is far greater than that of humankind.
But they are not immortal. Several of Eirne's people have been
killed by the Crow Folk, one of them during my time here. And
she fears that their number will dwindle until the clan cannot
survive. That is why Gentle-Foot's child is so precious. It is why
Eirne will not welcome this other child, the strange one I hold
in my arms now. But I have learned that the Long Path is not
what I thought. It leads to different realms and different clans,
all within the Otherworld. I knew they must exist; what of my
parents' friend, the fey nobleman Conmael, who brought me
to their door as a newborn? His clan is in the north of Dalriada,
that is, in the Otherworld kingdom of those parts. My parents
have known him since before I was born. But exactly how that
realm links up with Eirne's, and with others across the isle of
Erin, I don't entirely understand, and the explanations the Fair
Folk offer can be confusing. Eirne once spoke of her realm as
beneath, above, beside, beyond the human world, and indeed,
one step can take a person over that border. But a human man
or woman can enter this world only through a portal, and generally those portals, whether they be hidden doorways or deep

caves or mushroom circles, open or close at the will of the Fair Folk. As for those of us who live in the fey realm, even half humans like myself and Eirne are supposed to comply with certain rules. Those rules are designed to keep us safe, and I respect them. Mostly. Sometimes, though, I believe rules must be broken. Perhaps that is the influence of Swan Island.

"Rowan, does the Long Path lead to healers? Healers as expert as Mistress Juniper but of the Otherworld?"

"The Long Path leads many ways," Rowan says. "Not all of them are easy. But yes, that is what I meant. True is a good soul; he would find help there."

"But he couldn't go alone, could he? What if he collapsed along the way? And how would he know where to go? Mistress Juniper is surely far closer."

Below us, between the trees, I see the lanterns of the gathering place, and folk moving about. "Rowan?"

"Those are questions for the queen," my companion says. "They'll see us in a moment. Are you ready for this?"

"No," I say, matching his honesty. "But I'll do the best I can. Show them your burden first. Let them see how cruelly someone has treated the creature. Perhaps that will lessen the shock of what I'm carrying."

"Perhaps," says Rowan in a tone that tells me he doesn't believe that any more than I do. Then we walk forward and enter the gathering place.

Rowan takes off the cloak, lays it on the ground, unfastens it to reveal the slain creature, wingless, mangled, marked with that strange symbol. He warns folk not to touch, tells them the claws can not only scratch but also poison, even when the being is dead. Eirne's folk are torn between fascination and disgust. None seem especially interested in who inflicted the wounds or why. The Crow Folk are their enemy. Perhaps they think whoever hurts the Crow Folk must be their friend.

Eirne is here, with Nightshade. She glances at the sad corpse, then quickly away, as if she cannot bear to see the thing.

"Another act of deliberate cruelty," I say. "This being did not die in a fair fight. It was not killed by someone defending their folk or their home. It's been tortured. That is wrong. No matter what we think of the Crow Folk, it's still wrong."

"Brocc." Eirne's voice has a troubling note in it. "What are you carrying?"

My arms tighten around the bundle, which lets out a squawk of protest, and suddenly all eyes are on me. "What I bear is . . . a child, a young one, surely an innocent." A pox on it, I sound as if I'm trying to convince myself that this was a good idea. It won't do. I clear my throat and do my best to sound like a leader. "True and Rowan found it crouched by the body of its parent." I nod in the direction of the wingless corpse, which still lies on the ground. Eirne's folk have stepped back; the dead thing has an empty space all around it. "There were no others of its kind to be seen in that place. Left on its own, the young one would surely have perished from hunger, cold, or fear. So we brought it with us." I loosen the cloth just enough for the being to poke its head out, probably not a good move since that head is all mad eyes and stabbing beak. That the beak is a very small one does not render it harmless.

"Why in the name of the gods would you bring one of *them* into the center of my realm?" Eirne is all queen now, commanding, furious. "Why would you show the vile creatures the least scrap of pity? How dare you risk our safety in this way!"

Her anger hurts me. It wounds me. But I will not sacrifice my conscience. I will not give up compassion, kindness, a knowledge of right and wrong. "If you wish," I say, "I will take the small one to Mistress Juniper. Now, tonight. Let it have at least a chance of life. The child is not responsible for its parents' ill deeds, whatever they may be, nor for the wrongdoing of its clan. Act on that and we show ourselves to be barbarians." I am astonished by my own words; that sounded like something my sister would say.

"It is the Crow Folk that are barbaric," Eirne says. The full chill of her disapproval is turned on me. Never mind that it was Rowan and True who decided to spare the young one. "We cannot harbor one of them here," she goes on, "be it infant or adult or featherless ancient. How could this creature grow to become anything but vicious and wayward? Its eyes are venomous. Its beak is a weapon."

Nightshade speaks. She is calmer; her words are measured. "Mistress Juniper would not thank you for such a burden. What is she to do, cage the creature for her own protection? Would you have her nurture it in her house until it grows to adulthood? Human folk come to visit her, Brocc. She is healer to the whole district. If you take this thing there, you place her at great risk."

"Will not its clan believe it a captive there?" asks Nimble-Swift. "They might descend on the wisewoman's house in an attempt to free it. You might find yourself responsible for Mistress Juniper's death."

It's a good point, and so is Nightshade's. I cannot bring myself to ask Eirne, or any of them, what they would have me do. I can guess what their answers would be, but I will not kill this small one and I will not abandon it. Perhaps there is one argument they will understand. "You say the Crow Folk might be angry, that they might seek out their lost one. That is one possibility, yes." Gods, I hope I don't have to stand here holding the thing all night while we argue the point. It needs to be somewhere warm and safe, with food and water. It's still trying to get free, and I'm afraid it may hurt itself. "But if we take some other course, if we let the creature come to harm, might they not then seek retribution? What if this were your child, lost in the forest, and someone came along, and instead of looking after it, they walked away and left it? Or did something unspeakable?"

After that, there is silence. Even from Eirne. I can't let this drag out any longer. What about True, sitting there so quietly while the Crow Folk's poison sinks deeper into his body? "With your permission, Eirne, I will take this creature to my hut for the night. I will put it somewhere secure; perhaps Rowan will help me. If it survives the night, then in the morning we can decide what happens next." Eirne still makes no comment, but Rowan nods and moves forward. "We'd best do that now."

"Shut it in well." Eirne's tone is icy. "If ill comes from this, it is on your shoulders."

"I need no reminder of that, my lady." My voice is as cold and remote as hers. I hate myself for that; this is not the man I am. "I ask you, or Moon-Fleet, to look at True's injury. It is serious. He needs expert attention, and quickly."

True rumbles a response. "It's nothing. Don't trouble yourself."

"The bard speaks the truth," Rowan says. "Our friend here was wounded by the adult creature's claw; there may be poison in his body."

"We will do what must be done." Nightshade sounds calm and capable, and I feel relief. I want to check True's wounds myself; I am the son of a healer and I do remember some of the remedies my mother uses. But I cannot be in two places, so I offer my wife what I hope is a courteous half bow and head off for my hut, with Rowan following. As we walk, I wonder if I have so angered Eirne that she will cast me out of the Otherworld, husband or no. She spoke to me as if I were a stranger, and one she did not particularly like. Can the bond between us have unraveled so soon?

Rowan finds a sturdy wooden box. One-handed, I fetch a sack and some strong twine. I cannot set the creature down until I have a secure place for it. Rowan brings in a pile of leaves and grasses; he makes a nest in the box. He finds a small bowl, fills it from my water barrel, sets that in one corner. "What will you feed it?" he murmurs.

It is crow-like. A crow parent might feed its young on worms, grubs, scraps of this and that. But we're in the hut, and in the forest darkness is falling. The being squirms in my arms, fighting to get away. I wonder, for a moment, if it would be kinder to let it go.

There's a tap at the door. On the step outside are two small beings, and each is carrying a lidded jar in its hands. "Worms," says one. "Bugs," says the other. "Baby will be hungry," they say together.

Rowan thanks them and takes the offerings. As soon as the jars are in his hands, the small ones vanish into the night.

We work well as a team, Rowan and I, despite our differences. He lays the sack over the box and ties it to leave only a small space open, a gap big enough to admit a creature the size of a half-grown chicken. With only one candle lit, the hut is dim; Rowan has closed the door. I edge with ever-slower movements toward the box. Rowan holds back the sack. I slip the bundle in, my hands still firm around the shivering body.

"Now," I murmur, and let the creature go, withdrawing my hands. Rowan whips the sack over the gap, and together we tie up the fastenings. Within the box there is fluttering, scratching, a flurry of sound and movement. We wait, eyeing each other, breathing hard. So far, so good.

When the box's occupant has quieted, I use my knife to make a small hole in the sack. I open the worm jar and extract a fine wriggling specimen. I do not speak an apology to this healthy creature, not aloud, but I say it in my mind. When I make to drop it through the hole, using my fingers, Rowan puts out a hand to stop me.

"Wait," he says, and fetches a pair of small sticks from the wood basket beside my little stove. "Here."

He is wise. When I lower the worm, held between the sticks, the creature's beak snaps up at lightning speed to grab it. I might have lost a finger. I feed the thing another worm, and a bug or two. It would eat everything the small folk brought, I think, but I don't want to make it sick. I want it to rest. I set the jars aside for now. There's squawking for a little, then silence. When I peer through the hole, taking care not to get too close, the thing is in a corner, nestled into the bedding, its head under its wing. I hope it will be warm enough. I'd best keep the stove going overnight.

"Well," says Rowan.

"Well," I say. "A strange day. Thank you for your help. You should go and have some supper, and then rest. Will you check on True for me?" Rowan will understand that I must stay here; I cannot leave until this creature's future is determined. It is nobody's responsibility but mine.

"I will, and if I am not satisfied I will come back and tell you. You also need supper and rest, Brocc."

"Don't trouble yourself about me. I'll see you in the morning."

Rowan does not return, and nor do the small folk, who on a different occasion might have brought me supper. I sit by my fire a long while, getting up from time to time to peer through the hole in the sacking, reassuring myself that the creature is still breathing. I ponder various courses of action and find none of them satisfactory. When the moon is up, I lie down on my bed, but I cannot sleep. Every small sound from the box has my heart jolting with fright or concern or something else, though when I check, the creature is only stirring in its sleep, as if troubled by dark dreams.

Late in the night it wakes, crying out. I feed it; it gobbles my offering enthusiastically. Afterward I sing it a little song, and at a certain point it starts a soft chirping. When I stop, it stops. When I pick up the tune again, it chirps again as if to sing along with me. The hairs on the back of my neck stand up. Something deeply magical is happening. This is not the Otherworld magic of charms and spells. It is the simple and powerful magic of trust. When I peer into the box, the creature is gazing up at me. Its eyes look more tranquil now. "Sleep time, small one," I say, and close the sacking over the gap. There are enough worms and beetles left for breakfast, I think. And plenty more to be found in the forest. Perhaps I can raise this little one myself. Perhaps, treated kindly, even one of the Crow Folk can grow up healthy and calm and wise.

Eventually I fall asleep. I wake at first light, taking a moment or two to remember that I am not alone in my hut; yes, that really did happen. I look over toward the box and freeze. The twine is undone. The sack is drawn right back. Where—? I glance wildly around, up to the rafters, into the dark corners, over to the stove with its banked-up fire. No sign. Nothing. The door is closed. With my hands up to shield my face from possible attack, I tiptoe toward the box and look down.

The creature lies on the bedding, its fledgling wings spread wide as if in flight, its eyes glassy, its head at an impossible angle to its body. While I was sleeping on my pallet not two strides away, someone has entered my hut and broken its neck.

11

LIOBHAN

There's at least one gaping hole in the plan to get Dau safely back home. Seanan's people haven't brought a healer with them, and neither Fergus nor Jabir is able to accompany them all the way to Oakhill—each is required elsewhere. The closest thing Seanan has is me, but I'm the last person he'd want as nurse for his brother, even if he knew I was capable. And Dau would hate it. He's gone silent in the way only a furiously angry person can. If I speak to him I may get a punch in the guts for my efforts. I thought I was helping. I am helping. Yes, putting my hand up to be an unpaid servant in what sounds like the worst household in the world is perhaps not the most sensible decision I've ever made. But why would Dau be angry? With me there, at least he'll have a friend. He'll have someone to watch over him, to make sure he's safe. I'm trained for that. I resolve to treat this as another mission and to acquit myself as well as I possibly can.

Illann and Brigid should be back with our possessions by the end of the day. They'll bring the extra horses we need. Dusk and Fleetfoot are not part of the arrangement; they'll be returned to their stables. We'll have other mounts for the long ride to Oakhill, horses whose price is within the figure agreed on. I trust Illann to find a suitable animal for Dau. The fact is, Dau's an excellent rider, far more capable than me, but a blind man needs a very particular kind of horse, one like Dusk that's not only calm tempered but also quick to understand what the rider wants and needs. Can I ask to be the one who rides next to Dau? Seanan heard me speak at the meeting. He must have realized then that I have a mind of my own. It would be better if Dau asked him. But he won't. He's put up that invisible wall, the one that keeps everyone at a distance.

It's a very long day. The two groups tread a difficult line between ignoring each other and maintaining an awkward civility. Dau has retreated to the room where he was waiting earlier, muttering about a sore head. Jabir is with him. Cionnaola and Archu are talking to Fergus in one corner of the dining room. Seanan and his advisers are in another corner. Guards are stationed discreetly at various points around Hawthorn House, both inside and outside. I'm not sure exactly what the threat is supposed to be. Perhaps it's me. Perhaps they expect me to bolt when their backs are turned. Or maybe it's that substantial payment in silver that's the issue—I assume it's coming back on the boat with Illann and Brigid, who took one of our guards with them.

I've been outside, walking. Not far; I'm not stupid. One of Seanan's men tailed me all the way. I wished I could bring out my whistle and play a jig, just to startle him. Now I'm back, and since I can hardly march over and start telling Seanan how things are going to be, I need to talk to Archu. I'm still a Swan Island warrior. I intend to remain one, in thought and deed, while I get through what will be a testing year. So I'll do the right thing and seek the elders' approval for my self-appointed mission while I can. After tomorrow morning I won't see any of the team for a very long time.

I go over and sit down beside the three men. They stop talking. Archu manages a crooked smile, though they all look grim.

"All right, Liobhan?" asks Cionnaola. "You surprised us. You'll be sadly missed on the island."

A shocking thought comes to me. I hadn't for a moment considered I might not be welcome back on Swan Island after what's happened. I can only bear this time away if I know my spot will be waiting for me.

"It will seem long," Cionnaola says. "Interminable, probably. And difficult. But even as we regret that you're leaving us, we're relieved that Dau will have a friend and advocate in Oakhill."

"Keep up your physical training," puts in Archu, who reads me very well. "Otherwise you'll have a lot of work to do when you get back." Perhaps I let out a relieved breath, for he adds, "You'll always be one of us, Liobhan. I wish we could keep Dau, too, but it seems that's not to be."

"About Dau. His brother hasn't brought a healer. That seems quite an oversight. I do have some basic skills, as you know. If they're not going to pick someone up on the way, I could at least keep an eye on Dau as we go. I could take some of Fergus's preparations with me and administer them when he needs them. I'm not sure anyone else in the party will take much trouble over Dau's welfare." None of them comments. I go on. "I think I should ride alongside Dau. We're used to each other. I know him well enough to see when he's ill, or when he's not coping."

"And will Dau welcome that?" Archu asks quietly. I don't think Seanan and his party can hear us, but it's wise to be careful.

"I doubt he'll welcome anything, even if he needs it," says Fergus. "But Liobhan is his friend, and if he listens to anyone, it will be to her. Shall I speak to Master Seanan? Let him know that Liobhan is the daughter of a healer and can be useful to him on the journey if he entrusts this duty to her?"

"Better coming from you than from Liobhan herself," says Cionnaola. "Perhaps from you and me together, Fergus. Let's see if Master Seanan is open to some polite persuasion. If I call you over, Liobhan, remember that your role right now is healer and nursemaid, not warrior or bard."

I grimace, then seat myself beside Archu, who offers me a cup of ale. We watch as the others approach Seanan's party. A conversation starts, of which we hear little.

"Liobhan," says Archu in an undertone. "About Dau. I don't believe in miracles. But strange things happen, and the man's sorely in need of hope. Once you're on the way and when you have an opportunity, let him know you're not the only one under instruction to keep up your physical skills. He may be blind, but if someone's there to keep him safe he can run, he can climb, he can do the daily exercises you learned as trainees. Should his vision return, he'll want to be ready to come back. Remind him how quickly a fine weapon loses its edge if it's not maintained. He's going to a chieftain's household. His father will have all the facilities required. Dau just needs some-one to keep an eye on him. If not a trainer, then a training companion."

I try to see it in my mind and fail. "That training companion isn't going to be me. The bond servant. The lowest of the low. Did you see the way Seanan looked at me? In the eyes of that family I've got guilt written all over me. It just isn't possible."

"Ah," says Archu, and I know what's coming next. "But that's what we do on Swan Island. We make the impossible happen. You are one of us, Liobhan, and we expect no less of you."

I bow my head, partly in respect and gratitude, and partly to conceal the tears that have welled up in my eyes.

"A brave decision," he says. "I'm proud of you. Also somewhat horrified, but keep that to yourself. I see Cionnaola beckoning, and it won't be me he wants. Remember who you are, Liobhan, both on the outside as you play your role, and inside, where only one of your own kind can see." A pause, then he adds, "After this you'll truly deserve Bran's Blade. We'll be keeping it safe for you."

I wonder, later, what Cionnaola and Fergus said to get Seanan's agreement. I wonder if Dau's brother has some kind of plan he's not telling anyone. It feels too easy. I play my part as well as I can, keeping answers brief and courteous, not meeting Seanan's eye for too long, playing down the skills I can offer while sounding—I hope—confident enough to be believed. When he says yes to my riding alongside Dau and taking on the responsibility of keeping him alive and well until we reach Oakhill, I'm too astonished to say a word. I manage a nod, then retreat. This is starting to feel like a bizarre dream. Fergus says he'll put some useful items together for me and talk to me more after he's done so. The healer's bag will need to go on one of the packhorses. Cionnaola asks if he may speak to Seanan further concerning the agreement on my personal safety while at Oakhill. It's quite clear I am not to be present for this conversation, though I wish I could hear it. As I depart I hear Cionnaola requesting, firmly but politely, that the terms be worked out in the presence of the two lawmen and that a written record be retained.

It's nearly dark and Illann's back with our belongings. I find a private corner to check my bag, out of sight of anyone who might be too interested, and I'm glad I took that precaution since my two good knives, large and small, have been rolled skillfully in a night-robe and stuffed in between other items.

Best that they stay there so Seanan's people don't decide to take them off me. My protective gear's been included, which is a surprise. I don't expect to be getting any combat practice at Oakhill. It's more likely to be floor-scrubbing or ditch-digging. At least those activities will keep me strong. Whoever did the packing was thoughtful. They've included a roll of well-washed linen rags. I won't be needing those until we're settled, since my moon-bleeding finished only days ago. I wouldn't want to have that complication on a ride with Seanan's crew, though my comrades on the island—male and female alike—are understanding about these things. The two whistles I had at the Barn are now in this bag, wrapped in a silk shift. There's no way I'm going a whole year without music. If Lord Scannal is so wealthy, I expect his household has its own band of entertainers. I wonder if a bond servant would be considered too lowly to join in, even if she was good at it.

Some of my possessions are not here. There's no staff. There's no bow and quiver. That makes perfect sense; I can't ride a horse, keep an eye on Dau, and carry either of those at the same time. Besides, they would mark me out too obviously as a fighter, and although Seanan knows that's what I am, I bet he won't want reminding of the fact. Stupid, really. I'd be more useful to him as a guard than anything else. I wonder if he treats his men-at-arms as cruelly as he treated young Dau? I wonder how he deals with his servants? But then, he's not the chieftain, his father is. I'm not looking forward to meeting Lord Scannal.

I pack everything back in. The bag is designed to go behind the saddle. That's another bit of good thinking. Means I can be sure my possessions are safe as we go. Now I need to check Dau's things.

In the small chamber, Dau is lying on the pallet with his

eyes closed. Not asleep: his fists are clenched. Jabir is packing a bag with vials and jars and packets of herbs. "For you to take," he says. "I have spoken to Master Naithí. I told him these things must be carried carefully. They must be available to you whenever the party stops. Everything is labeled clearly. You will be limited in what you can prepare along the way, unless you stop at a house with a stillroom. This powder, taken in a cup of warm water, will help relieve pain. At night, enough to cover your thumbnail. That will aid sleep. By day, only a small pinch, since Dau has to ride."

"A man may be blind," Dau observes in a drawl, "but that does not also render him deaf."

"Liobhan is the healer." Jabir remains calm, as always. "My instructions are for her. For you to administer a dose to yourself would be most unwise."

There's a silence, then Dau says, "Was that a joke, Jabir? I did not believe you capable of such a thing."

"This is no joking matter, my friend, as you well know. Liobhan, if time or place does not allow you to exercise your skills as you would wish, a cool, damp cloth on the brow, with those herbs you know to be effective, will give at least some relief. And if at any time you are seriously concerned for Dau you should make that known to Master Seanan, whatever your reservations."

I grimace, saying nothing.

"Or to Master Naithí, who, I believe, may be more ready to listen."

"My father's puppet," says Dau, sitting up and opening his eyes. "Lackeys, all of them. What is the point?"

I march over and sit down on the bed beside him. "Dau," I say, "the point is to stand up and be strong. Not to let this beat you down. The point is to hold on to hope. It's stupid to refuse help. All right, perhaps these remedies only relieve the pain and swelling for a short while. But perhaps they're part of a long, slow healing. Jabir and Fergus have said they don't understand your condition. So they don't know if it's permanent or not. Now listen. I've chosen to come with you, whether you like it or not. I may not be a skilled healer like Jabir, but I can help with this. How is it going to look if we have a fight every time I try to apply a compress or give you a dose? Do you want to provide cheap entertainment for our traveling companions? No. So stop doing this right now, will you?"

I wait for him to point out that he's the one whose future has been snatched away, the one whose brother is a monster, the one whose hope of recovery is so slight it's cruel to speak of it. But he doesn't.

"You sound like a nursery maid scolding her disobedient charge, Liobhan," he says. Can that possibly be the hint of a smile? "Don't think to try that approach on my brother. He doesn't respond well when provoked." If it's a smile, it's a bitter one. "Jabir, I owe you an apology. You are a patient man."

Jabir gives a little bow, which Dau can't see.

"Dau, I just checked the bag they packed for me. Shall I go through yours, so you know what's in it?"

"If you want. I can guess. No sharp items, nothing I can hurt myself with. Nothing you wouldn't give to a two-year-old child."

"They would surely return the weapons you brought with you when you came to Swan Island." But they haven't. Dau had a beautifully crafted sword, so well-balanced that using it felt like playing a fine instrument. It wasn't a gaudy, showy thing, just perfectly made. It was given to him by his mentor, Garalt. And he had his own good bow, too, with a tooled leather quiver. Neither is here, and when I unpack the bag, nor are his knives. I tell him what's here as I lift each item out. Clothing, mostly. Protective gear, the same as mine. A favorite cup. Right at the bottom, a strip of worn leather that looks like rubbish. I'm on the verge of discarding it when I see that it's a collar. An old, worn dog collar. Stained dark here and there. Now I want to cry. "And this," I say, putting it in Dau's hands. I can't look at him. "No sign of a sword or bow?" I ask, glancing at Jabir.

"Nothing. But they may be elsewhere. Since neither of you travels as a warrior, perhaps Illann has kept them aside to be loaded onto the packhorse. You should ask him."

"Maybe." Not the knives, though. They'd have been in the bag, as mine were. Unless Illann or Brigid feared Dau would use them on himself. "I'll ask. Or rather, I'll ask Cionnaola or Archu to ask. Shall I pack this up again, Dau?"

He passes Snow's collar to me, then wipes his eyes. "Who'd have thought it?" he says lightly. "These eyes are still perfectly good at shedding tears. Put this somewhere safe, will you?"

"I will. Right at the bottom, wrapped in a handkerchief. Which is something you've always unfailingly produced when it was most needed." I lay my hand over his for a moment. Only for a moment, or I'll cry, too. Didn't I just lecture him about being strong? "As for your weapons, I suppose your brother will want them returned, if not now then later. They're valuable."

"Unlike the man who used them." As quickly as that, Dau's mood has changed again. "The sword should stay on Swan Island. It was never Seanan's or my father's. Tell Archu that. You should have it. When you come back."

I have to leave the room. I find my way right outside, dark as it is, and stand in a corner where nobody can see me. I cry until I have no more tears. I splash my face in a water barrel. I take a few deep breaths, reminding myself that I am a Swan Island warrior, I am strong, I can do this. Nobody is going to see me defeated. Not tonight, not tomorrow, not before this wretched year reaches its sorry end and I can come home. And if, at the back of my mind, a question lingers—what sort of homecoming can that be, if I must leave Dau behind at Oakhill?—I'm not ready for the answer.

12

DAU

My brother has decided I am no longer a man. I deduce this from the fact that he does not speak to me direct. As we make our way toward Oakhill he converses with his lawman and his councilor, as well as addressing his head guard when appropriate. If he needs to communicate something to me, he speaks to Liobhan. Only it's not a request or a suggestion, it's a barked-out order of some kind, and he doesn't use her name. To him she's nothing but a bond servant, and he calls her "girl."

I know Liobhan pretty well after those months of training and the mission in Breifne, which threw us together and taught us a hard-won trust. In my mind I see her face tight-jawed, fierce-eyed, and I'm furious on her behalf. But I don't challenge Seanan. The way I am now, I'd only make a pointless exhibition of myself. I want to shout, to punch his jaw, to break something over the man's head. Every time he speaks, the old hate wells up in me. But I hear Liobhan responding to his commands with scrupulous politeness—I bet the blind man is the only one who can tell she's fuming—and I feel obliged to match that.

On the first day of riding I acquit myself reasonably well. I think I do. I can mount on my own, provided Liobhan leads me to the right position. I can dismount unassisted. My horse, though no match for Dusk, is well-mannered and compliant. The midday stop and rest, in the shelter of some woodland, is awkward. When a blind man has to take a piss, it wouldn't be right for a woman to accompany him. The problem is solved when one of the guards, Donn, suggests we go and do the necessary together. Whether this is his own idea or whether Liobhan has signaled to him in some way, I don't know. His manner is relaxed; he speaks to me as if I were an equal, able-bodied and capable. I thank him.

"Anytime," he says. "Must be hard to get used to. You being a fighting man and all."

"It is. Have you been at Oakhill long? In my father's household?"

"A year or two. Before that, at the court of Dalriada. Left there in pursuit of a lady, but all in vain, sadly. She wed another man."

"My sympathies." Liobhan and Brocc lived near the court of Dalriada before they came to Swan Island. Might not this man have heard them playing and singing in that district, perhaps even at court? Liobhan's not the sort of woman you'd forget quickly. Still, I won't say anything if he doesn't. I'll mention it to her quietly. Perhaps it's of no consequence, since she's not under cover here. I'd rather my brother doesn't find out where her parents live.

"Ah, well. It wasn't to be," says Donn. "I'm content enough where I am, for now at least. Better be getting back. The ground's pretty uneven here; put your hand on my shoulder." As we make our way back, he adds, "Pays to be careful in the woods. Especially as we head south. Have you heard of the Crow Folk, Master Dau?"

"In tales, yes." I won't mention that Liobhan and I have fought them and survived. The Crow Folk haven't been seen anywhere near Swan Island. But there have been continuing tales of attacks in the southwest.

"There's a lot of them in the forest south of Oakhill," Donn says. "Makes it hard for the farmers to protect their stock. And sometimes they'll attack travelers, too. They do stay away from your father's house. You'll be safe there."

Oh, the irony in that. If only he knew.

We stop for the night at the home of a nobleman known to my brother. We're still in Dalriada, but sufficiently far south to be well clear of the court and of Liobhan's home at Winterfalls, where she and I went after Brocc's departure. That is a good place. Homely, safe, quiet. It's far enough away from other dwellings to be restful, but near enough so folk can reach both of her parents when they're needed, which is often, since Mistress Blackthorn is a healer and Master Grim seems able to turn his hand to almost anything, though his principal craft is thatching. Sometimes, when I've been lying awake at night, I've wondered if Liobhan's mother might know of some remarkable, obscure way to restore a man's vision, something two expert physicians have never heard of. I've wished I was back in Breifne, difficult as that time was, so I could visit Mistress Juniper and spill out everything to her, as I did once before. She is the only person who has heard the full story of what my brothers did to Snow. Even Liobhan knows only part of it. I can't hear Seanan's voice without seeing that day in my mind. I can't hear it without wishing I had my knife in my hand and just enough vision to find my brother and kill him. Who cares what happens after that? They can string me up from the nearest tree. A quick ending that would break my neck but not my promise to Liobhan. I can't do it, of course. That would leave her at my father's mercy.

I'm given a small chamber to myself. Very small; when I stretch out my arms I can touch both walls. There's a narrow pallet, a chest, a shelf. The room is cold. It feels damp. Somewhere along the way, as they were bringing me here, I lost Liobhan. Where have they taken her? I think of a lot of questions I don't want to ask, such as how do I get to the privy at night if I need to, and what happens if I wake with my head throbbing—a common occurrence—and need help. "A bucket might be useful," I say. "A jug of water and a cup, if that can be managed." I think I succeed in sounding polite. Is there anyone still here from our own party, or am I with strangers now, servants in this household?

"That will be arranged, of course," someone says.

"Thank you. Is there a healer or physician in this house?"

A silence that feels awkward. "Not in the house, no. Are you unwell?"

I swallow bitter laughter. "No more so than usual," I say. "The woman who traveled with us, Liobhan, has been tending to me along the way. Do you know where she will be accommodated?"

There's a muttered consultation, which tells me that these are household serving folk and that all they've been told is to bring me and my bags to this room. "She'll be in the women's quarters," one of them says. "Over at the eastern end, quite a walk from here."

I could make a fuss. But that might bring my brother. There's a rich aroma of roasted meat wafting by; I imagine these folk will give us supper. Perhaps, after that, I will have a night without dreams. "Could you show me where the privy is? If I'm on my own, I'll need to be able to find my way there and back."

I don't hear the answer, because Liobhan's voice cuts through the others, full of energy even after the long day's ride. I hear her footsteps as she strides along the hallway toward us. "There must be some mistake. Are you aware that Master Dau is Lord Scannal's son? He's recovering from an injury and he needs a more appropriate chamber, with enough space for me to tend to him if required." A silence. "If you please," Liobhan adds.

"We had instructions to bring him here," one of the men says.

"Instructions from whom?"

"Liobhan." I try to convey a subtle warning. I can guess who gave the order, and I know I don't want Liobhan clashing with my brother so soon. She doesn't know Seanan as I do. She doesn't know how deep that streak of cruelty goes. "I've slept in worse places."

"Who's going to measure out a draft for you if you wake in pain? I've been told there's no healer in the place and nothing else arranged."

"I expect I'll survive one night."

"And get on your horse and ride again all day tomorrow?"

One of the servants clears his throat. "We're just carrying out our instructions."

"Might I speak to the household steward?" asks Liobhan. Although she's still courteous, the tone she strikes is that of a grand lady, someone whose orders everyone will jump to obey, and in front of these people I can't tell her to shut up and leave this alone.

"It's not for us to question—" the man begins, then falls silent as a new voice is heard from along the hallway.

"Is there a problem here?" Seanan has a manner with servants that sends them scurrying to do whatever he asks.

"A slight difficulty, Master Seanan." That's Liobhan, her tone quite different now, hushed and almost servile. "Your brother has not been sleeping well. He often needs attention during the night—someone close at hand to administer drafts or bathe his eyes. This chamber does not have space for that, and there's nowhere for me—or whoever will be looking after him—to sleep nearby. Also, he needs a comfortable bed." A pause. "One appropriate to his station in life," she adds.

"Isn't he a warrior now?" If anything, Seanan sounds amused. "I thought fighting men were used to hard beds. You, too, if what they tell me is correct. This seems entirely appropriate. I advised our host that Dau would likely wake at night, perhaps several times. That he might shout, scream, and become aggressive. That was made plain enough in the testimony we heard. Now, *that* was a definition of uncomfortable. I'm grateful to our host for accommodating our whole party overnight. I don't wish to cause his household any inconvenience, so I requested that my brother be housed in an isolated chamber. These two fine fellows are doing exactly what they've been ordered to do." Another silence. I imagine Seanan lifting his brows, showing Liobhan *that* face. "Surely I don't need to remind you why Dau is in this situation," he says. "If you wish to be at his beck and call night and day, so be it. I know nothing of your relationship before this, except that you enjoy hurting each other in front of an audience."

I imagine Liobhan clenching her fists, tightening her jaw. I wait for her to bite back, but she says nothing at all.

"You two, bring the girl's bags here. Ask my men-at-arms which ones they are. Get her a blanket. She can sleep on the floor."

The servingmen depart. My brother does not. I feel his presence as an animal might, with some sense I cannot name. I feel danger. I feel menace. I feel a creeping terror that is oh so familiar. And I'm angry. But showing that will only make things worse.

"Odd," I remark, "how losing one's vision makes folk leap to the conclusion that one is suddenly also deaf and lackwitted. I suppose I will grow accustomed to being treated as invisible. Liobhan, you have a long ride ahead; if the steward can offer you a good bed in the women's quarters, take it. I will get by until morning."

"The floor's fine," she says. "Thank you, Master Seanan."

Another silence. In the distance, I hear the sound of platters and knives being set on a table, and folk talking. Seanan is still here.

"Cozy arrangement," he observes in his silkiest tone. "You and the girl, I mean. A tight squeeze on that narrow bed, but you'll find ways around that. Was that how it was in that place, fighting on the field by day, a wrestle in the sheets by night? My baby brother, hmm? Never would have thought you had it in you, little man. Scared of an unkind word. Spooked by your own shadow."

"Enough!" says Liobhan. Her tone has changed completely. "You speak nonsense. Vicious nonsense."

The sound of a blow is sudden and shocking in the quiet of the house. I feel Liobhan flinch beside me, and my hand goes up instantly to lock itself around Seanan's wrist. If I weren't so furious I'd be pleased I got it the first time, guided by sound alone. I say very quietly, "No."

"I'm all right, Dau." Liobhan speaks with perfect calm. "An open-handed slap, that was all. Master Seanan, you have an agreement with the Swan Island elders, signed and witnessed, that my personal safety is assured while I live in your house. I didn't anticipate that you would break that agreement quite so soon. Is this the way you expect to continue?"

"Let me go, little brother." Seanan's speaking through gritted teeth.

"Answer the question first."

"The agreement has not been broken. This is not my house. I warn you, girl, that if you speak out in this way, if you challenge my decisions or those of my father, you will quickly find yourself in serious trouble. I do not believe for one moment that Dau's injury was accidental. From now on, do not ever forget that you travel with me not as a guest or as a healer or even as a companion for my wretched brother here, but as a bond servant making amends for a crime against my family. In my household you will be the lowest of the low. You will work as you have never worked before. When you address me, it will be in a manner appropriate to my status and yours. Do I make myself understood?"

"Perfectly, Master Seanan. Do you make a habit of striking your servants when they speak the truth?"

He moves, perhaps to deliver a matching blow on the other cheek, but my grip is firm. Not firm enough to crush his bones, but close. And now I have the other wrist, and I push him back until he stumbles and almost falls. "*I* do not have such an agreement, brother. And although I am blind, I am still a warrior. Do not forget that."

"Guards!" Seanan calls, not in the tone of a man who fears for his safety, but in the tone of a person who expects instant obedience. When I hear the footsteps of booted men along the hallway, I release my brother's wrists and step back. Liobhan puts a hand on my arm lightly.

"My lord?" A man's voice; one of the guards.

"My brother is not himself. I just witnessed a fit of violent behavior. Can this chamber be locked from the out—"

"Something amiss, Master Seanan?" A new voice; thank the gods, it's Master Beanón, who knows all about that agreement, and with luck will not believe that I've gone suddenly mad.

And now another voice, calm and practical. "I hope all's well here, Master Seanan. Young lady, my people are bringing your belongings over from the women's quarters; I'm told you need to be close to the invalid during the night. This may not be the ideal chamber. We do have some quarters that are used from time to time when folk get sick, far more capacious and, as luck would have it, not currently occupied. Oh, I am Gáeth, steward to the household. Master Seanan, supper is about to be served— you might leave this problem with me and go through to the dining hall with Master Beanón? Master Dau, welcome. I will arrange for supper to be brought to you—a long day, you won't want a lot of fuss and noise. Come this way, please. And you, young lady."

Liobhan offers an arm and I take it. Gáeth is clearly a person of much authority; even my brother has fallen silent, perhaps wondering if someone will ask how Liobhan got a mark on her face—that blow may have been open handed, but it sounded hard enough to leave a bruise. Beanón murmurs something to Seanan, and when Liobhan leads me off after the steward the two of them do not follow, and nor do the guards. I silently offer Gáeth my profound thanks.

Some time later, Liobhan and I are seated in a far more commodious chamber, with an antechamber large enough to take a pallet where she can sleep. The main room has a hearth with a fire; there's a table holding a jug and cups and a lamp. There's a bucket of fresh well water, and she's been given the items she requested to make up a wash for my eyes. Our bags are here; Liobhan has checked them to make sure our possessions are intact. My bed, perhaps one on which folk have lain in fever or dropsy or wasting sickness—it may have seen a corpse or two—is twice as big as the one first offered, and furnished with linen sheets and goose-feather pillows. All this I know because Liobhan made me walk around the place while she described it.

A servingman has brought us food on a tray: roast beef, root vegetables in a bread sauce, a pudding with fruit, and ale. Liobhan describes that as well, though the smell is clue enough. Now we sit and eat before the fire. It feels as if we're suddenly in a completely different world.

"The calm before the next storm," I say.

"Mm. We should be glad of it while we have it," says Liobhan.

"How's your face?"

"It was nothing."

I knew she would say that. "Sounded like a hard blow."

"I expect I'll have a bruise tomorrow, and if anyone asks me how I got it, I'll tell them the truth."

"He'll be watching every move," I say. "Remembering every word. You've already provoked him into hitting you. Keep going the way you are and you won't survive the first week, let alone a year." Gods, I wish we could make ourselves disappear. If only I could see, if only I was myself again, we could use what we've learned on Swan Island to escape our escort somewhere between here and Oakhill. We could get right away to someplace where nobody's heard of us. Make an entirely new life. But that's not possible. Blind, I'm no comrade to anyone. I'm a burden. How could I ask Liobhan to toss away her whole future for me? If she can get through the wretched year, she can have her old life back. That's what matters.

When the meal is finished we sit awhile, enjoying the warmth of the fire. I'm tired; I have aches and pains that don't bode well for tomorrow's ride. It's dawning on me that when I ride blind I hold myself much tighter than I should. I should ask Liobhan for a salve. But I don't want to. It would make me feel weak.

"Don't know about you," she says, "but I could do with a

good wash. And I'd best apply some salve to my face. It wouldn't hurt for both of us to put something on our joints, too. Another long ride tomorrow. I'll see if I can procure some warm water, yes?"

"Good idea." She's made it all right to speak out. I wonder if she's inherited some special skills from her wisewoman mother. Mistress Juniper often had a surprising insight into my thoughts, and I daresay Mistress Blackthorn is the same. "I'd be glad even of some horse liniment. I'll take more care how I sit tomorrow."

"Stack those platters for me, will you, and I'll take them when I go."

I manage the job without dropping anything or cutting myself on the knife. "Here."

"Thanks. Bolt the door. I'll knock three times when I get back. You don't want uninvited guests. Though you dealt with your brother pretty well, I thought. Quick response, remarkably accurate. Not that I'd advise doing that sort of thing again unless you're in fear for your life. As you said, he'll remember every word. And every move."

I don't point out that she was the one I feared for in that moment. "Go, then."

Nobody comes; for today, it seems my brother has had enough of me. I ponder the fact that Liobhan has left her bag here with her knives in it, and that I could make good use of them before she returns. But a promise is a promise. Besides, I can imagine what Seanan would make of my blood-soaked corpse being found in this comfortable chamber where Liobhan and I have just enjoyed supper before the fire. She'd be blamed, she'd be found guilty, she'd be the one strung up from the nearest tree, and Seanan would laugh as he watched, having rid himself of us both with minimal effort. This sends my thoughts down an unwelcome path. A pox on my wretched family! I can sit here and let the shadows overwhelm me, or I can get up and do something. Bend, stretch, make this aching body work for me. Be a warrior. Hah!

As I work my body through a modified version of the exercises Archu taught us—I am in a confined space and must avoid breaking things—I think of Snow and I think of Liobhan. My brothers always knew how to torment me. They were quick to identify a weakness and exploit it to the fullest. I loved Snow, and they turned that love into a tool to break me. If Garalt had not left that household when he did, they would have used the bond between us in the same way. I hear a similar intention in Seanan's voice as he speaks to Liobhan. I can't let that happen. Liobhan and I must don new masks, the masks of folk who care nothing for each other. She will work out her year of servitude and return to Swan Island. Until that happens, I will do my best to stay out of her way. I will be coolly courteous, no more. I will not play Seanan's foul games. A year in my father's house. May the time pass quickly.

Liobhan comes back. At her knock I unbolt the outer door then retreat to the main chamber. She and a servingman bring things into the anteroom; I hear the clanking of buckets, the sloshing of water. Liobhan tells him she'll put the items outside the door later and her helper departs. I realize, listening, that I don't want to lose whatever it was that held us in its spell as we sat before the fire. Mistress Juniper would have a name for it. It was a good thing. It was like the feeling I have when Liobhan sings, something deep and sure. It was like an anchor or the strong roots of an oak. I cannot bring myself to be cold to her. Not yet. Not tonight.

My companion is busy; the sounds suggest she is filling some kind of bath. "You go first, Dau," she calls through the open doorway. "Come through, I'll show you where everything is."

I make my way into the anteroom.

"Here's the tub," Liobhan says. "Though it's more of a shallow pan. There's a stool here with soap and a brush. A scoop for rinsing. And over here on the shelf is a cloth for drying yourself."

"Thank you. I'm sweaty; I stink. You should go first."

"Bollocks. You go first. I'll be in the other room. Not looking until you have your clothes back on. I didn't see a nightshirt in that bag. What do you want me to fetch?"

I'm accustomed to sleeping in nothing at all. "Shirt and breeches, I suppose. They'll have to do for tomorrow as well."

She finds them, brings them in. "Here. Call me if you need anything. I'm not talking about personal services such as having your back scrubbed, you understand. My nursing assistance goes only so far."

I strip and wash; it feels good after the long day. In the other room, Liobhan is quiet. Until I'm getting dressed.

"Dau?"

"Mm?"

"I could offer to keep doing this after we get there. Be a sort of assistant to you, I mean. I know your father may have a resident healer, but you won't need that sort of expertise all the time."

I'm astonished by how badly I want to say yes to this. The fire and the food and the good company are even more dangerous than I thought. "That's not a good idea," I say, donning the shirt with some difficulty. Why are the armholes so hard to find?

"No? It sounds practical to me. Your father would get my moderately expert services for free. And it would keep me out of people's way."

"It wouldn't get you out of the way, it would put you right in the middle of my family, which is not a place you want to be, believe me. Besides, you're the last person they'll listen to. Don't suggest anything. Make yourself as unobtrusive as possible." I picture Liobhan's tall, athletic form, her flowing red-gold hair, her vivid expressions, and know I'm talking rubbish. "Bath's free," I say, trying to sound matter-of-fact. "The floor got a bit wet."

We exchange places. She bathes, I sit before the fire. We seem to have run out of things to say. After a while I hear splashing sounds as she scoops the water back into the buckets, then metallic ones as she hefts everything back out into the hallway. The outer door closes.

"If the floor wasn't sopping wet before," Liobhan says, "it is now."

The anteroom was already getting cold when I bathed. With the fire banked up, this room will be far warmer. As Liobhan comes back through, treading so lightly she must be barefoot, I say, "Bring your bedding in here. There's room in front of the fire. It's not as if we haven't shared close quarters before." I recall a night spent in an outbuilding at the court of Breifne, and Liobhan falling heavily asleep with her head on my knee.

"I'll be all right out there. If your family is so terrible, I may need to get used to sleeping somewhere cold and damp."

"It's no laughing matter. Please. Bring your bedding in and sleep before the fire. Or take this bed and I'll sleep on the pallet."

"That's ridiculous," Liobhan says, but she sounds as if she's smiling. "What would your brother think? All right, I'll sleep on the floor in here. It does make sense for both of us to get a good night's rest. Another long day tomorrow, and who knows where they'll put us after that."

She settles by the fire. I lie down on the soft bed, knowing I'm exhausted and need to sleep, but unable to still my tumbling thoughts. I try to think of good things, but instead my head is full of dark imaginings. I cannot see the future in Oakhill. I cannot imagine what they will do with me. They never wanted me, even when I was whole and healthy. I was a daily reminder of my mother's death. Why are they bringing me home now that I am nothing but a burden? And what might my brothers do to Liobhan? I remember Garalt, who found me one day with a noose around my neck, ready to kick away the stool I balanced on. Garalt, who saved my life and my sanity, who found me a safe haven, who taught me hope. What price that hope now? I remember Snow, and I think of Seanan's laughing reference to dogs. My jaw aches; my head throbs. I can't stop grinding my teeth. I turn one way then the other; I can't keep still. I listen to Liobhan's steady breathing. I can't wake her. I won't wake her. But it's so dark. It's like the darkness when my brothers shut me in the root cellar and left me there; it's like the darkness when they stuffed me into the old oak chest and said they'd kill me if I made any noise. It feels like the end of the world. I wish it was the end of the world. Let it stop, let it stop . . .

I wake. Heart nearly jumping out of my chest. Head screaming. Body tight as a coiled spring, everything hurting.

Someone holding my hand. Someone singing in the dark.

> *Often he mourned the loss of light*
> *The blaze of sun, the candle bright*
> *Yet there was joy in touch and sound*
> *The wet nose of a loyal hound*
> *The joyful laughter of a child*
> *The cry of birds in forest wild*

A lover's kiss, a friend's strong arm
To shield him, safe from . . .

She falters; the song ends. "You're awake."

She's sitting on the bed, her hand in mine. I try to say something, anything, but all I manage is a strangled, meaningless sound. As she releases my hand, I realize my face is wet with tears and my throat hurts nearly as much as my head. I want her to go on singing. I want to lie here and listen and not have to ask if I've been shouting or crying or otherwise making an exhibition of myself. I try again, rasping out, "Sorry. I'm sorry."

"Don't." Liobhan sounds fierce. "Don't apologize, I can't deal with that. Stay there while I fetch a cool cloth for your head and set the kettle on the fire. And if you're worried about making a noise, don't be. There haven't been any knocks on the door. Let me fix your pillow—that's better. Now stay there. I won't be long."

I hear her poking the fire, putting more wood on. Pouring water, doing something with the kettle. Going into the anteroom, coming back again. "What was that you were singing?" I ask.

"Made it up as I went along. A lullaby of the 'Sleep, Little One' variety didn't seem appropriate."

"Sorry I woke you."

"Stop it! Why do you think I chose to sleep in here? Now I'm bringing you a cool cloth. Lie back again and I'll put it on your brow, yes, that's it. Stay like that while I make you a draft. Or better still, I'll make an ordinary brew, something calming, and we'll share it. It's a thing I learned growing up. If you're out of sorts with someone, sharing a brew is always a good idea."

"Not out of sorts with you," I murmur. "Only with my wretched body."

Liobhan says nothing.

"Funny," I say. "I wanted to hear you sing. But I couldn't ask."

"I've missed it," she says after a silence. "And I'll go on missing it for a while, I imagine. Whatever work I'm supposed to do when we get there, it won't be music."

13

LIOBHAN

It's worse than I expected. When we arrive there's no sign of family waiting to greet their long-lost son. Instead, as soon as he dismounts Dau is hustled off somewhere by Seanan with a couple of guards following. Beanón and Naithí speak to a man who looks like a steward, then head indoors. Dau's family home is as substantial as either of the royal establishments I've visited. The main house is huge. It sprawls across the center of a well-kept domain, all encircled by a high stone wall. If I ever doubted that the family was wealthy, I doubt it no longer. At some distance there are outbuildings, including stables. Servants are unloading our horses, and grooms are waiting to lead them away. Before I can retrieve my bag or Dau's I'm confronted by two guards, both armed and both big even by my standards. Like the rest of the men-at-arms here, they're wearing blue tunics.

"This way," one of them barks.

"My bag," I say, holding my ground. "Where did they take it?"

"This way," the man repeats, seizing my arm. I could wrench free and punch him in the jaw, with a kick for the other fellow, but I resist the urge. They're obeying orders, I suppose. I breathe slowly and walk on with my escort, away from the

house, away from the pretty gardens, down toward the furthest of the outbuildings. Beyond the outer wall I glimpse a
stretch of farmland on rising ground and, at a distance, forest.
It's probably good if they put me somewhere away from
the house, provided that means away from Dau's family. I
might even be able to play the whistle occasionally. But what
about him?

"Down here."

We pass a stable block with a well-kept courtyard and neatly
walled exercise area. We pass a barn, where several men pause
in their work to give me a thorough look-over. I could smile. I
could stick out my tongue. I could make a crude gesture. Instead, I take careful note of what I see: walls to hide behind;
doors to use for escape, should that ever prove necessary; lad-
ders that might be handy for one thing or another. In one field
there's a big bull that doesn't look friendly. I see an enclosure
with geese, and further away there's a pigeon loft. My companions are grim-faced and silent. They keep up a striding pace,
which I match despite my saddle-weariness.

"You'll be in here, and you're not to move until someone
comes to talk to you." *Here* is a hut of mud and wattle, with a
thatched roof that's badly in need of repair. It's a sad little place
that brings to mind the term *hovel*. The hut stands alone at the
edge of a low-lying area, and there's a smell. Impressive as the
main dwelling is, I suspect the drains are not very good; or
maybe this is where they empty the contents of the privy. Ah.
That'll be my job, sure as sure.

"Next door to the cesspool." I can't hold the words back.

"We're just following orders. Lord Scannal wants you separate from the household."

"Would this be your choice of accommodation for a young
woman? Your sister, for example?"

"Not for me to say," the first guard responds, but the other speaks over him.

"It would depend on what she'd done," he says.

"And what have you been told about that? About why I'm here?" Gods, the smell is truly vile. My father would be horrified. He always did believe in good drains.

"Enough," says the first man, and I don't know whether he's shutting the other one up or making a comment on my misdemeanor, whatever it's supposed to be. "Go in and stay in until someone comes to fetch you."

I peer in the doorway of the hut. No lamp. No hearth, which is perhaps just as well considering the hut's poor state of repair. A crude shelf with one rough blanket. An empty bucket in a corner. No sign of food or drink. No fresh water. I choke back the first comment that comes to mind. They can't plan to leave me down here. Whoever is coming to talk to me must surely tell me about meals and washing and what work I'll be expected to do. I'm grubby after another day's riding and I'm tired. But it doesn't seem wise to complain.

"Thank you," I say, striding into the hut only to find the ceiling is so low I can't quite stand upright. "What about my bag?"

"Can't answer that question." The first guard frowns. Perhaps this is the first time he's seen inside the place. "If you give your word you'll stay put, we won't lock the door. The smell's pretty bad."

I don't point out that the smell will still be there whether I'm locked in or not. He's being kind and probably disobeying orders. "I'll stay put. If you can, please ask someone about my bag. There are . . . there are things I need in it. Personal things."

The guard grunts a response that could be anything, and

the two of them depart. I see them gesturing to each other as they walk back up the rise. It looks as if they're arguing, perhaps about what evil deeds I might get up to if I'm not safely under lock and key.

Between the long ride, the stink, and the tide of sadness that would overtake me if I weren't so angry, I don't have the least inclination to get up to anything. I'm hungry. But thirst will be the killer. I could walk back up to the stables, where there'll be a well or a pump. But if someone's taken a risk on my behalf, even a small one, I don't want to get him in trouble by taking advantage of it. I do go outside to piss, making sure I'm out of obvious view from those working areas. Now that I'm down on cesspool level, I can't get much of a view over the wall, which truly is massive. It's at least as high as the one at the court of Breifne, which was of wooden stakes, not stone. It must have taken an army of folk to build this one. Dau hasn't said anything about his father's lands being under threat, disputes with other local chieftains, or anything of the kind. I wonder how long this house has been here.

Back inside, I test whether the smell is worse with the door closed or open and decide it makes no difference. I close it for privacy. It doesn't lock from the inside. If this really is where I have to stay, I'll do something about that. I'm not my father's daughter for nothing.

I lie down on the shelf bed, rolling up my cloak as a pillow. I think about the night when Dau started shouting in his sleep, then screaming, then sobbing, and I held his hand and sang to him until he quieted. For a bit, in the middle of all that, I wished I'd given in to the mad impulse that seized me during today's ride, to snatch Dau's reins and gallop off while our escort's attention was elsewhere. To lose ourselves in the forest before they had time to act. To ride and ride until we found a safe place, and never to go home again. Yes, it was crazy. If we'd tried and Seanan's men had caught us, the consequences would have been dire. I was tempted, all the same. But I couldn't do it. I stood up in that hearing and promised I would go to Oakhill for a year. A person doesn't break that kind of vow. Dau needs the sort of help only a rich man can afford. There's no way I'd be able to provide for him properly, and even if I could, he'd be too proud to accept. It would be the leap from the clifftop or the sharp knife in the dark for him, and a lifelong burden of guilt for me.

They'd better look after him properly here. If they have someone like Fergus or Jabir, expert and kind, he should be all right. They need someone who's physically strong, too. Dau is both strong and quick—the way he grabbed his brother's arm so fast, even though he couldn't see, is evidence of that. They must do the right thing; they're his family. And this place attests to what I already know: that they have the resources to do so very well indeed. Yes, they hate and resent him. But the house is big, the grounds are expansive, they could set him up with his own healer and someone to act as body servant and companion. He wouldn't need to see his father or brothers unless he wanted to.

I force my thoughts away from Oakhill, away from Dau and his poxy kinsfolk, and over the miles to my own family. *Mother. How much I wish you were here to give me some wise advice, though you'd hate this household, and since you're even worse than I am at keeping your mouth shut, it's just as well you're miles away. Father. You'd know how to fix the drainage problem. But first, I'd like a big hug, I'd like a warm smile, I'd like to know that I am a good person and that I can keep on going, no matter what. Galen, my big brother. I'd love a joke, a laugh, a wrestle, good company and good conversation. I wouldn't mind being a little sister, just for a bit. Brocc. Oh, Brocc, where are you and what are you doing? I miss you so much. I miss your wonderful voice, your magical hands on the harp, your wit and your kindness. I hope you're all right. I hope you're safe. I hope you found happiness in that strange realm. While I'm lying here waiting, I might make up a song for you. Because if you were in my place, that is exactly what you would do.*

14

DAU

"S o," says my father. "You return at last. Would that the circumstances were different."

Six years, it has been, and these are his first words to me. I'm
taken aback by his voice. He sounds old. Old and uncertain. We
are in a council chamber, where I sense other people are present. My father has not taken the trouble to tell me who they
are, though I heard Seanan's voice as I came in, and that of
Naithí the councilor. No Liobhan. No Ruarc, as far as I can tell.

This house makes me sick. It makes my gut tighten and
turns my skin cold and clammy. Every room is full of old nightmares. It takes only one sound, one smell to bring them flooding back. I must hold myself together. I will be strong. "As you
see, Father." I will not refer to the incident that blinded me. I
will not apologize for being a burden. I will not ask where Liobhan is. "If I said I was glad to be home I'd be lying. I agree
that the circumstances are unfavorable. But my brother negotiated a generous price on your behalf. You will have more than
adequate resources to keep a blind man in your house, even in
the unlikely event that I live to fifty or more."

Seanan mutters something; someone responds with a muted
chuckle.

"We'll look at other possibilities for you," says Father. "At the time of your abrupt departure, it was clear that you had no interest in returning to your home and family." Not a word of sorrow at what has befallen me. Not a trace of apology for things past.

I count silently to five. "What do you mean, other possibilities?"

Seanan speaks; perhaps Father has indicated that he should take over. "You could go to Ruarc at St. Padraig's. The monks have a facility for the crippled, the maimed, and the indigent. That would be more appropriate."

I count to five again. "Indigent," I echo. "With over seven hundred silver pieces paid for my upkeep."

"Better that money goes to the monks, who surely need it more than I do," my father says. "St. Padraig's has an infirmarian, healers, folk who can provide what a blind man needs." Even as he speaks these practical words, his voice is unsteady, almost quavering. I remember him as confident, strong, fierce in his authority. This sounds like a different man. "They would welcome you."

I hear what is unsaid. *And we wouldn't.* "Did you say Ruarc is at the monastery? You mean my brother Ruarc? In what capacity?"

"Sit down, Dau," says my father, using my name for the first time since I came in. "Someone guide him to the bench."

Someone does; I want to shake off that careful hand. "I cannot believe that Ruarc, of all people, has become a monk." Ruarc, Seanan's obedient servant in everything, whether it was hunting or hawking or bullying the defenseless. Ruarc, who held me back while Seanan tortured Snow to death. How could such a man call himself a follower of any god? How could he take up a life of prayer?

"Yet that is exactly what he is, little brother." There's a

sneering amusement in Seanan's voice. "We anticipate that he will rise within the Church and one day hold a position of great influence."

Wonderful. When Father is gone, we'll have Seanan as chieftain of Oakhill and Ruarc as prior.

"Of course," Father puts in, "we know your heart was never in your prayers. I don't imagine that has changed."

I see no need to respond to this, so I remain silent. I'm still reeling from that news. Ruarc in a religious order. He must have told a lot of lies; so must the rest of the family. Perhaps Father made a generous donation to the monastic foundation. I shouldn't be so surprised. As for the infirmary and healers and so on, in a way that would be a reprieve. Even with Ruarc close at hand, St. Padraig's would surely be better than this house full of dark memories. But I cannot pretend to be a Christian. I lost any vestige of faith years ago, when I was still a child. I do not want monkish attendants spouting their doctrine in my ears day in, day out. They'd probably tell me my condition is God's punishment because I'm too proud, or because I ran away from home, or because I did not obey my father. And I would become so angry I would be tempted to acts of violence. Besides, there's Liobhan. She certainly won't be going to any monastery. She's stuck here with my father and Seanan for the next year. If I'm not here, who will make sure she's safe?

I promised myself I wouldn't ask. But I do. "What provisions have you made for Liobhan? Where is she accommodated and what work will she be required to do?"

This is greeted first with total silence. Then Seanan starts to laugh, and others join in.

"Your friend is not here as an honored guest," Father says after the amusement has died down. "Have you never heard of a bond servant, Dau? Both her accommodation and her work will be appropriate to that status. Whether you stay here or go to St. Padraig's, you will see very little of her. In the light of what happened, that is just as well."

"I see." I won't give them any more ammunition to use against me. It was stupid to ask. I'll find out what I want to know later, from someone else. There must be a household steward here. *Your friend.* I want to tell Father she's a warrior. I want to say she could probably beat any of his men-at-arms in combat without making much of an effort. "That is most interesting, Father. I am rather weary after the day's ride. Might I retire now to wherever you intend to put me? Or were you planning to send me off to St. Padraig's straightaway, before we've had the opportunity to discuss it properly? A night's rest under this roof would seem appropriate. A meal, if you can stretch to that. And I would like a word with your steward. I don't suppose Torna is still here." Torna was steward when I left here. To my thirteen-year-old self, he seemed ancient. But he was kind.

I hear Father rise to his feet; other folk do the same.

"That place has taught you an insolent manner, if nothing else," Father says. He clicks his fingers. "Iarla, show Master Dau to his quarters." He raises his voice. "Clear this chamber!"

I feel the room change; there's a sound of soft steps and the rustle of fine clothing as the occupants depart. None of them are talking, though this is sure to be the subject of gossip outside my father's hearing.

The steward comes—another gentle touch on the arm—and I'm guided out of the chamber and through various hallways. Either Iarla is naturally more talkative than the others I've encountered here or he just has better manners. He introduces himself. He refers to me as Master Dau. He asks me if I'm hungry, and whether I'd prefer to eat before or after I wash off the dust of another day's riding. I'm so grateful I could cry. Which just goes to show how low I've fallen.

I thank him and answer his questions. If Iarla was here before I ran away, I don't remember him. He sounds young. Back then he'd have been a junior servant of some kind, scrubbing pots or cutting up onions. He might have known nothing about the trials that saw me flee from home.

"You understand, Master Dau," he says quietly, "that Master Seanan has given us precise instructions as to what is to be provided for you and what we may or may not discuss."

"If I'm to have a chamber to myself, might we go there and talk briefly behind closed doors, Iarla? I won't push you to break the rules. I can imagine what the penalty might be." I keep my voice to a murmur. He can see if anyone is about, but I can't, though I'm finding that my hearing serves quite well.

He's good. Just as good as the estimable Gáeth in his own way. When we reach the chamber that is to be mine, there's a guard at the door, and Iarla asks him politely to go and speak to someone about water for bathing, then takes me inside and closes the door behind us.

"What would be most useful, Master Dau? Should I describe the room to you? Lead you around so you can find what you need?"

There must be a hearth; the chamber feels warm. "Later," I say. "Show me where to sit down, you sit, too, and if you can answer some questions for me, please do. I will understand if your orders forbid that."

We sit on a bench. I sense the room is quite small; if I'm to have a personal attendant, I doubt he'll be sharing my quarters. "My father spoke of sending me to St. Padraig's. If that didn't happen, Iarla, what would be available for me here? A companion, a guard, a healer? Where am I to eat, to exercise, to spend my time? Am I a member of the family, or am I to be shut away?" When Iarla does not reply, I say, "I'm sorry. Perhaps you could answer the practical questions. That seemed quite a long walk."

"This chamber is at some distance from the family apartments. It's on the eastern side of the house, near the stillroom—you will remember that, of course. This wing is partly closed up at present; it serves as additional accommodation when there are many guests."

"If I need assistance, who do I call and how? In time I will relearn my way about, I expect; that's if I stay here. But for now I will struggle. The privy, the bathhouse, and wherever I am to take my meals—I will need help to find all those. And . . . up until now, since I lost my vision, I have had a healer in attendance, or someone who could perform nursing duties. If this is close to the stillroom, I wondered . . ."

"I've been given no instructions on those matters, Master Dau. Perhaps your father anticipates that you will move to the monastery almost immediately. I will find you an attendant, someone who can stay close and help you find your way to the bathhouse and so on. And perform such tasks as tending the fire. I will do that straightaway." He hesitates.

"But it will require my father's approval?"

"I'd need to ask Master Seanan. He's in charge of the arrangements. But I won't trouble him with it tonight. There's a young man I have in mind; he's working in the kitchen at present but will welcome a change, no doubt. As for healers, we rely on the infirmarians from St. Padraig's. They provide for the whole community, this household included. They will visit if their services are required."

"Thank you. Perhaps you would walk to the privy with me now, so I can learn the way." This is humiliating, even when it's a kind man who's doing the favor. The rest of my life is

going to be like this—one step forward, two steps back. Trapped
in a world whose boundaries seem ever shrinking.

Iarla walks me to the privy and back. I count the steps we
take; I commit to my mind the left and right turns, the paths
that slope or wind about, the obstacles that must be avoided.
Back at my allocated chamber, he shows me the bed, the small
table, the bench, the shelf for my belongings. My bag is here;
someone has brought it in. Iarla offers to unpack for me.

"I'll manage, thank you. Iarla, before you go, can you tell
me where they've accommodated the woman who rode here
with our party?"

Another silence. Then he says, "I'm not sure I can answer
that, Master Dau."

"Please. I do know this house; just a hint will be enough."

I wait, and after a little he says, "The old hut downhill from
the stables would have been here in your time, wouldn't it?
Near that marshy spot."

I nod thanks, and Iarla leaves, promising to send me the
servant he mentioned. I think of the old hut down from the
stables and the area beside it. Marshy? Unless it's changed in
the years since I left, that's a place not even a frog would want
to inhabit. Though any frog that ventured there would be well
fed, since the spot is rich in insect life. I imagine Liobhan writing a verse about that, a comical one that would send her after-
supper audiences into gales of laughter. Or a whistle tune. It
might be called "Bullfrog's Delight." But it's no laughing matter. That hut is not fit for anyone to stay in. She'll get sick. She
won't be able to work. Maybe that's Seanan's plan. Make her ill
then punish her for not working hard enough. That would be
just like him. They've put us at opposite ends of the house.
That must be deliberate.

When the boy from the kitchen comes, he brings my supper
with him. He's nervous. Eager to please. But awkward, especially

when I need help. I remind myself that this is by no means the worst they could have done for me. The chamber is comfortable, though small. The food is good. One important thing is missing, and I doubt anyone's mentioned it to this boy.

As I eat, I try to engage him in conversation. His name is Corb and this is his first position in a noble household. His family are on a smallholding to the south. He has two brothers who work the land, so he ended up here, thanks to a family connection with Iarla. I wish I could tell him to go back home and tend to the sheep or goats or whatever it is, and not stay under my father's roof. My guess is he's not much older than I was when I left. If he's been given the duty of attending to me, he's right in the path of every weapon my brother has.

"Shall I take the tray back to the kitchen, Master Dau?"

I'm going to say no, but I change my mind. This is a good opportunity not only to gain some information, but also to let Corb know what he might be in for. "Before you do that, go and see what's in the chamber next to this and any others close by. Find somewhere you can sleep. I wake at night sometimes and need attention—a draft to dull pain, a wash for my eyes . . ." I pity the lad. How can I expect him to take charge? He probably expected no more than clearing a tray or two and folding my clothes. "I'll speak more to Iarla in the morning," I say. "But do fetch your bedding and find a spot, somewhere you can hear me if I call you."

Corb takes himself out. I wonder if I should have offered to share my meal with him. He comes back in not long after. "Master Dau? The chamber next but one is empty. I'll bring a broom. There are spiders."

Why am I not surprised? "Good work, Corb. Take the tray now, and fetch what you need from your own quarters." What am I doing to the poor lad? Who'd want to be stuck with me, at my beck and call night and day? I should say yes to St. Padraig's and swallow my pride. That would be best for everyone. Except Liobhan.

"Thank you, Master Dau." Corb sounds hesitant.

"For what?"

"I've never had a room of my own to sleep in before. Always crammed in with my brothers, or with the other serving boys here. I'll do my best. I promise."

Oh, gods. "Off you go, then," I say, hoping the sinking feeling in my heart is not a premonition of things to come.

15

LIOBHAN

I scratch another mark on the wall of my extremely modest new home, using a rusty nail. My knives vanished on the first day. It was no more than I expected. They must have been removed between the bags being taken when we first arrived and my getting them back in the hut. Who has them now? Those are my own good knives, the ones I've used for years. They know the shape of my hands. The smaller one was my only weapon in a battle with the Crow Folk, those pestilent bird-like creatures that haunt the forest near the court of Breifne. Dau fought alongside me that day, and so did Brocc, not with knives but with his voice. That was the moment when I really understood, deep down, how strong the fey part of my brother was. I was shocked. But also impressed. I'd hardly begun to understand what was going on before Brocc took himself off to live in the Otherworld. We were so close, he and I. It made no difference that he was given to our parents as a tiny infant, not born to them. We grew up like twins, almost the same age, doing everything together. I wish Brocc was here now. I wish we could play some music together. At least whoever took my weapons left me the two whistles. Could be I'm far enough from everyone here in my swampy corner that playing a tune won't draw attention. I want to play. Music gives me heart. But if someone hears me they might take away the whistles. I can't risk that.

I'm sitting outside the hut on a makeshift bench I've constructed from some bits and pieces I found on a scrap heap behind the barn. My markings on the wall add up to six days, which is not much when you think of a whole year ahead. But every mark is one day closer to Swan Island.

For the first three days I worked on the drains. As a bond servant I don't question orders, so even though I knew a better way to do the job, I couldn't suggest it. I couldn't say the plan was rubbish. But once the fellow in charge—a hard-faced individual named Berrach—saw that I was capable of doing the work unsupervised, he took himself off and left me to it. So I changed the method, not so much that it'd attract attention, just enough so there'd be a better outflow from the cesspool and less of a buildup of household waste day by day. It meant a lot of digging at the start. I had to borrow a hurdle and a couple of sacks from the lads at the stables so I could bring down a load of small stones to line the bottom of my new drain. It's done now, it looks good, and it works. My back and shoulders hurt, but I don't mind that.

I thought for a bit that they weren't going to feed me. On that first day I worked all morning and although folk turned their heads to look at me from a distance, nobody called me to breakfast. Berrach hadn't come back and he hadn't said anything about meals, just told me to keep working and not wander off. When I started feeling dizzy, I disobeyed that order and walked over to the stables. As soon as the workers up there saw me, one of them told me to sit down and another fetched a cup of water and put it in my hands. I must've been looking as strange as I was feeling. And smelling like the cesspool I'd been working in. I sat and drank and pretty soon there was a small crowd around me. No women among them, of course. I saw an older man walking over, a person with an air of authority, and I thought I was in trouble. But he asked my name and whether I'd had anything to eat, and pretty soon I had a slab of bread and cheese in my hand and they were all introducing themselves and each other.

"I'm Fionn. Head farrier. Mongan's away today. He's our stable master, a good man, very fair in his dealings."

"I'm Padraig. Like the saint. And he's Caol. And the fellow with the dark hair is Torcan."

"A fine warrior name," I said, grinning at Torcan, who was tall and straight as a young oak. "Means wild boar, doesn't it?"

The young man smiled. "They're saying you're a fighter. Is that true?"

"Not right now. If you've heard what I was, then you'll have heard what I am now and why I'm here digging drains instead of cleaving enemy skulls. But yes, I am a fighter. Don't say it's an unusual profession for a girl or I might feel tempted to give you a demonstration."

They laughed, which was good. I wasn't even supposed to be talking to them, let alone showing off my combat moves.

"I'd better get back to work now." I'd demolished the food with extreme speed. "I'm not meant to be up here."

"You wouldn't have lasted long on an empty stomach and no fresh water," observed Fionn. "That was a hard morning's work. You dig as strongly as any man."

"My father taught me. Thank you for the food and for your kindness. I don't want to get you in trouble."

"You've got to eat," Fionn said. "I'll see if Mongan will have a word with Berrach, make some kind of arrangement for you. Breakfast with us up here, a bite to eat in the middle of the day. We take supper in the hall with the household."

"Mm." I got to my feet. "I shouldn't think bond servants take supper in the hall. Can you tell me what Berrach's position is in the household? Who else answers to him?"

The farrier looked surprised. "He's one of Master Seanan's men. Does whatever Master Seanan needs him to do. Didn't he explain?"

"No." Maybe Lord Scannal didn't know I was down here living with the stink and the insects. Could that be? "Fionn, please don't take any risks on my behalf. None of you should do that. Easier for all if I just do as I'm told." It was hard to say that, true as it was. A kind word, a simple meal, a bit of friendly company can make a person long for more.

"Leave it to me," Fionn said. "Now, sure you're all right? Looked like you were going to pass out for a while there."

"I'm fine now, thank you. I must get back to work." I picked up the pail of water they'd brought me, bestowed a general smile, and headed off back to the hut. Behind me they were quiet. But I felt their gaze. I felt their thoughts, full of things that could not be said, full of opinions too dangerous to speak aloud. What a place to work. What a place to live. No wonder it drove Dau half-crazy.

Somehow, Fionn and the stable master, Mongan, worked magic for me. I'm allowed to walk up to the stables in the mornings and share the food that's provided for the workers there. That feels a little weird, because on our last mission Dau played the part of a farrier's assistant. And he had to pretend he was mute. I keep thinking of that and thinking of him. I haven't seen him at all. I don't know where he is and I can't ask. I suppose he eats supper in the great hall with Lord Scannal and his circle, enduring the company of his awful brothers. I don't know if he has a healer to look after him. I don't know if that person has any idea of what preparations Fergus and Jabir were using. I don't know if Dau's all right. The fellows from the stables bring me food every evening after supper, leftover bits and pieces from their own platters, and I could ask them if they've seen him. But I don't. I want to know and I don't want to.

For now, the best thing I can do for Dau is keep my head down and work hard. I've seen almost nothing of his father and brothers, though they must visit the stables from time to time. That suits me just fine. If they think working hard and getting filthy will dent my spirits, they think wrong. I want to be busy. I want to stretch my body and stay strong. Right now, what I'd like to do is climb a particular tree that stands close to the stone wall encircling Lord Scannal's stronghold. From up there I can get a better look at the woodland in the middle distance. I wish I'd studied a map before we left the Barn. Archu said this place was almost as far south as Breifne, only further east. I don't know how big Eirne's forest is—the forest that conceals a certain portal to the Otherworld—but I wonder if what I see is the far eastern edge of that same forest. Is that possible? It would have to be huge. But then, uncanny folk and places are changeable. Even time is unreliable in that realm. I know many tales in which someone wanders into the Otherworld and has a fine old time for a few days, then goes home to find a hundred years have passed and everyone they know is dead. Or the other way around, which would be even stranger. So maybe, in a place full of magic, a forest can shrink or grow in size to fit the circumstances.

I won't get the view I want unless I climb almost to the top. I have a strong urge to climb. There are no trees on Swan Island. If they dare to shoot up, the wind soon beats them down and the salt spray finishes them off. Our climbing practice takes place on cliffs high above the crashing waves, at first with ropes and later without. I miss the thrill of it. But climbing this particular tree could get me into big trouble. I've been lucky so far, despite getting smacked in the face by Dau's brother and ending up living in a swamp. People have been kind to me. I don't want to risk that. On the other hand, if I do climb up, not only might I catch a good view of the forest, I might also get a glimpse of Dau with whoever is looking after him. The weather's good, and they must take him outdoors sometimes. He'd insist on it, wouldn't he?

Ah. There's a party of folk on horseback, heading for the gates. I see Seanan, with a substantial escort of guards. That settles it. There's nobody much about at the swampy end of the holding, and the work I was allocated for the day is done. I don't let myself think too hard. Instead I practice something they taught us on Swan Island, which is how to cross open ground with stealth. You use everything you can: shadows, small bushes, crumbling drystone walls. You watch everywhere and choose your moment for each dash from one place of half concealment to the next. You keep your footfalls quiet, because if you happen to startle a wandering sheep or duck, the noise they make will draw attention.

The tree is a magnificent ash. The late spring foliage should provide good cover as I go up. I'm surprised the tree has survived so well in this damp spot. Maybe the drainage problem is of recent times only. I can't imagine there's a lack of funds to do these things properly. Is Lord Scannal neglecting his responsibilities? Or does he simply not care? Judging from what Dau told me, his father either chose to ignore the older brothers' persecution of the youngest, or truly believed the whole thing was Dau's fault. Either way, Lord Scannal apparently took no steps to find out the truth. Perhaps he's lazy. Perhaps he doesn't like conflict. Perhaps, when the letter came from Swan Island telling him his son was blind, all he thought was, *Oh, God, another problem to deal with.* I may never get the opportunity to find out. I haven't been called to speak to Lord Scannal or to any figure of authority other than Berrach.

I climb as high as I can in the ash tree. I find a secure perch that allows good views. The stone wall lies below me, but there will be no leaping over this one; it's about three times my height and there's no corresponding tree on the far side, so unless I could do something with a rope—which would be too visible anyway—an attempt would end in broken bones or worse. *Sorry, Dau,* I think, remembering how he took a risk to help me escape another fortress in pursuit of justice. That won't be happening here.

I turn to look toward Lord Scannal's establishment with its tower—there's a blue banner flying there, with the sword emblem I saw on Seanan's tunic—and the substantial buildings around it. There are gardens at the far end, sheltered by low drystone walls. I see a couple of folk working there, a man digging, a woman with a basket over her arm, harvesting something. I wonder if there's a stillroom. If so, it would probably be nearby, since that sheltered garden is the obvious place to grow herbs. And might not an invalid be housed conveniently close?

I'm tempted to go over there and see for myself. I bet I could do it without being spotted. *No, Liobhan. Keep your head down.* I look back the other way, toward the tract of forest just visible where the farmlands end and the terrain rises more steeply. Even supposing I could get out of here, even supposing I was foolish enough to try, that would be a longish walk. Not something I could do without being missed.

I'm about to start my descent when a tiny bird flies in to alight on the branch next to my hand. The forest may not look familiar, but this little creature does. It's finch-sized, but not a finch or a wren or any sort of bird I can name. It's just like the ones I saw at Mistress Juniper's cottage, and again in Eirne's realm. An Otherworld bird. A messenger.

I clear my throat, wondering if I can use the creature the way Eirne's folk do, the way the remarkable wisewoman, Mistress

Juniper, does. Can this creature read my thoughts? Does it report back on what it sees? Or can I speak to it as I might to a human messenger?

The bird chirrups, a delicate upward statement. *So?* Its feathers are of many shades of blue, with here and there a touch of gold. I imagine its picture in an illuminated manuscript, something old and rare.

"Please tell my brother I love him and I miss him, and I hope all's well with him and with Eirne's folk," I say quietly, wondering if I've chosen some perfectly ordinary bird to talk to. I think not; this one is perched barely a handspan from me but stays perfectly calm. It puts its head on one side, as if in question.

"Please tell him I hope he is still singing and playing."

The tiny one seems to be waiting for more. It burbles a miniature cascade of notes. Looks at me, bright-eyed. Can it be requesting a song? Nothing springs to mind. I'll have to do what Brocc does and make it up as I go along, the way I did the night Dau woke me with his screams.

> *With your voice so pure and high*
> *You sing the moon across the sky*
> *You sing of joy, you sing of pain*
> *Of loved ones we won't see again*
> *Of courage, faith, new lives begun*
> *You sing the rising of the sun*
> *Sky's messenger, with your sweet call*
> *You bring down blessings on us all.*

It's the best I can do on short notice. The bird seems happy enough. It warbles a response, then lifts its wings and flies off. I watch until it is too far away to see. It's heading toward those woods. So that might be Eirne's forest. Whether the creature can pass the message on to my brother, who knows, but at least

I've tried. And I've sung a song, which feels remarkably good, even if my creation was no masterpiece. I can improve both verse and melody. It'll give me something to do during the long evenings when I'm sitting alone in the hut. Who knows, when I go back to Swan Island I might have tripled my repertory. It will be good to sing for the community there again; to play the whistle while Archu drums, to hear the voices of my comrades.

I hear a voice now and I'm suddenly reminded that I've broken the rules. Berrach's down there shouting my name, and I have no choice but to climb down—the last bit is more of a scramble—and front up to him. An explanation is on my lips, but he doesn't wait for it. I get a slap on the left cheek, and I have to clench my fists tight to stop myself from hitting back. I know I could knock him down. He's on his own. But it's not worth getting in trouble for this.

"Explain yourself!" Berrach demands.

"I've finished chopping and stacking the wood, which was my task for the day." I stand very still, resisting the urge to put a hand up to my face, which is stinging. "I wanted some fresh air. Up there, the stink from the cesspool is not so bad."

"Are you complaining?"

"No, Master Berrach. Just stating facts."

"Your orders are simple enough. You stay where you're working or at the hut. You want to be locked up again? No? I thought not. Master Seanan doesn't want you nosing about. He'll be notified of this episode."

"Yes, Master Berrach. By all means inform Master Seanan that I was sitting quietly in a tree minding my own business, with all my work completed."

"Don't speak to me in that tone, girl! You may have won yourself some privileges, thanks to whatever unsavory sort of trade you've set up with the fellows in the stables, but when you're at work you follow my orders, understand?"

"Yes, Master Berrach." I wonder if he's afraid of Seanan? Perhaps he's experienced the man's dark side, as Dau did. If I step out of line, maybe I'm not the only one who'll be punished. I'd hate to bring down Seanan's wrath on Fionn and the stable crew.

"Lord Scannal's got enough to worry about without you causing strife," Berrach says now. "Keep to yourself, do as you're ordered, and get your nose out of other folk's business."

There it is again, the suggestion that I'm spying. I don't know what he means about Lord Scannal, and I can't ask. "Yes, Master Berrach." This time I can't keep the exasperated sigh out of my voice.

"I don't like your manner," Berrach snaps. "I don't care what you were before. Here you're a servant, and if you forget that, you risk a beating or worse. It seems you find yourself short of work today. There are some fellows mending a wall down by the horse field. You can go and carry stones for them. Other side of the barn, down the track between the apple trees. Tell the man in charge that I sent you. You're to work until that crew stops for the day. Don't try to weasel your way out of it. I'll know."

I'd heave stones anytime rather than listen to this bollocks. If I stay here much longer I won't be able to resist the urge to hit him. As for a beating, just let him try. "Yes, Master Berrach."

I got used to spying when we were on our mission. I wasn't great at it, but I did learn to get information out of people without seeming too curious. There are two things I want to know. One, where is Dau and is he all right? Two, what's worrying Lord Scannal, beyond his least favorite son coming home blind? Seems to me he'll be viewing that as no more than a minor nuisance, especially with that hefty payment in silver. Do they see anything of the Crow Folk this far east? Stock losses, random attacks, folk too frightened to go out of doors? If that's the same forest, I'd think the pestilent creatures would be found on all sides. But nobody's mentioned them to me.

The wall crew consists of three men, and at first they're not delighted to see me. But it doesn't take long before the one in charge, Niall, realizes that I can work as hard as his two assistants, so he tells me what to do and we all get on with it. It's heavy work, and I've already spent the morning cutting and hauling firewood, but I'm strong and I'm used to keeping going even when I'm tired. Swan Island training does that.

It helps that I've done this job before. My father was sometimes called to help with drystone walls, both building and repairing, and he taught me how to lay the stones to keep the thing strong and even. The four of us work well as a team. For a while I set aside my worries and enjoy the rhythm of the job.

Niall is a better taskmaster than Berrach. When we've done a bit more than half of the repair job, he tells us to stop and rest for a while. We sit around and Niall unwraps a parcel of bread and mutton, which it seems we're all going to share. I don't have my own knife, so he cuts a portion off for me and hands it over. Someone lends me a cup; Niall has also brought ale in a stoppered jug.

"You're a good worker," one of the lads observes. He doesn't add, *for a woman*.

"My father taught me to mend walls." Gods, this food is wonderful. I try not to wolf it down. "And dig drains. Never thought I'd be doing both."

"Must be hard for you," says Niall. "Being here like this. They say you were a fighter, before."

"Mm-hm." I won't talk about Swan Island. "Harder for Dau. Master Dau, that is."

There's a brief silence. Then, "Couldn't say," mumbles one of the lads.

"I just thought . . . because he's a fighter, too, and he's come home hurt . . ." I can't push this any further.

"Must be bad," says the other lad. "Corb said—"

"Hush," says Niall, frowning, and there's silence from the helpers.

"Who is Corb?" I ask.

"Never mind that." Niall speaks without quite meeting my eye. "We do our work, we mind our own business."

The rest of us mutter agreement. I should have known better than to mention Dau. That's perilous ground. I've got to let it go and hope I happen to find him, or happen to hear something useful without needing to ask. Gods, this year is going to be long. At least there's work to do. At least my fellow workers treat me like an equal and not the scum of the earth.

It feels wrong to turn my back on a comrade. It feels so wrong.

16

DAU

Darkness all around. Shadows. Ghosts. A hive of bees in my head, buzzing, swarming, stinging. My eyes burn. What is this? Someone's shouting, a young man, an old man, yelling at each other. The words don't make sense. Crashing sounds, breaking sounds, hurting my ears. I shout, I scream, but nobody comes, there's only me and the pain, the knife through my skull, the writhing snake in my head, the pounding beat of a great drum inside me . . .

Wasn't there a boy here? A boy with a kind voice? What happened to him?

My hand is burned. My hand was in the fire. When I fell. Why did I fall? Where am I? Why doesn't anyone come?

Hot. Cold. It hurts to breathe. What is this garment, a monk's habit, a night-robe, a shroud? It's wet. It smells vile. Oh, gods, my eyes! Help me! Help!

No. Don't shout. Don't bring them here. Their scornful voices. Their cruel hands.

* * *

Every part of me aches. My knife . . . my weapon . . . Make this pain stop. Make it stop.

A sound. A door opening. I curl up tight. A hedgehog, all sharp spikes. A hard-shelled sea creature. I will make my own fortress. I will . . .

17

BROCC

There's nothing to say. What is the point of accusations? The bird is dead. I could ask questions all day and not find out who slipped into my hut and murdered it while I slept. To do so would not bring it back to life. A dark mood is on me as I dress then wrap the corpse in a cloth and carry it out into the forest. I will lay it to rest now, before too many folk are stirring. I cannot speak to them yet. I know I could not hold back my anger.

I don't try to find the area where Rowan first saw the little one. The forest is vast and his description was vague. Instead I walk well clear of the habitations of Eirne's folk, then look for a spot where the small one's remains are unlikely to be disturbed. It feels so light in my arms now. I have wrapped the cloth over its head; I cannot bear to see its eyes so dull and lifeless.

It takes me some time to find the right place. At last I come across a fearsome stand of holly bushes growing around a small rock formation that somewhat resembles a crouching cat. It is possible to slide the bundled remains through a narrow gap, then edge them up until the rocks hide them from view. I hope this is good enough. I kneel there for a little, and sing softly about flight and freedom and hope. Odd how a bard can summon such words when his heart is full of doubt. Does that mean the song is a lie? I do not know, only that I am heartsick and weary, not in the way of a man who has completed a long day's work, but in the manner of one who wrestles with unanswerable questions. A man in danger of losing his way. Oh, Liobhan, how I wish you were here.

The song is done. I walk back to the gathering place, where Eirne's folk are preparing the morning meal as usual. It is as if nothing at all has happened. But perhaps they do not know—after all, I took the body and went off without a word. Still, at least one of them must know the truth.

Folk bid me a good morning and I wish them the same. Eirne is nowhere to be seen, but when Rowan appears I tell him quietly what has occurred. His shock seems perfectly genuine. Of them all, he is the one I could least believe to have done this deed.

"You should speak to the queen," he says in a murmur. "Let her know about this before anyone asks you how the creature is." He glances around the gathering place. The assorted folk of Eirne's clan are setting out leaf platters, piling various foodstuffs on them, bringing little jugs of water. They look so innocent. They are like something from a sweet childhood song, perhaps the one I sang with Eirne, verse for verse, on the day we first met. Not all are here. "Where is True?" I ask Rowan. "How is he faring?"

"Resting in my quarters. Troubled by pain. Moon-Fleet sat with him overnight. She tried her wash to reduce inflammations of the skin, and her draft to banish ill humors. He is no better this morning. His wounds are beyond her ability to treat. The matter needs urgent action, Brocc."

I hear the words he does not speak aloud. *Whereas the death of the bird, sad and strange as it is, requires no action at all.* "Moon-Fleet must be exhausted," I say. Moon-Fleet is the nearest thing to a healer that Eirne's folk have. She is a human-like being, notable for her flow of silver hair, her large shining eyes, and her delicate, pale features. Of all the clan, she is the one most like the image I always had of the Fair Folk, back in the days when I had not encountered them in the flesh. The one exception being Conmael, my parents' friend, who brought them the entirely unexpected gift of a newborn infant. But Conmael, like me, like Eirne, is of mixed blood, one parent fey, the other human. Or so my mother has told me.

"Eirne cannot help True?" Eirne has her own powerful magic. I've seen what she can conjure up in her scrying bowl.

"The queen is unwell." Rowan sounds somber. "And she has said this is beyond the abilities of any in our clan to heal. True must walk the Long Path. I will go with him, Brocc, if you think that wise. Only . . . it would leave our patrols short, unless there is another who could take my place." He knows, and I know, that only the three of us are strong enough to act as guards and protectors.

"Perhaps Moon-Fleet could go with True. Or Nightshade."

"The queen needs Nightshade by her side. And Moon-Fleet is too slight to support True if his strength fails along the way."

We look at each other, neither of us willing to put the other possibility into words. In the end, this will be decided by Eirne. As queen, she has that right.

When all are assembled, including a shaky-looking True, I tell them what has happened with the bird. I make no accusations and they ask no questions. All are unusually quiet. Perhaps that has something to do with the look on Eirne's face.

Rowan asks if he and I can speak to her in private after breakfast, with Nightshade, True, and Moon-Fleet, and she nods assent. I notice that she eats almost nothing. There was a time, not very long ago, when I'd have been able to sit next to her and coax her to eat, choosing the choicest morsels. I should do that now. But she is shutting me out, not with an oaken door and a bolt, but with eyes full of distrust and a tight, ungiving mouth. Is it because I do not comply unquestioning with her will? She is not always right. She is fallible, as I am. I came here to be her warrior, her bard, her helpmeet. But not her slave.

With breakfast over and the smaller ones heading about their day's business, we gather in Eirne's retreat, which is spacious enough to accommodate even True. He, too, has eaten little, and he moves stiffly, as if in constant pain. How long is the Long Path? A walk to fetch help might take many days.

"Well, Rowan?" Eirne's tone is cool, even toward her most loyal retainer. But then, he has become my friend and comrade, and perhaps she no longer trusts him as she did.

"True needs expert help, my lady. You spoke last night of the Long Path. I believe he should go now, this morning, while he has the strength. One of us should go with him."

"True?" Eirne's expression softens as she turns toward the stony being. This morning his mossy hair has a brownish tinge, as if the Crow Folk's poison is starting to kill it. How will his tiny passengers fare if that happens?

"I can go on my own. It would be better."

"No!" Rowan, Moon-Fleet, and I all speak together.

"No, True," Eirne says. "You must take a companion, for the way can be long, and you are not your strong self right now." There's a silence. Eirne looks at each of us in turn: her indispensable companion and sage; her stalwart protector; her delicately built healer; her husband, the warrior bard. As her eyes light on me, a frown appears on her brow. Gods, she's pale. I wonder if it is she who should travel the Long Path in search of healing. "You will go, Brocc," she says. "I must have Nightshade here by me. The patrols will cease until you return, though some of our winged beings will watch from above. Rowan, you will make a plan to keep the gathering place and all the dwellings of our folk safe until True and Brocc return. There are some who can help you. Make use of them. And no more forays out into the human world. Not for anyone."

She wants me gone. That hurts, even though I had been about to volunteer my services, knowing this was the best plan. I am strong enough to support True. I have skills that might be useful on such a venture; I am a healer's son, and I am a Swan Island warrior. Or was, until last summer. Eirne's folk will miss me less than they would Rowan. My wife will miss me less than she would Nightshade. There, I've said it. Not aloud, but I think all present understand it.

"Very well, I will go. I may need some instructions, having never ventured down that path before. I should speak with Moon-Fleet about True's injuries. I should pack a bag."

"Brocc," says Eirne, "you are a warrior. Prepare yourself calmly, as you would for a mission. When you are ready, I will show you the doorway."

I'm used to packing quickly and efficiently. It's one of the things they taught us on Swan Island. I talk to Moon-Fleet, who gives me a jar of salve and a cloth-wrapped bundle of dried herbs. She has never traveled the Long Path and does not know how far we will have to walk or whom we might ask for help along the way.

Rowan puts his bone knife in my hand. "You'll need this," he says. And when I make to protest, for I know it is a prized possession, he adds, "Look after it carefully. We'd best see about making you one of your own after you return. Be safe, my friend."

"And you, comrade." Gods, when I first met Fox Boy—that was my crude name for him before I learned the real one—I would never have dreamed we would become so close. "I hope this won't take long."

"It will take however long it takes." Nightshade casts her owl eyes over the bag I will carry, which holds both my necessities and True's. "The Long Path is changeable. Your music will help you, Brocc. A shame you cannot carry the harp, but your voice will open doors for you. If not that, then your quick wit. May good spirits attend you."

Eirne is out of earshot, talking to True by the council oak, so I say, "I know you will look after the queen; give her good counsel; help her in all things. Nightshade, I am concerned for her. She seems so distant, and she looks so pale."

The sage gives me a look I cannot interpret. Quizzical? Pitying? "The queen will be among her own people," she says. "Think first of True, who needs you most. He does not like to admit weakness, Brocc. He finds it hard to accept help. But the walk will be testing for you both, and you must be the strong one. Do not lose sight of the small folk who dwell on him, for they, too, will need care."

I had imagined perhaps the tiny folk would stay behind, moving from the chinks and crevices of True's body to similar spots on tree trunks or stony outcrops. "They travel everywhere with him?"

"They have not taken the Long Path before and neither has True. I wish you a safe journey, bard, and a swift return. I think the queen is waiting for you."

Eirne has said good-bye to True, who stands in the shade of the council oak, gazing around the gathering place as if to commit it to memory. Now she comes toward me. A smile trembles on her lips. Are those tears in her eyes? She looks like a flower chilled by the first frost of winter.

I will not say good-bye without touching. I cannot. Too much is unknown about this journey. We might never come back. How can I not embrace my wife, kiss her cheek, murmur words of love? But the wall is still up, for all her smile, for all her tears. I reach out and take her hands in mine. They are cold. "I wish I could sing you a song," I say, ignoring the fact that we are not alone. "But I know we must leave now. I will sing to you when we return, and I hope it will be a song of love and hope, wisdom and courage. Be well, my queen. Be safe, my wife." I lift her hands and kiss them gently. I close my eyes and remember how we were on our wedding day, brimful with love and joy and fun. That was a day of singing and dancing, of flowers and feasting and laughter. "Will you show us where to find the path?"

Eirne does not embrace me. She does not kiss me. But she holds on to my hands, and her eyes are searching as she gazes up at me. "Fine words, bard," she says, and I do not know if she means the words are lies, or if she is telling me she, too, still believes in hope and courage. "I will look forward to that song. Come, I will show you. Reaching the Long Path is not so much *where* as *how*."

We walk northward through the woods, Eirne, True, and I, with Nightshade following. I have the bag on my back. True carries a staff. On this journey he'll more likely be using it as a support than as a weapon. I have no idea what we will encounter, and none of the others is particularly helpful.

"How will we know where to stop?" I ask. "How can we know whom to trust?"

"There will be signs," Eirne says. "You seek a healer. Do not expect that healer to be much like Mistress Juniper, who, despite her knowledge of this realm, is a human woman. If I believed she could help True, I would have sent you to her."

I'm not sure if this is the truth. When I suggested Mistress Juniper, when I needed help for the little bird, Eirne said no.

But I don't challenge her. Right now it's True's well-being that matters.

"Here," says Nightshade. The terrain has become more hilly, rising and falling through beech woods, and there are many streams. We have crossed several bridges, some consisting of a single log spanning a watercourse whose width was twice my height. Those were a challenge for True. As a warrior, his greatest assets are his strength and his sheer bulk. But he is heavy and a little awkward in his movements. Now we are at the top of a rise, and down the hill before us is a bigger body of water, perhaps a lake. "The entrance is on an island. There is a ferry." Nightshade glances at True.

"This is the only way?" I ask, imagining the sort of ferry that might be designed to take passengers such as the slender Eirne or the bird-like Nightshade, or our small folk such as Thistle-Coat and Gentle-Foot. On that kind of vessel, a tall man such as myself might well have difficulty.

"It is the only way," says Eirne, stepping forward to look up at me. "Go now, Brocc. May good fortune walk with you. For this journey, my bard, your fey blood is your friend. Use what you have learned in your time here. Do not give answers too freely. Do not trust in outward appearances. Be measured in your approach." She turns to True. "Be strong, my friend. Help is in sight. For you and for your small passengers. I wish you well."

"Thank you, my lady," rumbles True, but I cannot find words to speak. I hitch the bag higher, glance at my companion to be sure he's ready, then head on down the path without a backward glance. It is all too easy to believe this whole thing is a trick designed to send me away from Eirne's realm, perhaps forever. In my mind is an image of myself lying dead under the trees, my eyes staring blindly upward, my neck snapped like the bird's. I see True drowned, his body reduced to a heap of rocks on the lake bed, a beard of water plants creeping across his face.

"Well," True says now, making me start. We're on the muddy shore, and out there on the water is a shallow vessel. A diminutive boatman is poling it toward us. "It's a ferry of sorts."

An old story comes to mind, one in which a man got onto such a ferry and was persuaded to take a turn with the pole. When the vessel reached the far shore the ferryman sprang to dry land and the man discovered he was ferryman now, doomed to pole the craft back and forth, back and forth, until he in his turn could trick a passenger into lending a hand. "If he asks for help, say no," I mutter.

As the boat makes its gradual approach I take a good look around. This is a smallish lake, not much bigger than a pond. Might there not be some other way to cross? But no. This is the Long Path. The ferry is here, and this is the way onward.

"Take you over, friends?" The boatman puts me in mind of a clurichaun, not that I've ever seen such a being, but I know of them from tales. This one stands a little higher than my knee, and he wears a jaunty green hat with matching boots. His tunic and leggings are nut-brown, and around his neck is a collection of acorn cups, dried leaves, and tawny feathers threaded on a cord. The fellow's face is human-like in its general proportions, but markedly Other. His hair falls to his shoulders in scrolling brown curls.

"Thank you," I say, eyeing the ferry, which is closer to a raft in shape. I wonder how such a small boatman can wield a pole long enough to reach the lake bed. This thing surely can't float with True on it; it'll sink or smash into splinters the moment he steps on. "As you can see, my companion is quite heavily built. I am not sure your ferry can accommodate him safely."

The ferryman lays down his pole. The boat is at the shore; he holds it steady with one green-shod foot. "Take it or leave it," he says. "It's all one to me whether you cross to the island or go back where you came from." When I don't reply straight-away, he moves his foot and picks up the pole as if about to head off without us.

"Wait," I say. "True? Do we try this?"

"The only way," he says, and his tiny folk echo his words in their high squeaking voices. I can't ask him to wade across; even if all of his passengers could climb up onto his head it would be risky. The lake may seem small, but this is the Other-world, where things are changeable. We don't know how deep it is. The length of that pole is no guide; it, too, may alter as the user wishes. "You go first, Brocc."

"No. You go first. I'll help you on." I can't go across and leave True to wait.

The ferryman holds the craft in the shallows. True steps on. "Sit," says the clurichaun, or whatever he is. "Careful, now."

True sits. The boat is dwarfed by his huge form. It seems impossible that it will stay intact under his weight, let alone remain floating. But it does. The ferryman pushes it further out, not seeming to exert himself much, though he utters a few choice oaths under his breath. True is staying extremely still, as if he fears the least movement will see him and his small ones sink and drown. With every dip of the pole, with every move forward, the lake seems to grow broader, darker, more mysterious. It's taking them a long time to cross. And now . . . now I see an island. It's all overgrown with brambles and bri-ars, and beneath that tangling wild abundance there's a tumble-down house of some kind, or maybe a rocky outcrop with a door-like opening.

It's not until they reach the shore of that isle and the stony man, with difficulty, rises and steps onto dry land that I can unclench my fists and breathe again. The ferry returns, while True waits on the island. The boatman holds his craft out on the water; it is two long strides from the shore where I stand.

"I'll be wanting payment now," the little fellow says, eyeing the bag I have set down while I waited. "That's the way these things are done. We don't give something for nothing. And we don't take without giving back. Fair's fair in our world, if not in yours, fellow."

I count silently to five, thanking my sister for recommending this trick. When I speak, my voice sounds reasonably calm. "This *is* my world, ferryman," I say. "As is the other. I do not care for tricks. But fair payment is something I understand. What is your price for our crossing both ways? When we have found what we seek, we wish to return to Eirne's realm."

The little man narrows his eyes, then looks down and fiddles with the acorns on his necklace. "For the crossing, the price is not high. For the wisdom you seek, it may be much higher."

"We'll deal with that when we find it." I'm watching True, who is moving awkwardly from one foot to the other, as if he may be in pain. We need to move on. "What price for the ferry?"

"A little bit of yourself," says the ferryman. "Just something small. A finger, maybe. A tooth, white and shiny."

Morrigan's curse! It's all too easy to imagine my finger attached to the clurichaun's necklace, among the leaves and acorns. I think of asking True to wrench out one of my teeth. "A song," I say. "I will make it up, I will sing it for you, I can craft it to suit your wishes. That is the only fee I will pay, but I will make sure it is the finest possible. I am the queen's bard."

"And another on the way back," the ferryman answers, quick as a flash.

"Done."

We are over the lake in a trice, but he won't let me disembark before I sing the song. It would seem that being the queen's bard is no guarantee of trustworthiness. On the way across I have distracted myself from the erratic passage and the possibility of getting very wet by writing verse and refrain in my mind. I'd like to put the boatman's name into the song. But I know better than to ask him for it.

> Oh, who will guard the Long Path, and who will guard
>   it true
> Oh, who will be the ferryman, so evil can't come
>   through?
> Not I, said one and two and three, Not I, said many more
> 'Tis a right hard job to pole the boat all day from shore
>   to shore.
> With a fa-la-deedle-deedle lift up your pole now
> Fa-la-deedle-deedle glide to the shore.

By the end of that verse and refrain, the ferryman is grinning. As I sing, True keeps time with a gentle drumbeat, hand on stony knee, and the tiny folk punctuate the song with rhythmic squeaks.

> They asked the folk of Ulaid and they asked the men of
>   Creagh
> Oh, who will be the ferryman, forever and a day?
> A hundred men, two hundred, and none of them agreed
> Till up there stepped a Green Man, saying, "I'm the one
>   you need."
> With a fa-la-deedle-deedle lift up your pole now
> Fa-la-deedle-deedle glide to the shore.

As I reach the end of this verse, the ferryman digs in the pole and gives the craft one last push, and we do indeed glide to the shore. I know better than to rise and step off before the song is done. By bringing me to land, the little man has shown trust. I must return that trust.

> They thought he was not strong enough because he was
>   so slight
> The Green Man took the pole in hand and pushed with
>   all his might
> The ferry shot from shore to shore, so swift and straight
>   and clean
> The finest boatman in the realm was that small man in
>   green.

This time, as I sing the *fa-la-deedle* refrain the boatman joins in, adding his husky but tuneful voice to mine. When I do not begin a fourth verse, he says, "And what happened next?"

"Ah," I say. He's smiling. He's pleased with the song, so maybe I can take a risk here. "I'll sing you that part on the way back."

There's a moment of silence. Things hang in the balance. Then the ferryman gestures me off the boat. "Go your ways, then," he says. "I'll be waiting. Three more verses, that's the price."

"With pleasure," I say, stepping onto the shore, and I'm not lying. I enjoy the challenge of making a verse quickly—one could hardly call it crafting when there's no time to think it through—and indeed when I first met Eirne it was over just such a challenge. That seems so long ago. Long ago in a time when I was filled with wonder. Long ago when I fell in love without needing to think. And yet, less than a year ago. "All right to walk on?" I ask True.

"I can walk, yes." As we move away from the water and under the dark trees, True adds, "The queen would like that song. It would make her smile."

I say nothing. I do not know if I will ever make her smile again.

18

LIOBHAN

Berrach moves me around from one task to another, always with a different crew. Perhaps he doesn't want me to make friends. Most folk are welcoming once they realize how hard I can work. So although I don't ask questions about Dau and his wretched family, I start to learn a few things. One of them is that when people talk about Master Seanan's men, they mean a small group that answers only to Seanan. They're spread across guards and house servants and folk like Berrach, who has the authority to interfere in anyone's work provided it's out of doors. The way I understand it, if you're one of Seanan's men, you're outside Lord Scannal's control and that of Lord Scannal's own folk, such as Iarla the steward, whom people speak of with respect, or Mongan the stable master. The stables seem to be an area where Seanan has no influence, which is just as well or I'd have died of thirst or starved or been eaten up by insects by now. Although Naithí the councilor and Beanón the lawman both came to Hawthorn House with Seanan, I think they are both Lord Scannal's men, and while they took a hard line in the discussions, they might be approachable. Not that I'm likely to get an opportunity.

The only woman I've spoken to is Fionn's wife, Íonait, who came out to the stables one evening with a plum cake for us to share. Íonait is an assistant cook. She greeted me courteously while giving me a good look-over. I wasn't exactly at my best, since there'd been precious little opportunity to keep myself or my clothes clean and in good repair. When you look and feel and smell like something the cat dragged in, you need a whole lot of pride and hope to go on standing tall.

Íonait didn't comment on my appearance, but the next night, when I went up to the stables to wash my hands and face under the pump and collect my supper of leftovers, there was a bundle waiting for me. "This and that," Fionn said, offhand. "Things that would have been thrown away or used for rags. If anyone asks questions, you found it by the midden. Íonait says if you want your things washed, bundle them up tomorrow and leave them with me. She'll see to it."

"I don't want to get anyone in trouble," I said.

"Then don't mention any names."

"I won't, Fionn. Thank you. And please thank Íonait from me. I'm truly grateful to you both."

When I went back to the hut that night, the stable hands carried down two buckets of water for me, one hot, one cold, and left me a cloth and a scrap of hard soap. In the chill of the small damp dwelling I gave myself the best wash I'd had in many days. When I was done, the water was dark with dirt. The bundle of clothes contained not only a skirt, a shirt, a tunic, and a pair of stockings, but also a much-laundered old night-robe. I put this on with my own shawl over the top, brushed my wet hair until my scalp stung, and went to bed feeling, if not like a queen, then at least like a semblance of my old self. I wondered how long it would be before this act of kindness made its way to Berrach's ears. How long would it be before he made someone pay for treating me like a human being and not a piece of dirt to be ground under his heel? Or might such a man not even notice the difference?

* * *

I'm working with the wall-mending crew again, closer to the
main house, in a spot where sheep graze under apple trees
and there's a good view of the gates leading out of Lord Scannal's domain. We're closer to that walled garden, and I see folk
come out from time to time to work there. Mostly I keep my
head down and concentrate on the job we're doing, which is
taking down a whole section of drystone wall that has become
unsafe after heavy rain shifted the earth around it. When it's
all down we'll do some backbreaking digging then re-lay the
stones.

Niall gives us breaks. I get a share of the food. Small kind-
nesses; I'm realizing how important they are, and I resolve to
offer them to others when I can. We're sitting there eating
when we see a plume of smoke rising from somewhere beyond
the fortress wall but not very far off. As we look, the plume
becomes a cloud, and the cloud darkens and becomes a fire,
with leaping flames visible at the base.

"St. Padraig's," Niall mutters. "Those poor fellows. Maybe we—"

A bell begins to ring, its resonant note a cry for help. Someone shouts from the top of the field where we've been working.
Now men are running in from everywhere, collecting buckets,
streaming down toward the gates, which are being opened by
a team of guards.

"They want us," Niall says, gesturing toward the man who
shouted. "Down tools, we'll finish this later. Pick up a bucket
if you can, or a sack, and get out there." When I rise to my feet,
ready to join the crew, he adds, "Not you, Liobhan."

I want to help. I'm strong. I'd be useful. But Niall's right.
Rush down there to help and certain people would assume
I was making a run for it. At the very least I'd draw a lot of

attention to myself. So I stay and watch as the flames grow higher and the voice of the bell is like a scream of panic. An army of men pours out of Lord Scannal's domain, while women gather on the sward by the house in anxious small groups. That's a big fire, and men with buckets can do only so much. I try to remember if a river flows nearby. Did I see a lake or pond on the way in here? I was concentrating so hard on the exhausted Dau that I wasn't as observant as I should have been. If they're relying on a single well, they haven't a hope of quenching that fire before it consumes the place.

Everyone's looking at one thing only. I can't go out there and save lives. I can't get on with the drystone wall on my own. But I can do something else. The women who were working in that garden are gone now. I can go up there and take a look around. Find a stillroom if there is one. Find the healer, perhaps, since that person surely won't have rushed off to fight the fire. Ask the healer about Dau.

I don't give myself time to think too hard, because deep down I know this is not the most sensible idea I've ever had. I move in the way Eabha taught us, darting from one point of cover to the next. The clothing Íonait gave me is in practical dark colors, gray shirt, brown skirt, dusky blue tunic—useful at such times. The skirt comes only halfway down my shins, no surprise as I have yet to meet any woman as tall as me, but at least I can move quickly without tripping over it. I'm in the walled garden before anyone's so much as turned their head in my direction. So far so good.

I stay in the garden only long enough to observe that there's a big bed of medicinal herbs set out in orderly fashion. Someone has left a basket behind; the contents are suited to the brewing of restorative teas. At one end of the garden is a door into the eastern part of the house, and I don't see a guard—I suppose they're all fighting the fire. I go in, working out what I'll say if I bump into some senior member of the household. I could tell them I feel ill. Collapse in a faint. With luck nobody's thoughts will be on me right now.

I hear muffled crying. It's coming from the chamber directly inside and it sounds like a man. I walk quietly to the open door. It's the stillroom; there's a steaming pot on the hearth and various herbs are strewn across the table. Seated at that table is a young man—a very young man, fourteen at most—with his head in his hands, sobbing. I tap gently on the door.

He starts as if struck. His head comes up, and I see the face of someone who is at his wits' end. He looks as if he hasn't slept in days. He's deathly pale, with shadows around his eyes, and those eyes are reddened and swollen. His right hand is red, too; that looks like a burn.

"I was looking for the healer," I say, keeping my voice low as I move into the chamber. "I hoped he—or she—might be here. My name is Liobhan." And when the young man stares at me wordless, a lock of brown hair falling over his brow, I add, "Is everything all right?"

He sniffs, then wipes his nose on his sleeve. "There's no healer," he says in a thread of a voice. "Only me. And I can't do it. I can't keep on doing it, I can't . . ."

"Take a deep breath," I say. He's trembling. Lack of sleep can do that to you. "Please, I mean you no harm." He draws in a shuddering breath and lets it out in a sigh. He won't meet my eye. "What were you making? May I help?" I cast a glance over the untidy table. I can do something simple with what's there. Chamomile and lavender; a soothing mix.

"Nothing works," the boy mumbles. "Nothing's any good. I've been trying my best, truly . . ."

I finish shredding the dried flowers, find a jug, fill it with hot water—at least there was a kettle ready on the fire—and tip the fragrant blend in. I look for honey, find a jar, add a spoonful. It smells quite good, considering the makeshift method. I let the boy weep undisturbed. As I'm stirring the brew I hear another voice. It's coming from further along the hallway. Not a sob this time, more of a low-pitched groan, quickly cut off. I freeze where I stand. "What was that?"

The boy shakes his head, then puts his hands over his ears and lowers his brow to the tabletop. I fill a cup and set it by him, warning him that it's hot. Then I'm out the door and along the hallway. The next chamber's empty. The one after it has its door shut, and the sounds of distress are coming from inside. What if I barge in and it's not Dau? What if I walk in on some complete stranger lying sick in bed? But it is Dau. I know his voice.

I open the door. The room is in darkness. The light from the hallway shows me a disordered pallet, and on it a man curled up on himself, with his arms shielding his eyes. He groans again, a sound of such awful pain that it's like a knife going through me. My shadow lies across the floor, and now it's joined by another.

"I tried my best," the boy says from behind me. His voice is still shaky, but he's pulled himself together. "For a bit, he wasn't too bad. But he kept on rubbing his eyes and saying his head hurt, and I didn't know the right way to help him, and nobody would explain . . . He got worse and worse. He can't sleep, and it makes him crazy. He screams and crashes about and hurts himself. When I try to help he fights me. He's really strong."

I won't waste time asking questions. "Fetch a lamp," I say. "Or some candles. And be quick. You're not in trouble. I know how to help. What's your name?"

"Corb, mistress." There's a note of profound relief in his voice now.

"Call me Liobhan. In this household I'm a servant like you. Hurry, please."

I prop the door open, praying nobody else will come until I've found out what in the name of the gods is wrong. I must stay calm, though anger is building in me every moment I look at Dau curled up there like a beaten child. The stink tells me he's been vomiting and voiding his bowels and hasn't been cleaned up properly for some time. I can't be angry with Corb. He said he's done his best and I believe him. I'm angry at who-ever thought his inexpert ministrations would be enough.

I sit down on the edge of the pallet, cautious after what Corb said earlier. "Dau," I say softly. "Dau, it's me, Liobhan. Are you in pain? Can you talk to me?"

He squeezes himself up as tightly as his long limbs allow. He's still hiding his face.

"Dau, it's all right. I'll help you." And a pox on anyone who dares try to stop me. "Turn this way, Dau. Turn toward me. Please." I want to see those eyes, though I dread it at the same time. "Dau?"

He doesn't move.

I reach out, put a hand on his shoulder, shake him gently. "Dau!"

In a heartbeat he's sitting up and his hands are reaching for my throat. I block him with my forearms just in time. "Get away!" he shouts. His voice is hoarse, but the words are unmis-takable. "Don't touch me!"

I push him back onto the bed and keep him there, my arms across his chest, my weight pinning him down. He's writhing and kicking, fighting to get free of me. Corb was right: sick as Dau is, he's still strong. I hold him down while Corb comes in with a lamp, sets it on a chest, then dithers by my side, not sure what to do. "A clean damp cloth," I snap. "And some water for him to drink. Do you have anything to give him for the pain?" Then, as Dau lets fly a stream of foul oaths, arching his back so hard he's likely to hurt himself, I say, "Never mind now, fetch the cloth and some water." I can't have the lad playing around with any of the herbs I'd use for a soporific draft. You need to know what you're doing for that. I have to get Dau calmed down some other way.

"Dau!" My tone is sharp this time. "It's Liobhan. Your friend. I'm here to help you. But I can't do that if you keep trying to kill me. Stop fighting me or I'll feel obliged to knock you out so I can give you a bath and get this room cleaned up. If you don't believe it's me, here's proof." Somewhat breathlessly, I whistle the first few measures of the jig we both know well, "Artagan's Leap." Then I sing part of the song I made up for him on the journey. It's something of an effort to do this while holding him down. If he's been like this with Corb, no wonder the poor lad was feeling so helpless.

> Often he mourned the loss of light
> The blaze of sun, the candle bright
> Yet there was joy in touch and sound
> The wet nose of a loyal hound . . .

"Aaargh!" groans Dau, with one last, straining effort to break free of my grip. Then, abruptly, he stops fighting me and goes limp. I don't let go. I'm used to all kinds of tricks. "Liobhan?" he whispers, and I know straightaway that this is no trick. Nobody could fake that haunted voice. It's as if the man is emerging from an unthinkable nightmare. "Is that really you?"

"Who else is strong enough to hold on to you and sing at the same time? Yes, I'm here, but I don't have much time. Corb is here, too, the boy who was looking after you. Or trying to.

Dau, I need you to help me. I know you're in pain, and I'll do something about that as soon as I can. I'm letting go now. I'm trusting you to cooperate."

I release my hold. At that moment Corb comes back with the items I requested.

"Who's that?" Dau turns his head sharply from side to side, sits up, then curses.

"It's Corb. He's helping me." How long before the fire at St. Padraig's is under control and the house fills up with people again? How long before someone comes marching in here and orders me out? "Corb," I say, "we have to get this room cleaned up. I need to make a draft to relieve the pain. As quickly as we can." Corb hands me the cup of water and I coax Dau to take a sip. He drinks, shudders, drinks again. I take the wet cloth but don't apply it yet. Best if I get him out of this filthy room. "I'll help Dau up and walk him through to the stillroom. Can you fetch enough water for him to have a good wash? A couple of half buckets of cold and top them up from the kettle. And he'll need some clean clothes to put on afterward."

Corb may be exhausted, but he's doing a good job now. Perhaps useful instructions were all he needed. I get Dau to the stillroom; he's able to shuffle along, leaning heavily on me. In better light I'm appalled by his eyes, which are swollen and reddened. He's been scratching around them, grinding his face against the pillow or rubbing with his knuckles, and he looks the worst I've seen him. Fergus and Jabir would be horrified. I feel red fury rising and make myself breathe slowly. One step at a time; it's the only way to handle this. Just let someone try to order me out. I'll kill them on the spot.

I settle Dau on a bench. "Stay there and don't move. Corb's fetching water for a bath, and I'm having a look around this stillroom. It seems quite well stocked. I'll find something to help with the pain and something to relieve the swelling.

While I do that, hold this cloth against your eyes. Two hands. That's it." He gasps with pain. "It hurts, I know. But just do it, please." He sits with elbows on the table and hands against the wet cloth, holding it in place. His whole body looks tense. As I search the stillroom shelves I keep on talking. "We have work to do. Not just me, both of us. Do you know what Archu told me before we left? He said I'm not the only one who needs to keep up my fitness while we're away from Swan Island. He told me to remind you that if your eyes get better you'll be wanting to step right back into your place there."

"Bollocks," Dau says from behind the cloth.

I find this oddly reassuring. "No, absolutely true. Just think how annoyed you'd be if you were cured but found yourself so much weakened that you couldn't go back when they had a place for you. All because you didn't bother doing a few exercises every morning. Ah!" A lucky find: not simply the herbs I want, but a dry mixture ready blended, so all I need to do is brew some of the stuff. I wish my mother were here. She'd know the safe dose so I don't end up killing my comrade. I remember the bath water and set a big kettle on the fire, taking off the small one.

"Ah, what?"

"Ah, I found what I was looking for. I'm going to make a draft and you're going to drink it. Also, from now on you're to leave your eyes alone. No rubbing or scratching. Don't even touch them. Your hands are filthy, and you're making things worse. The draft will relieve the pain and help you sleep, but you can't have it whenever you want. It's too powerful for that."

There's a silence, in which the only sounds are of me scooping out a cautious amount of the herbal mix, finding a cup, and pouring hot water over the dried leaves and berries.

"What happens if I drink it whenever I want?" Dau inquires.

"I'm not having that discussion. You drink it when I say you can, in quantities measured by me. When a person can't see, he shouldn't play apothecary. End of story." Maybe that's harsh, but this is Dau, and under present circumstances it wouldn't surprise me if he decided poison would be a quick way out. "You can take that cloth off your eyes now. I'm straining this so you don't get a surprise mouthful of vegetable matter. It needs to cool before you drink it."

"It smells vile."

I refrain from giving him the obvious answer to this. Instead I observe Dau's strikingly handsome features with their mask of reddened, puffy skin. He's a shadow of himself, hollow cheeked, the bones prominent. I'm not letting anyone but a skilled healer look after him from now on. Just how I'll manage this when I'm the lowliest person in the entire household remains to be worked out.

No sign of Corb. Where's that water? I need to get Dau clean and dressed.

"Liobhan," he says.

"Mm?" Gods, those eyes look bad. I wonder if Master Naithí would get a healer if Dau swallowed his pride and asked for help. I wonder if Lord Scannal doesn't realize how sick his son is. Surely he would have provided Dau with better care.

"I can't do this anymore." Dau's voice is flat, exhausted. "I can't pretend that things will get better. That I'll one day have my sight back. That I'll be what I was. I'm tired, my head aches, I just want to go to sleep and never wake up again."

"Bollocks," I say in my turn, thankful that he can't see me wiping away sudden tears. "What kind of attitude is that for a Swan Island man? How about a wager?"

Wan and hopeless as he is, Dau can't keep a fleeting smile from crossing his features. "Don't you ever give up, Liobhan?"

I count silently to five. "You know me, Dau. You don't need an answer to that."

"What wager?"

I must word this carefully. "I wager that if you cooperate, I can get you back to perfect fitness in—let's say two turnings of the moon."

"That doesn't include my eyes, I assume."

"I'd be stupid to promise that, Dau. Stupid and cruel."

A silence. "You forget one important thing," Dau says. "And that's my brother Seanan. I don't know where you've been all this time, but I've been stuck in that chamber, under orders to stay there. I had one or two visits from my brother. They were not exactly pleasant. When the boy was occupied elsewhere I did some blundering about on my own, with not very successful results. Stuck my hand in the fire at one point, and the boy burned himself helping me. As for the wager, there's no way in the world you could win. Seanan wouldn't let you anywhere near me."

"Dau."

"What?" He's drinking the draft now, making faces as he does so, but getting it down.

"Where is your other brother? Ruarc, is it?"

"Hah! I can tell you, but you won't believe me."

"Try me."

"He's a monk. At an establishment close by, St. Padraig's. My father must have offered a hefty bribe for them to accept him. I could hardly believe it when they told me, but it's true."

St. Padraig's. Which is currently on fire. I'm searching for the right way to tell him when Corb returns with a bucket in each hand and a garment of some kind over his shoulder.

"Dau, Corb is here. He'll help you have a good wash. You're to let him do it, understand? I'll be in the other room cleaning up, and I'll hear if you cause trouble. Corb, quick but thorough, all right? With soap. Any sign of folk moving about outside?" I'll have to say it. "Does it look as if the fire's under control?"

"What fire?" asks Dau.

"Still a lot of smoke," says Corb. "I couldn't see much. A girl told me what happened. Doesn't look as if the fellows are back yet."

"The fire is at St. Padraig's," I say, watching Dau's face. "Just about every man from the household has gone out to fight it. That's the only reason I was able to get in here and find you. And the only reason Corb and I have been able to help you without interruptions."

Dau says nothing. He looks as if someone has hit him.

"I didn't know your brother was there," I go on. "At the monastery. They've put me right at the other end of the place, with strict rules about where I can go and what I can talk about. People don't tell me anything. I didn't know where you were, Dau. I didn't know what arrangements they'd made for you. Someone said the healers from the monastery come over regularly to tend to anyone sick in the household. But they can't have seen you or your eyes would have been treated properly."

Corb makes to interrupt, but I forestall him. "I know you did your best, Corb. They shouldn't have asked this of you. Now get on with the bath, you two, and I'll tackle the other room. Is there a mop? Out there? Thanks."

The bedding's in a vile state. I bundle everything up, haul it outside, and leave it lying for now. I get the chamber as clean as I can. By the time I go back to the stillroom Corb is doing his own mopping up, while Dau has moved outdoors to sit on a low wall in the sun. He is clad in a nightshirt, with a blanket around his shoulders. His hair is damp and stands up in little spikes, dark gold in the sunlight. Corb comes out to empty his buckets over the vegetable plot. I stretch my arms and ease my shoulders. I'm weary all through. I have no idea what to do next.

Men's voices, approaching fast. I move quickly to stand beside Dau, trying to look as if I have every right to be here. "We have company," I murmur. "Stay calm."

A group of men appears, heading straight for us. In the lead is a tall person in a monk's brown robe. Apart from his tonsured red hair, he's the image of Dau. This can only be the missing middle brother, Ruarc. Right now he looks harried, as well he might. It's clear he's not expecting to see Dau; he stops short in shock. Behind him are two other monks and a couple of guards wearing the blue tunics denoting Lord Scannal's household.

"By all the saints! Little brother!" Ruarc does not stride forward to offer an embrace, just stands there staring.

Dau rises to his feet. The night-robe and blanket don't make the most dignified of attire, and I know he's still in terrible pain; the draft doesn't take effect so quickly. But I see my friend doing precisely what he's often counseled me to do in difficult situations. He straightens his back; squares his shoulders; lifts his chin. It wouldn't matter if he was in rags or naked. He's a warrior through and through. "Ruarc," he says calmly. "I heard there was a fire. Is all well?"

"It's Brother Íobhar now. I've set the old life behind me. As for the fire, we've lost several buildings, including the infirmary. Two men killed. Who's in charge here?"

A tense silence. I swallow hard, then say in my most courteous tones, "Corb here and I are looking after Master Dau, Brother Íobhar. I believe most of the men of the household went out to fight the fire."

"And you are?"

"I'm Dau's friend. Liobhan. I came to Oakhill with him."

Brother Íobhar's eyes widen. One of the blue-clad men

comes up and murmurs something in his ear. The monk looks from me to his brother and back again. "You surprise me," he comments. "Never mind that now, we need these premises to house the folk displaced from St. Padraig's, including a number of old and infirm men. The stillroom, the chambers beyond, pallets, bedding, serving folk to tend to the sick and injured. If you've been accommodated here, Dau, you'll be moving elsewhere, and your attendants with you." He turns to me. "Clear his belongings out now and find somewhere else to take him, will you? We have folk in great need."

I open my mouth, then close it again. Dau hasn't said a word. What am I supposed to do, leave him here on his own while I run around following orders that will enrage Master Seanan? I can hardly take Dau to the hut by the cesspool.

"I'll clear things out, Mistress Liobhan."

Bless Corb, who goes quietly back inside to fetch the saddlebag containing what's left of Dau's possessions.

Brother Íobhar is consulting with the other monks, making plans to turn this whole part of the house into an infirmary until a new one can be built at St. Padraig's. If that means we'll have a skilled healer at Oakhill, it's a good thing. But where am I to take Dau, and how long before someone realizes I'm not meant to be with him at all? "Dau?" I murmur. "Got any ideas?"

"Hah!"

Not helpful. "Come on," I say, taking his arm. "Let's go."

But I've waited too long. Into the garden comes a new group of men, and among them is Master Seanan.

"You!" He strides toward me, pointing an accusatory finger. "What are you doing here?"

I drop a graceful curtsy and say in a voice so sweet it's sickening, "Brother Íobhar asked me to help clear out the area, Master Seanan."

"You're supposed to stay in your quarters or be under supervision. And you"—Seanan turns on Dau—"you should be in your chamber, not out here half-naked. Has this whole place gone mad?"

Perhaps he's forgotten about the fire and the deaths and the imminent arrival of a lot of people needing help. The man's priorities are sadly skewed. And where is Lord Scannal in the midst of all this? Out fighting the fire himself? Or closeted away somewhere while his sons make a hash of things?

"Master Seanan," I venture, hoping he won't bite my head off before I finish, "Brother Íobhar has explained that Dau— Master Dau—must be moved from this building so the sick from St. Padraig's can be tended here. Master Dau is very unwell. He has not been adequately cared for, despite Corb's best efforts. If the infirmarian from the monastery will be here, it might be better for Master Dau to stay close by, in one of those—"

"*What?*"

I take a step back. If Seanan tries to hit me this time, I don't trust myself to stand here and let him do it.

"You dare to give me instructions? Have you forgotten so soon the circumstances under which you came here, girl? Have you forgotten who is the cause of my brother's lamentable condition? Have you? Have you?"

Dau is about to speak, but I tighten my hold on his arm and he bites back the words. "No, Master Seanan," I say, hoping I sound calm. "I thought you and Brother Íobhar should know that your brother has not had suitable care. I imagine you want him to get better as much as I do."

"Hah!" The explosive sound shocks me; for a moment Seanan sounds just like Dau. "How likely is that, young woman? You've ruined him. You've destroyed him."

"That's not true." It's my turn to hold my head high and

straighten my back. How dare he say such a thing with Dau right there listening? It's appalling. "Your brother was a fine man before this happened, and he is still the same man. Not ruined. Not destroyed. Fighting hard against ill fortune and now neglect as well. Does Lord Scannal know about this? Does Master Beanón know? A simpleton could see that Dau needs better care than this." They're all staring at me with various degrees of horror on their faces. Dau clears his throat. I interpret that as a subtle warning that it's time I shut my mouth.

"Seanan," says Brother Íobhar quietly, "we have a number of sick and injured men on the way up here, and work to do before the place is ready to receive them."

"You're in the way," Seanan says, not taking his eyes off me. "And I don't like that. Since you're so clever that you think you can tell a man of my rank how to conduct his business, let's see if you can do it better. You look after my wretched brother. You tend to him and see how long it is before he drives you crazy. Find some corner out of the way. Somewhere I don't have to see either of you." He thinks for a moment. "The stables. Down the far end. Dau's familiar with the place. Go. Now. And don't forget for one instant that you're a bond servant in my household. Speak to me that way again and I'll have you whipped."

It's not the moment to remind him, again, of that signed and witnessed agreement ensuring my safety while in this house. I want to be sure Corb won't pay the price for my outspokenness. But I think Seanan has forgotten Corb, who is pretending to pick vegetables further down the garden. I want to ask if I can use the stillroom. But if I don't ask, I can't be told no. "Understood, Master Seanan. I'll do my best."

With a jerk of my head I signal to Corb to come with us. As we head for the stables, Corb and I supporting Dau between us as we move against the flow of people returning from St. Padraig's, I'm thanking my lucky stars that I wasn't ordered to look after Dau in my wretched, insect-infested hut. The area at the end of the stables is quite spacious. The lads will let Corb and me clear it out, I'm sure. It's sheltered, there's access to clean water, it's well away from the main house, and I'll be able to take Dau outside when he needs fresh air and exercise. Gaining access to the stillroom will be a challenge, but I'll find a way.

We're almost there when I remember that the far end of the stables is the place where, when Dau was thirteen years old, Seanan took a knife to his beloved dog while Ruarc held Dau back and made him watch.

19

BROCC

I have lost count of the days since we crossed the lake and moved onto the Long Path. True is tired, and I am growing heartsick. I had hoped for answers sooner. Now I fear my comrade may die before we reach help. Often he walks in silence, as if saving his flagging energy to move his great lumbering body ahead. Perhaps he is trying to spare his tiny folk, for when he is sick or weary or sad, so are they. I wonder what will happen if he dies. Will they, too, perish? And if not, how can I find them a new place of safety? If they could live on a rock face or the bark of a tree or on a riverbank, then he would not have brought them on this journey, surely. Perhaps they are part of True himself, linked in ways I lack the capacity to understand.

The forest through which we travel must lie only within the Otherworld, for I know of no wooded tract so large on any map of Argialla or Ulaid or Dalriada. There is no sign of human habitation here, no high forest edge from which we might see villages or tilled fields or grazing cattle, no chieftain's fortress, no mill wheel or granary or stable. The only roads are narrow pathways under the trees, as branching and complex as the limbs of an ancient elm. The streams run clear. We fill our waterskins often, for the walking is hard even for me. We forage for food and soon grow hungry.

At night we find shelter and make camp. Where it is safe we make a small fire, as much to give us heart as to keep us warm. At True's request, I sprinkle water over his little folk, where they nestle in his rapidly drying moss, and the small ones lift up their hands and dance about. These last few days they have become slower to respond to this refreshing bath, and one or two of them do not rise but stay curled up, sleeping on as the droplets fall on them.

"They live still," True says. "Perhaps tomorrow we will reach help."

Neither of us knows what form that help may take. A settlement of uncanny folk, maybe, with a healer of particular skill and a cooperative turn of mind. A person like Mistress Juniper but of fey descent. Thinking of Conmael, whom I know to be a nobleman among his clan, I wonder if there are grand establishments to be found, the Otherworld equivalent of the court of Dalriada, with kings and queens, councilors and stewards, and whole teams of physicians and healers ready to help us. Eirne has said almost nothing of other clans within the Otherworld. I do not believe she has ever met fey folk beyond her own small tribe. But if the tales are to be believed, the Tuatha Dé Danann make marriages outside their own clans, they conduct wars and rivalries, they make long journeys, including perilous sea voyages. At least, they did all those things back in the time of the great stories. Are they entirely shrunk to small, isolated groups like Eirne's, which ended up with a half-human girl as their queen for lack of any other candidate?

We have seen creatures on our way, birds flying overhead or busy in the trees, squirrels scampering and climbing, a cautious badger, a wild pig all tusks and bristles. Not the Crow Folk; not so far. And no folk like Eirne's people, or indeed like the Tuatha Dé of the tales. If they are here, they are avoiding us. As True and I sit to rest under a monumental oak, I ask him why this may be. I think sometimes I talk only to distract myself from the fact that we have been walking for so long, with True finding it harder each day to keep going, and harder to sit down and get up again, and harder to recall where we are and why we have come here. His tiny passengers sleep much of the time now, and I fear for both them and my companion.

"I remember the day you came into Eirne's realm," True says. "You sang, she sang, and in time the portal opened for you."

"And when my sister came, she, too, used music to find the way." Liobhan had to wait far longer than I; she sang and played for hours outside the wall before Eirne decided to let her in. "I did think of that, True. But it seems too simple. Besides, we are already in the Otherworld. If I sang a song, we might end up out in the human world. The charm or spell might work in reverse."

True does not reply. I open the pack, get out the pot of salve, and gently minister to his wounds. My supply of this stuff will not last forever, and I did not ask Moon-Fleet what was in it. Around the injuries, True's skin is no longer red and swollen. It's turned an unnatural chalky gray. He does not flinch when I touch the marks of the bird's claws. I almost wish he was still in pain; I do not like these signs.

"I am the son of a wisewoman," I mutter, as much to myself as to my comrade. "I should know what to do. I should know how to help. But when my mother spoke of her craft my mind was on tunes and verses, and I did not listen as I should have done."

"You've got your own sort of wisdom," True says. His tone has become a curious blend of growl and whisper. He's needing to catch his breath often. "That'll give you answers, if you let it work for you."

I'm concerned for him and his tiny folk. I'm fearful for Eirne and the clan back home, with only Rowan to keep them safe from the Crow Folk. For no real reason, I'm uneasy about Liobhan. My mind turns in circles. It will not quiet and let me breathe. Troubles grip me so hard I cannot find the wisdom True sees in me.

"A song," True says, so quietly I can hardly hear. The small ones' echo is a wispy squeaking. "Or a tale. A tale of finding what you need, or a song of fixing something broken. That might do it."

His words open a window in my mind. Through that window I hear splashing water, and I see a wall of stone, many times higher than the one that holds the portal between Eirne's realm and the human world. There are shapes within that stone, curious forms that I wish I could see more closely. The air of that place is damp; a fine watery spray fills it. Mosses grow thickly on the stones at the cliff's foot, and tendrils of green climb its face, forming delicate lacy nets. Is that sound a great waterfall? My vision does not show it, only the stones and the green, brightening as somewhere high above the sun emerges from cloud and strikes down to light the watery air to a golden haze.

"You tell a story, True," I say. "Are there other folk like you? What is their tale?"

"I can't recall," my comrade murmurs. "A wall of stone, maybe, and tall folk. As tall as the sky . . . but maybe I was small then. Water falling down, someone carrying me in . . ."

So it was his dream or his memory that came to me a moment ago. A long-ago memory. "I thought I heard that place. Or half saw it. Your home? Before you came to Eirne's realm?"

"I can't recall. They are gone, maybe. The tall ones." After a moment he adds, "Just hum if that's easier. A song would give us a bit of heart."

The tiny ones are all lying still; they neither move nor echo
True's words. We must find help today, before nightfall. If True
is not close to death, surely they are, and I do not know if he
can survive without them. So I sing, another of those songs
made up on the spot. When no answers are to be found, a man
always has music.

> Beside the plunging waters in a deep secluded vale
> There dwelled a clan whose folk were named in many
>   an ancient tale
> Their bodies sturdy, strong as stone, their hair of
>   mossy hue
> The tiny friends that rode on them spoke high and clear
>   and true.
> Long years they lived there undisturbed, creatures their
>   only guests
> Fish darted in the rocky pool and night owls made
>   their nests
> Within the shielding oaks that served as guardians to
>   the clan
> Peaceful they were, and wise, in tune with spirits of
>   the land.

There I halt. I know nothing of True's people. If I invent a
tale of, say, the coming of man or indeed of other races of uncanny folk to disturb their idyllic life, how can that ease his
mind? I can imagine various dramatic events that might have
led to the stone folk being dispersed around Erin or drastically
reduced in number. It's even possible that True was taken elsewhere as a tiny child, just as I was. He might have grown up
among Eirne's people. How could he remember? I have lived
nineteen years; he might have lived nine hundred. I cannot

remember the day when the mysterious Conmael first placed me in the arms of Mistress Blackthorn, who was my mother from that moment on. I cannot remember the expression on Master Grim's face as he first beheld his new son, though I know exactly how it would have been—his plain, strong features would have been alight with joy and wonder. But I have a clear memory of times not so long after that. Playing with Liobhan in the fallen leaves, scrunching them under our feet, throwing acorns at each other. Holding my brother Galen's hand as I learned to walk. Singing with my sister. Oh, I remember that.

"That place," murmurs True. "I wonder if it's still there. That would be the spot. To get a cure."

My skin tingles. "Now, you mean? Is it possible? Can it be reached from here?"

"In this realm, paths can lead anywhere. They can change as they please, or as the earth pleases. Sing as we walk, Brocc. Sing of those old times and the good folk who lived in them."

It feels like lies. I cast True's ancestors as wise and peaceable since, although I have used him as a warrior, he is a being of calm and thoughtful nature. From that, my bard's imagination conjured a whole race of such folk. But perhaps they were at war; perhaps there were unlawful killings, struggles for power, injustices never put right. Perhaps they were like humankind. That makes me sad. It is not what True needs to hear at this moment.

"A good idea, friend." My hearty tone sounds a little forced, but True gets up and prepares himself to walk on. He murmurs something to the small ones nestled in his hair, and I think I hear the very faintest squeaking response.

"Tell me as soon as you need to stop and rest," I say. "I don't want to press you too hard."

"Sing well, bard, and we will find the place before nightfall."

I wish I had his confidence. How good it would be if one could conjure up one's destination simply by picturing it or thinking hard about it. Or by singing of it. As we set off into the woods once more, I remember something. Didn't my father once tell me that when my mother needed to talk to Conmael she went off to a quiet place and turned her thoughts on him? Didn't Father say that Conmael usually did appear, unless he was in some far kingdom fighting evil or performing brave deeds or whatever Otherworld princes do? My mother may be a wisewoman, but she hasn't so much as a drop of fey blood. Whereas I, though far from wise, am of both human and fey descent. Could I, too, do this? Could I summon a healer, or an elder of True's clan? Or would that be overreaching myself?

While I ponder this I sing. I give the song about the stony tribe many verses, in which True's ancestors perform acts of kindness to the creatures of the forest, and nurture the young trees as they grow, and lay to rest the bodies of birds and animals fallen victim to early frost or winter storm or the weary bones of old age. I walk, I drink from my waterskin, I stop to tend to True's injuries. We pause by a stream and I splash water over the little ones at True's request. The sun passes across the sky. A rain shower comes, and True stands in it with arms outstretched, while his passengers enjoy a real bath. I see True smile. But he is tired, and there is pain somewhere deep inside his strong body; he says nothing of it, but I see it in his eyes. Dusk approaches and we have not found the place.

"We'd best make camp," I say, unable to keep the defeat from my voice. "It's fairly open here. We could have a fire."

True just stands there.

"There is one more thing I could attempt," I tell him. "I don't hold out much hope of success; the only magic I can work, it seems, is through music. But I can try."

"To take us there?" He sounds so full of hope. My eyes fill with tears.

"To summon help. To summon a friend. Only, when my mother does this, it's in silence."

I stand in the middle of the clearing, with pale-trunked birches all around me, their foliage shining in the last daylight. I close my eyes and stretch out my arms with palms upward. I fix my thoughts on Conmael, hoping beyond hope that if he does appear, he'll feel like helping us. I keep it up for what seems like an eternity. But when I open my eyes, there is only True, watching me gravely.

"You should sing," he says. "Sing while you're working the charm. The magic is in your voice and in your hands when you play."

My treacherous mind fills with ridiculous possibilities to sing, all of them too bawdy or too silly or too inappropriate. That's what comes of a past existence as a traveling minstrel who must be ready to respond to an audience's requests, even in a packed drinking hall. I order myself sharply to concentrate. I recall the times when I used my voice to keep off the Crow Folk—the only times, I think, that my singing made magic, save for that one remarkable performance at the court of Breifne, when I did Eirne's business. I lift my voice in a word-less chant, and as I do so I think of Conmael, because he is real, he is alive, he is my mother's friend, and if anyone is going to help, he's a more likely prospect than anyone else I can think of. In my thoughts is an image of Conmael carrying the infant Brocc to Mistress Blackthorn's door and entrusting him to her care for the next eighteen years. And a far older image from the story my father told me, of how young Blackthorn, who had a different name then, protected and befriended an outcast boy who was tormented and reviled because he was neither one thing nor another. The changeling, the other children had called him, little realizing how close that was to the truth. That kind deed won my mother his lifelong friendship, and at one stage saved her from certain death, though my parents do not talk about that dark time. I think, if it were I who bore wounds and needed healing, where would I want to be? The answer is simple. At home. Not at home in the Otherworld with my wife. At home in Dalriada, at Winterfalls, with my family. This thought is uncomfortable, but I keep on singing.

I hear True murmur, "Good, Brocc." Birds in the trees join me in the incantation or prayer or charm, their voices sweet and high. I think True's small people are singing, too, in tones still higher than those avian trills. My eyes are closed, but I feel the moment when things change. The sensation is so odd I have no words for it. I open my eyes.

He's here. Conmael is here. Tall, pale, solemn, his dark cloak swirling about him, though I feel no breeze. I have seen him a few times before, at a distance, but now I feel like a stranger, and I wonder if I am presuming upon the bond between him and my mother. I feel like some hapless youth who has got into trouble and, instead of solving his own problems, has called up an Otherworld prince to save him. Which is odd, since I am the husband of an Otherworld queen. I should stand tall, greet Conmael with confidence, thank him for appearing. I hesitate a little too long.

"My lord," says True, and creaks into a bow.

But Conmael has his eyes on me. "I did not anticipate such a summons," he says quietly. "Are you in need, Brocc, son of Blackthorn?"

He knows me. I bow in my turn. "Greetings, Lord Conmael. I regret—I apologize—" I pull myself together, wishing I had True's natural dignity. "My friend here urgently needs the services of a healer. He has some injuries that are beyond the ability of anyone in our . . . in our clan to deal with. Eirne—our queen—directed us to take the Long Path. We have walked for many days, but it seems to me something further is required. I would not have called for you, but . . ." I don't want to put it into words. Not with True listening. *But I fear my friend will die.* "I sought answers. True told me a little of his ancestral place, and I tried to put it into a song. Later, I sang of healing, of peace, of hope. But it was not enough."

Conmael has listened with a somewhat bemused expression on his noble countenance. I would like to sing of *him* one day, but I would not dare. "If it is your friend's folk that you seek," he says, "why call on me?"

"You have always helped my mother. I hoped you might also help me."

He smiles. It transforms the man completely. "You crossed over into the Otherworld," he says. "I expected many things of you, but not that. Not so soon. Was it love that drew you so far away from home, Brocc?"

He knows more than I thought. How? Perhaps my mother has told him what happened; I imagine the Swan Island elders sent Liobhan to Winterfalls to break the news that I had turned my back on the human world. But Liobhan did not know all of it. "Love played a part," I say, thinking that Conmael, too, grew up in the human world. He seems to move easily from one realm to the other. But his home is here, in the Otherworld. Did love play a part for him, too? I cannot ask. "But also a need that I could meet. Eirne's people have been plagued by the creatures we call the Crow Folk. She and I . . ." I did not plan to tell him this. Why can't I stop talking? "She and I are at odds as to why they stay in our region wreaking havoc on Fair Folk and humankind alike. But . . . she asked me to help her. To use all the tools at my disposal to keep her people safe. I have many

friends among them." *But I miss my human family. Oh, so badly.*
"True's injuries were caused by one of the Crow Folk. I think
there is poison in those gashes. And the small folk who live
on True's body are also sick. I thought . . . I know that my
parents hold you in deepest respect, Lord Conmael. Will you
help us?"

A half smile still lingers on his face. I think of the other
questions I could ask him, the ones about myself. Who were
my parents? Why did they give me up? How was it that Conmael brought me to the human world when I was an infant
no more than a few days old and left me there? It was never
spelled out that he was not my father, simply assumed. Now
is not the time for those questions. Perhaps the time will never
come.

"As a bard," he says to me, "you know, I am certain, that in
the Otherworld every gift comes with its price. So it is with the
gift of knowledge. I myself will demand no recompense from
you, Brocc. In one way or another, we are family. I will guide
you and your friend to a place where his injuries can be healed.
As for those you call the Crow Folk, they are a puzzle; an
enigma. You are a warrior, a bard, and a man of compassion.
Perhaps you are the one who will solve that puzzle. Follow me.
The path will not be long."

I am wary of such statements. This is the Otherworld,
where everything is changeable. We walk behind him, True
resting his big hand on my shoulder. He cannot keep going for
much longer. I feel the tremors in his body. After some fifteen
paces Conmael walks off the track toward what seems an im-
penetrable tangle of thornbushes. He does not slow his pace.
The dark cloak moves in a wind that is not here; the bushes
part, leaving a gap just wide enough for True to pass through
unscathed, with me coming behind. Before us opens a vista

that surely was not here before, for it is the place from my vision, the green land at the foot of the great waterfall. Here it is not dusk, but day. I see the cliff; the tracery of soft growth across its face; the pool below, full of light. In a few steps, we have passed from one realm into another.

20

DAU

Somewhere in that time before Liobhan found me, I lost count of the days. Everything slipped away but the pain and the darkness and the longing for it all to end. If I could not keep a tally, if I could not even tell light from dark, what sense was there in living? At the worst, my head felt as if it would burst apart. I wished it would. I wished it would split open like a rotting fruit and spill out my brains to make a feast for rats. I struck it against the wall, trying to make that happen, and someone hauled me back. I thrust my hand in the fire, and someone stopped me. Corb. It was Corb, who is scarcely older than I was when I first left this house. But I did not know him. I was a stranger to everything. They tell me I screamed, shouted, smashed things, hurled objects at the walls. They tell me it was lucky I did not set the whole place on fire. Lucky. I'm glad something was lucky.

Liobhan is here and I will count the days again. She tells me she has been marking their passing on the wall of the wretched hut where they made her stay. I ask her to make fresh marks on the stable wall and she agrees. Not that I can see them, but I want them close by. She says she will carve them deep so I can read them with my fingers.

I thought she might be locked up or even dead. She thought

I must be in the house, tended to by physicians, fed and shel-tered in a manner befitting the son of a chieftain. Now she is brisk, making decisions, taking charge in the way only Liobhan can, and I am glad of it. She made me apologize to Corb, and I did. I was cruel to him. I scared him. I scared myself. If I believed in God, or gods, I would pray never to feel pain like that again.

We are in what used to be the harness room. In this place Snow was put to death. In this place I was forced to watch as my brother executed the only being I ever loved. In this place the man who is now mild-voiced Brother Íobhar held me back while Seanan wielded his knife. I hope Ruarc made his peace with his god and has truly become a better man. Is such a re-markable change possible? I doubt it. I do not trust him. Per-haps, in the quiet of his monastery, Ruarc is able to set aside the cruel part of his nature. But here, with Seanan and my father close by, that will be a higher mountain to climb.

It is evening now. Corb and Liobhan have set up our new quarters with the help of some stable hands. Liobhan makes friends wherever she goes. It's a remarkable gift. The fellows have walked over to the house for supper, taking Corb with them. The draft Liobhan gave me earlier sent me to sleep all afternoon, and when I woke, my head remarkably clearer, she had arranged a basic stillroom on a bench at one side of this area, which is separated from the stables proper by a partition with a door. There's a shared privy out the back, and it's all close to the pump. People have lent her things, and she's al-ready organized a source of herbs from the garden. There's a good smell here, part horse, part fresh greenery.

"I've got a poultice for your eyes," Liobhan says now. "Damp, cool, with healing herbs in it. You'll need to lie down. That's it. Hold it firm."

"You're expert at this," I murmur, feeling more than a little useless. The wet cloth is a blessing against my swollen eyes.

"An overstatement," says Liobhan. "I did occasionally take notice of what my mother was doing, though I wish now I'd paid more attention. But please don't start telling me I'd have been better off pursuing the calling of healer and not that of warrior. The fact that you're lying down with your eyes covered doesn't mean you can say whatever you like."

I respond with a grunt. I did once say something of the sort to her, though it was the calling of musician I recommended, having heard her remarkable singing voice.

"Dau?"

"Mm?"

"This must be where it happened. Snow, I mean. It must be hard for you." The joking tone is gone from Liobhan's voice.

"This is the place, yes." *Where I watched, where I sat holding her. Where she screamed and whimpered and fell silent. Where she bled on me until there was no more blood left.* "I think I'm cursed. I bring down evil on anyone who dares get too close. When the pain is bad, it's easy to believe what they say about me is true. That I don't deserve to live, because when she gave birth to me my mother died. If she had lived, maybe they would have been different. Seanan. Ruarc. My father."

I hear Liobhan moving things around on her bench. There's a thud and crackle as she drops another log on our little fire, then a clank as she stirs the embers with the iron poker.

"Small steps," she says eventually. "Small steps toward getting you well again. And small steps toward setting your ghosts to rest. Your recovery does seem to be my business now, since your brother challenged me to do it better than his people could. And for all the bad memories, I'm glad we're here, and together. I wish I could be sure Seanan won't come marching in and change the arrangements on a whim, but while I can, I'm planning to do this job well. And you're going to help me. As for the ghosts, how you deal with them is not up to me. But

I did wonder if you might make your peace with Snow in some way. Maybe something of her is still here. You loved her and she loved you. Her passing was cruel, I know, but that love was stronger. When they let you go, you didn't run away and hide. You made sure she was sheltered in your arms when she breathed her last. She would have known that, Dau. Deep inside, she would have known."

The poultice masks my tears. It can't quite take the effect of them from my voice. Never mind that. I'm sure it's no surprise to Liobhan. "If it were your dog that had died, what would you do?"

"Can't you guess?"

I imagine her and Brocc at home, perhaps mourning the passing of some beloved old family dog, a sturdy fellow who might have lain by Mistress Blackthorn's feet as she brewed her remedies, or padded at Master Grim's heels as he walked out to work his magic on a neighbor's roof—when I visited them he had a dog like that, a sturdy black-and-white creature. Why couldn't I have a family like Liobhan's? A sudden startling thought flashes through my weary mind. *You could, Dau. You still could.* Because a man who lacks the love of a father, a mother, a brother, can still himself become a husband and a father. He can make a family anew. I don't want that thought in my head. How could a blind man hope to keep his children safe?

"Dau?"

"You'd sing a song," I say. "You'd make one up to suit."

"I can, if you want. Now, while there's nobody else around. Or another night. Only, if I do it now, this place will hold good memories of Snow straightaway. And they will be stronger than the bad ones."

"It's too simple," I growl, angry with myself for dreaming of a future I never even wanted and now can't have.

"Simple is good," says Liobhan. "Like the love of a faithful dog. Tell me about her. That way I'll know what to put in the song."

"May I take this off while I'm doing it?"

"Why?"

"It's easier to talk without it. Easier to pretend I can see you."

A long silence. "All right. Pass it to me—there. But you must put it on again afterward. I'll soak it some more while you're talking." Sounds of quiet splashing. "Now tell me what made Snow such a good dog. What were the things you loved most about her?"

So I do, and I cry without my eyes covered, and Liobhan sits on the floor beside the pallet and holds my hand. And it doesn't feel stupid to be behaving like a child, it doesn't feel weak. It feels good. It feels right.

There are many things to tell her. Snow's soft ears with their little tufts; her tail that wagged so hard that sometimes her whole body moved with it. Her delicate paws. How she would put one foot up on my knee as if asking politely to be stroked. Her bright eyes. The way she would sleep curled up on herself so neatly. Her running form, a streak of pure white against the darkness of the trees. Her pelt shining in moonlight. The neat way she ate, not bolting her food down but savoring each morsel with delicacy. The collar I made for her with Garalt's patient help. She was wearing that collar when she died.

Liobhan works her magic with the song, putting in everything, making it rhyme, singing it in the voice I so loved to hear when we were at the court of Breifne and she performed with the band every evening after supper. I have missed that. I am no musician, but when she coaxed me to sing along with her on one or two memorable occasions, I felt proud to earn her approval. Now she keeps her voice soft, perhaps thinking of the drowsy horses next door in their stalls, perhaps not wanting to attract the attention of anyone who might be wandering outside. This household does not know she is a bard as well as a warrior.

She reaches the last verse of her song.

> *She walks beside him pace for pace*
> *In dappled light he sees her face*
> *Her bright keen eyes, her tufted ears*
> *Faithful through strife and joy and tears*
> *Her lovely spirit still burns bright*
> *The best of dogs, his heart's delight.*

She pauses for a while, then says, "I hope that was all right. Brocc could do it better." It sounds as if I'm not the only one crying.

"It was fine. Thank you." I almost believe Snow is here listening, in some incorporeal form. I wish I could believe it.

"Now I'll put the poultice back on," Liobhan says, clearing her throat. "And if I sing anything else, it'd better be something silly like that song Brocc wrote about the lady with the skirt. Or the one about the fisherman—you know all the words to that."

I pull myself together, to the extent that I can while lying on my back with a cloth over my eyes. "Hah!" I say. "I can just imagine my brother happening to come in when we were singing a bawdy song together. He'd put two and two together and make nine-and-twenty. Or he'd decide I must be quite well and no longer in need of your attentions."

Liobhan snorts. "I'm almost tempted to try it and see what happens. But on second thoughts, maybe not. I have a plan for you and I don't want it disrupted before we've even started."

"What plan?"

"Tomorrow," she says. "I think I hear the fellows coming back, and they should have some supper for us. Eat, sleep, and tomorrow we'll begin."

The curious thing is that when I'm sitting up at our table a while later, eating some quite good food the stable hands have brought back for us, I can feel Snow's warm body at my knee. I, the blind man, can see her hopeful eyes looking up as I eat my mutton pie. I can hear the slight movement of her claws on the hard slate of the floor. A tear trickles down my cheek; I lift a hand to wipe it away.

I know Liobhan is watching me. But she doesn't say a thing.

21

LIOBHAN

Fear never won any wars. In Dau's presence I show confidence. Poultice on, poultice off. Draft swallowed down to the last drop. I've warned Corb that if he has any doubts about our patient's recovery, he should air them only when we're out of Dau's hearing. We have an agreement, Corb and I, that one or other of us will always be with him. We won't ever leave him on his own. Word is that the monks have a lot of very sick people in their makeshift infirmary, including several suffering burns. Folk are saying none of the brethren has a moment to think of anything else. But I don't trust Dau's brothers, even the more approachable Brother Íobhar. I don't trust Lord Scannal and I don't trust Seanan's men. While I'm close at hand I can keep Dau safe. As for Corb, he's no warrior but he's willing and able and he'll call me if he can't cope.

The potion is allowing Dau good sleep at night, without the nightmares that plagued him earlier. The poultices and washes are reducing the swelling around his eyes. If he keeps his hands away from his face, the scratches will heal and the bruises fade. He's eating quite well. Our friends in the stables provide for us during the working day, and an unnamed person in the kitchen is supplying extra rations so they can bring us a satisfying meal in the evenings. I warn Fionn that this arrangement may draw

Master Seanan's displeasure, and find that Iarla the steward has approved it. Seems that since meals have to be conveyed to the infirmary for the patients there, it's considered reasonable for us to be supplied at the same time. Common sense—who'd have thought it?

We've seen nothing of Seanan, which is both good and bad. Good because if the man comes here, it will only be for some ill purpose. Bad because it makes me suspicious. He loathes Dau. He despises me. He enjoys tormenting people. I feel as if I'm just waiting for him to charge in and ruin the delicate process of restoring Dau to health. Health of body and health of mind—that's what I'm aiming for. I won't let Seanan get in the way. Not even as a shadow in my mind.

I let Dau spend three days resting, while I treat his eyes and give him the twice-daily draft. During that time I find out which of the women from the household know the most about herbs and healing. They're unlikely to be treating the injured men from St. Padraig's, but they'll still have access to the garden. I discover that a woman named Miach makes up remedies for the women and children of the household. She's said to know a lot about herbs and potions. Miach is the sweetheart of one of the stable hands, Torcan. I do wonder how many folk I might be getting into future trouble, but with Torcan's help I meet Miach near the stables one morning—she's a tiny thing with a shock of dark curls—and she offers to fetch me the herbs I want from the garden and to find me some of the other supplies and equipment I'll need if I'm to provide for Dau properly.

On the fourth day, after we've had breakfast and cleaned things up—Dau may be blind, but he's capable of scouring dishes in a bucket of water and tidying up the bed he's slept in—I say, "Right. Today you don't rest until later. It's fine outside and we're going to start some exercise. There's a place that should be suitable. It's out past the grain store, a little yard that doesn't seem to be used for much. Partly grassed, partly packed earth. Reasonably secluded. Ideal for some training. Let's find out how much ground you've got to make up." I'm changing into my trousers as I speak. Since Dau can't see me, I don't bother going behind the makeshift screen the stable hands have put up for us. They seemed to think this necessary once they realized I was planning to sleep in the same area as Dau. Corb has a pallet in the stables proper, not far from our door. If the men think this arrangement odd—why would Corb not share with Dau?—they make no comment, which I appreciate. I'm not planning to waste time and energy explaining that he and I are comrades, and that the kind of work we do means a person can't be fussy about the living arrangements. Or that if he wakes at night to find his demons waiting, I'll be the one battling them by his side.

I plait my hair tightly and pin it up into my combat style. I put on my boots. I take a deep breath and let it out slowly. "Let's go."

Dau is very quiet as we walk to the training yard, if indeed it can be called that—it's more of a forgotten space that has suddenly come in useful. It's not overlooked by any building; it's out of most folk's way. It is fairly close to a spot where Lord Scannal's men-at-arms sometimes conduct their training, but I've seen little activity there of recent times and I judge we'll be unobserved. I've asked Corb to come and tell us if anyone seems to be showing too much interest.

"We start slow," I tell Dau. "No rushing into the full set of exercises we were doing before we left the island. We build up gradually. On the ground to start with, on your back, ready to stretch. This patch is all packed earth. It's about five man-lengths north to south and three east to west. Right now you're facing south. On the north side there's a patch of grass. No obstacles within the area. Ready?"

Dau has sat down on the ground. He looks deeply skeptical. "What are you going to do, stand there and shout orders? Laugh at how weak I am?"

"Don't go out of your way to annoy me, Dau, or I'll have to start acting like Archu. I'm going to do everything you do. I'll be damned if I go back to Swan Island any weaker than I was when I left the place. I've been missing this. But I can't do it without a training partner."

"How do I know what to do? Are you planning to execute the routine and talk while you're doing it?"

"Want to make a wager that I can't get through it?"

"I'd have surer odds if I wagered that I couldn't get through it," he says with some bitterness, though he has lain down on his back and is stretching out his arms, preparing to start.

"Don't tell me you've lost your competitive streak, Dau. You were scheming to beat me from our very first day on the island."

"Hah!"

We start. Stretches first: arms, legs, back, shoulders. Exercises on the ground. Exercises standing. I've wondered how much running and jumping Dau should do; wondered if that might make his eye condition worse. But Fergus and Jabir did allow him to ride here from the coast, so it should be all right.

"How's your head?" I ask casually.

"Not bad, so far."

"Think you could jog around the edge of the area, maybe with a hand on my shoulder? Or just using what you can hear?"

"You expect me to say yes."

"I expect you to say yes provided you can do it without

hurting yourself. The aim of this is to restore you to fitness, not do more damage."

"I'll do it. No hand on shoulder; we can't run properly like that. You go first, I'll follow."

We start slowly. When it's plain Dau can do this remarkably well, we speed up. I make the pace, he follows. We complete twenty circuits of our smallish training ground, then gradually slow until we stop and stretch again. Compared with our morning routine on Swan Island this is child's play.

"More?" inquires Dau when he has his breath back.

"We need to take it gradually. That may be enough for the first day."

I pass him the waterskin. He drinks and gives it back. "How about a walk?" he suggests. "Are there folk around?"

"This place doesn't give the best of views. I suppose I could take you on the scenic tour of my hut next to the cesspool." I pause to drink. "Dau. We do need to be careful. Seanan told us to stay out of his way. You know what he's capable of."

After a moment Dau says, "How many days left until the year is up?"

"Too many." I can't keep the chill from my voice. There's no way Seanan's going to leave us alone for the best part of a whole year. I'll be lucky if we get one turning of the moon. "So let's make each of those days count, Dau. Let's do something good with every single one. Adding a new exercise to our routine. Singing a new song, telling a new tale. Finding a friend. Inventing a joke. Making each other laugh."

"How do you do it? Where do you find that relentless hope?"

"I can't tell you that. Just that it's always seemed like the right way. The only way. Part of trying to be brave, I suppose."

"Trying? Seems to me you can't help being brave."

"I have my weak moments, Dau. I just try not to show

them. You're right about the walk. Archu would approve. Shall we go?"

On the way down to the hut I explain in an undertone what I can see around us and warn him of obstacles in our path. When we're about halfway there I stop suddenly, and he curses under his breath, narrowly avoiding a stumble.

"Sorry," I murmur. "Come over here, under cover." I've just seen Seanan out riding, beyond the wall, all by himself. He's heading south along the valley, with the forested hills to his right and on his left a patchwork of walled fields dotted with small clusters of trees. Dau and I keep still in the partial cover of a furze bush. I watch as his brother rides up toward a stand of willows. There's an old byre or outhouse there; I can glimpse crumbling walls under the trees. The fields in that area lie fallow—no creatures graze there, and from the look of it, the soil hasn't been turned over in years. It's all long rank grasses and deteriorating drystone walls. It must once have been a farm, but there's no dwelling house in sight. Is that still Lord Scannal's land?

"What are you looking at?" Dau whispers in my ear.

"Shh. Later."

Seanan dismounts and leads his horse in under the trees. Both he and the animal are out of sight now. Has he gone inside? We can't stay here too long; someone could be watching us. It's odd, though. Seanan's not equipped for hunting, and he doesn't seem the kind of man who'd go out to visit the poor on his own. Perhaps the old outhouse is not derelict after all; I see a curl of smoke rising from the place now. If it's some kind of assignation—I try and fail to picture Seanan with a lover— that is hardly the most appropriate of trysting places. "We'll walk down to the hut now," I tell Dau. "We'll talk when we get there."

Inside the hut are my markings on the wall, my first count

of days. I take his hand, put his fingers against the scratches. "I used to think people who count things were odd," I say. "But I'm understanding now how it helps. If we add these to the ones in the stables we'll have every day since we came here."

"Let's not start with these," Dau says, surprising me. He always keeps count of everything, from how long it takes to clean a weapon or set up a target to how many times each of us has won a single combat.

"Then where do we start?"

"From the day you found me," says Dau.

Oh, gods. Tears well up too fast to deal with. What is this? How can so slight a thing make me weep like a child? I turn away quickly. Not that he can see. But he's close enough to hear it in my voice and in my breathing. "All right," I say. In my mind I make a promise that may be impossible to keep. It has to do with Dau's eyes and the unpalatable knowledge that at the end of my year's servitude I'm supposed to walk away from Oakhill and leave him behind. It dawns on me that our friendship is changing in a way neither of us ever intended. That's an uncomfortable insight. "It'll feel long enough even without those extra days." This seems a good time to change the subject. "Dau, I saw something odd before, when I stopped on the path."

"Mm?"

I tell him about Seanan and the old crumbling farm building and the empty land around it. "Is that part of your father's holding?"

"It was. Probably still is. There was a tenant farmer there. I remember the place as well looked after. But a lot can change in six years. Corb might know. I think his family farm is up beyond there."

"It did seem rather odd. Not that it's any of my business what your brother does in his spare time. But Swan Island trained us to be observant. To take note of anything out of the ordinary."

"Maybe he went for a ride and needed to relieve himself somewhere private. Maybe he's getting tired of a house full of monks."

"Stopped for a piss and lit a fire on the hearth while he was doing it?"

"Maybe he was feeling cold."

I give this remark the silence it deserves. Seanan is master of his own domain. Folk jump to obey him. He can arrange things any way he wants. If he wants to be left alone, surely all he has to do is say so.

"Swan Island doesn't teach you to stick your finger in a wasp nest so you can find out what happens," Dau says. "If he's not bothering us, be glad of it. Whatever he's up to, it's no concern of ours." He wrinkles his nose. "How did you bear the stink in here?"

"It's not as bad as it was before I fixed the drains. But it's time we went back anyway. We don't want to overdo things."

"Spoken like a stern parent admonishing an unruly child."

"I'd prefer to sound like Archu working with a wounded warrior. Give me time. I may get it right before we're finished."

We walk back. I keep an eye out for Berrach, though he's stopped giving me work since we moved to the stables. We're almost back there when Dau says, "I'm sure I'll be cursing you before the end of this. But so far you're doing a pretty good job."

"Of being Archu?"

"You'll always be yourself, Liobhan. But you're like him. You're like him in more ways than you probably know."

I feel my cheeks flush with pleasure. He's surprised me yet again. "Thanks," I say. "As for the cursing, I expect we'll both be doing it before we're finished. It goes with the job."

* * *

Day by day we work on strengthening our bodies and sharpening our minds. We don't see Seanan at the stables. If he wants to go riding, it's his practice to have a groom prepare his horse and lead it around to the front of the house. We don't see Berrach. The sick, injured, and frail from St. Padraig's are settled in that part of the house where Dau was before. The infirmarian and his assistants are caring for them, but the other brethren are gradually returning to their damaged monastery, where rebuilding will soon be under way. Brother Íobhar does not come to visit Dau. I assume that's because he's busy overseeing the arrangements for the sick—he seemed to be a figure of some authority—but I learn soon enough that I'm wrong. Miach passes on something she heard from the apothecary monk. Brother Íobhar has been sent away on monastery business. He left suddenly and he's likely to be gone for some time. In his absence Brother Petrán, the senior infirmarian, is in charge. He's agreed that Miach can continue using the stillroom for her own preparations, provided she lets him know what she's doing. Useful for me, since Miach is the source of the materials I use for Dau. I ask if she knows where Brother Íobhar went—it seems odd to me that he would leave at a time of such upheaval for the brethren. Miach doesn't know. But she tells me there was a row between Íobhar and Seanan the day before Íobhar left. Something about the household arrangements and who was really in charge. She slipped away out of the garden when they raised their voices, not wanting to be accused of eavesdropping. I wish she'd heard more.

As for Lord Scannal, he must have made a decision not to interfere. I didn't expect to see anything of him. But Dau hasn't seen him since the first day, and that is a surprise. Despite the history of ill will, there's no altering the fact that Dau is his son. His silence is distinctly odd.

None of this is reassuring. I know Seanan's not far away; I know how deeply he hates Dau and how much my manner irks him. I thought he'd act sooner. Does he not realize that by sending us to the stables he's done us a big favor? The man's not stupid. If he's waiting for us to lower our guard, waiting for us to feel safe before he strikes, Seanan has underestimated us. We're getting stronger and we'll be ready.

By day fifteen I'm seeing a marked improvement in both Dau's strength and his attitude. I can tell that he's decided whatever I can do, he will match, even though he's blind. Stubborn idiot. If he thinks I'm going to have a full-on bout with him, he's dreaming. I'd be mad to risk delivering another combat injury.

All the same, when he suggests we practice deflecting a surprise assault—imagine, for instance, that a person was walking along a hallway, perhaps heading calmly to supper, and someone reached out from an alcove and grabbed them—I agree without allowing myself to think too hard. It's a situation we could easily face here with Seanan's men, and if it happened in the dark I'd have the same challenges to meet as Dau would.

We can't practice this effectively in our small open area so we do it in the stable yard. Dau's getting to know his way around here, though people do have an unfortunate habit of leaving buckets or pitchforks or brooms up against the wall. I check that there are no such obstacles present. I check that there are no hard objects on the ground, then check again.

"Count slowly to ten," I tell Dau. "Then walk along next to this wall as if you were heading to the privy. And be ready." As he counts, I slip as quietly as I can into the second of two open doorways along his path.

I expect him to walk slowly, finding his way with caution.

Instead he strides, so I have to lunge out from my hiding place in a less than perfectly controlled move. I manage to get a good grip, but in doing so I topple both of us to the ground, which was not part of my plan. With a heave and a twist, I make sure I'm the one who lands underneath.

"Cease," I gasp, being Archu again. Dau may have got thinner, but it's still uncomfortable to have his full weight sprawled on me. After that awkward twist my back hurts.

Dau rises. In keeping with the protocols of Swan Island, he reaches out a hand to help me up, judging my position precisely. It's then that I see Corb at the pump, watching us round-eyed, and a couple of stable hands behind him, apparently much diverted.

"We have an audience," I tell Dau in a murmur. "Corb and a couple of the lads. Your turn now."

"If you say so," says Dau. "We should make this quite even, yes? Corb! Find me something for a blindfold, will you?"

It's fair enough. Corb brings a scarf and, under Dau's instructions, ties it over my eyes. This feels weird. It's only an exercise, and we know not to hurt each other, but my heart is suddenly racing. No time to consider why, because Dau says, "Count slowly up to ten, then do the same thing I did. Only we'll start from the other end this time."

I count. I don't stride out but I walk at a brisk pace, feeling how my balance is affected now I can't see. I have just time to think, *This is what it's like for him all the time,* when he grabs me, not around the chest as I expected, but by the legs—he's been crouching down, and he throws himself at me. I'm not ready for it, and I stagger, fighting for balance. I try to grip his clothing, but he holds on and rises to his feet with me over his shoulder like a sack of flour. Morrigan's curse! Has he been practicing secretly, to have so much strength back? Dau drops me, and I land on the ground in a humiliating heap. He helps me to my feet. Again. Corb and the stable boys cheer, startling the horses.

"That was a low trick," I say, reaching up to untie the blindfold. The first thing I see is the triumphant grin on Dau's face.

"Precisely the sort of move you might use," he says. Then the grin fades. "You didn't let me win on purpose, did you?"

"Hah! Hardly. I don't enjoy being hauled about like some hapless maiden. My only concession was taking steps to make sure you didn't hit your head the first time around. And now my back hurts, so we'd better leave it at that. A stretch or two and I'll be fine." I remember our audience. "Thanks, Corb." I pass him the scarf. "The show's over, fellows."

With some reluctance they go back to their work. Perhaps they didn't believe I could really fight, before this. In view of what just happened, maybe they still don't believe it. Never mind that. Dau has done well. I take some pride in that. And he was happy, for a bit at least. Small steps.

When we're back in our quarters, Dau offers to salve my back. I accept, since I can't reach the spot myself and the only alternative is Corb. I shut both doors first, the one into the stables and the one that leads outside. The special salve my mother gave me when I was last at home is all gone, but I've made up a fair imitation from materials Miach got for me. I'm in shirt and trousers, my usual attire for training. I pull the shirt awkwardly up out of the way. The only thing I have on under it is the band I tie around my breasts when I'm doing something active.

"This isn't going to work," says Dau, standing next to me with the salve jar in his hand. He knows where I am, but I can't keep my clothing out of the way with one hand, and I can't indicate where the sore spot is without guiding his hand there.

"Lie on the bed, facedown. And if you're concerned about your modesty, don't be. I can't see a thing."

No, but you can feel plenty, I think but don't say. Since it makes perfect sense, I do as he suggests. I take off the restricting band, then lie down with my shirt pulled right up. I wait while he touches different parts of my back with fingertips so careful I think of a butterfly on a flower, which under the circumstances is utterly ridiculous. "There," I say, and his fingers pause. "You need not use much. It spreads quite easily. Rub it around that spot, over an area about the size of your palm. Mm, yes, that's good. Not sure what I did to myself, but it hurts. Maybe no training tomorrow."

"Just a walk, perhaps." Dau's hand keeps up a steady motion. The salve warms my skin and the pain starts to subside. I must remember to thank Miach again.

"I wish we could go walking outside the walls," I say. "Up to the woodland."

"And spy on my brother's unusual activities?"

I wasn't thinking of that at all, only of how good it would feel to walk in the forest, just Dau and me, pretending for a while that things are as they were before. But it wouldn't be like that, of course. He'd still be blind. "Not that. Just to be somewhere different for a while. Somewhere we didn't need to be so careful."

Dau says nothing for a while. He keeps rubbing my back gently. I wish I could stop time for a little bit, just lie here and enjoy the sensation.

"Liobhan," Dau says. His hand stops moving. "Would you ever lie with a man because you felt sorry for him?"

"*What?*" I start to sit up, then think better of it. "Of course not! That idea disgusts me." What is he thinking, to ask me such a question?

Now he's gone silent again. I squirm around to see his face and don't much like the shuttered look on it. It reminds me of how he was sometimes, in those first days on Swan Island. Those days when I had no idea about his past and his family and the nightmares he wore like an invisible garment everywhere he went. I clear my throat. "Let me clarify. Lying with a man is somewhat appealing, given the right circumstances. But not because of feeling sorry for him. It would have to be for other reasons."

"What reasons?"

"Must we have this conversation?" Even as I ask this, it occurs to me that at some point or other, perhaps we do. Because things are changing between us, whether it suits us or not. It's there in the way he touches me, and the way my body responds. The way I can sing to him and hold his hand in the dark, the way we can cry together. The way I feel when I see him hurt, and when I see him brave. The way his voice softens, sometimes, when he speaks to me. It's a development fraught with complications, and right now complications are the last thing we need. "Forget I said that. Now's not the time, that's all." But it feels like the time, as I lie here with Dau's hand warm against my back, and the sweet, pungent smell of the salve filling the room, and my mind pleased out of all proportion by our little training exercise, even if I did end up on the ground with my back on fire.

"Feeling more comfortable?" Dau withdraws his hand, stands up, and moves away. "You might want to put more clothes on before Corb decides to walk in."

"Dau?"

"Mm?"

"Thanks."

"Anytime."

I look across and see a smile on his face, not the supercilious smirk he used to favor us with on the island, but a natural sort of smile. Maybe I should offer to sleep on Corb's pallet in the stables, especially now Dau is getting through the nights quite well. It would be easy enough for Corb to fetch me if I was needed. But I don't offer, and Dau doesn't make the suggestion. As I adjust my clothing and tidy up my hair, he sits on the bench saying not a word.

22

DAU

The thirtieth day since Liobhan and I came to stay at the stables, and spring is advancing into summer. There are new foals out in the fields, so Corb tells me, and lambs. I am getting stronger. Liobhan and I spend a good part of the morning on our exercise. We rehearse some carefully planned throws and contests of strength, but those feel more like dancing than fighting. I'm ready for a proper fight, I know it. But Liobhan says no.

She's seen Seanan riding out to that place several times, sometimes with one of his henchmen, a big fellow called Ultán; sometimes on his own. Sometimes smoke rises, sometimes not. Sometimes he stays there for an hour, two hours; sometimes he returns quickly. I hear in her voice that she scents a mystery and is driven to solve it. I tell her to leave it alone and to be glad my brother is well occupied.

When we work in the stable yard—not all our activities can be carried out in the makeshift training area—we usually get an audience of two or three, whichever of the fellows happen to be working there at the time. Sometimes they ask Liobhan to demonstrate a move or teach them one. When she agrees, I suspect it's only so she can make me rest without having to give me an order. I'm sick of being reminded to take things slowly, not to risk damaging my eyes further, and so on. All right, I can't see. But I know where things are; I can feel and hear and make decisions for myself. Liobhan's caution is becoming irksome.

It's started to rain, just lightly. We're going through our exercises in the stable yard so that if the drizzle becomes a deluge we can get quickly under cover. Working in the wet is part of the training on Swan Island, since we must be able to perform capably under any conditions. The ground beneath our feet is slippery now, but we know how to adjust for that.

There's quite a bit of noise. While we push up and hold, push up and hold, Liobhan explains without a trace of breathlessness that there seems to be a leak in the thatch, just above the stall allocated to my father's prized broodmare. The mare is being moved, and the fellows are putting a ladder against the wall outside so someone can climb up and attempt a repair job, even though the rain's still coming down. "Morrigan's britches," she mutters as we extend our hold to a count of twenty, "the way they're going about it, someone will end up with a broken leg. Or neck."

Just after she says that, there's a shout from up on the roof, or more of a scream. Gasps from the lads down close to us, and then Mongan's voice, shouting, "What's wrong?" And someone up there yelling back, "He's cut himself! Bad!"

One moment Liobhan's still beside me, and the next she's out of her pose, up and away. I hear her running across the yard.

"Give me that cloth! Quick!" It's an order. Then the sound of someone scaling the ladder, fast. I don't need to be told who it is. Isn't her father a master thatcher? There's a babble of talk all around me now, so I get a running account of what's going on. Liobhan up on the roof, balancing like a cat. Liobhan getting one of the two men up there to press a wadded-up cloth on the other one's wound—a thatching knife is sharp—while she ties on a makeshift bandage. I can hear her voice, but not the words. Her tone is calm, practical, intended to convince the injured man that despite all the blood, he's not going to die; he's in safe hands.

Then they have to get him down, and he doesn't want to come. Shocked, no doubt, sent up there to do a job he wasn't trained for. There's absolutely nothing I can do to help, except maybe holding the base of the ladder while they get down. But they don't need me; other men, men with eyes that work, are already in place. I stand there, completely useless, listening to the fellows around me.

"Frozen. Can't move."

"How's she going to get him down?"

"Morrigan's britches, if he keeps struggling like that he'll have all three of them over the edge."

I taste blood: I'm biting my lip. I want to be up there. I know exactly how it should be done. I could do it, even the way I am now. But who would say yes to a blind man?

Mongan shouts, "Liobhan, you and Lughan get him over toward the ladder between you! One of you fellows climb up to the top and wait. You can brace him as he comes down."

Sounds of movement up there. The injured man is whimpering; terror has turned him into a small child. I know that feeling. I could help him. I could help save him. But I can't move.

"Dagda's bollocks, that woman is strong," someone comments.

"Not scared of heights, is she?" observes someone else.

A subdued cheer goes up. I gather they've reached the top of the ladder, where a brave volunteer—I think Caol—is waiting to support the injured man on the way down. Brave because there's a strong possibility the man will thrash about and send both himself and anyone close on a fast drop to the courtyard.

"Stand underneath," Mongan says. "Be ready to catch."

Some of the men around me go to do this; I stay where I am, knowing that even this simple duty will be considered beyond me. I stand there as Caol and the injured man reach the ground without mishap. I stay there as Lughan comes down, and lastly Liobhan, whose arrival is greeted with more cheers, as well as offers of ale or mead.

"Will you see to his hand?" asks Mongan.

"He's best treated by the infirmarian from St. Padraig's," Liobhan says. "The wound may need stitching up. I'm not trained to do that kind of thing." A pause. "You should take him there straightaway."

"Will you come with us?"

"I'm not welcome in the house. Corb will go." Her tone changes; becomes warm and reassuring. "Take a few deep breaths, Tomas. You're going to be fine. The monks will look after you. Can you walk over to the house if Corb helps you? Good man."

And just like that, it's over. Liobhan lets the fellows congratulate her and go over what happened for a bit, then the rain gets heavier. She tells them she wants to wash her hands and change her clothes, and they let her retreat to our quarters. I follow; I can find my way now. When I get there, there's nothing for me to do but sit on the edge of my pallet while she goes out to the pump to wash, then comes back in and puts the kettle on the fire.

"Danu save us," she observes mildly. "You realize the hole in the roof still isn't fixed. I should go and do it now, while the ladder's up. Just needs a couple of pegs replacing, and I've got them. Stuck all of Tomas's bits and pieces in my belt before we came down."

I don't say anything. Right now, my thoughts are darker than they've been for a long while. I'm not sad, I'm angry. Just who I'm angry with—myself for being so useless; Liobhan for doing everything so capably and for charming everyone, and for sounding so bloody cheerful; or fate for completely wrecking my life—I don't know and I don't care. Who cares about the wretched roof?

Liobhan's changed her mind about making a brew; I hear her take the kettle off the fire. "Now," she says. "Before someone else decides to have a try and ends up with a slashed hand or worse. Dau?" She's moving about, fetching things, getting ready.

I say nothing.

"Will you come and hold the ladder for me?"

She thinks she's being kind. Letting me feel useful. "There'll be plenty of lads lining up eagerly for an opportunity to help."

"They'll have realized they've still got their own work waiting to be done. Come on, Dau. Let's get this finished."

Despite myself, I follow her back out into the rain and across the courtyard. Maybe she's right about the lads; I hear a voice or two in the stables and the sound of hoofbeats as someone leads a horse out, but nobody speaks to us as we go over to the ladder. I know nothing about thatching. It does seem unwise for Liobhan to go up there by herself, especially now it's so wet, even though she seems to be able to turn her hand to just about anything and make a success of it. But I'm not going to start an argument. I hold the ladder as instructed and she climbs. What happens if *she* cuts herself? How is it she's so sure she won't make a mistake? Was I like that before I went blind?

Liobhan's on the roof now; her weight is off the ladder. Something falls, striking my shoulder before landing with a thud on the ground by my foot. She curses from up above. I reach down and grope for the fallen object. The thatching knife. Dagda's bollocks! Just as well it didn't fall blade first.

"I'll come back dow—" Liobhan calls, but I'm already climbing. A pox on all of it, I'm going to be useful if it kills me. Which, one might say, it just nearly did.

"Dau—" she protests, then falls silent. I reach the top of the ladder. Holding on with one hand, I pass her the knife, handle first.

"No comment," I say. "Do you need me to stay up here and hold things for you?"

"Go back down. Please. You're making me nervous."

"Your father wouldn't be impressed by your safety measures."

"Shut up, Dau. Go back down." She's furious. That makes two of us. I climb down with a red rage in my head. I didn't count the steps coming up, and I don't judge them right going down. I'm only a couple of rungs above the ground, but I slip, I drop, my foot slides out from under me and I crash down in a heap. A sharp pain shoots through my ankle, and when I get up the leg won't hold my weight. Shit! Just what I need right now. I haven't called out. I won't. I won't be weak. She said stay and hold the ladder, and that's what I'll do. I sink my teeth into my lip. I clutch the ladder so hard my hands hurt. My ankle's throbbing. I feel dizzy, as if I might pass out. Let those men in the stables not see me making a complete hash of the one simple job I was given to do. I imagine grabbing the thatching knife when Liobhan comes back down and using it to slit my own throat. Ending the pain in one flamboyant burst of red. I imagine my brother Seanan talking, afterward. *Oh, Dau. He was strange even as a boy. You know he killed his own dog. With a knife. Something wrong about him from the start.*

"Done, as best I can." Liobhan steps down beside me. "It'll need fixing properly later, when the weather clears. But at least I've stopped the leak. We'd better get this ladder—" She falls abruptly silent. "Dau? What is it?"

"Nothing." My voice comes out as a growl. I try to walk away, but I can't. The best I can manage is a hobble, and I can't do it without gasping in pain. "Curse it!" As if the humiliation weren't enough, now I have to endure her sympathy, her strong arm in support, her brief lecture on not overdoing things because that will only set back my progress. I let her help me. I let her talk. It's only when we're safely back in our own quarters with the door shut behind us that I pick up the first object I can lay hands on, an earthenware bowl from the table, and hurl it at the wall, where it smashes into a thousand pieces.

23

LIOBHAN

Wretched Dau! He was doing so well. Now he's sunk in his dark place again and refusing to make the slightest effort to climb out of it, with or without my help. He puts me in mind of some trapped creature, either spitting and snarling when anyone approaches or shut off in a terrible silence.

I've tried to be patient. I've had to, to stop him from damaging the ankle further instead of resting it. But my patience is running thin. What is it with him? We were working as friends, fighting this fight side by side. We were getting somewhere. I thought we were. Now he won't even try to conduct a normal conversation. He has to be bullied before he'll wash himself properly. There's a struggle over the drafts every time he takes them, an argument about whether there's any point to any of it and why don't I go off and attend to my own business. I hate this. I hate being angry. A Swan Island warrior doesn't get angry about this sort of thing. Besides, Dau's a Swan Island warrior, too, and he should know better.

I make sure the drafts go down. I tend to his eyes and endure the muttering commentary about how useless it is. I try not to spend too much time alone with him, because seeing him like this makes me feel like a failure. It makes me sad. And if I'm sad I can't get myself through this wretched year.

The lads from the stables, Caol and Padraig and the others, take turns keeping an eye on Dau so Corb and I can escape from time to time. That means I can run through my exercises or go for a brisk walk or help the grooms with holding a difficult horse. Rescuing Tomas and mending the thatch won me Mongan's approval. As long as the lads get their own work done, he doesn't have a problem with them helping us.

The stable crew learn that I can sing. They've already overheard me telling Dau stories. Now, eight or nine of them come over most evenings, bringing our supper and staying on afterward. I sit out in the stables with them, leaving the door to our quarters open and Corb in there with Dau, and I tell a tale or sing a song while they enjoy a jug or two of ale. Night by night the audience grows. It grows to include men-at-arms and gardeners as well as grooms and stable hands. Once or twice the master-at-arms, a spare, keen-eyed man named Fergal, comes to join us; from what he says, I gather someone's been telling him about Dau and me and our combat practice. Sometimes I coax one of the men to tell a story. I ask all of them to join in the refrains of the easier songs, and if they don't know tune and words, I teach them. There's a magic in it. Not the kind that conjures up visions or turns something to gold or makes toads jump out of a person's mouth. The kind that lifts hearts and sets a hopeful beat in them. The kind that coaxes a smile to a sorrowful face, and dries up tears, and tells a lonely man he has a friend.

It doesn't work on Dau. While the rest of us are gathered in our circle by lantern light, with the soft sounds of sleepy animals in the stalls behind us, he stays in our quarters. I place myself where he can hear me. That's deliberate. And Corb makes sure the door stands open, even if Dau wants it shut. But Dau remains hidden. Doesn't show so much as one little finger. Doesn't speak of this to me or to Corb; doesn't say a word to

Caol or Padraig or Torcan, just lets it flow past as if he's in some other world, a world where you can be bitter and silent and furious, but never happy. Never content. Never accepting.

Would I be accepting if I were in his shoes? I hope I'd grit my teeth and get on with things. But I can't be sure.

One of the men-at-arms from our journey to Oakhill, Donn, is a regular visitor to our storytelling sessions. His two friends come with him, big, sturdy Canagan and bristle-bearded Morann, a man with a wide smile and a tuneful voice. It's from them, one night, that I get some news.

I've just finished telling a tale about the Otherworld. In it, a man with a withered leg hobbles into the woods, looking for flowers to weave into a garland for the girl he loves. His plan is to put it on her head at the midsummer revels and ask for her hand in marriage, though he fears she will say no—he's a cripple, unfit to do a full day's work, and she's the prettiest girl in the village. Either Davan's got foolish hope or he believes in miracles. He's heard of some very particular flowers that grow deep in the woods. These blooms have a scent about them that fills a person's mind with happy thoughts. No ordinary bluebells or snowdrops or primroses for Davan. Of course he wanders in too deep and finds himself in a mushroom circle, and all around him are strange wee folk with big eyes and long noses and straggly beards. One of the wee folk asks him what he's doing on their land, and Davan explains about the flowers and the sweetheart and the withered leg. So the wee folk—clurichauns, without a doubt, and full of tricks as such folk are—offer to show him where the special flowers are and to point out the smelliest of all. Davan, being an unworldly sort of man, goes along with this. They pick him a big bunch of flowers and wish him luck. He bursts into tears. That sets all of them sobbing and wailing until the forest rings with it. When they've all calmed down, the clurichaun chief asks

Davan why he was crying, and the lad explains that even if the flowers were the most precious thing in all the world, Flannat will never agree to marry him with his leg being the way it is. He can't walk straight, he can't dance, he can't safely carry his children about—not that he has any children yet, but Flannat is sure to be thinking ahead.

The clurichauns are not impressed by this. They suggest Davan look for a girl who doesn't care about the leg. But it's Flannat he loves and wants. They're all set to play a trick on him. Mend his leg, then tell him the price is an eye or a hand or his old mother's happiness or something of the kind. But they feel sorry for the man. All he's asked for is a bunch of wildflowers. And his tale made them cry; some of them are weeping a bit now, just from the memory of it.

So they walk him to the spot where he can cross back into his own world, and they make sure he's got a good hold of the flowers, and they bid him farewell, and as he steps out of the mushroom circle, the clurichaun druid gives a wee flick of his magical staff, and lo! Davan's withered leg is as straight and healthy as his other leg, and he can walk as well as any man. Maybe there's a price. Isn't there always? But they don't ask for it then. They watch Davan hop and skip and jump his way home, happy as a lark, and they go back to their secret clurichaun business.

My audience likes this story, and now it's finished they sit with ale cups in hand discussing what would have happened next. What would the price have been? Davan's first child? A kiss from the new bride? Her weight in silver pieces? When they've finished debating these questions, the talk turns to other matters.

"Heard Ross of Fairwood's heading this way," Canagan says. "Him and his daughter, with a body of guards and atten-dants. They're all talking about it up at the house."

"Who is Ross of Fairwood?" I ask. "A local chieftain?"

"Mm-hm. His territory's to the south of Lord Scannal's. The two of them used to be on better terms, or so folk say. But Ross hasn't been here in a long while."

"I know a fellow who joined Lord Ross's guards," says Caol. "Maybe he'll be in the escort. When are they expected?"

"Five or six days, I've been told," says Mongan. "We'll get a message when they're one day out—they'll stop a night at Underwood Bridge, not wanting to make the ride too taxing for the young lady. I suppose she'll be keen to look her best."

An awkward silence follows this. As it draws out, a horrible suspicion creeps into my mind. A young woman, riding all that way with her father. There's only one noble son in this household whom Lord Scannal would consider marriageable, and I wouldn't wish such a husband on my worst enemy. I don't ask the question. I wait for someone else to speak.

"How big a party?" asks Torcan. "Might need to move things around in here if it's a lot of horses."

"I'd expect at least twelve," says Mongan calmly. "Ross and his daughter, a couple of attendants for her, perhaps a councilor or companion for him, a good presence of men-at-arms. The Crow Folk have been seen in those parts, and we all know what that means. Ross is no fool; he'll want good protection. I believe the son may be coming, too. Weather's set fair; we can put some of our animals out in the field and give Ross's mounts the stalls."

"Kitchens will be busy," says Caol. "Wanting to impress."

Morrigan's britches! I don't know what question to ask first. "The Crow Folk. You have them here, too? On Lord Scannal's land?" They were a curse back in Breifne, destructive, unpredictable, a menace to farmers and travelers with their fierce attacks. I've seen no sign of them here.

"Some," says Mongan. "We've kept them at bay, more or less. It's worse in other parts, folk say."

"You use fire? Ordinary weapons?"

"Seen something of them, have you?" Mongan's question is casual, but it occurs to me that I should consider my responses. My brushes with the Crow Folk took place while both Dau and I were under cover on a Swan Island mission.

"Once or twice," I tell him. "They're hard to get rid of, or so I've been told." I can't mention magic. I can't talk about fighting the Crow Folk, and how Brocc used music as a weapon to save our lives. But I do want to know Oakhill's answer to the scourge. *We've kept them at bay.* How?

"Master Seanan sets traps," says Canagan. "Him and his men. Up in the woods. Seems to be working."

What sort of trap could work on the Crow Folk? They're big, they're strong, they're malign. Their beaks can stab your eyes out. Their claws can rip you to shreds. They can fly. I try to picture such a device and fail. A magical trap, maybe. But Master Seanan's not likely to be dabbling in the uncanny. With questions threatening to spill out of me, I go back to the other matter, which may be equally important.

"This visit by Lord Ross. None of my business, I know, but is it to do with a possible alliance? Through marriage?"

A silence again. Seems all of them feel the same as I do, but nobody's going to put that heavy feeling into words. They can't; in every way that matters, this is Master Seanan's household.

"From what I heard," Canagan says, looking down at his hands, "that's why they're paying Lord Scannal a visit. They'll be hoping my lord will think the girl a good match for Master Seanan."

I bite back words I can't let myself utter. I hope this girl takes one look at Seanan and tells her father she'd rather marry a pox-ridden beggar. Sadly, she probably won't, even if she feels that way. She'll be bound to do what daughters of noble families do: wed a man her father chooses for her, with no option to refuse. "The house will be full up," I say. "What with the men from St. Padraig's and their attendants, I mean, as well as these visitors." Dau and I are accommodated in what is usually the harness room; a lot of equipment was moved out to make room for us. And there's Corb's pallet taking up even more space. "I suppose you need us to move." But where? Is the hut by the cesspool the only option?

"We've got a few days," Mongan says. "Might be better if you stay here, even if it's tight." Meaning, move anywhere else and I'll be back under Berrach's eye. "But I suppose Master Seanan may have ideas about that, too."

"Mm." Gods, the idea of Seanan with some young girl makes my guts curdle. Imagine that man as a father. I force myself to smile. "Well, I'd best say good night. You'll have a busy few days ahead."

"One last song?" Donn pleads, but I shake my head, then retreat to the quarters, nodding to Corb that he's free to go. He slips away without a word.

Dau is awake. His supper is on the table, untouched. Our lamp is burning and the fire on our small hearth is still glowing, though it needs more wood. I busy myself with that, putting off the moment when I have to speak. Knowing that if I say something obvious, such as "Not hungry?" he'll either snarl a bitter response or ignore me completely. How can I help him if he won't help himself? He told me that I had relentless hope. Right now, my hope is feeling like a worn-out cloth, full of holes and fraying at the edges.

I make a brew. I pour a cup for each of us, set them on the table, push Dau's platter to one side. Out in the stables it's getting quiet as the lads give the horses one last check then head off to their beds. Danu's mercy, how much I want to go home! Home to Swan Island, with the wild wind and the waves and the good fellowship, the tests of strength and endurance, the music and laughter, the understanding of comrades. I imagine myself on the practice ground, facing off against Hrothgar or Yann in unarmed combat. Will I be able to stand in that spot and keep my full attention on my next move, my opponent's next move, staying one step ahead? Or will I forever be thinking of the moment when Dau fell and hit his head? Will I carry that memory inside me until the day I die?

"Liobhan," he says.

I start as if struck. Just as well he can't see. "Mm?"

"Those tales. The ones about folk being cured by magic. Is there any truth in them?"

I wanted him to talk to me. I wanted him to make an effort. I was going to ask him about Ross of Fairwood and his daughter, and whether he shared my horror at the thought of anyone marrying Seanan. But this? From Dau of all people? I scramble for the right response. "We can talk about that. Come and sit at the table with me. There's food here. And a brew that's especially designed to give us heart."

"Hah!" Despite the derisive response, he gets up. Corb has made him a crutch, shaped wood padded with sheepskin and very nicely finished, but so far Dau has refused to use it. I haven't bullied him about this; the ankle must still be quite sore. But it's not broken, only twisted. I've strapped it up well, and it's time he started exercising it a little. He needs to get over feeling humiliated and just do it.

Dau finds the cup, lifts it to his lips, takes a tentative sip. "Morrigan's britches. What's in this?"

"Chamomile. Lavender. Calamint. And a few other things, honey included. Tastes just fine to me."

He sips again. "I'd prefer ale. But never mind that. Is there any truth in those tales of magic?"

Before Dau and I went on the mission to Breifne, before certain strange things happened, he wouldn't have dreamed of asking such a question. The old Dau would never have given credence to the possibility that magic existed in our time, or indeed ever. He didn't go to the Otherworld with me and my brother. He waited for me outside the portal, waited for hours with stoic courage. He saw enough to give him pause for thought. But this? I weigh my answer: it needs the right balance between truth and hope.

"It's a no, isn't it?" Dau sets down his cup. "Or you'd answer straightaway."

"The question can't be answered with yes or no. Some things I can say yes to. The Otherworld exists: I've been there. Magic exists: I've seen it and so have you. When Brocc played the Harp of Kings. When the portal opened and I went in. When Brocc sang to keep the Crow Folk away."

"But?" Dau picks up a piece of bread and takes a bite. He's listening properly for the first time in days.

"As a bard, I have a theory about the old songs and tales. Some of the things that happen in them are truly odd. Remarkable. Impossible, you'd think. And probably a lot of those things are . . . just made up. Invented by a bard who needed something exciting for a special occasion. Or someone who had spare time and a wild imagination. But bards don't pluck their ideas from thin air. They draw on an ancient fund of knowledge. Tales that have been told a thousand times before, tales that change a little with every telling. Stories that gain new parts and shed old ones, stories that mix the everyday and the deeply magical, the ordinary and the extraordinary. I believe every one of those old tales has its roots in something real, something true."

For a while Dau says nothing. I think over my lengthy answer and wonder if I've boxed myself into a corner. I can't promise a magical cure for his blindness, even if I were free to go off looking for such a thing. Yes, I know of a portal to the

Otherworld, though it's far from here. But Dau has seen with his own eyes how hard it is to make that door open. And if you ask for a favor once you're in, they make you pay. If it's a big favor, the price is high. I lost my brother. Brocc lost his life in the human world.

Dau's still sitting there, silent. I can't tell him any of this. If the hope of a cure has got him off his bed at last and swallowing a little food and drink, I'm damned if I'm going to point out how hard it would be to pursue such an idea and how slim the likely chance of success.

"I'm not sure what you mean," he says. "Are the things that happen in those tales possible?" There is such hope in his voice.

I feel like I'm balancing on a very narrow bridge. "When I was in that place, the fey queen showed Brocc and me visions in a scrying bowl—remember what I told you about that? They were of the future, or rather two possible futures, depending on how we acted with the Harp of Kings. I saw it clearly, and when things happened later on it all made sense. That could only be magic. And if magic exists, a lame man might have his leg healed by clurichauns. Perhaps at some time in the distant past, something resembling that may have really happened. Hence the tale."

Silence.

"Dau, there are all sorts of obstacles—"

He thumps his fist on the table, making platter and cups rattle. "That place. That place where you went through the wall and I waited for you. A person could get there from here. We could go. We could find the doorway." His voice is shaking. His fist is white-knuckled on the tabletop.

"Many days. Without weapons. Without horses, unless we steal them. Without supplies. With your father's men on our tail, most likely. Have you forgotten the small matter of my debt bondage? Can you imagine how your brother would respond if you and I just vanished? Even supposing there was some way we could get out of here?"

He sits there tight-jawed, scowling.

"Not the most practical idea you've ever had," I say. And when he does not respond, I add, "Needs some work."

Dau brightens. The tight fist relaxes. "You would consider it, then?"

Oh, gods. "I'll give it some thought. We couldn't attempt it now. It would have to be later, after my year is up. And I'll consider it on one condition only."

"That I stop being an ass?"

"Correct. And you start looking after yourself properly. However we do this, it's going to require the ability to walk, to run, to climb, and probably to fight, too. Work on getting well. Use the crutch when you need to, practice walking, and when you're ready, we start the exercises again. And be civil to Corb."

"Chief combat trainer of the future," Dau says, lifting his cup in a mock toast.

"Unlikely, if I head off for the Otherworld right when I'm due back on Swan Island."

He's silent again, the cup cradled between his hands now. He has beautiful hands, long-fingered and elegant.

"But I will," I say. "If that's what you want."

24

BROCC

We come to a halt, gazing in wonder. This is a place of true magic. The cliff stands strong and proud, the ferns and creepers drape a soft green garment over the weathered bones of the ancient rock. And the waterfall! I could write such a song about the music of its tumbling veil, its cloud of fine droplets, the glint of sunlight on the moving water, the calm pool below. This place is a haven of rest. The pool's surface shows me patches of blue, a scudding cloudlet, a soaring lark. Its beauty robs me of breath.

True lets out a great sigh. "Old ones are here," he says. "My eyes do not see them but my heart feels their presence."

When I can speak, I murmur to Conmael, "What should we do? Are we to summon them?" This is not like the portal to Eirne's realm, where a bard's quick wit and tuneful voice provided the key. This is a place altogether older and more solemn, and I do not belong here.

"True," says Conmael, "do as your heart bids you."

After a long silence, True steps forward. He lumbers down to the place where the water is not dashing and splashing but lies tranquil and still. At the edge of the pool he stops. "Brocc," he says quietly. "Will you sing?"

I go to stand beside him, following my own heart. An image of Liobhan and me as children comes to my mind, a brother and sister without a drop of blood in common, yet as tightly bonded as twins. True is my friend, my comrade. Here in the Otherworld, he and Rowan are my brothers. I draw in a breath, open my mouth, and sing for him. There are no words in it; to couch such a deeply solemn request in the rhyming verse I so often use would be an insult to the invisible elders. But as I sing my wordless melody, I think of True, so staunch, so patient, so strong, and I think of ancient times and how a people formed like stone might live so long they would watch kings and queens rise and fall, and see the land beaten by storm, starved by famine, and drowned by flood. They would witness the dwindling of magic in the age of humankind. I try to convey that True has been wounded while performing an act of kindness; how his sickness cannot be cured in the human world, or in Eirne's realm, but only here.

I realize I am no longer singing alone. True has added his deep voice, chanting on a single note in a tongue unknown to me. His tiny passengers add a high descant, faint as the distant chirping of baby birds in a nest. Only Conmael is silent as our music rings out over the pool and across the open space, echoing back from the high walls of stone. I do not know who will answer or how. I do not know what will happen. But as we sing on, the cliff before us shifts and moves, and I see in it the shape of a huge being, something like True but many times taller and broader, a creature that dwarfs the tallest trees and looms so high his shadow darkens the clearing. It is as if dusk has come while the sun is still high.

The stone man steps out of the cliff to stand on his two enormous feet. The pool lies between him and us. He does not speak; I can only imagine how thunderous and deep such a creature's voice might be. He gestures with a huge hand. It is a sign of invitation, graceful despite his bulk. He wants True to move forward into the water.

True turns to me. He lays a fist against his heart and inclines his head, and I return the grave salute. I hope we are not saying farewell. I hope we are acknowledging the bond between us. Respect. Affection. Fellowship. I am not singing now; the voice of the waterfall is the only music he needs. "Be safe," I say as True turns away and wades into the pool.

Is this water itself a source of magical healing? I do not know. I watch as True goes deeper; I wonder if the elder will ask him to immerse himself, and if so, what will happen to his tiny folk. But no. The deepest part of the pool comes only to my friend's waist. The elder guides him up the stream toward the spot where falling water smashes down on the rocks from up above. Beside this ancient stone man my friend looks small. True is sick; he was growing too weak to walk. How can he withstand that fierce torrent? I glance at Conmael, wondering if I should rush in there to support my friend. Conmael appears unperturbed; his pale features are calm. He shakes his head slightly, as if to say, *No cause for concern.*

True walks forward, steady and sure now. He passes through the tumbling water and out of sight. My fists are clenched, thinking of the small ones. How can they not be scattered everywhere? I wonder if my friend is gone forever. I've done something foolish, I've made an error somewhere along the way, and now both True and his little ones will die. If I had not asked for compassion toward the Crow Folk . . . If I had not agreed to follow this path . . . If I had sung differently . . . I know nothing of True's people. Perhaps I offended them.

Time passes and True does not reappear. The elder has melted back into the cliff face, becoming one with the rock. But I can see where he stands; my bard's eye shows me the jut of his nose, the hollows that are his eyes, the swath of greenery that drapes itself across his massive body. If there is an expression on those monumental features, it is of grave acknowledgment.

A flock of birds flies over, so high I cannot tell what kind they are. True steps out from the waterfall. His arms are stretched wide, his palms upward as if to catch the flow. As he comes down over the rocks toward the pool, I catch my breath. There are no wounds on his body. He is healed. I want to weep, to laugh, to sing a song of triumph. Instead, I kneel and bow my head. Something remarkable has been wrought here today, something beyond the understanding of the cleverest of bards, the most scholarly of druids. My friend is well, and I have seen an ancient power such as I had believed long gone from this green land. The only true response is deep silence. By my side Conmael, too, is kneeling.

Someone speaks. Not True, not Conmael, but a far deeper voice, surely that of the elder. I cannot look; this, surely, is for True alone.

"You are healed, friend, and we wish you well on your journey. Our gift is powerful. It is rarely bestowed. But you are the first of our own kind we have seen in many years and we know you to be wise and good."

"Thank you," says True, and his little ones chorus "Thank you!" in their high voices. How they hung on under the fearsome pelting of that water I do not know, but it seems they, too, are healed.

"There will be a price." The old one's tone is measured, calm. "Not for you, friend, and not in return for your healing. We are not merchants; we are guardians. But when you leave the Long Path, your friend will be asked for a payment. That is for passage along the path and out into your own realm."

"I understand," I say, still maintaining my bowed pose. It seems important not to look up.

"Good," comes the deep response. "Walk out past the Cave of Dreams. It grows late; you may stay in shelter there until morning. Those who sleep in that place are visited only by good dreams."

"Thank you," says True. "From the bottom of my heart, thank you."

Then there is silence. I hear Conmael rising to his feet; I copy him, opening my eyes. The elder is still visible within the cliff face, and all around the falls I can see others: here a strong arm, here a pair of eyes fringed with ferns, there the hint of a jaw, a shoulder, a great bare foot. True's people. His ancestors. How did he come to be with Eirne's folk? Are there more of his kind out there somewhere in the Otherworld? Those are not my questions to ask.

"I will accompany you to that cave," says Conmael quietly. "Are you ready to go, True?"

True turns around slowly. He nods but does not speak. His eyes are bright with wonder.

The Cave of Dreams is floored with soft earth. We settle there, the three of us, for Conmael has promised to take us to the spot where I summoned him, then set us safely on the path back toward the portal. We do not make a fire; shadowy trees stand tall beyond the cave mouth, and they are alive with birds returning to their roosts for the night. We do not want to frighten them.

True is very quiet. I think he is exhausted. His mind must be full to bursting with what he has seen. He closes his eyes and is soon asleep, lying against the cave wall. I sit awhile with Conmael, thinking of all the questions I want to ask him and unable to get even one of them out. Without him we would not have reached that place and my friend would not have been healed. What happened was remarkable. It was wonderful, and I am happy for True. At the same time I am full of misgivings.

There is Eirne, who now seems to question my every decision. There are her people, who are also my people, needing my protection. And there are the Crow Folk, a puzzle, a problem, a threat. I have fought them. I have killed them. I have seen the vile work they can do; I know them to be prone to acts of unpredictable ferocity. And yet, and yet . . .

"You're quiet," says Conmael. "What is troubling you?"

"Questions of right and wrong. An enemy I believe might become less hostile, if only I could find a way to talk with them. If only I knew their story."

"You speak of the so-called Crow Folk?"

I tell him something of my history with them. He seems to know a fair amount about my life without the need for more information. That is disconcerting. "We saved a young one whose parent had been cruelly killed," I tell him. "That was how True got his injuries. I had the fledgling in safe confinement, with food and water, and it was eating well, though still distressed. I needed a little time to work out what I should do next. It was night. I fell asleep, and when I woke someone had entered my house and killed the creature. I do not know who it was; only that it must have been one of Eirne's folk. But Eirne's folk do not tell lies. They do not scheme and play power games as human folk do."

Conmael takes his time in replying. "The Otherworld has more than its share of lies and games, Brocc," he says. "You are a bard. Are not the old tales full of tricksters, jealous lovers, betrayals, feuds, and wars? Even clurichauns have wars, often quite fiercely fought. The killing of your creature—might not that have come about because of fear? Folk want to protect their own. If that leads to the death of the innocent, some would say that is simply the way of the world."

"Then the world should be better. Gentler. More compassionate."

"The world needs its bards and its philosophers. It also needs its warriors, its heroes, its bold voyagers. Like your sister."

This silences me. It fills me with conflicting feelings: pride that he holds Liobhan high in his esteem; astonishment that he can know her so well when he has never met her; disquiet that he watches over us so closely. Sadness for opportunities lost. A small twinge of jealousy.

"Do you regret your choice?" Conmael asks quietly. "To quit the world in which you grew to manhood and cross over into the world in which you were born? If you had the opportunity, would you go back?"

"I have a wife. I have folk who depend on me. I cannot go back."

"Some men would. But you, I think, must act in keeping with that world you described. A world where justice and peace prevail."

There's a lump in my throat. "If we do not strive for that, we are less than we should be," I say.

"You are a fine young man, Brocc," Conmael says. "I wish you well. And I hope your wish to help your friend there does not cost you too dearly. Over that, I have no influence at all. I cannot go all the way to the portal with you."

"I would not expect that. But I thank you again for answering my call for help." I wish I knew about his life. Whether he lives alone or within a clan; what role he plays; whether there are others he has saved as infants and watched over from far away. My mother said he is a lord, here in the Otherworld. Lord Conmael of Underhill. But she was never sure if that was only a name he gave himself for a short time and a particular purpose, and I will not ask him. "I hope that we will meet again."

"I, too, Brocc. We should sleep now. A hard bed. But the dreams will be good."

* * *

Next day, Conmael leads us to the spot where he first appeared to us and bids us both farewell. He puts a hand on True's shoulder and speaks kind words. He gives me a brief, hard embrace. "Keep to your straight path, my boy," he says. "There is darkness all about, in this world and the other. Your singing is remarkable. It is a powerful weapon for good. May your light shine bright, Brocc."

"Farewell." I fail to keep my voice steady. "Thank you again. I wish you a safe journey."

And he is gone, vanishing under the trees as swiftly as a cloud shadow.

True is well and strong again, his old self. His small folk ride on his head in the soft moss and exchange excited squeaks when they see a pair of martens, a patch of bluebells, a cobweb catching the light. My mood brightens as we go. Soon we will be home, and perhaps Eirne will be feeling better. Maybe she will throw her arms around me, smiling. I will feel her soft body pressed against mine, and smell the sweet scent of her, and stroke her dark hair, so silken and shining. Perhaps she will welcome me back to her bed and to her heart.

We walk by day and camp by night, as before, but we are much quicker now, and in only three days we reach the lakeshore. No need to call for the ferryman. His boat is drawn up in readiness, and the wee man in green waits beside it. I have more verses ready to add to the song about the best ferryman in the land. I suspect that will not be enough.

"Ferry you over, friends?"

True takes a step forward, but I say, "Wait. Ferryman, what is the price?"

"For him"—the wee man jerks his head toward my companion—"the price is as agreed: three more verses to end the song. Get on, big fellow."

I make to speak, then choke back the words. True must cross safely first; right now, that must be my priority.

True steps onto the raft-like boat and seats himself. The ferryman digs his pole in and they're off to the far side of the lake. I'm shivering now; my gut clenches in unease. True disembarks. The ferry returns. The wee man holds it out on the water, two long strides from dry land.

I sing the three verses. In them, the man in green deals with a troublesome passenger who causes the vessel to capsize and tumble all on board into the water. Before they have time to drown, a magical fish appears and swallows them, only to vomit them up onto the shore a moment later, somewhat sickened by their experience but otherwise unharmed. A happy ending for all concerned, with a rousing refrain to finish.

The clurichaun is grinning; that is a good sign. But he does not bring the ferry in to shore. I have paid only for True's safe passage.

"Coming across, bard?" he asks, brows up. The grin has become malign, with a display of many sharp teeth.

"First I would know the price, friend."

"What do you love dearest in all the world? What is it you can't do without? What is your most priceless treasure? What is your most powerful weapon?"

I am silent.

"What will you give me, bard? A finger off your harpist's hand? That would look fine on my necklace, don't you think? Shiny and white it would be in the moonlight, when the flesh is all rotted away."

"No!" shouts True from across the water. "You can't ask that!"

I signal to him: *Quiet*. He must stay safe or this venture will have been for nothing. If I do not survive this, or if I am trapped on the Long Path, he can still go home.

My heart is hammering. My skin is all cold sweat. *Think, Brocc. Use your wits.*

"You are wed, are you not, bard? Your firstborn child, then, to stay with me and keep me company, and to be ferryman after me."

"I will not pay such a price. Passage across this lake is a matter of perhaps ten dips of the pole; it takes less time than it did to sing three verses of the song. The life of a child for that? It is a most uneven bargain."

"Your singing voice, then." His own voice has turned night-dark, iron-strong. If there was a playful note in it before, now it is entirely gone. The finger, the firstborn child, those were spoken in jest. But this is no joke.

In the space of three heartbeats, as my blood turns to ice, I consider my options. Jump in the water and swim across to True. No. I am still on the Long Path, and though he is so close, chances are I would swim and swim and never reach that shore. Wade two strides in, seize the ferryman, and wring his poxy neck. Or dunk him in the water, give him a good shake, and tell him not to be ridiculous. That's what Liobhan would do, and he'd probably tip his hat to her and wish her a safe journey home. Say yes and lose my very soul. I can't do it.

"Answer quickly, bard, or you will have no choice at all."

"Brocc!" calls True, despite my warning. "Don't do this!"

With an effort, I stave off blind panic and gather my wits. In the Otherworld, everything has its price. He has set the price too high. I have to haggle it down.

"That is extravagant, ferryman." My voice comes out as a strangled croak. I clear my throat and continue. "Your assistance on our journey has been most welcome, but what you name is inappropriate for so short a passage. I offer you a more fitting payment. From today on, for one turning of the moon, I will give up my singing voice."

For a moment he is completely silent. He has not expected me to fight back. Then he opens his mouth and roars with laughter, making the lake surface ripple and setting True's small folk squeaking in fright. "Ten years," the ferryman says, quick and sharp as if he's an old hand at this sort of thing.

"Three turnings of the moon." I can't believe I'm doing this. My voice is my heart, it is my self, it is comfort and solace to my clan. It is our strongest weapon against the Crow Folk. Our only real weapon.

"A paltry offer, bard. Five years, no less."

"Too long, ferryman. Too long for a tribe to go without music. Too long for them to miss the tune that lifts the spirits, the song that brings healing tears, the rallying march of courage. Two seasons, no more."

"Three years."

"Three seasons, then."

"Two years, bard. My final offer." The ferryman is enjoying himself; his eyes have a mischievous glint.

I want this to be over. I cannot bear it a moment longer. "One year," I say. "One year without song. Please take me across the lake now."

He poles the craft to shore. I step on. The boat crosses the lake in silence, and I step off on the far side, where True stands as solemn as if this were a deathbed.

"Farewell, bard," says the wee man, and he does indeed take off his green hat and make a little bow in our direction. "Farewell, big fellow. I'll be away now."

I do not return the courtesy, though True gives the ferryman a nod. We turn and head for home. We walk in silence. There's no need to try my singing voice. I know it is gone. A year. A whole year. What have I done?

25
DAU

A promise. She's given me a promise. Foolish as I know it is to hope, I find myself doing just that.

The scratches on the wall change. Not in appearance but in meaning. I'm not counting the dark days until Liobhan's departure, when I'm released from my earlier promise and can make an end of myself with whatever sharp implement first comes to hand. Now I'm counting the days until she takes me up into the forest and through that portal and maybe, just maybe, I open my eyes and see again. See Liobhan's bright hair and her steadfast gaze and her smile full of courage and heart. See the pathway opening before me, once more full of possibilities.

A man does not so soon begin to believe in the uncanny. Not if he's a man like me. But living at such close quarters with Liobhan, who finds hope even in the darkest places, seems to be brushing off on me, just a little. The stories are ridiculous. Clurichauns. Tiny staff-waving druids. Miracle cures. But I cannot dismiss them as I would once have done. I have heard Brocc sing to save our lives in battle, then sing to win another man a crown. Liobhan is right. If those things can happen, then perhaps, just perhaps, if a blind man tried hard enough, he might have his sight restored. I have done little to deserve such a gift, and Liobhan says all such favors must be paid for in some way. I wish I had been a kinder man. I wish I had been braver. I wish I had stood up for myself when my brothers tormented me. I wish I had made my case well enough to be believed.

I use the crutch. I thank Corb for taking the trouble to make it. It is remarkably comfortable, just the right height for me, and well crafted. I apologize to him for all the times I have cursed him and fought him and thrown things. I think he is embarrassed by this, for he says very little. Or is he troubled about something else? I am the last person he would want to confide in, I should think. But I am starting to wonder if there is something wrong. I choose a time when Liobhan is off doing her exercises—my ankle is mending, but I cannot join her yet—and Corb is clearing the ashes from the hearth.

"Corb? Could we go for a walk?"

I hear a clank as he drops the poker. He must have been deep in thought. "I'll just finish this," Corb mumbles, and there's more clanking.

"When you're ready."

Not long after this, we're sitting on a low wall near the field where the horses are let out for exercise. It's a sunny day. I like the warmth on my face.

"Anyone around?" I ask. With the visitors expected soon, the place is a hive of activity and it's hard to have a private conversation. Corb says there are two grooms out with the horses but nobody close by. I'm not sure what to say next. Could be there's nothing wrong at all.

Turns out I don't need to ask. We haven't been sitting here long when he says, "I heard something. Not sure if I should pass it on."

"To me? Or to someone else?"

"To anyone. Could be only gossip. But I can't help thinking about it."

"Tell me, if you want."

"It's about Master Seanan. You may not like it."

I wait. Corb is aware of the animosity between Seanan and me. He can't imagine I would be upset, or even surprised, to hear something ill of my eldest brother.

"One of the lads from the kitchen heard him talking about the young lady, Lord Ross's daughter. The one Master Seanan's going to marry. What this lad heard was—it was vile, Master Dau. It was too shocking for me to repeat. About what he would do to her once they were wed; about how he would . . ." I can't see Corb's face, but I imagine it's scarlet with embarrassment.

"How he would what, Corb? You'd better get it out. I doubt whatever it is will shock me. And call me Dau, please. We're friends, aren't we?"

"That when he'd had her, lain with her, he'd share her around his men. Let them all have a turn. I suppose it was meant as a sort of joke—surely nobody would ever really do such a thing— but none of the folk in the kitchen laughed, they all just looked at him, and he got angry and lashed out, and a pot of hot soup got tipped over. One of the cooks was scalded all up his arm." He falls silent for a while. "Dau, I know he's your brother. But that was . . . it was just wrong. All of it was wrong."

I find that after all I am shocked, though I have no trouble believing this unsavory story. "It's good that you told me," I say. "A very poor kind of joke. Don't speak to anyone else about this, and if you see your friend from the kitchen, warn him to keep quiet. Not that I want to cover up for such oafish behavior, but if my brother hears this has become the subject of gossip, he'll be quick to punish anyone who's suspected of spreading it." A pot of hot soup, gods! Men do engage in crude humor from time to time. That I've experienced before. But such an act of impulsive violence goes far beyond that. Seanan is usually controlled in his anger. This troubles me badly.

"Would he do what he said?" Corb sounds hesitant now. "When he's wed, I mean. Would he do such a thing?"

Oh, yes, I think. *My brother is cruel to the core. To abuse others excites him.* "I must make sure he's denied the opportunity," I say with a lot more confidence than I feel. "A pity my father believes me to be a liar and a troublemaker. I cannot go straight to him. But perhaps someone else will listen. Don't worry, Corb, I won't divulge where I heard the story, and I will take action to protect this young woman."

Corb doesn't ask how I can possibly do that, or who I will speak to, or anything of the sort. He just says, "Thank you, Master Dau. I mean Dau." I find his trust in me frightening.

Lord Ross and his party are expected in two days' time. There's activity everywhere, including on the training ground. Maybe our men will invite Ross's to engage in a few practice bouts. Or shooting at targets. I miss that kind of thing; I miss it more than I can readily admit to myself. If Liobhan gets me to that place . . . if there truly is a cure . . . I must set that aside. Wait until her year is up. I must apply myself to a more immediate task.

I've been selfish. I heard them talking in the stables about Ross of Fairwood and his daughter and I let it wash over me because my mind was all on the tale Liobhan had told about the magical cure. Now I must act. The marriage can't go ahead.

I can't march into the house and tell my father the truth—that if Ross's daughter weds Seanan, her life will be destroyed. Father never believed me when I was a child. Why would that have changed? If I confront him, he'll support Seanan. I can't tell any of his people. They're all under Seanan's thumb. No, this must be treated like a mission. I must put a strategy in place. First things first. I need a foothold in the house. My father's councilor, Naithí, seems an appropriate choice. I don't expect an open-armed welcome. I haven't set foot in the house since the day Brother Íobhar moved me out to make way for his ailing monks. But, like it or not, I am Lord Scannal's son. I will put on the guise of a nobleman and move boldly forward. "Corb," I say. "We're going up to the house."

Corb insists we return to our quarters first. He makes me put on a clean shirt and brush my hair, and he shaves off my untidy beard, managing not to cut me. Liobhan's not back yet. I wish she could come with me, but that can't happen. Corb still officially has the job of nurse and keeper, though surely most of the household must know who's been doing the bigger share of the work.

I hate behaving like the nobleman I was born to be. I can't help the fact that I resemble my brother Seanan, but acting like him makes me feel soiled, degraded. I will try to balance the confidence of privilege with courtesy and restraint. I will push down the dark shadows. I will not let the memories undo me. It's a test. I'm a Swan Island man. Blind or not, I like a challenge, and I will meet this one bravely.

The guards on the door are surprised to see me and Corb. I hear it in their voices. Someone calls the steward, Iarla; I remember him speaking to me with courtesy during those difficult first days.

"Master Dau! You look well. What can I do for you?"

"Iarla. I did not have the opportunity to thank you earlier for your kindness in welcoming me when we first arrived here. Were I ever to establish a household of my own, I would want just such a man as yourself to oversee it."

"Thank you, Master Dau. I wish the circumstances had been different. We're required to follow orders, as I expect you understand." He clears his throat. "Have you been comfortable out there in the stables? Well cared for?"

"We do well enough, thank you. Corb here has been an excellent companion and assistant."

"And will you now be returning to the house? Should quarters be prepared?"

"Not yet, Iarla. I'm here to speak with Master Naithí, in confidence. I hope he can make time for me. He's not expecting me." I lower my voice. "I'd be glad if this can be managed as discreetly as possible."

Iarla is expert at what he does. "Certainly, Master Dau. Follow me. If you'll just wait in here, I will find Master Naithí for you."

For this visit I've dispensed with the crutch. With one hand on Corb's shoulder I follow the steward along the hallway and into a chamber. I recall the place. In the past, this was where folk waited for audiences with my father or the other senior members of the household.

We've barely begun to settle ourselves when Iarla returns. "Master Dau. Master Naithí will see you now. This way."

The councilor is in a different chamber. It feels much roomier, and it's warm. Was this once a scribe's workroom? I can't remember. Naithí greets me, ignores Corb, thanks Iarla and dismisses him. The door closes.

"Please be seated, Master Dau." Naithí's tone is measured, careful. I wonder if every word I say will go straight to my father. Perhaps that's one of the duties of a chieftain's councilor: to report back in meticulous detail. "How may I assist you?"

The situation is strange. If I had lived a different life, if I had grown to manhood in this household as a respected son of the family, this man would have listened to my concerns without question. As it is, I am an outsider, unknown to him before that awkward meeting at Hawthorn House. I could understand if he were not prepared to trust me with anything.

I haven't thought how I am going to put this delicate matter to him, save that I will give less detail than Corb gave me. Hint at some concerns, maybe, without mentioning the source. Suggest that everyone take more time for reflection. But I realize that isn't going to work. To achieve what I want, I'll have to do something every part of me shrinks from. I'll have to be my father's son.

"You know we're accommodated in the stable block, yes?" I go on without waiting for an answer. "I heard that Lord Ross of Fairwood will shortly be visiting my father, along with some family members and an escort. You probably know that Lord Ross has a son of about my own age. He and I were friends long ago. Someone mentioned that Cormac might be a member of this party. If that is so, I would like to renew my acquaintance with him during the visit, especially as it seems possible we may be kinsmen by marriage at some point in the future."

"Indeed," Naithí says. "This visit is for the purpose of discussing that possibility, Master Dau. And I have been informed that both Master Cormac and his sister, Sárnait, are on the way here with Lord Ross."

"Yes, I gather it will be quite a large party. I and my two assistants are currently accommodated in an area that was formerly the harness room. I doubt that the visiting horses and grooms can be housed in the manner Lord Ross would expect unless that area is opened up again. Which leaves the three of us with nowhere to sleep."

I wish I could see Naithí's face. He's not stupid; he knows where this is heading. But he's not dealing with the man who sat shocked and helpless at that hearing back in Dalriada. He's talking to his chieftain's son, and he knows it. "Go on, Master Dau," he says.

"I imagine Lord Ross would think it strange that a son of the house and his attendants were banished to the stables or to an outhouse solely because that son is blind. I can get about well enough with the assistance of Corb here, or of Liobhan. Liobhan understands the treatment I require for my eyes and the headaches that sometimes visit me. And, being a trained warrior, she has the expertise to help me maintain my strength." I pause. Naithí makes no comment. Corb holds the silence appropriate to his position in the household.

"I have jarred my ankle slightly, but that occurred while attempting an everyday task and it is almost better. I am eager to stretch myself; on occasion, a little too eager. You will understand, Master Naithí, how frustrating it is for a fighting man to find himself weakened as I was for some time after the accident."

"I was never a fighting man, Master Dau. But yes, I understand. And I also understand your argument where Lord Ross is concerned. If Master Cormac was your friend, he will expect to see you; it is widely known that you have returned home." He draws a long breath, then lets it out. "It would indeed be better to accommodate you in the house. You and your helper here. I will have a word with Iarla." And when I don't reply, he goes on, "You would take the evening meal in the great hall. Sit with the family."

There's a *but* in his tone. "But my brother won't care for that arrangement?"

"Master Seanan will understand how important it is that matters are arranged appropriately while Lord Ross's party is here. The betrothal—" He falters; he's said more than he meant to.

"Is Lord Ross's daughter promised to my brother, Master Naithí? Or is that only under consideration?"

"The latter. It's been discussed. The young lady has met Master Seanan only very briefly in the past. This visit will provide further opportunities. Your father hopes the matter may be settled while they are here. An alliance with Ross of Fairwood would greatly strengthen Lord Scannal's position."

I want to ask if he thinks my brother a suitable match for a young girl. Or for anyone. All I say is, "How old is the prospective bride, Master Naithí?" I may have met her once or twice back then, but Cormac had several sisters and I have no memory of them as individuals. In those times I did not go out of my way to make friends, since doing so seemed likely to place them in jeopardy.

"I believe she's in her fourteenth year, Master Dau."

Corb makes a little sound of shock, quickly suppressed. I swallow a curse. So young. This can't be allowed to happen. "Thank you, Master Naithí. Please do speak to Iarla about suitable quarters for us. Not just me and Corb. Liobhan as well. I need an attendant available day and night, and it's too much for one. Besides, only Liobhan has the required nursing skills."

"You press me hard, Master Dau. I'm well aware that Master Seanan has barred your friend from the house. She is not your personal nurse. She is a bond servant."

"I don't recall any law stating that a bond servant cannot sit in the hall with other serving folk at mealtimes, provided she conducts herself appropriately. And Liobhan *is* my personal nurse. When Brother Íobhar and his monks came to stay in this house, Seanan passed my care over to her, stating very firmly that if she doubted his capacity to have his folk look after me in an appropriate way, she could do it herself. Which she has, very capably, or I would not be fit enough to sit here talking to you now, Master Naithí. I require her to be accommodated with Corb and me. The ideal arrangement would be a room with a large antechamber. That way we can observe the proprieties. And she's to be allowed in and out of the house without challenge."

He clears his throat. "Your brother—"

"Master Naithí. Is this my father's house still? To the best of my knowledge, he remains chieftain of Oakhill. Or does he no longer make his own decisions? If the common sense of this suggestion eludes you, please take it to him. And don't forget to remind him how odd it will seem to Lord Ross and his family if I am not accommodated as a son of the household should be." I pause. "Liobhan is included in the agreement or I sleep in a horse stall and make sure our distinguished visitors know about it. Tell my father that."

Naithí clears his throat. Time passes, and neither he nor Corb says a word. I wait. Eventually the councilor speaks. "Your father relies increasingly on Master Seanan to act for him," he says. "I will pass on this message, of course, but the chances are Master Seanan will be dealing with the matter."

I find myself shocked. Whatever I may have thought of my father's refusal to believe me when I told him the truth, he always seemed well respected, not only by the highborn folk who came to speak with him, but also by the more lowly ones who worked for him. It's hard for me to believe he would trust that weasel Seanan to make important decisions on his behalf. "My father is surely still in his right mind and well enough to perform his duties as chieftain of Oakhill," I say, not making it a question.

"In his right mind . . . yes. But Lord Scannal has been somewhat distracted of recent times, Master Dau. Increasingly forgetful. Easily tired. Since Master Ruarc entered the monastery, more and more matters of strategic planning have been passed to Master Seanan."

This is deeply troubling. "Has my father seen a physician? Is it known what ails him?" I may loathe this place. I may be counting the days until I can leave it. But the thought of Seanan as chieftain has never been a good one, and that it should happen sooner rather than later paints a grim picture for the folk of this household and of the region. I came into this room playing the part of Lord Scannal's son because it suited my purpose. But like it or not, I *am* Lord Scannal's son. Perhaps it is for me to do something about this.

"I don't believe a physician has been consulted, Master Dau.

When a family member is unwell, the head infirmarian from St. Padraig's, Brother Petrán, generally pays a visit. And, of course, Brother Petrán is in residence here now, until such time as the rebuilding is complete. But busy. Very busy. It is unfortunate that Master Ruarc—that is, Brother Íobhar—was called away so suddenly." A pause. "I will instruct Iarla to prepare sleeping quarters for you and your young man here—what is his name?"

"Thank you. His name is Corb. His family works one of the neighborhood farms." I pause for a count of five. "And Liobhan?"

Naithí sighs. "I am certain Iarla can find something appropriate. I will explain to Lord Scannal that perhaps the situation has not been assessed quite correctly. But I cannot answer for Master Seanan. If your friend is able to . . . blend . . . with the household . . . to be discreet . . . not to draw attention to herself while the visitors are here . . ."

There's a silence then, and I imagine both Naithí and Corb are thinking what I'm thinking: that Liobhan tends to draw attention even when she's not trying to. "We might make an agreement, Master Naithí," I say. "You speak to my father on this matter, stressing the need to present a calm and united household during Lord Ross's visit. And I speak to Liobhan about being discreet. Mm?"

"A calm and united household is something to strive for, Master Dau."

"I imagine it is, Master Naithí, though I may not be the best judge, never having lived in such a household. Thank you for your time and for your discretion. We will return to the stables until we receive word that our new quarters are ready for us."

Liobhan is back in the harness room. She's in good spirits after a challenging round of exercises—she informs me that three of the guards completed the sequence with her, with master-at-arms Fergal watching—and she smells sweaty. It occurs to me that if she's going to be living in the main house and eating supper in the hall, she'll need another change of clothing. And so will I.

"Where were you?" she asks.

I clear my throat. I feel oddly nervous. "Up at the house, talking to Master Naithí. Liobhan, Corb told me something I didn't like, and you won't like it either." I pass on the unsavory little story. She greets this with deathly silence. "We can't let this betrothal go ahead," I say.

"The marriage has probably been planned since this poor girl was an infant." Liobhan sounds grim. "What can you and I do about that?"

"Corb," I say quietly, "you need not stay if you have other things to do. Just let me know if a message comes from Iarla, will you?"

Corb understands that he's been dismissed and heads out into the yard.

"When Corb told me what he'd overheard I was tempted to rush in boots and all," I tell Liobhan. "I wanted to spew out every foul thing I know about my brother and tell my father such a man should never take a wife or sire children. But I know Seanan inside out. He would convince everyone that this was all in my mind, that no such events had ever happened, that I have been spinning wild tales since I was a small child. He'd probably think of some way of blaming you, perhaps for putting these notions into my head. I've promised Corb I won't expose him as the source of the information."

"Didn't someone get burned in the kitchen? Weren't there witnesses?"

"Fear of the repercussions will keep them silent. That's the way it's always been in this household."

A charged silence. "This is not all right, Dau," says Liobhan in her fierce voice.

"I've known that for a long time. I lived with it every day for thirteen years. But yes, we have to warn this girl. And not by charging in to the rescue or making a big public scene."

"Mm." Liobhan bends to poke the fire back into life. If she has any suggestions she keeps them to herself.

"I do have an idea."

"Tell me. I'll make a brew, help us think better."

"When I went to see Naithí I didn't have much of a plan. But one thing's obvious and that's our leverage. Neither my father nor Seanan will want Ross or his daughter to see any signs of trouble in the family. They'll know I'm back home; news travels fast, and Ross's son Cormac was my friend in the early days, to the extent that my brothers made it possible for me to have friends. Cormac and I shared a love of dogs. I don't know what he was told about Snow's death, but I do know he'd never believe the story that I went crazy and killed her."

Liobhan is busy setting the kettle on the fire, finding cups. "And is Cormac coming here with his father?"

"That's what Naithí told me. So Cormac provides our opportunity. Provided I am living in the house, taking meals with the family at the high table, and comporting myself in an appropriate manner, there's no reason why I should be prevented from having a private conversation with my old friend at some point. I'll tell him the truth—not only what Corb shared about Seanan's gross remarks, but also something of my brother's true nature. I'll ask him to pass it on to his father in confidence. Suggest they leave with the betrothal arrangement not settled, then find a tactful way of withdrawing later."

"Mm-hm. Ross is not likely to think the alliance with your father more important than his daughter's future happiness?"

I shake my head. "He'd have to have changed a lot since I last met him."

We fall silent again while Liobhan finishes making the brew

and sets the cups on the table. "What if Seanan refuses to have you in the house?" she asks. "He can surely overrule Naithí."

"He won't. I fully expect to be sent back out here, or somewhere worse, as soon as the visitors leave. But anyone would think it odd if a son of the house, an injured son at that, was not treated as part of the family." The brew smells good; like mint with a dash of something spicy.

"Can you do it?" Liobhan asks. "Act as if you're all on good terms, stay calm and collected with your father and brother right there? Ross might decide to stay awhile."

I straighten my back and square my shoulders. "I can do it. It can't be harder than staying mute for weeks." But it will be. Of course it will.

"What about me?"

"You stay in the house, too. Next door to me and Corb. All perfectly proper."

Liobhan gives a low whistle. "Might have been better to leave me over here on my own," she says. "Seanan will be watching my every move. And if not him, then Berrach or another of Seanan's men."

"I don't want you over here on your own. I want you close by so—" I come to a sudden halt, not sure how I want to finish this.

"So you can watch over me? Do I seem like the kind of woman who needs protecting?"

"You seem like a comrade I care about. I would prefer you not to be in harm's way." Gods, how stuffy I sound! Of course I want to protect her. She's Liobhan. She's irreplaceable. "I want you close by so we can look out for each other," I say. "You might even get a chance to have a word with Cormac's sister."

"I'm not big on sisterly advice, Dau. Especially not when she's the daughter of a lord and I'm a bond servant."

I think about circumstances under which Liobhan and

Sárnait might become sisters and wish my thoughts had not gone down that track. The conversation is getting out of hand. "All the same, she might be more prepared to listen to another woman. Girls don't always take notice of their brothers."

"That's certainly true. You've surprised me, Dau."

"What, by caring about what happens to this girl?"

"By deciding to take things into your own hands. By standing up for yourself. By being prepared to act like you belong here, when I know you hate the place."

"You realize you'll have to do the same. Play a part. The obedient servant who never speaks out of turn. Unobtrusive. Scuttling about with her eyes averted."

"Unless she needs to be a warrior," Liobhan says.

"Unlikely, surely. The plan is this: I speak to Cormac when I can, you and I both keep our heads down, Cormac passes on the message, Ross's party leaves with the matter unresolved, and we return to what we were doing before. At some later point Ross informs my father that the betrothal is off."

"And you hope Seanan never finds out why Ross suddenly changed his mind."

There are flaws in the plan and that is one of them. But I can't turn my back on this. I can't let Seanan destroy another life.

26

LIOBHAN

I thought my Swan Island training meant nothing could surprise me. But this does. Not the arranged marriage and
wretched Seanan thinking he's a suitable husband for this poor
girl; that is entirely what I would expect. But Dau snapping out
of his contrary moods and deciding to take control—now, that
did startle me. Especially since it means pretending he's happy
to be in the house, surrounded by his unpleasant family and
needing to be polite to everyone, Seanan included. But maybe
I shouldn't be surprised. Dau's had the Swan Island training,
too. He's shown himself to be excellent at maintaining a role.
The strange part of this is why he's doing it. It's the faint hope
of a cure that's turned him around. Gods! If we escape this
place, if we get to Eirne's realm and it turns out they can't help
him . . . I can't bear to think of what might happen then.

Iarla's good. Not only excellent at doing his job, but quick to
understand what isn't being said out loud, and adept at smooth-
ing the way whenever he can. So here we are, in a capacious
chamber within the main house. We have our own hearth;
Dau explained to Iarla why this was important. Dau and Corb
are supposed to be sleeping in the main room, with me in the
anteroom, where a body servant would usually be accommodated. Since I'm the one who does the nighttime nursing when

it's required, it's more likely Corb will take the anteroom. That way he at least can get a good night's sleep. As it is, Dau's ankle is almost mended and he's been sleeping well these last few days. But in here, surrounded by all sorts of memories, it may be a different matter. Clearly best if we keep our arrangements to ourselves.

We're unpacking our possessions, few as they are, when Seanan appears in the open doorway.

"Your brother," I murmur to Dau. He straightens up. His face becomes a mask of composure.

Seanan strides in uninvited and halts a few paces from us. "Fine accommodation for a bond servant," he observes, taking a good look around. "This chamber has housed chieftains and kings. I am amazed that my father approved it."

I hold back the obvious retort. *Dau is the son of a chieftain. And a son of the house. Why wouldn't Lord Scannal approve it?* I don't say a thing, just stand there hoping I can control my features as well as Dau does his. I unclench my fists. Every time I see Dau's brother I get an overwhelming desire to punch him in his supercilious face.

"Indeed." Dau sounds as calm as he looks. "It is pleasing to be housed as the son of a chieftain should be, in a comfortable room with my people close by. You might pass my thanks on to our father, should you have the opportunity. I have not yet been able to do so in person." A calculated pause. "I understand you are more or less acting as chieftain now, Seanan. Is Father unwell, that he no longer undertakes his full range of duties?"

I didn't expect this. Wasn't the plan to keep our heads down?

"Why would that be of any interest to you, brother?"

"He is my father as well as yours and Ruarc's. We have been estranged, yes, but I am here now, perhaps for the rest of my life. If Father is afflicted with some malady, it would be appropriate for you to inform me of the details."

I try to imagine myself speaking to Brocc or Galen in such a frostily formal manner, and am possessed by a sudden urge to laugh. I put a hand over my mouth and cough instead. Corb is standing in the shadows by the wall, doing his best to be invisible.

"May I sit down?" Seanan seats himself on the bench, not waiting for an answer. "Boy, shut that door."

Corb moves with near-silent steps to do so.

"Had I known in advance that our father would approve this arrangement, I would have raised objections. The girl should not be in our house. She should not be sharing your chamber." Seanan speaks as if I were not here. I'm watching Dau. I see him take a deep breath and let it out slowly. He's counting to five. Maybe ten. "But it's a sound strategic move," Seanan adds, surprising me. "I need not go into the reasons why I do not wish you, brother, or either of your serving folk to create any disturbances while Lord Ross and his party are in this house. You will behave impeccably from now until our visitors have departed. Not one step out of line. Not one word misspoken. Do you understand me?" He's glaring in my direction.

"Yes, Master Seanan," Corb and I mumble together.

"You haven't answered my question." Dau's voice is like a well-honed blade, cold, clear, and sharp. "What ails my father?"

A moment's hesitation. It's the first time I've seen Seanan without an immediate rejoinder. Then he says, "Are you not aware that a man's faculties deteriorate with his advancing years, brother? There is no malady afflicting Lord Scannal but old age. It comes to us all in time."

Dau's response is whip-quick. "To the best of my knowledge, our father is now five-and-forty years old. Getting on, yes. But hardly a faltering graybeard."

Seanan smiles. It's not a pleasant look. "Indeed not. But old, all the same. Forgetful sometimes. And not only in matters such as where he set down his handkerchief or his mead cup. In important matters. He cannot rule alone."

Don't mention the betrothal, I will Dau. We must give Seanan no hint that it interests us. Can this be true about Lord Scannal? My parents are older than that. My father is the furthest thing from a faltering graybeard that anyone could imagine. And my mother is simply . . . herself. So much so that, looking at her, a person would think of courage, wisdom, a lively mind; never of age.

"I see," Dau says.

"Judge for yourself when you have the opportunity to observe him," says Seanan, rising to his feet as if about to leave. "And while we are on that topic, if you are to be in the hall for supper and mingle with our distinguished guests, you will need something better to wear." He glances at Dau in his serviceable, well-worn clothing. He casts his eye over Corb. "I'll send someone to assist you with that. The lad should be in the household livery. He'll stand behind you at table; act as your body servant." He spares a glance for me; there's open contempt in it. "The girl will eat with the other serving folk. That gown is too short. Unseemly. You'll wear something more appropriate in public, girl."

"Yes, Master Seanan." I'm wearing the clothes Miach found for me. My everyday gown is being laundered right now. And in my bag, still rolled up, is the outfit I used to wear when Brocc and Archu and I performed as a band, the russet gown with the embroidered overdress. A bond servant doesn't wear garments like those. She doesn't wear her hair loose and sit at the table laughing with her friends over a jug of ale. When the band plays, she doesn't get up and dance. I remember Dau and me, hands clasped, circling each other amid a crowd of dancers. It's like something from a different life.

"Dau," says Seanan. His tone has changed. "You understand

that failure to comply with this will result in consequences. For your boy, dismissal from this household. For the girl, punishment appropriate to her situation."

For a moment, I might almost believe that Dau can see Seanan, such is the look on his face. His voice is very quiet as he asks, "And for me? Do you still mete out punishment to your brother?"

"I will leave the possible consequences to your imagination," says Seanan, matching Dau's tone. "I don't suppose there's anything wrong with your memory. Now I'll take my leave of you."

None of us says anything as he departs the chamber. Once he's gone, Corb shuts the door. I fetch my flint and start to lay a fire; Corb fills the kettle and gets out herbs for a brew. After a little, Dau sits down on the bench. "You know what I'd like to do?" he asks.

"Might be better if I don't answer that. I can think of a few things." Most of them include acts of violence, and as I've just promised to behave impeccably, nothing of that kind is going to happen. After that little scene, it's easy to imagine how silver-tongued that man could be if he wanted to ingratiate himself with folk like Lord Ross and his daughter. And I'm forced to admit that Seanan is a handsome man, tall, broad shouldered, golden haired, and fair of complexion. Many young women would find him attractive, at least on first acquaintance. He looks like Dau. But he is not like Dau; he is a vile, scheming bastard.

"I'd like us to dress in our best and stride into the great hall arm in arm, and after supper I'd like us to dance as if we had not a care in the world," Dau says. "I'd like every eye to be on us and folk to say, *Don't they look happy?* I'd like my family to look on and know they can't bring us down, no matter what they do."

Danu save us. I can't find words. It's possible I may have tears in my eyes. Corb is staring at Dau openmouthed.

"Have I shocked you?" Dau asks.

"A little, yes." I clear my throat. "But only because I was thinking along the same lines myself."

Surprisingly soon, a manservant brings the promised clothing. There's a blue linen tunic for Corb, along with a new shirt and breeches. Dau's tunic is a deeper shade of blue. The fabric looks rich, and the family emblem is embroidered on the breast in silver thread. His shirt is of fine silk, his breeches high-quality wool. I had wondered if Seanan planned to humiliate him by providing something inappropriate, but these look like quite princely garments. They could even be Seanan's own; that way they'd be a perfect fit. No sign of a plain gown with a longer skirt for me. Seems I'm supposed to produce that by magic.

When it's time for the midday meal, Corb goes to the kitchens and fetches food for the three of us on a tray. Tonight we'll be expected to eat with everyone else in the hall. None of us is feeling talkative now.

"I suppose we're free for the rest of the day," I say. "I'm going to go mad shut up in here, comfortable as it all is. A walk would be good. I want to see Miach if I can. It would be too awkward— and messy—to make up your draft in here. She'll need to do it for me." Curse Seanan and his stupid rules! I could pick everything I need in the kitchen garden and make up the brew quite quickly in the stillroom. I wouldn't be in anyone's way.

When we've finished eating, Dau gets up and reaches for his stick—he's dispensed with the crutch. "Maybe we'll all go for a walk," he says. "Strength in numbers. We might go and visit the infirmary. Corb, can you take me to the privy first? I re-member where it is, but I'll need to learn the way again." When I don't comment, he adds, "Liobhan? Are you coming?"

"You shouldn't push yourself too hard. You need to be at your strongest and most alert while we're in the house."

"Now, that's a first," says Dau. "You telling me not to exert myself. I'll employ the good judgment I learned on Swan Island. Does that answer satisfy you?"

I can't help smiling. "It'll do. Now who's demonstrating relentless hope?"

It's Dau's turn to smile, though his has a twist to it. "Your mad ideas must be catching. Shall we go?"

I haven't been to the kitchen garden since the day of the fire. Today is warm; I can feel a hint of the coming summer in the air. A monk is gathering herbs and two others are sitting on the low wall, deep in conversation. They fall silent as we approach. I'm not sure what the rules are, only that I know Miach has been using the stillroom, so women must still be admitted even though the monks are in residence. I murmur to Dau, telling him where we are and who else is present.

"Greetings," he says now as we halt next to the brethren, who both rise to their feet. This courtesy most certainly isn't for me or Corb. They must know who Dau is, though he's not yet clad in his new finery. But of course they know: the three brothers are peas in a pod, almost. "I thought it was past time I paid you a visit."

"Welcome, Master Dau," the elder of the two monks says. "I am Brother Petrán, infirmarian at St. Padraig's. This is my assistant, Brother Pól. And over in the garden is our apothecary, Brother Martán." He glances at Corb, then at me, brows up. But Dau can't see it.

"We're Master Dau's personal attendants," I say. "This young man is Corb and I am Liobhan. We perform the required nursing duties, help Master Dau get about, and make up whatever preparations he needs." *Stop talking, Liobhan.*

"Ah, yes," says Brother Petrán. "I believe we have been

supplying you with various materials for that purpose. Brother Martán makes our stillroom available at certain times to the young woman who prepares tonics and the like for those who need them in the house. I must say you are looking remarkably well, Master Dau."

"Thank you," says Dau. "We appreciate your assistance. I was hoping I might be shown around your temporary infirmary. I trust the men who were hurt in the fire are improving."

"Of course, Master Dau. Brother Pól, will you . . . ? I will join you later."

Brother Pól makes to usher Dau inside.

"Corb, you should go with Master Dau." I don't want Dau to go in there without one or the other of us to keep an eye on him. "I can wait out here in the sun and maybe have a look around the garden."

Quick to understand what I'm not saying, Corb follows the others in, leaving me with Brother Petrán. The herbalist, Brother Martán, comes over with his basket on his arm, and we are introduced. I notice something in the basket that I didn't know could be harvested in this garden. The sleeping draft I gave Dau in those first desperate days had a small amount of that particular fungus in it. Whoever first made up that dry mixture labeled the container with every component listed and the quantities, for which I was extremely grateful. I stopped using it as soon as I could. If you get the dose wrong you can kill your patient. If you keep it up for too long, even in a dilute form, the patient can become dependent on it. It has unfortunate side effects. The fungus itself is small and dark and has strange protuberances like stumpy toes.

Brother Petrán sees me staring. "You know what that is, Mistress Liobhan?"

He rises in my estimation immediately. It's the first time anyone has addressed me that way in a very long time. "Devil's-foot. Effective but deadly. Only to be employed in situations where nothing else will give the patient rest, and then only by a skilled healer. Best in combination with several other less potent herbs, made up in a tea. To be taken warm, ideally, with honey to mask the bitterness."

Petrán's smile is friendly and unguarded. It strikes me as quite unmonkish. If he knows I'm the wild warrior woman who blinded a son of the house, he's not letting it bother him too much. "Very good. Where did you learn your herb lore, may I ask?"

"My mother is a healer. Folk call her a wisewoman. I didn't expect to be practicing what little I picked up from her, but there was a need, so I did the best I could. I was pleased I re-membered enough to do a reasonable job. As for the mixture that contains devil's-foot, I was glad to find it ready-made in this stillroom when I needed it for Master Dau. But I wouldn't attempt to make it myself. Fortunately, he did not need it for long. There are risks."

"Indeed. It was partly because of that kind of risk that Brother Martán and I recently established a new system for the labeling and storage of all our preparations. You may be inter-ested to see it."

"Thank you, I would like that." I try not to sound as sur-prised as I feel.

"I hope you know that as Master Dau's carer, you are wel-come to visit the stillroom anytime you wish. If there's any difficulty finding what you need, just speak to me or Brother Martán. We keep a record of what goes out, since we supply not only our own patients and Lord Scannal's household but also those of our brethren who have returned to St. Padraig's— our stillroom there is unusable at present. We also provide remedies to a scattering of local folk whom we visit, those with chronic ailments mostly."

"No wisewoman in the district?" I ask as we go into the stillroom, which is markedly neater than it was the day I found Corb weeping there.

"Sadly, no."

"Sadly? Don't your folk distrust such local healers as . . . unreliable? Ungodly?"

He gives me a sideways glance as he takes a bound book from a shelf and opens it on the immaculately clean workbench. "It depends whom you ask, Mistress Liobhan. I can speak only for myself and those who assist me in my duties. When a case is perplexing, when symptoms do not allow a clear diagnosis, when established learning provides no answers, then one may need to step beyond the usual pathways to understanding. At such times, the advice of a local herbalist might prove useful. It would at least help a physician such as myself to clarify his own thoughts. It's clear to me that Master Dau is much improved. Some of us were dismayed when we learned he would not be in our care. We were doubtful of his recovery. It seems you know what you are doing."

I smile in my turn. "I've simply used what little I do know and improvised when I needed to. I can't cure his blindness; two expert physicians were consulted and neither had any answers. All I could do was relieve the swelling and the headaches."

"What are the components of your draft to relieve pain?"

I list them; all are herbs that grow in this garden, and none produces adverse effects in the amounts I am using. "Master Dau needs it less often now," I say. "Fresh air and exercise have helped him greatly. Just as well, since he's often reluctant to take the draft. Men do not like to appear weak."

Petrán nods sagely. The fact that I'm a woman doesn't seem to bother him. But then, he lets Miach use the stillroom, so perhaps this establishment has different rules from the usual monastery. The brethren may even be enjoying the relaxation of their discipline. I think of the druid community in Breifne, where Brocc was a welcome guest—a man, a musician, a scholar of sorts—and no woman ever set foot inside the gate.

"I'm grateful to you for speaking with me like this," I say. "I know how busy you must be. Especially with Brother Íobhar away."

"True, Brother Íobhar's sudden departure did set our arrangements back somewhat—his leadership would have allowed us to put our full energies into tending to the sick and injured. But by the grace of God, we manage well enough. Let me show you this book. I've been keeping it for a few weeks now. We make a record of what comes in and what goes out. At the monastery we were somewhat less rigorous, but . . . let's say there is greater cause for concern here, where our facilities are more open." He shows me the neatly ruled lines, the lists of materials and quantities taken, who needed the supply and for which patient. "I require whoever takes from our supplies or makes up a preparation to sign their initial in this column, something I did not do previously. Young Miach cannot write, but I showed her how to indicate her name." He points to a shaky but recognizable *M* in the appropriate column. "This will allow Brother Martán to keep track of things even when we are at our busiest. His *M* is in a different style, of course."

I can see it; an elegant small capital in a script whose name I do not know. I run my eyes down the list. Some initials are such a scrawl they might be anything.

"And if you were to use our facility you would do the same, of course. It's generally easy enough to find someone to write down the details for you." There's a hint of a question in his voice.

"I can read and write, Brother Petrán. I wouldn't have helped myself to that rather potent mixture when Dau was first ill if I'd been unsure of the components."

"I'm glad you are careful, Mistress Liobhan. Before we came here, I believe there had been no such records kept in the house for a considerable time. I hope that those responsible for the stillroom will maintain this system once we have returned to St. Padraig's." He's looking worried now; the ready smile is nowhere in sight. I want to ask what sparked the change in recording methods. *Cause for concern,* he said. I don't think he means me or Miach. He's treated me with respect, explained things as he might to a colleague. And if he didn't trust Miach, he'd surely stop her working in the stillroom and have one of his brethren provide what the household needed instead. Who else would be making up cures, apart from the monks who tend the sick here? I wish I'd had a better look at the book.

"I understand your caution, Brother Petrán. You keep some items here that could be perilous for someone who did not understand their uses. Not only devil's-foot, but several others I can see, thanks to your excellent labels. Deadly in the wrong hands. You wouldn't want someone just wandering in and helping themselves while you and your brethren were other- wise occupied." In fact I'm amazed that he would trust me enough to let me use the place, record book or no record book. I hope Brother Íobhar doesn't overrule him when he returns from wherever he's gone. It sounds as if he's a figure of some authority. Perhaps being nobly born allows a man high status even in a religious order, wrong as that seems. Seanan wouldn't approve of my being here. I'm quite sure of that.

Could they be setting me up for disaster? Giving me enough rope to hang myself? My Swan Island training makes it all too easy to imagine how they could do that, using my obvious knowledge of wisewomen's business and my freedom to visit garden and stillroom to concoct a theory about a poisoning plot. I blinded Dau, didn't I? So I'm wayward and violent, or at the very least heedless of other folk's safety. That's how it could be argued in a legal hearing. I was going to ask if I could make up the dried mixture for Dau's draft now and save Miach the trouble, but I don't.

"You look concerned, Mistress Liobhan." Petrán sounds so kindly, I wonder why I doubted him. I must be going a little crazy.

I'm trying to form a response, something about Master Seanan that doesn't sound too critical, but I'm spared from speaking because I hear Dau's voice and Brother Pól's as they make their way back outside. And in the distance I hear something unexpected, a sound that brings a big smile to my face and makes my feet want to tap in time. Music. More precisely, someone playing a complicated dance tune on the small-pipes. Someone else is beating out a complex rhythm on the bodhrán. The drummer is not quite as good as Archu, but good enough. The piper is expert. Seems there might be entertainment in the hall after supper once Lord Ross's party gets here. Someone has hired a band. I wonder if there will be dancing. Probably yes, considering the reason these visitors are coming. An image shines bright in my thoughts: Dau's hand in mine, both of us smiling as he turns me under his arm. Both of us surprised to find that we dance well together. Curse it, now I have tears in my eyes. And a stupid thought in my head. Why shouldn't a blind man dance?

27

BROCC

We come safely home. The trees in our forest are clothed in many shades of green; squirrels are busy finding food for their young ones, and fledgling birds venture out on their first wobbling flights. Berries ripen on bushes; flowers open their faces to the sun. I judge it to be not yet full summer, but it cannot be far off. What seemed to us a journey of less than one turning of the moon has taken more than twice that time in Eirne's realm. I am a bard, I know my tales, and I know the oddities of time in the Otherworld. Still, this jolts me.

Eirne's folk greet True with smiles and embraces. The smaller ones shriek with excitement, jump up and down, dance about. Rowan claps True on the shoulder and kisses him on either cheek, then gives me a brotherly embrace.

Eirne looks better. The rose has returned to her cheeks and the light to her lovely eyes. It does me good to see her, even as I so much dread telling her my news. As she takes True's hands in hers, tears fall down her cheeks. "Dear friend," she says. "We have missed you so. And now you are well again. Later you shall give me the whole story, if you can. A wondrous journey."

We are weary, True and I. He goes off to rest. I hesitate; I can make no assumptions.

"Come with me, Brocc," Eirne says. "A bath, some food, a

rest . . . That is better done in my retreat, where we can be quiet. Moon-Fleet, will you make the preparations?" She takes my hand and leads me away from the others. We walk slowly; I am weighed down by what I must tell her. I should be full of gladness. We are home, True is cured, and it seems Rowan has single-handedly kept all of Eirne's folk safe during our lengthy absence. The summer is upon us, the forest is full of joyful life, and my wife seems kindly disposed toward me. But . . . but . . .

Somehow, by the time we reach her little house, the bath stands ready, the water warm, and everything I might need close at hand. No sign of Moon-Fleet. She has done what was needed, then departed to leave the two of us alone. I should tell Eirne now. I should get this over. But I cannot bear to see the warmth drain from her eyes. I cannot bear to lose the tenderness of her touch, the sweetness of her voice.

I do not tell her as I soak in the warm water and she scrubs my back and massages the hurt from my shoulders and kisses my wet body here and there. I do not tell her as we share mead and sweetmeats and gaze with longing at each other, or as we lie down together on her bed. I do not whisper the truth in her ear as our bodies renew their friendship, or as we come together in long-held-back passion, or as she cries out in delight. Nor afterward, as we lie quiet in each other's arms and a song forms itself in my mind: a song that cannot be sung until a full year has passed. So much can happen in a year.

"You are frowning, my bard. What troubles you?"

I cannot tell her. I cannot bring myself to say it. But I must. Tonight, the small ones will want music. But . . . the story is True's, for the main part. He should be the one to tell of the place we visited, the place of his ancestors, and of how he entered the falling water and was healed. If he wants to tell. My part in this journey was small. I paid a price, yes; I will tell of that when the time comes. I cannot bear to shatter this contentment. Eirne lies in my arms, warm and relaxed, her head on my shoulder, her body against mine. It has been so long. Not only the time of our absence, but before. "Nothing, dearest," I say. "I am a little tired, that is true. Out of practice at such activity." I reach to stroke her hair. To find her so well, so full of life, so much her old self, feels like a miracle and I rejoice in it.

"Sleep then, dear one," Eirne says, and we do.

28
DAU

Corb and I walk around the temporary infirmary with Brother Pól, who talks as we go, explaining what I cannot see. The chamber where I tossed and turned and endured such pain that I wished for death now houses a survivor of the fire and a quiet attendant. Pól will not say the man is dying, not when the patient can hear him, but I understand this from his tone and his carefully chosen words. Other chambers hold various invalids, some suffering no more than old age and frailty, some recovering from burns, some with different conditions. It's clear that when my brother Ruarc is here, he's in charge of it all. That seems bizarre. Ruarc as head of an infirmary; Ruarc responsible for the sick, the injured, the frail. When we were young, it was always Seanan who led and Ruarc who followed. Seanan who gave orders and Ruarc who obeyed, even if those orders were to commit acts of vile cruelty. And yet folk here speak of Brother Íobhar with what sounds like genuine respect. Can a man change so much in a matter of a few years? Can it be that my brother truly found God and saw the error of his ways? I cannot believe it.

In one of the rooms there is a man I remember. He calls my name as we come to the door. I would know that voice anywhere, though there is now a wheezing, shaky quality to it that reminds me, uncomfortably, of the way my father sounded on the day I came here.

"Master Dau!"

We halt. "Is it Master Fiachna?" I ask, knowing I'm right. He is—was?—my father's scribe, back when I lived here. What I learned of letters and numbers, I learned mostly from him, outside the hours of formal tuition. When Seanan was present I could learn nothing; my terror made it impossible to think. I am glad Fiachna is here. I had forgotten him and his kindness. But perhaps not glad, for this must mean he is sick or hurt.

"It's Fiachna all right, Master Dau. Come in and talk to me. I'm laid low with my leg in a splint and nothing to keep me amused but these brethren with their tales of miracles—no offense, Brother Pól, you tell them well enough. Come in, sit down."

Corb steers me to a bench; sits me down. I suggest to Brother Pól that he might leave us for a little, since he must be so busy, and that Corb can walk me back out. He thanks me and departs.

"I heard you lost your sight, lad," Fiachna says. "I'm sorry."

It delights me that he's dispensed with *Master Dau*; that person has never sounded real to me. "My half uncial was never neat enough for you, Master Fiachna, and sadly now it never will be. What happened to your leg?"

The scribe sighs. "Best not spelled out, my friend." He's dropped his tone as if afraid to be overheard. "I fell foul of certain folk in the household. Not long after, I had an unfortunate accident on some stairs. Fell awkwardly, broke a bone. I've been well tended to by the brethren, I'll say that. Brother Petrán did the bonesetting himself and splinted the leg. They give me a draft for the pain. Tastes vile but deadens the worst of it. I'll be walking again soon enough. Lucky, you might say."

I'm trying to piece together what he said. Does he mean someone pushed him down the stairs? I don't know who might be within earshot, and I'm not sure what to ask anyway. "My father must be missing your assistance. I remember how much he valued your skill."

There's a silence. Then the scribe says, "Master Seanan's in charge now. I've seen very little of Lord Scannal for some time. As for my skill, such as it is, I believe I may be exercising it elsewhere once this leg is sufficiently mended to let me travel. But enough of that. Tell me, is the malady that affects your eyes permanent? Brother Petrán's very skilled. Might he be able to help?"

I explain the situation, thank him for his concern, and don't mention magical cures. I don't want to talk about myself and my eyes and my awkward situation. Or about Seanan and his impending betrothal. But there is something I can ask about. "I was much surprised to find my brother Ruarc as a member of a monastic community. What I remember of him does not match with that at all. I would have liked to talk to him"—a lie—"and I'm sorry he was called away so suddenly. Do you know where he went and for how long?" I hope that sounds natural enough.

"He surprised me, too, but I believe his faith to be genuine. As for the sudden departure, there was an argument. With his brother. Raised voices in this part of the house carry clearly to those of us trapped in our beds and unable to shut our ears. I would not pass on details of the conversation, since it was intended to be private. But . . . it touched on your own care, and that of Lord Scannal, who has been poorly for some while. Shortly after that, Brother Íobhar was sent away on priory business. For how long, I do not know."

I try to take all this in. I can't ask probing questions. I can't get Fiachna embroiled in my family's unsavory affairs any further. Is Seanan's answer to anyone who challenges him to send them away from Oakhill? To dismiss them from his service?

But the monks don't answer to him, unless my brother has even the prior at his beck and call. Could he threaten to withdraw funds from St. Padraig's if the prior does not do his bidding? Unlikely, surely. Perhaps, deep down, Íobhar is still that boy who always obeyed his older brother, no matter how vile and cruel the instruction. Most certainly, I cannot look to him for support, even supposing he's back by the time Lord Ross's party arrives.

I'm rising to leave when I decide to ask one more question.

"You mention my father has been unwell. I've only spoken with him once since I arrived here. What is wrong with him?" I wait for the same answer Seanan gave me.

"You haven't spoken with Master Seanan?" asks Fiachna.

"I'd prefer to hear your answer," I say.

"Your father keeps himself to himself these days. We take our instructions from Master Seanan. I cannot give you an expert opinion. I gather Lord Scannal does not wish to consult Brother Petrán, though he has done so quite often in the past over less significant ailments. It's unfortunate. But your father is his own man and will not be pushed."

"I see." But I don't. Not fully. This doesn't add up. "Thank you for being so honest, Master Fiachna. I hope the leg mends quickly, and I wish you safe for whatever comes next, whether it is at Oakhill or elsewhere."

"Alas, I cannot rise to bid you farewell in the manner most appropriate." His tone tells me Fiachna is wearing a wry smile. "But it's good to see you, lad, even under such circumstances. I'll be in hopes that you regain your sight, if only so you can see that your half uncial is not as bad as you remember. As for me, Father Eláir always has room for one or two lay brethren, and if a man can turn his hand to illuminated capitals, so much the better. Farewell to you for now, Master Dau. And you, young man."

As Corb and I walk back out, my mind is teeming with questions. I knew Seanan was ruthless. I knew he cared nothing for the feelings of others. I knew he was ambitious. But to take over my father's responsibilities almost completely? If that is necessary, Father must be seriously ill, perhaps dying. And yet he's refused the aid of a physician. It makes no sense. What am I not understanding? What am I missing?

29

LIOBHAN

The musicians are rehearsing outside, taking advantage of the good weather. They've settled themselves on a level patch of grass to the eastern side of the house, the drummer and harper sitting on stools, the piper and whistle player standing. An audience of household workers has been drawn by the sweet sounds. Seems Lord Scannal is sparing no expense in his effort to impress this girl, or more likely her father. Dau, Corb, and I come to a halt at the back of the small crowd as the band launches into "Over Fox Hill," a tune I know like the palm of my hand.

I can't keep still. The music thrums through my body, setting my feet tapping. The fellow with the small-pipes is taking the main melody, with the whistle player joining in for the refrains. When I play this piece I add different embellishments every time the refrain comes around. It keeps me and my bandmates on our toes. This band has a woman on the whistle; she's doing a good job, but her approach is rather workmanlike. I wonder if I'm too showy? No doubt Seanan would think so if he ever heard me playing.

When the musicians reach the end of the jig, we all applaud. "More!" someone shouts, predictably. They run through a few songs. Each of them takes a turn singing; they're adequate for the job, and the woman has a nice pure tone, but there's nobody outstanding there. Nobody like Brocc. When they play "High Days of Summer" they invite their audience to join in the chorus, which is a soaring melody full of heart, expressing the poet's longing to return to his home valley where he met the love of his life many years before. So we sing, and the sound fills me with the same deep yearning for home. It's good to set my voice free. There'll be no more singing in the evenings until they send us back to the stables. I'm happy that Corb and Dau are joining in now. Both of them can hold a tune, though Dau has the better voice, rough-edged but true. I wish he'd sing more often.

We reach the end of the final refrain and the musicians put down their instruments. Seems the rehearsal is over. I become aware that quite a few people are looking at me, including the piper and the bodhrán player, and I understand rather late that I've made an error. For a little, I forgot that here at Oakhill I'm not a musician in front of an audience, I'm only one step up from a slave. I should be invisible. Inaudible. But I'll be damned if I sing in an apologetic whisper.

The band members are in intense discussion now, their voices lowered. I have a feeling we should move on, but we can't, because folk are coming over to greet Dau with bows or curtsies, to comment on how well he looks, and to wish him their best. I realize that most of his father's people have barely seen Dau since we came to Oakhill. We've been living in a much smaller world, that of the stables and the practice yard. Why am I so surprised that people want to be kind?

Now here comes the piper, straight toward us, and I can't avoid him. Curse it! Dau's speaking with an older man, a gardener by the looks of his hands, and Corb is by his side.

The piper is a slight person with curly hair, sharp features, and bright blue eyes. He looks as if he's stepped out of some fanciful tale. His smile reveals a pair of charming dimples. I bet he's popular with the female members of his audience.

"Greetings!" His manner is equally charming. "I'm Cian. Lovely singing voice you have. Have I heard you play somewhere before?"

"My name's Liobhan." I think fast. Does it matter if he knows who I am? "I did belong to a band once, a couple of years ago. With my brother. We don't play together anymore. I miss it, that's the truth. How long will you be here?"

"We've been hired for seven nights, perhaps a little longer. Been on the road awhile, just wanted to air ourselves out, so to speak, though we're not required for entertainment until tomorrow night." He gives me an appraising look. "You live here? Fancy a turn with our band? We're short of a strong singer at present."

I clear my throat. Look at the ground. Silently curse fate for making it impossible to say yes. "The way things are here," I say in an undertone, "I can't. I'm a—I'm a very lowly kind of servant and it's not even worth my while asking. But it's been good to sing along." I have tears in my eyes. I pretend they aren't there. "If you're practicing some other time, I'd love to come and listen."

Dau has extricated himself and walked over to stand beside me. "This is Master Dau," I say, "Lord Scannal's youngest son. Dau, this is Cian, who was playing the pipes."

"Welcome to Oakhill," Dau says, sounding like the nobleman he was born to be. "I don't believe there's been much music here for a while—I've only recently returned after a long absence. I hope you'll be well accommodated. Ask Iarla to give you a space to practice, if he hasn't already done so. Outside is all very well in fine weather, but you'll need to store your instruments safely."

"Thank you, Master Dau. I wish you could persuade the young lady to join us. Her voice is remarkable."

"She's handy on the whistle, too," Dau says. "You should hear her version of 'Artagan's Leap.' If anything is remarkable, that is. Like something from another world." A pause, during which I just manage not to kick him. "But Liobhan's right, there are reasons why she could not join in your performances."

"Ah well, we can live in hope," says Cian smoothly, and takes his time to introduce the other members of the band to Dau. Dau explains that he is blind, thus relieving me and Corb of that duty, and talks with each of them in turn. I stand there feeling awkward until he bids them a courteous farewell and turns away. As we head toward our quarters I say not a word. But what I'm thinking is, *You're the one Sárnait should be marrying. You're the one who should be the next chieftain of Oakhill.*

The next day Lord Ross and his party arrive. Corb sees them ride in and comes back to report to us. Lord Ross, his son Cormac, and his daughter Sárnait are accompanied by a larger body of men-at-arms than the fellows in the stables expected, and they have a councilor and a lawman with them as well as several ladies. Seems Ross is serious about this possible betrothal, which makes me wonder how much he's seen of Seanan over all the years since Lord Scannal's sons were boys growing up and Cormac was something of a friend to the hapless young Dau. But then, Seanan is expert at putting on his best face. That face may be the only one these visitors have ever seen.

We've got through one supper in the great hall. Even without the complication of important visitors it was bad enough: Dau seated at the high table next to Seanan, with Naithí on his other side, and Corb standing behind him looking less than relaxed. I was in a corner with serving folk and stable hands, so it was easy enough to keep my head down. I did watch Dau. He talked to Naithí; between him and Seanan was an invisible wall. Lord Scannal looked unwell. His skin had a gray hue to it and his manner struck me as odd. Distracted. He played with his knife rather than using it to cut his meat. He stared into the distance as if not seeing what was right before him. When his servingman, standing behind, bent forward to speak to him or offer any kind of assistance, Lord Scannal waved him away. He hardly spoke a word and he hardly ate anything. Seanan spoke to his father quite often, perhaps encouraging him to drink his mead or to sample the fruit-laden pudding. The attention looked kindly. If Seanan keeps his performance up, he may well convince Lord Ross that he'd make a worthy son-in-law.

Now the visitors are here and I must curb my wish to sing and dance and my deep desire to give Master Seanan the beating he deserves. I must behave like the little mouse I once pretended to be when in the company of a frightened child. Only I'm damned if I'll stay in our quarters all day, and with so many folk in the house it's impossible to go out and in without being seen. I may be good at walking softly and keeping to the shadows, but a tall, strongly built woman with bright red hair is never going to blend in with her surroundings. As I'm thinking this and getting into my working clothes I imagine my brother making up a silly song about a woman like me finding the perfect spot to hide: a forest in autumn, among the tall, russet-leaved trees. I miss Brocc. I wonder if it's really possible to walk all the way to Eirne's realm through that forest we can see from here, or whether there are mountains and lakes and chasms between us and that place, not to speak of hostile territories. Dau and I might die before we ever reached the portal. And I'd have to guide him all the way.

Dau has woken with a headache. He hasn't even tried to get out of bed, and it's plain he's not well enough to go to breakfast

in the hall. I send Corb off to fetch us some provisions. Dau
is ashen pale, lying back on the pillow and trying to keep his
breathing steady.

"We need more of the draft," I tell him as I boil the kettle on
our little hearth. "I'll brave the stillroom later, since they've
given me permission. I have enough of the dry mix to make
you a cupful for now."

"A pox on the draft," Dau mutters. "It'll send me to sleep all
day. What's the point in that?"

"The point is it takes away the pain." I keep my voice calm
and level. "And then you can do the things you need to do. And
keep yourself under good control while you're doing them."

He falls silent while I get on with making the draft. I brew
a peppermint tea for me and Corb as well. I've made sure we
have cups and a jug here, as well as the kettle and the strainer.
It's not until I carry Dau's cup over to him that he speaks again.

"Would you marry a man because you thought he needed
looking after?"

I nearly drop the cup and its contents. With extreme care, I
set it down on the stool beside the bed. "Same answer as I gave
you last time. Not if that was the only reason. And not if the
man was grumpy and uncooperative."

"Not the same question as last time." Dau manages a smile,
though his face still has that white, pinched look.

"I noticed. In fact I have no plans to marry anyone, now or
in the future. Swan Island doesn't exactly make allowances for
it. That's cool enough to drink. You want me to hold the cup
for you?"

He doesn't, but his hands are shaking. I have to hold the
thing and tilt it so he can take one sip at a time. Not long ago
this would have made Dau angry. Now, he lets me do it.

"Your brother's situation must be playing on your mind," I
say after a bit. "Or you wouldn't be talking of marriages. I don't

imagine Sárnait will see her intended husband as someone who will ever need looking after. More as a man who will look after her."

"Hah!"

"Careful, you'll spill it. I share your opinion on that issue. So drink the draft, rest until your head feels better, then go and do something about it. Calmly. It's a mission. Keep that in mind, hard as it is at times."

He drinks. After a while he says, "I've heard folk say that Brigid and Archu were once a couple. Never made it official, but I suppose they found opportunities where they could."

I'm silenced, trying to imagine those two hard-bitten warriors as loving companions or even as passionate bedmates. There are married couples on the island, several of them. Eimear, who plays the whistle, is married to one of the younger warriors. But none of those couples is made up of two fighters.

"But they're not lovers now," I say, not quite making it a question. Brigid and Archu are certainly old and true friends. But if there's anything else, I've seen no sign of it.

"The only way to find out would be to ask them and risk a clip around the ear," says Dau.

"None of our business anyway."

There's another silence. It's not the right time for that conversation, the one we need to have at some point. Perhaps it will never be the right time.

"Liobhan—" Dau begins, but I don't find out what he was about to say because at that moment Corb returns bearing a laden tray.

"Master Cormac sends his regards, and so does the young lady," Corb says with some delicacy as he sets out various food-stuffs on our small table.

"What is she like?" I can't help asking. "Sárnait, I mean."

"Not for me to say."

"Oh, come on, Corb. You're not a servant here, you're one of us." This from Dau, who wouldn't have dreamed of saying such a thing scant weeks ago.

Corb turns pink in the cheeks. "Small. Very pretty, with long fair hair. Friendly. Courteous. A real lady."

Far too good for Seanan, I think. But we knew that already.

"And Cormac?" asks Dau. "I haven't seen him since we were children."

"Fine-looking man. Very polite, same as her. They said they'd brought you a gift, but they didn't say what it was. I told them you were indisposed. And I explained to Iarla."

"Thank you, Corb. We'd best eat. There's porridge, Dau, and oaten bread, and some soft cheese. And berries in honey. What would you like?"

Dau passes me his empty cup and lies back against the pillows. "Nothing right now. You two have it."

We save him some bread and cheese, but eat the rest. When we're done I head off to the stillroom. I suspect the headaches will persist until Dau has dealt with the issue of his brother's betrothal and the visitors are gone. I need to be sure I have an adequate supply of the dry mix so I can make up his draft every day while they're here, if that's what he needs. And since he's going to be resting this morning and Corb can stay with him, now is the time. As I walk over I think of different answers to that question about marriage. Would I marry a man because I thought he needed looking after? Most certainly not, if that was my only reason. You marry someone because you love them and they love you. You marry someone so that you can look after each other. Be equal partners. You marry someone because neither of you can imagine the future without the other. Like my parents. Though, from what little they've told me, it took them quite a while to learn all that. I can't imagine them without each other. They're like two startlingly different parts of one remarkable whole. We're so lucky, Galen and Brocc and me. So, so lucky. And I suppose that's another part of marrying someone: to make children together. Not part of the future I plan for myself. There's no way it could be made to fit.

In the stillroom I find my ingredients then record everything in Brother Petrán's book. This time I have a better look. All the entries I see have initials against them, mostly ones I can match with the folk I know use the place: Martán, Petrán, Pól, Miach. There's a scrawly one that might be *A*; but then, there may be other monks who help here. As far as I know, Miach and I are the only folk from the household who use the place.

Dau hates the taste of his draft. There's a fungus that would give it a better flavor without lessening its efficacy. I look along the shelf where dried mushrooms and toadstools are kept, and as I reach for the jar that holds what I want, I notice a paring knife balanced across another jar, the one labeled *devil's-foot*. Someone's been careless; there are still traces of the black fungus clinging to the blade. I make sure the jar is properly closed, then clean the knife, wondering who could have been so careless. Devil's-foot is not a substance you leave lying around. I'm about to check the book again when Brother Martán, the apothecary, comes in and we bid each other a polite good morning. I should tell him about the devil's-foot. But I hesitate. What if it was Miach and I get her in trouble? What if Martán takes offense at the implied criticism? I might get myself banned from the stillroom.

The apothecary fetches his basket, already full from an early morning harvest, and begins to unload and sort the contents. He's got some plants there that I'm fairly sure don't grow in this garden, and I consider how easily the monks come and go through the gates. Pity that doesn't apply to me. I could make up something a lot better for Dau if I could wander in the woods to find a few of my mother's more obscure choices. I could use fresh wild-picked herbs. Never mind that.

Dau's odd questions about marriage are still on my mind when I start chopping and grinding my materials to the required fine powder. They're bothering me far more than they deserve to. I find myself wielding my knife and then my pestle with more speed and violence than is strictly necessary. From time to time Brother Martán glances over at me with brows raised. Too bad. I've promised not to draw attention to myself while the visitors are at Oakhill. So I can't still my wayward thoughts in the way I usually would: by going for a run or working my way through our exercise routine or climbing a tree. Cutting things up with a very sharp knife is the way my mother calms herself when she's wrestling with a problem. If it works for her, it should work for me.

My mixture is complete and safely stowed in a drawstring bag; I've made enough for several days, in case Dau's headaches continue. Brother Martán is putting things away on the shelves. It would be all too easy for an unscrupulous person to misuse these materials, meticulous records or not. I have to speak up, even if it gets me in trouble.

"Finished for the morning, Mistress Liobhan?"

"I am, thank you. But there's something I must tell you." I explain what I saw, and that I made sure the jar of dried devil's-foot was securely stoppered and the shavings cleaned off the knife. "I used an old rag; you'll find that and the residue in there." I motion to the basket where debris is dropped before it's consigned to the fire at the end of the day. I don't want him thinking I'm covering for an error of my own. Because he's looking very serious now, I add, "If you want to check what I'm taking with me against what I wrote in the book, please do."

"I'd best do so, I suppose." Brother Martán opens the little bag I pass to him, sniffs at the mixture, then closes the string and gives the bag back. "Thank you. Your vigilance is appreciated. If you notice anything of the kind again, please let us know straightaway. Just a careless error, I expect. But troubling."

Troubling, I think, *because you know none of your trusted brethren would make such a glaring mistake. So who's been using devil's-foot?*

30
DAU

"D au?"

I swim up through mists of sleep. Someone's shaking me by the shoulder.

"Dau, there are visitors at the door. Master Cormac and his sister."

Sitting up feels like shifting a block of stone. My head is dizzy, my limbs are leaden, all I want to do is lie down again and shut out the world. But Corb is urgent. "They have something for you. I couldn't just send them away."

Cormac. I remember what I'm supposed to be doing, why it's important to talk to him. Cormac and his sister. Gods. Maybe Liobhan can take Sárnait off somewhere while I . . .

"Where's Liobhan?"

"Not back from the stillroom. Here, let me comb your hair. That's better."

I look a wreck, no doubt. A ruin of the boy they once knew. Not that Sárnait will remember me, but Cormac will. I was never sure how much he understood, back then. "Let them in, Corb. We shouldn't keep them waiting."

"Dau!" Cormac's voice is a man's now; we are of an age. He speaks with what sounds like genuine warmth, and no trace of shock. "Welcome home! Do you remember my sister, Sárnait?"

"I imagine you've both changed somewhat," I manage. "I wish I could see you. You find me less than perfectly prepared for visitors—I had to take a sleeping draft earlier and my head is not as clear as it might be. I'm happy to make your acquaintance again. Old friends and good ones. I hope you've been well accommodated." There's something in the room that troubles me. Something I can't identify, a smell, some small sound, something . . . And none of them is speaking now, not even Corb.

"Corb, will you go and fetch us some refreshments, please? Just something light." How long did I sleep? Not long, surely, or Liobhan would be back.

"Yes, Master Dau." Corb is being a servant. "And something for the . . . ?"

"A bowl for water," Sárnait says. "She doesn't need food. Not until later."

All of a sudden I'm very still. The faint smell, the little sound, the slight difference in the room . . . And now, before I can utter so much as a word, someone is putting a living, breathing creature into my arms and I have no choice but to take it. A warm, wet tongue licks my cheek. The small body wriggles a bit, then settles against my chest. A dog. They've brought me a dog.

"You remember Father's bitch, Fleet? This pup is from Fleet's daughter's last litter. She only had two. Sárnait's keeping the boy, and we thought you'd like this girl." Cormac's tone softens. "We haven't named her; that's for you to do. You must have been sad to lose Snow. I know how much you loved her."

You are a Swan Island warrior. You will not weep. You will not be sick. You will not order these kind people out of your chamber and you will not tell them rudely that you cannot have a dog, you will never have a dog, you can't be trusted with a dog. You will find a solution. You will make the impossible happen. "This is . . . very thoughtful of you," I say, working hard to keep the tremor out of my voice. The creature on my knee is quite small. If she's old enough now to leave her mother, I don't think she'll ever be a massive animal. Her muzzle is delicate, pointed; her ears flop down, but that will likely change as she grows. Fleet held her ears high. The puppy's tail is thumping against my knee. A dog. A hostage to fortune. A treasure I cannot afford to have. She leans against my heart, warm, alive, perfect. "What name did you choose for your dog, Sárnait?"

"I'm waiting to ask Seanan what he would like."

This cannot happen. This is not going to happen. "Fleet's granddaughter," I say. "A good line. Is this dog all white?"

"She has a dark patch over the left eye," says Cormac, "and another on the lower back, near the tail. Otherwise pure white. The sire was an excellent hunting dog, compact and wiry. She'll be easy to train. And strong."

He cannot have heard the manner of Snow's death. I want to ask if he knows why I ran away from home all those years ago. But I can't; not in front of Sárnait. Gods, if only I hadn't taken that draft. I can't think clearly. Of course they're assuming I will go on living here and Sárnait will marry my brother and this little dog and her own brother will run around together all day and be happy. Hah!

I manage to chat about inconsequential things until Corb comes back. No sign of Liobhan. What is she doing? I avoid saying anything about Seanan, even though it's plain Sárnait wants to ask me about him. I set the dog down on the floor for a bit and hear her exploring in all corners. I ask Corb, more than once, to make sure she can't get out. If my tone sounds rather fierce, too bad. She may not be mine for long, but while I have her I will keep her from all harm if it kills me. A plan starts to form in my mind. Too risky? I hope not.

I snatch an opportunity to speak to Cormac alone as my

guests are leaving. The little dog is feasting on a piece of cheese someone has dropped under the table. While Sárnait is coaxing her out I draw him aside in the anteroom.

"I need to talk to you sometime. Not here. Somewhere on our own."

"Of course, Dau, if you wish. We're going out riding soon, with your brother. Tomorrow morning?"

"Thank you. It's important, Cormac. And . . . please don't tell anyone. Not anyone."

I can't see his face. He may well be thinking I've gone a little crazy as well as blind. But he sounds calm as he says, "I'll be discreet. The stables perhaps? I might take you over to admire my new mare; she's a fine girl with a beautiful temperament. A gray."

"I'd like that, Cormac. And then a walk, away from listening ears."

"I'll meet you after breakfast, all being well."

They leave, and I find I no longer want to crawl back into bed. I have a problem. Two problems. That's on top of the existing situation.

Corb has set down a bowl of water for the dog. I hear her lapping. "Corb," I say. "If I gave you a couple of days' leave, could you get home to the farm and back easily?"

A moment's silence before he replies. He's surprised, thinking it out. "The walk isn't long. I could be there and back in less than a day. Why?"

"I can't keep the dog here. She wouldn't be safe." I imagine her sleeping on my bed, a small, warm presence to keep away the nightmares. I imagine her running in the field, walking by my side, a companion, a friend. Someone to take care of. "If you took her to your parents' farm, would they keep her for me? I would pay them well. I don't know how long she'd need to stay there." Until Liobhan's year is up? That is too long.

I would be a stranger to the little one. I would miss the best time to work with her, learn her ways, start to train her. "It might be a good while. But I can't have her here in the house. And don't suggest the stables." I feel my body tense, hear my voice become sharp. I make myself count to ten. Why doesn't Liobhan come back?

"If that's what you want." Corb sounds doubtful. "Only . . . mightn't it be best to wait until after the visitors have left? You'd have to explain to them why the dog wasn't here. And who would stand behind you at table while I was gone?"

He's right, of course. I have no doubt Seanan would use the creature as a weapon against me. But he's not likely to act while Lord Ross's family is here. He'll wait until they're safely out of the way. Then he'll strike. I think of a dozen ways she could be hurt in what appeared to be an unfortunate accident brought about by having a blind owner. My brother is both devious and imaginative. But Corb is wise. To send him home, I'd probably need Iarla's permission. And I'd need to explain why it was necessary. A visit to his parents might be sufficient excuse, but not if he rushes there and back in a single day so he's here for supper.

"As soon as they're gone, then. And in the meantime, I'll need you and Liobhan to help me look after the dog. And . . . Corb, I want her kept away from my brother. You don't know the story, but . . ." I don't want to tell him. He's only a lad. "The dog I had before, Snow, died at the hands of my brothers. That was why I left home. That and some other things."

"I'll help, of course. That's . . . it's terrible, Dau. How old were you?"

"Thirteen. Around the age Sárnait is now."

There's a silence, then Corb says, "I'll go and find a leash later, something very light. She's wearing a good collar. She's small, though; maybe she'd be better in a harness."

"When you take her to the farm you'll have to carry her most of the way." What in the name of the gods am I doing? Under what circumstances could I possibly keep this little dog? Wherever I go when Liobhan's year is up, I won't be here at Oakhill. Even if I were, this is the last place for the creature. She's too delicate for the long and unpredictable walk through the forest to find that portal. As for Swan Island, there's a rule—no dogs, because of the sheep. I should have said, *I am a blind man and cannot look after an animal.* I should have said, *Look what happened to Snow. I can never have another dog, or a sweetheart, or a child, or anything else while men like Seanan walk the earth. I cannot let it happen again.*

"Dau? Are you all right?"

As Corb speaks, I hear the patter of the dog's neat small feet on the wooden floor, and then she is beside me, putting her paws up on my leg, thrusting her nose into my hand for attention. And even though I am not alone, I let my tears fall. For me. For Snow. For this trusting creature who does not know I'll be sending her away. For Sárnait. For a world full of men like my brother, and for dreams that can never be.

31

LIOBHAN

The musicians are practicing again. I think they're in the hall itself, perhaps getting things set up for their supper-time performance, though it's only morning. I resist the urge to go in and listen. Cian would most likely repeat his invitation to be part of the performance, and I don't want to have to say no again.

On the way to our quarters I have to duck into an alcove to avoid a group of people that includes both Lord Scannal and Seanan. Once in our chamber, I find an added complication in the form of a small dog. I should be glad that Dau's headache has abated and that he's up and having some late breakfast. But he looks tired and troubled, and it's plain that Corb, too, is upset. The dog doesn't care. She's under the table eating morsels from Dau's own platter.

My mind has been on other things. It sounded as if the monks already have serious concerns about the stillroom supplies. Am I putting two and two together and making something considerably greater than their sum? Am I acting like a spy when my job here is something quite different? I must speak to Miach, if I can find her. But privately, or I risk getting both of us in trouble.

Corb makes a brew; he's well trained by now. He and Dau

explain the presence of the dog and what they intend to do about it. The plan they present me with is full of holes. What happens when I leave Oakhill? Or when Dau and I head off to try to find Eirne's realm? And, more immediately, how are we supposed to conceal the animal from Seanan when he can walk up and knock on our door anytime he wants? Besides, surely the girl, Sárnait, is going to mention to her prospective husband that she brought his brother a surprise gift. She'll have no idea why that wouldn't be a wise move. Dau should have said no. Of course he should. But looking at him now as he gathers the creature up onto his lap and strokes her tiny ears, I understand perfectly why he didn't. And in a way, I'm glad of that.

I drink half my tea before I make any comment. "How's Corb going to get out without drawing attention?"

"He'll have Iarla's permission to visit his family for a night. If anyone asks awkward questions about the dog, he tells the truth: that I've ordered him to take it to the farm." After a moment he adds, "Corb knows what happened with Snow. He understands why this is important."

I wish I could think of a better plan, but nothing comes to mind. I change the subject. "Corb, I need to go and see Miach. Where would I find her at this time of day?"

"When she's not in the herb garden or making up cures, she helps with the linen. Sorting and mending and so on. They work in a room near the kitchen, where the morning sun comes in."

"One of you should take the dog out first," says Dau. "To do what dogs do."

"That won't be me," I tell him. "Corb can do a far better job of being unobtrusive. You'd better find that lead first, Corb. I'll stay here until you come back."

"I'm not an infant," Dau snaps. "I expect I can manage not to burn the house down or trip and break my leg for as long as it takes."

"Don't I recall your promising recently not to be an ass?"

His hand tightens around his cup, then very deliberately he relaxes it and lets go. "Stay, by all means. These are your quarters, too."

Corb goes. I make a neat stack of the dishes and put them on the tray. The dog sits on Dau's knee, her bright eyes watching every move. I wonder how big she's going to grow.

"Does she have a name?" I ask with some hesitation, knowing Dau's mood to be volatile right now.

"No."

"She needs a name. If not now, then soon. Or we'll have to call her Dog." Which, to me, seems rather the same as being called, Hey, you! or Girl.

Dau doesn't respond. I wait, and after a bit he speaks again. "Did I tell you Sárnait has one, too? This one's littermate, a male. Not here, thank the gods, back at Lord Ross's holding. But she would bring it here if . . ."

"Another reason to speak to Cormac soon. Was he friendly? Do you think he will listen?"

"I'll make him listen."

"Dau. Don't forget you're a chieftain's son. You've been doing a good job. A remarkably good job. Hard as it is, you need to keep that up until these people have gone home. And probably after that, too, unless you want to go back to the harness room. So, speak to Cormac nicely. Don't push him, negotiate with him. Explain calmly."

He attempts a smile. "Cormac's still a friend. We may be men now, but he's not much changed. As for the harness room, I'm coming to think I like it better than these comfortable surroundings. I never was suited to being a chieftain's son."

"Really? That's a pity, in a way. You'd make a good chieftain."

The look on his face makes me want to laugh. Or maybe cry. I'm not sure which.

"Better than Seanan, maybe," Dau says with some bitterness. "But you could say that of almost anyone. Cormac knows I want to talk to him alone. We're meeting tomorrow."

"Good work." I won't tell him about what happened in the stillroom. It's none of my business, it's not part of the job I'm doing, and there's no reason Dau should add it to his troubles. I'll have my own private conversation with Miach, and with luck that will be an end of it.

Miach is folding newly laundered sheets and laying them in a storage chest with sprigs of dried lavender in between. There are one or two other maidservants in the long chamber, but they're at the other end and it's safe to talk quietly. I make myself useful folding, one of the tasks where being tall comes in handy.

"May I ask you something? It might seem a little odd. It's about the stillroom and Brother Petrán's book."

"Ask away. I probably can't answer, though. I never learned to read and write. When I need to set down what I've used or what I'm taking away, I tell Brother Pól and he writes that part for me. I just sign with my letter, M for Miach. I don't know what else is in the book."

"How about other people's letters, like the M for Martán or P for Pól? Do you notice those? Could you tell me how many different people take supplies away? Perhaps what sort of things they take?"

Miach frowns. She has a stalk of lavender in her hand; the sweet smell is all around us, setting an image of my mother's stillroom in my mind. "Not many people do," she says. "From the infirmary, only those three: Martán, Pól, and Petrán. If something is needed at St. Padraig's, one of them takes it over there. They're in and out quite often."

"Only the three—not Brother Íobhar?"

"Brother Íobhar isn't a healer or herbalist. When he's there, he's just . . . in charge. Oversees everything."

"And from the house?"

"Only me, officially. And you." Miach hesitates.

"Nobody else? What if Lord Scannal needed a draft? Or Master Seanan?"

"They'd send someone to ask the monks. Same as they used to do before the fire, but here in the house. Only . . ." She breaks the stalk, puts the lavender bloom down on the sheets.

"You said you use it officially. Is there anyone who uses the stillroom unofficially, Miach?" At the far end of the sunny chamber the other women are having their own conversation, but I lower my voice further anyway.

"It might be better if I didn't say." Miach speaks even more quietly. She glances around the room, one way, the other way, then turns her attention back to the linen.

"When I was there this morning, someone had left a knife out. With traces of rather a potent substance on it. Something the monks wouldn't be careless about. I haven't used that item, and I know you haven't. So I wondered if there might be someone taking without signing."

She doesn't ask me what the item was and I don't tell her. The less she knows about this the better.

"If Lord Scannal needed something prepared, or if Master Seanan did, who would they send to ask the monks?" That's an easier question for her to answer.

"One of their body servants. There's Ardgan, who attends to Master Seanan, or Lord Scannal's man, Gobán. They'd come back to fetch the preparation when it was ready and they'd sign for it in the book. The monks don't go into the main part of the house." She hesitates.

A for Ardgan. Seanan's man. *Don't leap to conclusions, Liobhan.* I might risk one more question. While Miach and I fold another sheet between us, I ask as casually as I can, "Have you ever used devil's-foot, Miach?"

Her eyes widen. "Is that what was taken?" she whispers.

"It looked that way."

"I have used it in a sleeping draft. But that was a long time ago, and I only used a pinch. It was for a woman who had a canker in the gut, something even a physician couldn't cure. She was in terrible pain. Brother Petrán came over from St. Padraig's and showed me how to make the draft. It was that same mixture they keep in the stillroom now."

"Mm. The one I used for Dau not long after we arrived here. Oh, well, I expect there is some explanation. But it did trouble me." How can I warn her without scaring her? This may be nothing. "You and I should take care that everything we use is recorded in the book. Every single thing. You should be all right if Brother Pól is writing the details in for you. Perhaps I should ask him to do mine as well. If there really is someone taking things they shouldn't, we might find ourselves called to account, Miach. We know we're doing the right thing, but persuading some person in authority of that might become tricky, since we're both women, and servants. Me in particular, because they blame me for what happened to Dau."

"Mm. Thank you for warning me, Liobhan."

"Don't trouble yourself unduly. It's probably nothing. I'd better go now; I should get back to Dau."

As I'm turning to go Miach speaks again, this time in a whisper. "Lord Scannal takes a sleeping draft. I had to make it up for him once, when Gobán was away. That was a while ago, before the monks were living here. Gobán used to brew it himself. There was no devil's-foot in it. But . . . Lord Scannal needs a stronger mix now, because of the nightmares. Gobán asked me what he could add safely, and I said he should ask the monks. I never suggested devil's-foot, Liobhan. I wouldn't."

"Nightmares? Lord Scannal has bad dreams, like Dau?"

"That's what Gobán said. I wouldn't know, myself. Lord Scannal does have that look about him. As if he's always tired."

"Mm, I noticed." We glance at each other, and in it there's an understanding neither of us will put into words. We're servants. Lord Scannal is a chieftain. We may be concerned, but trying to do something about this can only get us both in trouble. Who would take us seriously?

"Thank you, Miach."

"Thanks for your help with the folding, Liobhan."

No need to tell each other to keep our mouths shut about this conversation. As I head back toward our quarters, I think that if I were to tell anyone—apart from Dau—it would be Brother Petrán. As for Dau, it's best if I don't mention it to him yet. Let him deal with Cormac and Sárnait and the whole wretched betrothal issue, and let Corb get the little dog safely away, and then I'll talk to him. One thing at a time. Step by step. There could be all sorts of reasons for this. I shouldn't jump to conclusions. But there's one possibility I can't set aside. What if someone's trying to poison the chieftain of Oakhill?

32

BROCC

True tells his story: how we followed the Long Path and met a guide who was a stranger to him but not to me. How that stranger led us to the place of True's ancestors. How True was healed under the waterfall. How he and his passengers are now back to full health. Eirne's folk greet this remarkable tale with wide eyes, gasps of amazement, murmurs of wonder.

"There is another part to our story," True says, looking at me. "We paid a price to step onto the Long Path, and a higher price to step off."

Eirne is seated on her willow chair. In honor of our return, tonight there is feasting and her folk are clad in their best. She wears a gown of buttercup yellow, and her hair is piled high, with flowers threaded through the glossy brown locks. She looks so merry and sweet. I cannot bear to say the words. But I must.

"What price, True?" Eirne asks. "Who demanded payment?"

I clear my throat. After this tale, Eirne's folk will expect music. I must speak. "I will tell this part, if you are in agreement, True."

True gives a nod and sits down; to the extent that I can read his stony features, I think he is relieved.

"There was a lake, with a ferry, as in the old tales," I say. "The ferryman required a fee to take us over. He was a . . . a small fellow, clad in green. Perhaps a clurichaun." My voice is shaking. I can't help it. I see the shadow cross Eirne's face; she has realized that something bad is coming.

"Go on, Brocc," she says. Her tone is cooler now.

"To step onto the Long Path, the price was three verses of a song. Not so difficult for a bard. The ferryman was pleased; he said he would expect three more on our return."

Nobody says a word.

"And he kept to that, as far as it went. When we reached that shore again, I paid for True's passage across with another three verses. The vessel was not large enough to carry us both at once."

Eirne has her arms hugged around herself. In every eye I see the same look. *The bard has made some awful error. He has been tricked. He has betrayed our trust.* I clear my throat again. "I had to bargain with the ferryman for my own passage home. At first he asked for impossible things: a finger, my firstborn child, my singing voice. And . . . in the end, I bargained him down. No finger. No child. But . . . for the next year I will be unable to sing." A great gasp goes up; tears roll down the faces of several small folk. One breaks into loud sobs and has to be consoled by Moon-Fleet. Eirne is very still. I dare not look her in the eye. "My voice would have been gone forever had I not haggled over the price. I'm sorry. I did the best I could."

There is a terrible silence but for the now-smothered sobs of the small one. Then Eirne says in the quietest of voices, "It is not only that you have robbed us of the delight, the joy, the consolation you bring, Brocc, though that saddens every one of us. It is the sacrifice of our only weapon against the Crow Folk. Without your voice, how can we defend ourselves? How can we protect our little ones?" She falls silent for a moment, and I know what is coming next. "Why didn't you tell me before?" *Before I welcomed you home gladly,* she means. *Before I lay in your arms and gave you sweet kisses, before our bodies were joined in passion and delight. Before, before . . .*

"Would you have had me give the fellow a finger, so I could not play the harp? Would you have had me refuse and stay forever on the Long Path? I am only a man, my lady. I do the best I can. Sometimes it is not enough, I know. But I can do no more."

Eirne rises to her feet. "The celebration is over. I no longer have the heart for it. I bid you all good night." And in the space of a breath, she is gone.

I expected something of the kind, but still it feels like a blow. For a few moments I close my eyes, wishing I were anywhere but here. Feeling more alone than ever before. Then a tiny voice speaks.

"You could play us a tune."

And another says, "You could play a jig. We could dance."

A third voice speaks. It is Nightshade's. Nightshade, the queen's sage, closer to Eirne than anyone. "Will you play a song, bard? We could sing."

"I will fetch your harp," Rowan offers. He heads off without waiting for a response.

For a little, I am dumbfounded. Is this a revolt? Didn't they see how furious Eirne was? She is the queen. She gives the orders. She makes the ultimate choices. In her eyes, I have erred. And I have challenged her. But her folk? Surely not. "The queen would be displeased," I say.

"The queen is sad," says Moon-Fleet. "Your singing gives her heart. We must try to sing with the same heart, with the same healing strength."

"With the same fun," pipes up a little one.

"That, too," says Nightshade in her hooting, musical voice. "In dark times, in times of doubt, it is hard to make room for fun. But fun unites us. It makes us one clan, one tribe, one family."

And so, when Rowan brings the harp, I set it on my knee and play. I play jigs and reels and capers for dancing. I play old tunes and new, and Eirne's folk clap and stamp and whistle along. I play songs, and although I cannot sing them—I have tested this, and all that comes out is a tiny, wavering thread of sound—I am surrounded by voices high as a soaring lark and low as an ocean cavern, voices sweet as the nightingale's and rough as the warty toad's, voices that sound from the highest branches of the trees and voices that peep out from between the roots. They sing of a sailor on a lonely voyage, who encounters wondrous creatures along the way. They sing of the woman who lifts her skirts to reveal she is not quite what she seems to be. They even sing "The Farewell," as I pluck the harp strings and feel the ache of loss in my throat, and in my heart, and deep in my spirit. This will be a long, long year. We end with something merry, the song about the animals joining the faery queen for a party in the forest. I sang this on the day I first met Eirne; it was her voice, matching me line for line, couplet for couplet, that drew me into the Otherworld. How different it is tonight. But her folk know every word, and they sing with such smiles on their faces that I cannot feel entirely sad. As we near the end, I glance across the gathering place and see that Eirne has not, after all, retired to her retreat and shut the door behind her. She is here, on the edge of the crowd, under the council oak, with her shawl tight around her shoulders. She's been crying; her eyes are reddened, her cheeks pale in the lamplight. But she's here, watching me. The song draws to a close:

Dance, my little ones, cried the fae,
Tomorrow is Midsummer Day!

I set the harp down. Eirne stays where she is, silent, and none of the others goes to speak to her. I wonder if they cannot see her. One by one Eirne's folk come up to thank me, to pat my knee, to touch my cheek, to wish me a good night's sleep. The smallest ones, excited by the music, are still twirling and bouncing as they bid me farewell until tomorrow. I thank them in my turn; for forgiving me, for welcoming me home, for singing in my place so we can all enjoy our music and the good fellowship it brings. Though I do not say all this. There is no need. They understand.

"Good night, Brocc," says True. "I owe you a great debt. I hope I can one day repay it."

"You are my friend, True. My brother. There is no need to repay."

"Sweet dreams, my friend," says Rowan. "You have been on quite a journey. Tomorrow we'll talk about other matters: the patrols, the Crow Folk, the . . ." He does not quite look at Eirne. He, at least, knows she is there. "You'll be wanting to make plans. Work out strategies."

"We must do that, yes." All my mind can take in right now is my wife, standing all alone in the shadows. Waiting to bid me leave this place forever, since I am no longer of use to her and her clan? Waiting to curse and weep and rail at foolish humankind, even though she is as much human as I am? Why is she here? "In the morning. Good night, my friend."

When they are all gone, Eirne moves. I stand like a scarecrow, still and silent, until she is right in front of me. Tears glint in her lovely eyes; I smell the sweet scent of her and do not know what to say.

Then Eirne puts her arms around me, and lays her head

against my breast, and says, "I'm sorry. Dear one, I'm so sorry. Come. You need sleep." And when she takes my hand and draws me after her, it is not toward the little hut where I work by day and sometimes sleep by night, but to her own retreat. So easily, it seems I am forgiven.

33

DAU

T hat was quite a test: to sit at table with my family and the
guests, then stay through an evening of music and dancing, unable to see a thing. If I'd had Liobhan next to me, at least
she would have made sure I knew what was going on—indeed,
I can just imagine what kind of commentary she would have
provided, and it would likely have got both of us in trouble.
Corb couldn't help much; he was standing right behind me, but
as a body servant he could only make sure I knew what I was
eating, where my goblet was, and when it was time to stand up
and move.

I had Master Naithí's wife on one side and a woman from
Lord Ross's party on the other. Neither had much conversation; I welcomed their silence. The prior, Father Eláir, had been
invited and sat near me. He passed the salt on request and
spoke to me courteously about the progress of the injured men
I'd seen in the infirmary. Further along the table I heard the
voices of Seanan and a man I took to be Lord Ross. I did not
hear my father speak at all.

Master Beanón the lawman greeted me and asked after my
health, and I told him I was still as blind as ever, but otherwise
well. Master Naithí did not speak of my condition; instead he
commented that he'd never enjoyed the pipes much but that

this fellow played them remarkably sweetly. I said I agreed on both counts. I did not say I wished Liobhan could be out there playing her whistle. That is the sweetest sound a man could imagine, save perhaps for her brother's singing.

Folk got up and danced. I remained at the table. I was not alone there, thank the gods—I would have cut a pathetic figure indeed before my father's guests. My father did not rise to dance, and neither did Lord Ross or Beanón, though Corb, whispering in my ear, told me Naithí and his wife were joining in, and so were Seanan and Sárnait. Several men in turn had approached Liobhan, where she sat among the serving folk and men-at-arms, but she was not dancing. My reaction to this information troubled me. I was pleased, not because my comrade was doing exactly what she'd promised to do, but because . . . because if she danced, I wanted her to dance with me. If she'd got up and started enjoying herself with any of those fellows, I'd have been hurt. I'd have been jealous.

We found a young serving boy to keep the dog company in our quarters during that supper. Not much of a guard, but at the very least a deterrent. We gave him two coppers for his trouble and he was well pleased. Later, the dog slept on my bed, curled up warm in the crook of my knees. I told Liobhan the little one had no name. But there is a name in my mind, of course. How can I think of this precious, fragile new friend as anything else? Her name is Hope.

It is morning. I go to the stables with Cormac, walking without my stick. Liobhan's wise advice is in my mind: *Don't push him, negotiate with him. Explain calmly.* But I can't help remembering what she told me later, when the dancing was over and we were back in our quarters. Seanan dancing with Sárnait, he the picture of a well-mannered young nobleman smiling down at his sweetheart, she with eyes full of admiration as she gazed up at him. They joined in almost every dance. What Liobhan observed has made me edgy, nervous, even though Cormac is my friend, one of the few from whom I always had both respect and kindness. If Liobhan wants an example of a good chieftain of the future, it's not me, it's Cormac of Fairwood.

The mare is indeed a fine animal, and since both Cormac and I have always loved horses, that's what we talk about. He doesn't ask why the dog is not with me. After some time we go out to the fields and walk. In the open it will be easy for him to see if anyone comes too close.

And I tell him. I make myself stay calm. I take time. I have made a list in my mind, from one to twenty, of the things that happened, the things my brothers did to me. I speak of the times I told the truth and was not believed. I speak of the times I was blamed for something they did, and how my father always believed Seanan before me. I mention that although Ruarc was a secondary player in those cruel games, when we were called to account he always supported Seanan.

Cormac listens in silence to the whole story. I reach the end without shedding tears. Indeed, I feel almost as if I am telling another man's tale.

"God's mercy," Cormac breathes. "Why didn't you say anything at the time? We'd have helped you. We'd have believed you. All those years . . ."

Now I could weep. But I will not. "Thank you," I say, and put my hands over my face.

"I wondered, sometimes. I wanted to ask you if anything was wrong. If your brothers were being cruel to you. But we were young . . . . A boy of eleven or twelve does not accuse a chieftain of concealing such terrible things. Or even the son of a chieftain. Can't you do something now, Dau? Can't you see your brother brought to justice?"

"He is an accomplished liar," I say. "Even as a boy he had that skill. Our father will always believe Seanan's word first."

"And Ruarc? A man in a holy order?"

"If you had asked me a year ago, I would have said he will be Seanan's accomplice until the day he dies. Now I'm not sure. But I can't trust him. If called upon to speak out, I doubt he would do so. Besides, he is away at present."

There's a long silence. We reach the end of the field and turn back.

"I understand why you've told me," Cormac says. "I think you've saved my sister from disaster, though I imagine she won't see it that way. How much do I tell my father? And how much, in turn, does he tell Sárnait?" After a moment he adds, "I expect your brother will be less than pleased. Best if he does not learn the true reason for a change of heart on the matter."

"Are you sure your father will refuse the betrothal if you tell him this? Might he, too, dismiss it as a fanciful tale concocted out of bitterness and failure?"

"My father is a good man, just and fair. He'd need to hear only a small part of this to decide the betrothal should at the very least be delayed, and most likely not go ahead at all. I'll suggest we stay another night or two, so as not to cause disquiet. I will ensure Sárnait is accompanied at all times."

A wave of relief passes through me. Gods, someone believes me at last. Believes me without reservations. "Thank you," I say again, and my voice cracks as I speak. I summon what little dignity I can find. "If Lord Ross is able to leave with the issue unresolved, that may be best for all concerned. I would not wish to upset Sárnait. Your father might then send a letter, advising that he has changed his mind. It would be best if his reasons were not those I have provided. Liobhan and I are bound to stay in this household until next spring, and . . . I will not let her become my brother's victim."

"Dau, I am so sorry. Sorry we did not understand at the time, and deeply sorry now. And . . . our gift was perhaps unwelcome? The manner of Snow's demise . . . If you wish, we can take the pup home with us."

My mouth twists. That would be entirely sensible. Except for Sárnait, who would be upset and would ask awkward questions, perhaps before she left this household. I find that after a day, a single day, I do not want to give up Hope. "A kind and wise suggestion," I say. "But I plan to send the small one elsewhere until such time as I can be sure of her safety. A local farm. They will look after her. Your gift was welcome. An expression of true friendship. I am sad that things have fallen out this way."

"I, too, my friend. Now, we are almost back at the barn and there are several men up there, so we should turn our conversation to other matters. I will speak to Father tonight, in confidence. Tomorrow I will keep Sárnait busy. And the next day, all being well, we will ride for home. Thank you, Dau. In time, my sister will understand how much she owes you."

There are two more suppers to endure, two evenings of music and dancing. On the second, Seanan has been seated next to Sárnait at table, not far from me, and I cannot help hearing some of their conversation. It turns my stomach. I want to leap up and shout out my brother's wickedness in front of everyone. It is just as well I am placed between Cormac and Master Beanón. Cormac is discretion itself and does his best to keep me occupied with horse talk. Beanón joins in once or twice, but seems otherwise content to listen. I suspect he is as much an observer as Liobhan is. The man is sharp, acute, as a lawman should be. I wonder if I may have an opportunity to ask him about my father. If anyone has been in a position to observe changes, failing health, fading memory, then surely

Beanón has. But how I could broach such an awkward topic, I cannot think.

I retire early. Thus far there has been nothing to indicate Cormac has spoken to his father. Sárnait, at least, did not know of any change to their plans; that much was plain when she spoke to Seanan of a ride tomorrow, perhaps as far as the forest edge. I can only hope Cormac's faith in his father's good judgment is justified.

Then it is morning again, and I learn that the plans have indeed changed. Lord Ross has an urgent need to return home; his entire party will be leaving as soon as their horses can be made ready. Corb brings this news with our breakfast.

I would like to bid Cormac farewell, but I know we should stay out of the way until they are gone. We take our time over the meal. Then Corb and I go to the bathhouse and enjoy a good wash. When we return, Liobhan takes the dog for a walk, promising to be cautious. I don't imagine either Seanan or my father suspects we had anything to do with the early departure of their guests, unless both Cormac and Lord Ross have been too honest about the reason for it. Even so, I don't want Liobhan or Hope to cross Seanan's path.

Corb tidies up the chamber, which doesn't take long. A serving-woman comes to the door to take away our tray. Another servant brings a pile of clean garments and removes others to be laundered. For now, I remain a welcome son of the house, and such services are considered appropriate to my station.

"Dau?" Corb is putting the clothing away in a storage chest. "Shouldn't Liobhan be back by now?"

He's right. My stomach tightens. The dog needs only a short walk, just sufficient to stretch her legs, sniff about a little, and do her business. Something's happened. Dark images flood my thoughts, pictures of where Seanan might have put her: down a bottomless hole; perched on a tiny patch of dry land surrounded by sucking bog; up a tall tree on a fragile branch. I order myself not to be a fool. Yes, my brothers did all those things to me, and worse. But Liobhan is not a terrified child, she is a warrior, brave, strong, resilient. More than a match for Seanan. "She's probably talking to the musicians," I say. "Or up in the herb garden collecting ingredients for a brew." But she wouldn't be. Not when she has the dog with her. Not when she said she'd come straight back.

"Should I go and look for her?"

Corb has guessed my thoughts. Is my face so open? "Thank you, Corb. Be discreet, please. Don't ask people, just have a look about. Don't go up to the stables."

He goes and I wait. The longer I wait, the deeper the chill moves into my heart. I tell myself this can't be anything serious. It's too soon for Seanan to guess the real reason Lord Ross's party is leaving early. They may not even be gone yet; they could still be making their farewells. But time moves on and neither Corb nor Liobhan reappears. I pace across the chamber and back, counting my steps, a pointless occupation, but better than tearing my hair out, and far wiser than rushing out to find them, since I have no guide. Curse being blind! Curse being useless! Where is she?

At last the door opens. My heart leaps. I turn, though I cannot see who it is.

A patter of little feet on the floor. The dog, at least, is safe. I crouch to feel her warm body, the rasp of her tongue. "Liobhan?" I ask.

"I couldn't find her."

It's Corb. I rise slowly to my feet, waiting.

"The dog was in the garden by herself, not far from here. Her leash was tangled in a bush; I had to set her free. There was no sign of Liobhan. I had a good look, Dau. Maybe the dog ran away from her and she's out searching. But . . ."

"But she'd have come to tell us by now. She'd have asked you to help search." My heart feels like winter. "Did you see anyone? Seanan or any of his men?"

"Only folk doing their work. This one can't have been there long or someone would have found her. She was frightened. Shivering."

I'm up and pacing again, until Corb says, "Sit down a moment, Dau. You're upsetting the dog. This could be anything. She may have needed to go to the privy. She may have been called to help someone with a task."

"She wouldn't have left the dog on her own." I sit, despite the urge to keep moving. I know staying calm is best. Be a Swan Island warrior. Make a plan. Take control. But that is not so easy. Inside me there is a panicking child. Alongside him, a blind man who wants to find Seanan right now and confront him. I know he's done something. I just know it.

"We should ask Iarla," Corb says. "Tell him she went out with the dog and didn't come back, say we're concerned. I'll do it if you want." The voice of common sense.

"We'll both go," I tell him. There's no way I'm waiting on my own again. "Only . . ."

"The dog will be all right in here," says Corb. "With luck we'll find Liobhan quickly. And if we don't, Iarla will know what to do."

Hah! He might know, but he won't be able to act. Not if this is Seanan's doing. I count silently up to five. "Good idea, Corb," I say. "I don't suppose we'll be long." I wish I could believe my own lie.

34

LIOBHAN

First thing is the smell. A stench so vile I want to vomit. Next thing is the dark. The utter dark. Where in the name of all hells am I? Third thing is the pain. Stabbing pain in my head and neck, aching wrists and shoulders, cramps in my legs . . . I can't move. What in Morrigan's name is this? I try to shout for help. But I can't shout. I can hardly breathe. I'm lying on something hard. There's a gag over my mouth, cloth stuffed between my teeth, and I can't get so much as a squeak out.

We're trained for this sort of thing. We practice it on Swan Island, though if they tried out this particular combination on any of us there'd be protests afterward. I know what to do. Focus. Concentrate my thoughts. Read the situation. Identify the challenges, put them in order of priority. Find solutions. But I can't stop shivering, from cold, from shock, who knows? I don't want to breathe through my nose, the stink is disgusting, like rotting fish, like dead things, but I have no choice. Whoever put this gag on did a thorough job.

Focus. Right. What happened? Judging by the splitting headache, someone's knocked me out. Didn't I fight back? Did I just let that happen? What was I doing? I was . . . I was walking the dog. Shit! What happened to the dog? If she's been hurt Dau will never forgive me.

Something screams. My heart thuds in shock. Is this Snow all over again? No; even a dog in its death throes couldn't make a noise like that, a crazy, ear-splitting screech of agony and terror. It was a bird. It was . . . Oh, gods. That stink, the scream, the wild scrabbling I hear now, claws against wire, something desperate to get out, something desperate to fly away . . . Can it be Crow Folk? They've been near Oakhill, too, attacking farm stock. That's what the men-at-arms said, and that Seanan's traps helped keep them away.

This makes no sense. I'm a prisoner, trussed up in the dark. The birds are close. I can feel the air move as they flail around. How many, I can't judge. They're scared, perhaps hurt. But not attacking me. They must be prisoners, too. Why?

I've got to get up. My wrists are tied behind my back. My ankles are hobbled. But I can do this. I roll, tighten my stomach, force myself to my knees. I wobble and fall sideways into the wall, and the screaming breaks out again, right in my ear. It's not a solid wall, only a flimsy barrier of twisted wire. I flinch away as something stabs between the strands. I've seen what kind of damage those beaks can do.

My eyes are getting used to the dark. At the far end of this place there are cracks of light, and I guess it's still day outside. Not underground, then. Am I still within the walls of Lord Scannal's domain? My bladder is not overfull; maybe I haven't been here so very long.

There's another smell. Something like an apothecary's remedy, a potion . . . It's familiar . . . Was there something my mother used that smelled like that? Something she kept on a very high shelf in a box with two locks on it? Morrigan's curse! I've been dosed to keep me quiet! Someone's been playing tricks. What in the name of all hells are they planning?

Assess strengths and weaknesses. I'm hurt, bruised, possibly

I've been fed a substance that will hinder my ability to help myself. I'm tied and gagged; I can't call for help. I don't know where I am. Against that I set the fact that I'm strong, I'm fit, I believe I'm still in my right mind. The bonds are tight, but they're rope, not wire. If there's time, I can work myself free using that mesh barrier. That's if the prisoners on the other side don't peck me to pieces while I'm doing it. I was lucky to recover so well after we fought them off the other time. Both Dau and I had injuries, but they healed. Other folk weren't so fortunate.

No point in worrying about the herbal smell and exactly what it is. No point in trying to guess what in the name of the gods is going on. Seanan must be behind it, though; who else? I struggle to my feet. My head reels. I steady myself. I can't waste time. There must be some plan here, or why take such pains to tie me up? That means my captors will come back. I've got to get out, and fast.

There's a rough section on the wire mesh. I stand with my back against it and rub the wrist bonds up and down. Seems the birds can't get to me here; they flap and squawk and flail around not far away, but nothing touches me. I remember Brocc singing to the Crow Folk, chanting a terrible wordless song that held them at bay. It was full of dark power, and it both saved our lives and scared me witless. I can't do that. Brocc's the one with fey blood. I'm all human. But my mother is a wise-woman. In those squawks and screams I don't hear an enemy putting up a challenge. I hear something driven mad by fear.

I can't sing. I can't form words. With the gag in my mouth I can't even manage a la-la-la. But I can produce a sort of stran-gled hum. I make the tune as soothing as a desperate woman can, the fraught kind of lullaby a person might sing when they're very short of sleep and the baby won't stop crying. Dau would laugh if he could hear me. Only he wouldn't. If he knew about this he'd be beside himself with fury. And if this really is Seanan's doing, that's not the way to deal with it. What's needed is cold calm. The cleverest, most well-calculated of traps. A merciless accounting, truth laid bare for all to hear. I swear by everything I hold dear, I'll see that happen before I leave this place. I'll make it happen if I die in the attempt.

35

DAU

We can't find her. Time's passing. Iarla seems to understand my urgency, but it's plain the household is not going to be turned upside down for a bond servant who—most people will think—has simply seized an opportunity to walk out the gate and leave. Iarla doesn't say this in so many words, but I get the drift, and it's a fair assessment. Unless you know Liobhan. Running away is not in her nature.

I feel the full weight of my blindness. I feel it even more strongly than in those feverish days after it first happened. I'm still a chieftain's son. They haven't thrown me out of the house yet. I could insist on a search, I could rally the good people of my father's household—despite my brother's influence, there are many—I could order the men-at-arms to look in every nook and cranny, every underground place, every hidden corner until she's found. At least, I could do that until someone with higher authority—my brothers, my father—stepped in to stop me. But a blind man cannot take control. Even if I could, that is not the way to deal with Seanan. Strategy. That's what I need. My eyes may be useless, but my mind works perfectly well. I must be calm. Make a plan. One step at a time. And remember that any member of the household who is seen to assist me might become a target for my brother.

Corb and I retreat to our quarters to talk in private. The dog is frantic with excitement at our return. We've left her alone far too long—the sun is nearly at its midpoint, and Lord Ross's party is long gone. I should have let Cormac take her back. That was a selfish decision and now it's an inconvenient one.

"Change of plan," I tell Corb. "I want you to take her to the farm today, now. Tell the gate guards the story about visiting your family. If you're challenged about the dog, tell them the truth—that I can't look after her and I've asked you to take her. You'll need to stay overnight; it's too late now for you to get back before dark." I could tell him not to come back at all. On the farm, he'd be further from Seanan's reach. Corb is a fine, unselfish young man. He doesn't deserve to be put in danger because of me and my wretched family. But I need him. I need him to be my eyes and help me get around. And I need him because he knows what this is all about; he understands the danger and the difficulties. He's the young brother I never had. The problem is, Seanan must have seen how much I rely on Corb. He's probably observed the bond between us. Which means I've given my brother three weapons to use against me: Liobhan, Hope, and Corb. "And be careful. Really careful."

"But what about you? Who will help you while I'm gone?"

"Get packed up now. You'll need some supplies from the kitchen, and don't forget something for the dog. While you're fetching those, I'll speak to Iarla again. I'll tell him where you're going and ask for a replacement. Now that Lord Ross's party is gone, with luck someone can be spared."

There's a silence. Then Corb says, "Are you sure? That this is the best thing to do, I mean?"

"I'm not sure of anything." Except that Liobhan's gone, and I'm not letting Seanan get his hands on Corb and the little one as well. With them away safely, I can stop being so careful. Gods, if only I could see! "But I do want you to go."

"I'll head back here first thing tomorrow," Corb says. "I won't need to take much. Might carry a pack of some sort, big enough for the pup to ride in. A long walk for her. Dau?"

"What?"

"Ask Mongan if one of the stable hands can stay with you until I get back. One of the stronger lads. They know Liobhan. They know all of us. They'll keep their mouths shut if you ask them. And they'll be more use to you than some boy fresh out of the kitchen."

That could be a description of Corb himself, when he took on the thankless task of being my keeper. I don't remind him of that. Nobody could have learned the job better or proven so stalwart. Except Liobhan, of course; but she already had all the skills she needed, and more besides. Gods, where is she? How can Seanan have made her disappear so completely? And so quickly? What am I missing?

While Corb gets his supplies, I stand at the kitchen entrance with the dog on her leash, talking to Iarla yet again. I explain Corb's errand. When Iarla offers to find me a replacement, I tell him I will speak to Mongan, since I will be more comfortable with a familiar person as an assistant. Iarla says he has continued to make inquiries about Liobhan, but to no avail. Someone spotted her in the garden with the dog, much earlier, but that was all. And someone suggested she might have left with the musicians, who were paid off and dismissed once Lord Ross's party rode out.

"Was she seen with them? After she went out with the dog?"

"Not seen, Master Dau. But I'm told your friend loves music and has a fine voice. It was thought she might have . . . grasped an opportunity."

"It was thought? By whom?" I can't help sounding fierce.

"One of the men-at-arms who had heard her singing. He said only that she was something of a musician. It was Master Seanan who suggested she might have joined them."

"And broken the terms of her debt bondage."

"That would be the implication. You did say you wished to hear any information that came my way."

"She wouldn't simply leave, Iarla. She wouldn't break the terms." *She wouldn't leave me behind.* "I've seen nothing of Master Seanan today. When did he make that remark? When did he hear that Liobhan was missing?"

"He came in briefly after Lord Ross had left. I'm not sure where he is now."

"Thank you, Iarla. I'm sorry if I was less than courteous. I am very concerned. Deeply concerned. I know Liobhan would not walk away with no explanation. Now I'd best see Corb on his way." I hesitate, then add, "It would be appreciated if you did not mention to others that Corb will be absent until tomorrow. Or the nature of his errand. I hope you understand."

"Of course, Master Dau."

At the stables, they've all heard that Liobhan is missing. The fellows are quick to offer sympathy and suggestions, but all the places they can think of have already been searched, including the hut down by the cesspool. Stable master Mongan takes charge. He dispatches Fionn to walk Corb down to the gates and see him safely through. I bid Corb farewell and he leaves, carrying the dog. Then Mongan asks for a volunteer to be my helper, and it seems quite a few of the fellows would be ready to do it, but Torcan gets the job.

"Might be overnight as well," I tell him as we walk to the open area where Liobhan and I used to perform our exercise routine. "And I'm sometimes wakeful." I'm not sure if Liobhan has left sufficient materials to make up the sleeping draft. Nor am I sure exactly how it's prepared—Corb is the one who steps in if required. Not that I want to take it tonight. I need to stay alert. But another idea comes into my mind. We did walk to the herb garden this morning, just to see if Liobhan was there or in the stillroom. The place was quiet; there was no sign of her. But I should go back there. I should speak to the monks. They might know something. Liobhan's on good terms with the ones who use the stillroom. I can't explain all that to Torcan. It's best if he learns only as much as he needs to.

"No sign of her around here," he says now. "Where's next?"

"The infirmary."

"Don't walk so fast, Dau. You'll strain that ankle."

The ankle seems of no importance. "There's no time to be careful," I snap.

"Rush things and you won't be able to go on. You know that. Common sense."

I bite back a snarling response. Like it or not I need a keeper, and making his life miserable won't help me find Liobhan. And if Torcan speaks to me as if I'm a fellow worker and not a son of the house, there's a reason for that. The same reason he volunteered to help. He's seen me at my useless, defeated worst. He's seen me try to pull myself back up. And he knows Liobhan. I slow my pace. I wish I could as easily control the dark visions in my mind.

As we enter the garden we hear raised voices. It seems Brother Íobhar has returned to Oakhill. The other voice is Seanan's. They're arguing about a book and writing in it, and something about the devil. I hear the word *father.* I assume it is our worldly father they mean and not the one looking down from heaven and making not the least effort to be helpful.

Torcan stops walking and I am obliged to do the same.

"They're in the stillroom," my companion murmurs.

This is not the time to be a warrior and charge in armed

with accusations for which I have no more evidence than my sound instincts provide. But I am not blessed with an abundance of time and I do want to speak to Ruarc.

"Wait," I say quietly.

The voices, which were loud—surely too loud for such a conversation—become quieter. But I have good ears.

"Do not think to accuse me, *brother*," says Seanan, using a particular tone I had thought reserved for myself. It sets cold fingers around my heart. "I am not subject to the rules of your little establishment, and even if I were, I have broken none."

"If your man breaks them on your behalf, you have as good as done so." Brother Íobhar's voice is surprisingly calm. But I am expert in these matters, and I can hear the uneven note in it. Man of authority though he has become, he's fighting fear. "How long has this been going on, Seanan? Since the very day we moved our sick and injured brethren here?"

"I have no intention whatever of justifying my decisions to you," says Seanan. "Talk to Ardgan if you must. Perhaps he can cast light on this. You'll need to be quick. I believe he is quitting my service in the very near future. It is possible he may already be gone. Unfortunate, but there you are."

A silence. How convenient it must be for Seanan to make people disappear when they are in danger of betraying his secrets. I have no idea what this is about, but one thing is clear: at long last our middle brother is standing up to Seanan, and if he's not careful there will be a terrible price to pay.

"Think hard before you act, Brother Íobhar," says Seanan. The way he speaks this name is an insult. "Your tenancy of these quarters is dependent on my father's generosity. And you have nowhere else to go."

"That, surely, would not be decided between you and me, Seanan, but between Father and our prior, Father Eláir." Brother Íobhar is shocked; that's plain in his voice.

"We'll go in now," I say to Torcan.

"Sure?"

"Yes. No need for you to speak unless you're asked a direct question, and play dumb if you can, especially where Liobhan is concerned."

As we approach the open doorway to the stillroom, Torcan murmurs, "Master Seanan," and then comes my brother's voice.

"Ah. Brothers everywhere. I cannot escape them. A new assistant, Dau? But, of course, your girl has gone missing. Absconded. Relinquished her delightful duties. Where is your boy?"

I count to five. "One person cannot carry out those duties night and day. I requested additional assistance. Torcan is helping me for now. The arrangement has been approved by the appropriate members of your household."

Seanan makes no comment. I wish I could see his face. "Since you already know Liobhan is missing," I say, working on a calm tone, "maybe you can tell me whether any of your men saw her this morning. She made no mention of a lengthy absence. We've performed an extensive search and failed to find any trace. You speak as if she ran away, left this household by choice. If that were really the case, would you not take some steps to pursue her and bring her back? I do not detect any concern in your manner, brother."

"I believe someone saw the girl speaking to those players this morning, the ones who were hired for entertainment. There was some talk that she might have gone off with them. You want me to send a party of men-at-arms to track your woman down? Are you so attached to the creature?"

I breathe. Beside me, Torcan is a strong presence, though he's not saying a word. "I imagined you would consider the issue of debt bondage important," I say. "For me, the concern is that I know quite well Liobhan would not act in that way. If she makes a promise, she keeps it. I believe she may have come to some harm, Seanan. And as you seem to be acting as head of the household in our father's place, I'm asking you to do something about it. Time is passing. If anyone has harmed her, they will be answerable to me." I draw breath again. "Do not refer to Liobhan as a creature. Whatever her status in your household, she is deserving of respect. Who was it saw her speaking with the musicians?"

Seanan's tone changes again. I know he is smiling. I remember that smile all too well. It's the look of a predator that enjoys toying with the victim, drawing things out as long as possible. "I was right, then," he says. "You and this girl are closer than you admit. More than master and servant. More than friends. She's wormed her way into your confidences and into your affections. Influenced every foolish decision, no doubt. You're better off without her, Dau. Dear God, this is the person who blinded you! And you allow her to share your living quarters and make up your sleeping drafts."

Before I can find a response, I hear the voice of Brother Íobhar. He must be standing behind Seanan. "Look more closely at your own folk before you accuse Dau's," he says. "If anyone is tampering with sleeping drafts, it's not this young woman. Brother Petrán keeps a close eye on the book; I have his word that she is scrupulous in recording everything she uses."

"Ah," says Seanan, quick as a flash, "so she *is* under investigation."

"Everyone is under investigation. Every person we know to make use of our resources. Every person who might send another to fetch a particular substance from our supplies."

"A person might steal," Seanan suggests. "Anyone with access to your premises might help himself. Or herself. A little slipped into a sleeve or a pouch. Easy, I should imagine. Especially for someone expertly trained in such tricks."

"This is nonsense," I say. We're wasting time; we should be

looking for Liobhan, now, quickly. What is this talk of sleeping drafts anyway? Are my brothers referring to my father's strange behavior, his old man's state of mind? Can Ruarc be implying that Seanan has a hand in that? I feel a new chill as I realize how easy that is to believe. Does Ruarc realize the danger of speaking out on such a matter? He was never so brave before. "If you will not help with the search for Liobhan, at least give me what information you have. Who saw her speaking to the musicians, and when?"

"How would I know?" I imagine Seanan making a comical face, shrugging his shoulders, spreading his hands wide. "It's of no consequence to me."

"Not even when she still has the best part of her period of debt bondage to serve? Not even when she has the expertise to look after me at no cost to the household? Not even when you pride yourself on your ability to act as chieftain, with the control and balance and wisdom such a position requires?"

"Little brother. If she's gone, she's gone. Good riddance, I say. She was a meddlesome creature. No wonder she got herself in trouble. It was a mistake to allow her the duties of nurse, and a graver mistake to let her into the house. She couldn't keep her nose out of other people's business, could she? This does not rest on me, Dau, but squarely on your shoulders. If you cannot keep your own people under control, it is no wonder these things happen. But then, you are hardly cut out for a position of any authority, are you? Now stop plaguing me with your requests for help and go back to your quarters. You're a sick man and should rest. Ideally somewhere we don't need to see you. Take him back!" This barked command must be addressed to Torcan, who tenses by my side but does not speak. I hold my own silence with difficulty. I am in danger of saying something I will regret. I will not give this vile specimen of mankind a single word more to use in his attacks. Not one word.

"Brother Íobhar, I'll bid you farewell for now," I say, hoping he is still there. "I wish you and your brethren well in your search for truth. We'll go now, Torcan."

I stay strong as we walk back to the house, as we encounter Iarla in the hallway to be told there is no further news, as we make our way to the quarters Torcan will be sharing with me at least until Corb comes back. Even when we are inside with the door safely shut behind us, and nobody else can see or hear, I do not weep. I do not curse. I simply put my hands over my face and stand there while my head fills and fills with visions of horror, of suffering, of dark and loneliness and pain and despair. I do not know if it is myself as a boy enduring this, or Liobhan somewhere right now, or Corb, or Snow, or little Hope, or even the young Ruarc years ago, perhaps too terrified to speak up, perhaps held so fast by Seanan's threats that he was compelled into the role of assistant torturer, silent, complicit, forced into the same pattern of evil. Gods, was my father as blind then as I am now, that he did not see it? And did Ruarc really just accuse Seanan of doctoring our father's sleeping draft? Meddling. Seanan accused Liobhan of meddling. Was she asking awkward questions in the stillroom? Or was Seanan talking about something else—the sudden departure of the distinguished visitors? He can hardly suspect Liobhan of a part in that. It's too soon, and besides, I was the one who spoke to Cormac. Did someone see us out in the field talking? See us and report back faithfully to Master Seanan?

"Dau?" Torcan sounds anxious. "You all right?"

"Mm." I lower my hands and take a deep breath. "Just thinking hard. I'm sorry you had to witness that unsavory scene." I start to shiver; I can't make myself stop. Liobhan. She's here somewhere, locked up, hidden, trapped. Or she's been taken away. And I can't do a thing to help her.

"You should sit down. I'll light the fire, then I'll fetch you some food and drink."

"I don't want anything." After a moment I say, "But you should eat. They'll give you a tray in the kitchen. Since I've been ordered to keep out of sight, I will. For now at least." If I could fly, if I could transport myself to that place where Brocc lives now, if this were a story of wonder and magic, I would speak to the folk of the Otherworld. I would beg to have my sight back. I would set aside my last scrap of pride; I would promise everything that is in my power to give. Then I would find Liobhan and I would tell her . . . Oh, foolish wayward thoughts. Thoughts that belong only in a song. A song in which the handsome blind prince gets a choice: he can have his sight back or he can win the release of the woman he loves. That is to say, the release of his dear, true friend. Which does he choose? If Brocc is writing the song, the man does not hesitate to save his friend. If Liobhan is writing it, the ending is left open, for the audience to argue about when the performance is over. Me? I am no poet. I am no hero. I'm here in the dark and I don't know what to do.

36

LIOBHAN

The wrist bonds are starting to give when I hear someone coming. They're moving furtively. I guess that means it's not a rescue party. I freeze with my wrists against the wire and my heart thudding so hard I wonder if they might hear it. One man murmurs to another; the second responds. Curse it! I should have worked harder, got the poxy bonds undone, been ready to strike as soon as they came within reach. But I'm as helpless as when I first came to. With the gag on I can't even spit.

A creak down the other end. Light spills in. The captive birds start screaming, flapping, scratching with their claws. It's full day. Over my shoulder I can catch a glimpse of open ground beyond the door. Trees. Then the door closes and it's dark again.

"Open the shutters," someone says. I'd know that voice anywhere.

The other fellow, the one who isn't Seanan, obeys, and there's light again, but not so much. The window is heavily barred. There'll be no getting out that way for woman or bird. I breathe carefully, harnessing what strength I have, though my options are severely limited. Making the impossible happen is all very well, but the circumstances weigh somewhat heavily against me right now.

I can't move much. I can't speak. But right now I can see, so

I take a good look at the place while I can. It's small. Door at one end, two shuttered windows at the side, a cold hearth. Along the other side, cages. In the cages, birds. Or more precisely, Crow Folk. I'm in a tiny space between the last cage and the back wall. While the creatures are flapping about, the men can't tell that I'm standing up. There's a bench at the far end, near the door, and shelves with jars on them, and tools in a rack. Knives and other things. A roll of wire. The man who isn't Seanan is big and broad. I think it's Ultán, whom I've seen with Seanan before, but I can't be sure because he has a mask on. It's made of leather and has holes for eyes, nose, and mouth. A torturer's mask. An executioner's mask.

Seanan sees me. Strolls at a leisurely pace past the cages of frenzied birds, stops two paces away, and looks me up and down. "On your feet, then?" His tone is pleasant, almost friendly. "Your disappearance caused my little brother a good deal of concern. Seems he has a fondness for you, not entirely appropriate considering your situation. Sore head?"

I wouldn't bother answering even if I could speak. I hope my eyes convey my loathing.

"We were able to put his fears to rest. Seems you were coaxed away to join the traveling musicians as they moved on. Took the opportunity to quit your debt bondage, to set aside the period of service you owe us and run for the hills, so to speak. They say you're a singer. Full of surprises, aren't you? Turn around!" Suddenly he's rapping out orders. "Why are you standing there? Show me your hands!"

I stay where I am, holding his gaze with my own. He moves, lightning quick, his fist connecting hard with my jaw. My head crashes into the wire, setting the birds flapping wildly again. I almost fall; my ankles are still bound together.

"Ah. Trying to break free, were we? But lacking in strength, or you'd surely be out and away by now. Ultán! Bring the rope."

This time they tie me with my back against the wire. For a reason I can't fathom, but which I'm glad of, they change the tight ankle bindings to more of a hobble arrangement. I don't interpret this as an act of mercy; Seanan wouldn't understand the term. Most likely it's so they can move me without needing to carry me. Where? And why? Would Dau really believe I'd run off with the musicians and leave him behind?

The two men light a fire on the hearth, then clank around with metal objects, talking to each other in murmurs. I do not like the way this is shaping up. I don't like it at all. I try to summon the wisdom of Archu. I imagine him in my situation. He'd have a solution, I'm sure of it. Maybe all he'd say is, *Be ready for your opportunity. Don't die because of a moment's inattention.*

I can't see them now, but I hear everything. They open a door further along the cage and drag a creature out. They must be wearing gauntlets or their hands would be pecked raw. Ah. Maybe that mask is not so much a disguise as a protection. Maybe Seanan's not doing any of his own dirty work. Apart from giving himself the satisfaction of hitting me, that is. Or maybe the big man does the catching and holding, and Master Seanan does the . . . whatever comes next. Morrigan save me. First the Crow Folk and then me. That's the plan. I will not wet myself. I will not make a sound. Not even the small sound a person might make through a tight gag if she was scared out of her wits. I will not shiver. I will show not the least sign of fear. I'll snatch that opportunity. When it comes, I'll be ready.

The bird fights. It shrieks. The sounds curdle my blood. Ultán curses a few times, but I don't hear Seanan speak now. I imagine his face, cold and focused, as he wields the instruments of torture with precision. I consider what I saw through that door, the direction of the light, the dimensions of this chamber, which may be the entire building. I think about the nature of what Seanan has here and why he might want to separate this establishment somewhat from the place where, in all but name, he is chieftain. I wonder what Sárnait would think if she could see this and am glad she does not need to. I'm almost sure I know where I am.

At one point, as I stand with my arms already aching and my heart thumping, listening as the sounds go on and on, there's a sort of lull, then a different sound. A heavy knock, as of an iron poker against boards. A brief muttered conversation between the men. Then the vile stench that is part of this place, the stink of rotting fish, the odor of an herb I can't quite name and others I know all too well, gains another component—the smell of burning flesh. The creature's scream is terrible. It wrenches at my gut, it hurts my heart, it fills my eyes with tears. Then, abruptly, it stops. In the sudden quiet I can hear my own breathing. The door to the cage clangs open; there's a thud as something is tossed in, and the door closes again. The other birds are silent.

Seanan's tone is so courteous he might be inviting me to dance. "Now your turn," he says.

37

DAU

I t's night and there's still no news. Torcan asks me if I need my sleeping draft—he knows our routine from the stables—and I tell him there would be no point. Nothing could bring me sleep tonight. My mind brims with waking nightmares. When I've picked at the supper Torcan fetched for us, I tell him to go and sleep on Corb's pallet. There's no need for both of us to keep vigil. He's reluctant but obeys, saying I should wake him if I need him, even if it's just to talk. He's a good man.

I can't keep still. I sit before the fire, I rise and pace around, I lie down on my bed only to get up and pace again. Once or twice I forget where I am and blunder into something, cursing myself. If Torcan's managing to sleep, it's a miracle. Gods! She's out there somewhere, I know it. Out there waiting for someone to find her. Waiting in the dark.

"Lie down awhile, Dau," Torcan says from the antechamber; the door between us is ajar. "You may not sleep, but at least you can rest. Save your strength for tomorrow."

"Another day of useless waiting." We've searched everywhere. We've spoken to anyone likely to be useful. I can't believe the theory that she left with the musicians, even though, to someone who doesn't know us, that sounds plausible. I'm sure the musicians would have liked her to join them; any band would. I can't believe she would go back to Swan Island, only a few moons into her year of debt bondage. Nor would she head for Dalriada and her family home, where she could be easily tracked down. She wouldn't leave without explanation, without good-byes. She simply wouldn't do it.

Torcan has banked up the fire so it will keep us warm into the night. I sit before it again, on the floor with my knees drawn up, and pretend I can see the comforting glow. My whole body is sick with tension, chill with fear, filled with a restless urge for action. But I can't act. It's night. I'm blind. The next step would be a search beyond the walls—in the local village, at St. Padraig's, perhaps out to the nearest farms—and if Seanan has anything to do with it I won't be allowed through that gate, with or without a minder. And even if I am, how likely are we to find her? If someone has taken her they must have done so covertly. Even so, surely at least one member of the household saw something. Sadly, that doesn't mean the person in question will be brave enough to speak up. Not if Seanan's involved.

Perhaps I should ask to see my father in the morning. Confront him with the truth. But he's never believed me before, so why would he do so now? He'd be infuriated that she's gone and all too ready to believe she's absconded. He doesn't know her. He doesn't know me. He hasn't asked to speak to me even once since the day I came here. And even if he did, is he in any fit state to help?

If I find her, if she's all right, I will talk to Master Beanón. I will ask him about Father's state of health and about sleeping drafts. I will ask to speak to Father with Beanón present. Naithí as well. I will . . .

I lie down on the bed again. Beyond the shuttered window I can hear a night bird singing. *Liobhan,* I think. *Be safe. Hold on, wherever you are, dearest friend.* And it comes to me that if ever we needed help from the Otherworld, if ever we needed magic, it is now.

38

LIOBHAN

They're gone. It's over. For now it's over.

I assess the damage as well as I can. Not easy, as they've left me facing the cage with my wrists tied up above my head. My feet are squarely on the floor, and I thank the gods for that bit of good fortune. The bad fortune is that my hands are tied to a wire door, and if I surrender to sleep or faint or lose my balance, the weight of my fall will open that door and release one of the Crow Folk. A cunning arrangement. The creature can't peck out my eyes right now; there's double mesh all down the area where I stand. But once the door's open the thing is free, and it's just waiting, moving along its perch and back again, its eyes never leaving me. Outside, the last light is nearly gone. The window shutters weren't fully closed when Seanan and his henchman left; a lucky oversight. If I can take advantage of that I will. But all's quiet out there save for the sounds of birds heading for their roosting places. Nobody's rushing to the rescue.

Right. Wrists chafed, but not bleeding. Shoulders already aching, and there's the night to get through in this wretched position. Then there's the mark he made on me, a brand, burned onto the flesh of my right arm. Hurt like shit when he did it, but I'm pleased I didn't give him the satisfaction of screaming, even though the gag was off at the time. I didn't make a sound as he pelted me with questions, not the ones I might have expected, but questions about who spoke to Lord Ross, who spoke to Cormac, who spoke to Sárnait. And accusations about how I might have influenced Dau. I didn't say a word. I'll have a fine crop of bruises to show for my silence. Thank the gods for Swan Island. Without the training, I'd never have got through it.

The burn hurts like hellfire. Needs a cool poultice; could be Seanan has the required components for that on his workbench over there, though more likely he doesn't. I'd lay a bet that everything he's collected is for the purpose of hurting, not healing. No prizes for guessing where the missing devil's-foot went or who took it. Not Seanan in person, I bet—he's too clever for anything so obvious. He'll have sent his man to steal it for him.

Worse than the burning was what they did after. Offered me water. Not to put on the burn. To drink. I was so thirsty, my throat on fire, my whole body protesting what they'd done to me. I drank without thinking, from the cup Ultán held out. It wasn't water. It was a concoction of some kind. I spat out what was in my mouth, spraying it everywhere. Seanan hit me. Then he made his underling grab my hair and pull my head back, and he forced my mouth open and poured the rest of the stuff in. Then clapped his hand over my nose and mouth until I swallowed it. I fought, as much as a person can with hands and feet tied. I bit him at least once. But the stuff went down, and now my head is getting fuzzy and my knees are weak and I'll have to use every trick I can think of to stay awake. All night. I have to last all night.

Can't scream. The gag's back on tight. Can't sing to pass the time. Not out loud anyway. But I do know a lot of songs and stories. I can go through them in my mind. Pity my head feels so odd. Gods, I hope I haven't taken devil's-foot. Seanan's no herbalist; if he had expertise in that craft the monks would know about it. I wouldn't trust any remedy that man put together. Why in the name of the gods does he have Crow Folk in here? They're an enemy of humankind, yes, and we know he traps them. But keeping them captive here, hurting them, terrifying them—there's no point in that.

Dau must be frantic. I hope Seanan didn't hurt the dog. That would be enough to break Dau, strong as he is now. At least the dog's not in here, another victim waiting for the slice of the knife, the rough kiss of hot iron. Maybe that burn on my arm is meant to be a brand. A mark of ownership. You think you can own me, Master Seanan? Not in your wildest dreams.

I run through songs in my mind, line by line, verse by verse. The war song with its rallying chorus: *To arms! To arms!* The song about the woman who lifts up her skirt, a ditty composed by my brother Brocc. The one about the fisherman and the seal woman. "The Farewell," with its bittersweet ending. I cry a little as I think my way through the verses. Only I mustn't cry, because my nose gets blocked and with the gag in my mouth I can't breathe, and if I can't breathe I'll faint, and then . . . Wake up, Liobhan, you stupid fool!

I think my way through some of the whistle tunes, imagining different ways of doing the ornamentation. Wondering if I might play "Artagan's Leap" just a little quicker, or whether that would tip exciting over into ridiculous. I hope Dau can look after my things. The skirt made for me by the washerwomen in Breifne, with its brave stripes. The whistles I brought with me.

It's dark now. I can't rub through these bonds on the wire; that might open the door and let the creature out. Wish I had Brocc's uncanny magic. Wish I could somehow let the thing know I'm not like Seanan and his helper. I don't mean it any harm. I'd set it free if I could be sure it wouldn't kill me the moment it left the cage.

I tell myself a story: the one about Davan's encounter with the clurichauns, and how they mended his lame leg out of kindness. That story got Dau thinking about magical cures. The story led me to agree, despite all my misgivings, that I'd go to the Otherworld with him once my debt bondage is over. The way things are right now, I can't see that happening. There's only one possible ending Seanan can have in mind for this unsavory episode, and that most certainly isn't me going back to his father's house and getting quietly on with my life of servitude. For that to happen, Dau would have to agree not to speak up about this. That's not possible. Seanan will use me as a weapon against Dau for as long as he can, then kill me and make my body disappear. What a depth of hatred he must hold for his youngest brother. Hatred that's surely tipped over into madness.

I tell myself a story from ancient times, about a god with a silver hand. I tell myself a tale about cattle raids, about warring chieftains, about kings and queens of old. Somewhere in the middle of it my concentration fails, I sag against my restraints, then jerk upright as the cage door creaks. It's opening—no! I slam my hands against the wire, sending a wave of pain through my burned arm. The bird is lifting its wings to fly out as the door crashes shut. It utters a cry so desperate, so furious, that tears come to my eyes again. Mustn't cry. Must keep breathing. Must stay awake . . . but it's hard. My head feels heavy, my thoughts are wandering, and I'm cold . . . Isn't it nearly summer now? Why is it so cold?

The fire's long ago dwindled to ash. I have neither shawl nor cloak. I'm in my working gown and the right sleeve has been cut to tatters. I must have wet myself at some point; my skirt feels clammy. Can't smell that, though. The stench of this place is so bad, you could throw a bucket of piss over it and it'd make no difference. I hear Dau's voice in my mind. *Only you could make a joke out of the current situation, Liobhan. Where do you find that relentless hope?*

I wish Dau was here. Only I don't, because that would put him right in Seanan's way. I imagine the two of us, Dau and me, walking out of here and, instead of going back to face his brothers and his father and the whole intolerable situation in that establishment, going the other way, along the forest's edge and then in under the cover of the trees to walk along the weaving pathways until we found a portal to Eirne's realm. I think of seeing my brother again. I think of Eirne knowing how to restore Dau's sight and being prepared to do so. What price would she set on that? Would it be more than I could pay?

My legs are going numb. I can move my feet, though they're hobbled as if I'm a troublesome horse that has to be kept from bolting. Not so terribly far from the truth. Give me the means to get these restraints off and I'll bolt all right. I'll be out of here and away as fast as my wretched body will let me. The windows may be barred with iron, but surely that door will give under enough pressure. Where will I run? Every choice has its problems. Back, I suppose. Because the one thing I know is that I won't leave Dau. One way or another, his fate and mine are tied together now. I move my feet up and down, a ghastly sort of march that gets me nowhere. *To arms! To arms!* I flex my feet, I bend them, anything to keep myself upright.

Is it nearly morning? Hah! The night has barely begun, you foolish woman. Come on, another story . . . There was once a man . . . no, a bird . . . perhaps a whole flock of birds . . . and they found themselves suddenly in an unfamiliar place . . . perhaps by magic . . . a mage had cast a spell . . . or maybe a wisewoman . . . and then . . .

Shit! I push the wire door shut again, just in time. One good thing about that, it wakes me up. It's as if someone stuck a blunt knife through my arm, hard, and then twisted it around. A pox on Seanan! How could I let the two of them do what they did? Why didn't I fight harder? I should have been more than a match for them. Archu would be ashamed of me . . .

I tell myself a story about Archu's fur cloak and how he first came by it when he was challenged to a wrestling match with one of those Norse warriors known as Wolfskins. I imagine a gathering of folk around a roaring fire in some cold land, even colder than this place, all of them laughing and quaffing ale, and a younger Archu accepting the challenge to shouts of approval, and the bout with a fierce-eyed warrior wearing a necklace of wolves' teeth and a grin to strike fear into the boldest of opponents. None of it's true, but never mind that. When it's done I can't think of another story. My head is swimming. I was stupid to think I could last the night out. The worst bit is the gag. Along with the stink it makes me want to vomit, and I know what the result will be if I let that happen.

I think of home. The cottage at Winterfalls, the woodland, the mysterious pool. My mother's stillroom, her capable hands busy chopping and grinding and measuring, her sharp features, her perceptive gaze. My father's garden, and him by my side, showing me the best way to harvest carrots. A giant with the gentlest manner. A guide and guardian. No scholar, but wise beyond scholarship. I wish they were here. But no, I would not wish this on anyone, least of all those I love. I must find my own way out. I will find it . . . soon, really soon . . . but now I must shut my eyes, just for a moment . . .

I'm falling. The wire door crashes down, there's a startled sound from within the cage, then something flies across my face, not the captive bird but something far smaller. Abruptly I'm awake, I'm up, I'm slamming the door shut, my heart going like a war drum. Shit! How could I let it happen again? And what was that—?

It's on my hand, up by the wire. I can't see it, but I can feel its tiny claws on my fingers. I can hear its little cheeping voice. It's a bird all right, but about the size of a mouse. It must have come in through the gap in the shutters. *Don't panic and fly into the cage, little one,* I will it. It could easily happen. It's small enough to fit through the mesh. Why in the name of the gods—?

The tiny bird flies up to perch on my head. There it settles as if waiting. And I understand. At least, I hope I do. The small visitor hasn't flown in here by accident. What just happened wasn't an accident either. It saw danger and saved me. It's one of those birds we encountered in Breifne. It may even be the same one I sang to in a tree during those first hard days at Oakhill. It can take a message to Brocc. But how on earth do I tell it what I need to say? I have no idea how Eirne communicates with them. They went between her realm and the court of Breifne, they visited the druids, they must have been able to understand somehow. A pox on this gag! I can't talk. I can't sing. I bet if Brocc sang they'd know what he meant.

The bird moves up my arm to my bound wrist. It applies its miniature beak to the strips of tightly knotted cloth. *A losing battle,* I think. And I wonder if I'm dreaming this whole thing. The story is far stranger than most of those I've been telling myself as this endless night wore on. A woman tortured, trussed up, drugged, trapped. Saved by a bird smaller than a finch. Nobody would believe it. I blame Seanan's potion.

My right hand is free. A ghastly wave of pain goes through my arm as it drops down; I make a muffled sound through the gag. The bird hops over to the left and starts to work again. And that arm, too, is free. Oh, gods, I can't believe it. *Undo the gag next. Oh, please.* There's no way I can do it myself; my arms are in agony, my fingers are beyond dealing with knots.

Ouch! What is it doing now? Instead of loosening the gag or the hobbles, it's back on my head, pulling out my hair. *Stop it!*

I try to say, but all that comes out is a grunt that could mean anything. *Stop! It hurts!* Because this feels like the last straw, the last little thing that will break me. A friend, a savior at last, and then it turns on me. I can't stand up any longer. My belly is queasy, my legs are like jelly. I collapse to the ground with the small one still busy in my hair. As I force my aching arms up to swat the creature off, there's a scuffle and scream from the cage next door. In a whirr of wingbeats, the little bird is away. A rustle and click as it makes its escape between the shutters, then silence.

I should try to get the gag off. I should try to untie my ankles. I should break the door down, I should run . . . But my arms are on fire, my head is swimming, all I want is to sleep . . . I curl up and give way to the dark.

39

EIRNE

The queen lies awake in her retreat. It is night; a lamp shaped like a hedgehog glows faintly in a corner, casting warm light over the leafy walls, the soft bed with its silken coverlet, and the sleeping form of her husband, his dark curls falling over his brow, his face at peace, his arm warm against hers. She has been watching him, allowing herself to dream of a brighter future, daring to hope. She has not given him her news yet, but she must do so soon. Her bard is saddened by the loss of his voice. He must feel guilty. And when she tells him, he will feel still more guilty. Brocc will have no voice to sing his child a lullaby. Not until that child is a few moons old—Eirne is not quite sure when it will be born, and although Moon-Fleet is a healer, her knowledge does not extend to the birth of a half-human babe. Perhaps it will be born on the night the year turns to the dark. The queen hesitates to ask questions of her scrying bowl. The answers might be too hard to bear.

She will sing to the little one herself, and her bard can play his harp. He has put them at risk, yes, for his voice is their only real protection against the Crow Folk. For a year, a whole year, her folk must keep the threat at bay without the weapon of song. She was wise to have the young bird killed, when Brocc brought it home in a moment of madness. What did he think, that such a wild creature might become some kind of pet to be stroked and admired and paraded about? A wise person does not invite the enemy into his house. But her bard is softhearted in nature; it is one of the things she loves about him. The human part of her delights in his kindness. The fey part reminds her that she is a queen and must be strong. She is responsible for the welfare of her people. She reminds herself, as she strokes Brocc's hair gently away from his eyes, that this is not forever. A year. They must keep everyone safe for a year. Before that year is up, her child will be born, so small, so precious. So helpless.

Eirne lies back, her head on her husband's shoulder. He murmurs something in his sleep, and she whispers, "Lie still, dearest. All will be well."

Tomorrow. Tomorrow she will tell him about the baby. And she will confess to ordering the killing of the thing he rescued. A queen should tell the truth.

As she closes her eyes to sleep, there is a rustling in the curtain of vines and creepers that forms the walls of this place, and a messenger flies in. Eirne is well attuned to these creatures, tiny birds in outward shape, but in truth far more than birds. She sits up, careful not to disturb Brocc. She reaches out a hand and the small one alights on her finger. What is that in its beak? Strands of hair?

The messenger drops its burden onto her open palm, and yes, it is indeed hair. Three strands, long, with a slight wave. The lantern light is dim, but Eirne sees the bright red-gold of it and knows from whose head it was plucked.

The tiny birds do not cheep and chirp out their messages. Theirs is a more subtle communication. While they touch Eirne, while they perch on her, she knows their thoughts and understands what they want to convey. Thus she can send them forth to gather information and they can bring messages back to her. This little one, with its plumage of sky blue and blood red, she did not send. Either it has come of its own free will, or someone else has sent it.

What? she asks. *What is wrong?* Perhaps the message is for her husband. That is his sister's hair. But she does not wake him.

In the bird's mind there is an image: the forest's edge, on the eastern side, and a ramshackle hut shielded by a copse of trees. With the bird she flies closer. It is night. The moon is a dim presence behind clouds. But the small one can see as it peeps through the shutters. It can see as it flies in, as it lands on Liobhan's shoulder, as it works on her bonds and as it flinches when, through the wire, a fearsome knife-beaked presence looms, sudden and dark. Eirne sees what the bird saw—a woman tied up, exhausted, helpless. A dark place full of horrors. She feels Liobhan shrink away as the small one plucks these hairs from her head. She knows the moment when the caged monsters flap and scream anew, and the bird takes flight once more, out of that house of pain and away to the forest.

There is no misinterpreting this message. If it were set out with pen and ink, it would read HELP. *Where is the place?* Eirne asks in silence. *How far? Show me.* By her side, Brocc stirs in his sleep, rolls over, and is quiet once more.

The bird shows her. East to the forest's edge, near the spot where Brocc laid one of the Crow Folk to rest and sang a song. It is the area where his patrols with Rowan and True most likely cross the border between her realm and the human world more often than Brocc would ever admit. From there, north to a place near a settlement of humankind, a chieftain's walled domain, a village, orderly fields. And on the near side of this habitation but at some distance from it, the crumbling building that houses those prisoners. The place where Brocc's sister, the woman who did not want him to stay with Eirne, is now trussed up and helpless. Why would she be there? It is far from that island where she and Brocc trained as warriors and spies.

A quick flight for a bird. The position of the moon in those images shows this little one flew both ways within an hour or so. How long for those who walk on the ground? She could wake Brocc, although it is night. She could tell him what she has learned. Then he would race off to save his sister and most likely take Rowan with him, and who knows when he would return? She missed him so badly when he and True were on their journey. She worried about him every day. Her bed was lonely. The evenings were joyless without his music. And there was the constant knowledge that if the Crow Folk attacked, she and the others would be vulnerable. Her own magic is useless against them, and her people are few. Without their warriors, they could not stand long against that enemy.

Frowning, Eirne twists the hairs between her fingers and makes a little ring. Liobhan is a fighter, isn't she? Brave, strong, able to solve her own problems. Their own need is far greater; the future of her realm depends on it. Besides, if she must bid Brocc farewell again so soon, her heart will break. What if he never came back?

She slips the ring of bright hair under her pillow, lies down, and soon falls asleep.

40

DAU

"D au! Wake up!"

I sit up, my heart thudding. Someone's shaking me by the shoulder. That urgent voice was not Torcan's.

"Corb? What's happened?" I struggle out of bed. Where are my clothes? "Have you found her? Is she all right?"

"Here." Torcan passes me my smallclothes, my shirt, my trousers. "It's still night, Dau, so we'd best keep things quiet."

"Corb, tell me!"

"I left the farm in the dark," Corb says. "Wanted to be back early. Came by a shortcut, past that old building with trees around it, used to be a farm shed. And I heard something. Not a voice, just a scrabbling sound, but it was coming from inside, and it's years since anyone housed animals there. It wasn't only that." He hesitates. I refrain from shouting at him to get on with it, since he sounds not only alarmed but badly out of breath, as if he's run a long way to get here. "There was a terrible smell. Like something dead."

My heart goes cold. I order myself not to panic. I am a warrior; this is a mission. "Did you try to get in? Could you see anything?"

"I tried the door. It was bolted. Peered in a window, couldn't see much, it was too dark. But there's something in there, Dau. Something alive."

I make myself draw a steady breath. Something dead. Something alive. Liobhan did see Seanan go into that place once. Why in the name of all the gods didn't I think of this before? "Torcan, do you know anything about that building?"

"Not much. We skirt around it if we're riding up that way. I think Master Seanan uses the place for storage; doesn't like folk going too close. No idea what would be stored in such a building. It's not in a good state of repair."

A body, I think. That's what he would put there. "We need to get up there now," I say. "Corb, were you challenged coming in the gate?"

"The night guard was too tired to ask questions. Let me through with no trouble. Might think it a bit odd if I go back out straightaway, though."

And it will certainly be noted if I go out before dawn. Noted and perhaps passed on to Seanan. I think fast. Who would be up and about at this hour? Bakers, busy with the day's loaves. Night guards. And—ah! Monks. They'll be up already, since their first prayers are made while it's still night and their next at daybreak. I have a plan. It's risky. With my voice kept low, I explain it.

"You understand, this could lose both of you your positions in the household," I add. "If you don't want to be involved, say so. I won't hold it against you."

Neither Corb nor Torcan points out the impossibility of a blind man doing this on his own. Instead they start quietly gathering what we might need. Both of them have good knives. We add the iron poker from our little hearth. My stick, which can both support me and be used as a weapon. Two waterskins, full. Torcan wraps up some food left from last night's supper. We won't risk a visit to the kitchen so early. At my request, Corb fetches Liobhan's warm cloak.

"That'll do," I say, knowing that the guise we intend to use will be pointless if we're festooned with weapons and supplies. "When we get to the infirmary, leave the talking to me. If anyone asks, tell them you're following my orders. Ready?"

The house is hushed; most folk are still sleeping. I can only hope Seanan is one of them. "How long until dawn?" I whisper as we go out a little side door and head for the infirmary.

"An hour maybe. The sky's lightening up now," Corb whispers back.

I hope the monks are not also fast asleep, snatching what rest they can before the next round of prayers. With their patients to tend to, it's likely at least some are wakeful. Archu wouldn't like my plan. It's fraught with risk. A blind man giving the orders. A stable hand and a kitchen boy as his team. What if Ruarc refuses to help us? What if he sends someone straight to Seanan?

We reach the garden beside the infirmary.

"Lights inside," murmurs Torcan. "Someone moving about."

With my hand through Corb's arm, I approach the infirmary door. "Master Dau," comes a man's voice, somewhat startled. "Here to join us for Lauds?"

"I am not, sadly. I wish to have a word with Brother Íobhar, if he is free. I regret the early hour, but the matter is urgent."

"Of course, Master Dau. Wait here, please."

We wait. Corb suggests I sit down. I am too restless to sit. Body and mind are full of tangling thoughts. Liobhan is strong. She is a warrior. But she should be here. She should be back. Something alive. Something dead. What would you store in such a place?

"Dau." It's Ruarc's deep voice. "What is it? I have just a little time to spare."

I explain in as few words as I can. He knows Liobhan is missing. I tell him I think I know where she might be. That we need to get there unobtrusively. In particular, that we need to get out the gate without drawing attention. That it really is urgent. I pray to the deaf ears of God that my brother will not go straight to Seanan.

"I'm not sure I can be of assistance," Ruarc says, and my heart turns to lead. "We are vulnerable here; ruffle the wrong feathers and we could find ourselves without a roof over our heads."

There are words on my tongue, hurtful words about cowardice, about bearing witness, about speaking out. Something makes me hold them back.

"Young man." Ruarc speaks in an undertone; I assume he is addressing one of my companions.

"Yes?" That's Torcan.

"Open that chest, will you? That's it. You'll find some useful items there; take what you need. Close the chest when you're done, please. I'd best go now, my brethren will be waiting." A pause. "I regret that I cannot help you."

I say nothing, and within moments it seems my brother is gone, because Corb is whispering to me, and the three of us are donning the garments from the chest: the hooded robes monks of this order wear about their daily business. Clad in these, we might be any three brethren making a routine trip over to St. Padraig's. Seems Brother Íobhar's words were not for me, but for anyone who might have happened to be passing by. Intended to clear him of complicity. So maybe he hasn't changed much. But he helped us.

"With the hood up," murmurs Corb, "you look just like your brother."

Nobody questions us at the gate. We walk through with our hoods concealing our faces. I do my best not to limp. Corb uses the slightest of touches to guide me—I thought that was the most likely thing to give us away, but perhaps the light is still too dim for the guards to see us well, or perhaps they are simply tired after a long shift.

We don't speak until we're well away. I'm still half expecting Seanan's men to appear in pursuit, though in fact we are committing no offense, unless it is an offense to dress as a monk when one does not believe in God.

"You all right, Dau?" asks Torcan quietly. "Ankle holding up?"

"Fine." It's not fine, but we have to keep moving, and if it hurts, it hurts. The uneven path doesn't help. I want to run. I'm tempted to send the others on ahead. If I had a pair of Swan Island warriors with me I'd do so without hesitation. "I can go a bit faster. If she's there, we want to get her out and away before . . . We want to get her out as soon as we can." If she is there, if she's hurt, we'll have to take her back to my father's house. I can't think beyond that. I can't think beyond *something dead, something alive*. I wish I believed in God. "Faster," I say.

41

EIRNE

At some time in the night, the queen wakes again and slips outside to relieve herself. It's cold under the trees; the birds are still, and the moon peers out through a veil of misty cloud. Eirne shivers in her delicate night-robe, wishing she had remembered her shawl.

She returns, parting the leafy hangings that shield her retreat, and meets her husband's stare. Brocc is sitting up in bed, and in his hand is the ring of red-gold hair.

"What is this?" There's a note in his voice that makes her forget she is the ruler of this realm, the one who makes the decisions, and turns her once more into the frightened child she once was, suddenly removed from everything familiar.

"A bird brought it. A messenger." There's no point in trying to dissemble; Brocc will know instantly, as she did, to whom the hair belongs. "Not long ago. I was going to wake you."

He's getting up now, stepping into his trousers, fastening his shirt, although it is still dark outside. "You know this must be my sister's hair," he says.

"I know, yes." She'll have to give him the message. Could she make it sound less urgent? He will want to go now, straightaway.

"What did this bird tell you, Eirne?" Brocc sounds fierce. He sounds like the warrior he is.

She tells him the truth. Softens her description, yes, to spare his feelings. But tells him the full story, the what, the where, the when. Sees the last color drain from his face; sees his eyes grow darker.

"I must go," Brocc says. "Now, and quickly. I can't leave her there."

"It will take some time on foot, Brocc. You would not reach that place until an hour or two after dawn at the earliest. Did you not say it was close to a habitation of men? Surely someone will find her."

"The same person who put her there, maybe. I'm going. Not on my own. I'll take Rowan or True with me, if one of them is willing."

Eirne says nothing. Will it always be like this for him, his loyalty to his human family coming before his duty to her folk, who are now also his folk? His action will once again leave them vulnerable to attack. But Brocc is beyond listening. As for her own glad news, that must wait yet again. She hugs it to her like a treasure as she meets her husband's cold gaze. "Very well," she says. "Wake them if you will. And go if you must."

Brocc is fully dressed, ready to walk out and start his mission. Every part of his body spells out the urgent need to be gone. But he's not finished here. He turns toward her, and it is not to say a tender farewell. "Why didn't you wake me?" he asks. "You weren't going to tell me, were you? You were just going to leave it, leave my sister there to rot." Unspoken but understood are the words *After everything she did for you.* True, Liobhan played a significant part in the quest to see the right king on the throne of Breifne, a quest initiated by Eirne's own people. But Eirne owes her nothing.

"You exaggerate," she says. "Let us not argue about this. I have told you now. Best be on your way." Thinking of her child, she cannot bring herself to add *Safe journey* or *I hope you find her in time*. Her heart is full of fear.

42

DAU

We reach the place before dawn. The smell hits me long before we walk between the shielding trees. Something dead, yes. And another stink I recognize: the foul fishy stench of the Crow Folk. I don't let myself think. "Check the door," I tell the others. "Check the window. Go carefully, we don't know what might be in there." If only I had Hrothgar or Yann or any of the Swan Island team with me. If only I could see.

Corb and Torcan report back quickly.

"Door's locked. But not strong; the place is pretty run-down. We could break it in, I think."

"The window's got iron bars," says Corb. "The shutters are open a bit, as I told you. But there's no shifting those bars. No getting in or out that way."

"What can you see in there?"

"Cages. Something in them, fluttering about. Bits and pieces around the place, stuff on the floor." A pause. "I don't see her, Dau."

"It'll have to be the door." Torcan's bigger and stronger than Corb, with good shoulders on him. And despite my obvious drawbacks, I'm probably a good deal stronger than either of them, thanks to all that training with Liobhan. "You and I will do it, Torcan. Corb, I need you to keep watch."

It's an untidy job—one-two-three-crash!—but under the circumstances we don't do too badly. The door groans and starts to give on our second assault and collapses inward on our third. We've made enough noise to raise the dead, but the things in the cages only flutter about weakly.

I want to rush in, search every corner. But I'll only be in the way. "Torcan, you go in first. Corb, you're my eyes. Walk me in and tell me everything you see."

"Shelves of jars and bottles. Like in the infirmary, but messier. Knives, pincers, small saws, all kinds of tools. A mask hanging on a peg. Two masks, leather, the kind that cover your whole face." Corb snatches a breath; his voice is shaking. "Things dangling from the rafters."

"Things? What things?"

"Bodies. Of creatures. A fox. A cat. A rabbit. They've got . . . they've got marks on them. Burns. And cuts. Limbs missing. There's dried blood all over the floor."

I curse under my breath. "What about the cages? I hear something alive in there."

"There's one on a perch. One of those birds, like a crow but really big. It's hunched over. Looks sick. There's another one on the floor, moving about. It's hurt, dragging a wing. And . . . dead ones, too, some piled up in a corner, and some just lying where they fell. Holy saints, Dau, who would do this?"

"Dau!" Torcan's voice is sharp. "She's here!"

A sound comes from me that I did not think I was capable of making. I stride forward, pulling Corb behind me. He slows me before I walk into something.

"Down at the end," Corb says. "She's on the floor, behind the last cage. On your left, just here. Torcan, is she . . . ?"

I crouch down, reach out a hand, touch a body through cloth.

"Corb," says Torcan, "pass me your knife."

I can't bear this. "What's going on? Is she hurt? Tell me!"

"Gagged, with her feet hobbled," says Corb. "Torcan's cutting off the gag now. She's . . . she's not conscious, Dau. And she's cold."

"I'm checking now." Torcan sounds commendably calm. There are small sounds; perhaps he is turning Liobhan on her side, or cutting the other bonds, or putting his fingers to her neck, where the heartbeat can be felt. If a person is still alive. "Corb, fetch that cloak, will you?"

To warm a freezing woman? Or to wrap a dead one? "Torcan," I make myself say, "is she breathing?"

At that moment there's a little gurgling sound followed by a wheezing cough, and sudden movement beside me. "Help me sit her up," says Torcan. "Corb, find a bowl or something, will you? She's going to be sick."

They are the best words I've ever heard. I don't care if anyone sees I'm crying. I edge around until I'm on Liobhan's other side, and Torcan and I support her in a sitting position. She's freezing cold, shivering hard. We wrap the cloak around her. Her hair feels wet and her clothing has a strange smell, as if she's had a draft of some sort spilled over her. But she's here, she's alive, we've found her in time, and a joy floods through me that is like the sun rising after a night of wild storm. I put my hand on her arm—her sleeve is in tatters—and she sucks in her breath, flinching. Before I can investigate, she starts to retch in violent, choking spasms. Corb brings a bowl and holds it in place as she spews up the contents of her stomach, then watery bile. The sounds go on for a while. We hold her, and I hear myself murmuring meaningless words of comfort, "It's all right, we've got you, you'll be all right," and so on. All the time wondering about those potions on the shelves, and my father's sleeping drafts, and where my brother gets his supplies. Liobhan's been drugged, I'm sure of it.

She gives one last shuddering retch, takes in a long, labored breath, then rests her head on my shoulder. "Morrigan's curse, Dau," she whispers. "If that was devil's-foot, I'm never using it ever again. Is it really morning?" She tenses suddenly, pulling away from us. "Who's here? Are we safe?"

"Apart from me, only Corb and Torcan. Nobody else. And yes, we're safe." For now.

"We should move out of this corner," Torcan says. "It's too dark to see properly. Can you get up, Liobhan?"

She can't support her own weight; she's been lying unconscious a long while in the cold, and there's the draft she's taken. If it's anything like what I was dosed with in those early days, it will leave her slow and confused for a while. We move her out to a more open area and find her a stool to sit on. There's a dark fury rising in me. My lovely comrade is filthy and sick and hurt. I don't want it to happen ever again. My brother must be stopped. I would relish punishing him with one or another of the vile acts he carried out on me, but that is not the way. My anger must stay hidden and bide its time, and when that time comes I must not act as he would.

"Water," Liobhan says. "Please."

Corb brings her one of our waterskins. "Take it slowly," he says.

She drinks, shudders, drinks again. Gives back the skin. "Dagda's bollocks," she says. "I'm starting to wonder if I dreamed the whole thing . . . only, there's this. Don't touch. Just look." She holds out her arm. "It's a brand. He did it to one of the Crow Folk, too. Hurts like hell."

"Sweet Mary and Joseph!" breathes Torcan. "He burned that onto you? You see what it is, Corb?"

"Sword and dagger crossed," says Corb. He sounds beyond being shocked. "The family emblem."

Now I'm the one who feels sick. "Those corpses you described," I say. "Hanging up. Are they marked the same way?"

"More or less." Torcan's up and walking about, I assume to take a closer look. "I'd say some of them have been here awhile. Some probably fought harder against it. But it's the same sign. A crude version of Lord Scannal's emblem."

Seanan may be cunning. He may be clever. But he's made a grave error here. Unless, of course, he's devised some plan to blame it all on me. It's my family emblem, too. "We need to make note of everything. Remember everything. When we go back, I'm taking this to Master Beanón. I want it all set out before my father." Deep down I know there's no way Seanan intended to let Liobhan live. Not with his brand on her arm. He must be meaning to come back and finish her off. Then make her disappear for good. "It's time," I say. "Time for the truth to come out."

"Seanan will lie," says Liobhan. "His supporters will back him up. I'm a bond servant. You're blind. And our friends here aren't high in the household order."

"I'll tell the truth." Bless Corb, he is a fine young man.

"I'll tell what I've seen, of course," says Torcan. "But it's hard to pass on what you've heard when it might get someone else in trouble. Like what I knew about this place and why we were supposed to keep away."

"And so men like Seanan continue to rule their households by fear," I say. "We should move. We should go back."

"Why are you dressed like monks?" asks Liobhan.

"Long story. A useful disguise for coming out the gate, but

it won't work for getting back in, since there are now four of us and only three habits. Will you be able to walk the distance, Liobhan?"

"Of course," she says. A moment later I hear Corb exclaim, there's a rush of movement and a crash as the stool goes over. Not only can Liobhan not walk the distance, she can't even stand up on her own without fainting right away.

I sit on the floor with her head on my knee. Corb covers her up with the cloak. Torcan gets out the food we brought and passes around a waterskin. Nobody says much.

I go through the challenges in my mind, as Archu would expect. However long we wait to set out, we'll still be slow. Liobhan's weakened by what they did to her. I need to be guided and there's my wretched ankle as well. Corb and Torcan are not fighters. Can someone carry Liobhan most of the way? I know I can pick her up and put her over my shoulder, I've done it before. But that was before the ankle, and one lift is not the same as bearing an adult's weight over a distance. Torcan would be struggling to manage and Corb simply isn't strong enough. Two people carrying her between them? That would really draw attention. And because I'm blind, I couldn't be one of them. Which would leave me to walk back without a guide. A pox on it!

"One of us could go back and fetch help," suggests Corb. "Or we could head up to my parents' farm instead, stay there for a bit while Liobhan recovers."

Neither is practicable. Sending Corb or Torcan to fetch help is too risky; we don't want Seanan to find out what's happened until I've had a chance to talk to certain people. Going to the farm is appealing—Liobhan could be properly looked after, and all of us would get some breathing space. But Seanan's going to come back here. He has further intentions for Liobhan or he wouldn't have left her alive. If we go and he finds the place empty, he may seize the opportunity to clean up and dispose of the evidence. Then, when I speak out, he'll accuse me of inventing the whole thing. Besides, he'd most likely guess where we were. I don't want to bring down disaster on Corb's family.

"Be fine soon . . ." Liobhan's regaining consciousness, struggling to sit up. "Should walk . . . need to go . . ."

"Shh." I stroke her hair away from her brow. "Rest for a while. It's all under control." A lie if ever there was one. But it's still early; we do have time. *Stay calm,* says the voice of Archu in my mind. *Make a plan.*

"So, we wait for a while," I say in the most confident tone I can summon. "One of us keeps watch outside under cover of the trees. The moment they see anyone coming, they slip back in here and warn us." This is the flaw; if we stay inside this building so Liobhan can be in shelter, we could be trapped, cornered. The broken door is the only way out. Seanan is ruthless. He'd cut us down one by one rather than have this exposed. Or he'd use fire.

"Bad plan," murmurs Liobhan. "Get out . . . now. Get . . . under cover . . . But not in here . . ." A hint of her true strength is creeping into her voice. "I can walk," she says. "I can. Dau, you can help me."

A silence. Nobody says, *Dau can't see.* Because Liobhan has a perfectly good set of eyes. "Good," I say. "Corb, pack our things up, please. Torcan, see if you can spot some bushes or a stretch of wall, somewhere clear of this building and big enough to conceal all four of us. We go there, we get under cover, and we wait until Liobhan's strong enough to walk down to the gate. Then we go. We're hardly going to be attacked in full view of whoever's on watch. Liobhan, you'll wear this habit I've got on.

Unless I walk right into Seanan, I should be able to talk us in the gate."

There are flaws in this plan, too. But it beats staying where we are and finding ourselves boxed in by Seanan's men. If he starts disposing of evidence, burning things, destroying things, at least the four of us can bear witness later.

43

LIOBHAN

We're crouched behind some bushes, still uncomfortably close to Seanan's charnel house. I feel like death, but I'm damned if I'll say so. We're taking turns to watch the track down to Lord Scannal's establishment. If anyone comes, we're hoping they'll walk on by without seeing us. The day's getting brighter, soon all sorts of folk will be about, and I'm liking this plan less with every moment that passes. It doesn't help that I can't stop shivering, and my head still feels as if it's been shaken around, and my arm needs a poultice badly. I'm about to make an inappropriate remark when I see them, not on the track but making a covert way on the far side of it, each going on his own, but all of them heading in the same direction. They're moving under cover of bushes or down behind the ill-kept drystone walls, using the natural rise and fall of the land for concealment. At least, they're trying to, but they're not very good at it.

"Men approaching!" I manage to sound calm. "Five, I think. One of them is Seanan." I feel sick. I want to kill that man, I want it so badly I'm gritting my teeth and clenching my fists and I can feel the fury right through my aching, poisoned body. Which tells me I'm in no fit state for a fight.

"Keep down," says Dau.

But it's already too late: they've seen us. My red hair, no doubt. One of them calls, points. Seanan halts as if turned to stone. Then shouts a command, and the six of them, yes, six, come pounding up the rise toward us.

"Knife!" I snap, and Torcan puts one in my outstretched hand. "They're headed straight for us, Dau, closing fast." Dau will be relying on gut instinct and hearing, and the other two aren't fighters. I'll do what damage I can before they overpower us. The odds aren't good. Among those men is a very big one. Ultán. I remember him from last night, before I passed out. But he's only my number two target.

"Hold fast, team." Dau's voice is iron-strong.

"Dau," I say. "Don't get yourself killed. Please. They're about forty paces away, Seanan in the middle, a man on either side of him, three behind. Staves. Knives, I think. One man with a coil of rope over his shoulder. You need a knife?" He doesn't seem to have any weapon but the stick he uses to support himself. Morrigan's curse, he won't last to the count of ten. Bollocks to this whole thing.

"Don't you either," he says. "Get yourself killed, I mean. I didn't rescue you so you could throw away your chances in some stupid fight."

"Thirty paces and gaining. You'll want Seanan alive, mm?"

"Not if it means letting him kill you. But yes. I want him to face justice."

"Twenty paces. Ready?"

And they're on us. I slash the first man's arm, then lose my grip on a knife slippery with blood. I use fists and feet, setting aside the pain in my body. I topple another man, and Torcan knocks him out with a length of tree branch. Corb is wrestling with a third man, doing better than I'd have thought he could.

And Dau . . . I can't see Dau. I turn, and there he is, striking one of the attackers with his stick, an awkward blow but strong. The man staggers; I kick his legs out from under him and he falls. Before I can knock him out, another man grabs me around the waist. An elbow strike smashes his nose satisfactorily and he grunts in pained surprise, slacking his grip. I wriggle free, punch him in the jaw, and he, too, is down.

I straighten to see Seanan standing on the edge of the melee, arms folded, a slight smile on his face. I'm breathless, feeling sick, dizzy from an effort that wouldn't raise a sweat under normal circumstances. Mustn't faint. Must keep fighting.

Corb screams. It's a sound to chill the heart, a death shriek, and it stops me in my tracks.

"Corb!" shouts Dau, but he can't help. He can't see Corb lying on the ground with his head on a strange angle and his hands loose by his sides and his eyes staring up at the morning sky, unseeing. The man who just killed him stands looking down at him; it's Ultán. He moves now, heading straight for me.

"Dau!" I shout. "Torcan! Run!" Because I know that the way I'm feeling right now, I won't be a match for him, and two of the felled men are showing signs of getting up to join in again.

Nobody runs. Dau is grappling with his opponent, using a familiar crab-like stranglehold. His attacker slumps, unconscious. But before Dau can regain his feet, a second man is on him, kicking fiercely. Further away, Torcan is wrestling with another man. His face is grayish white and he's struggling for balance.

Ultán hurls himself toward me. There never was time to run. I wait, shaky on my feet. There's no way I can withstand a frontal assault. He's huge. My only hope is trickery. I glare and ball my fists. Let him think I'm going to meet force with force. He lunges for me, hands outstretched, going for my neck. I wait until the last instant, then turn aside and try to hook a foot under his. But he's more agile than I thought. He jumps over my leg. His hand snags my sleeve. He yanks me

sideways and we fall in a tangle of arms, scrabbling for a hold.
He rolls astride my hips and, before I can fully protect myself,
lands a glancing blow to my head. Shit! I'm dazed. My ears are
ringing. He rises and hauls me to my feet. *Be strong, Liobhan.
Why can't you be strong . . .*

For a bit, everything swirls around. All I can do is breathe
and hope I don't pass out. *Dau. Dau, don't be dead.* But no, he
won't be dead. Not yet. Because this is Seanan's doing, and now
I see Seanan in front of me with a knife in his hand, and someone is holding me from behind, and Seanan calls out, "Little
brother! I have your girl here. Shame you can't see this. But
she'll sing for you soon enough."

I'm going to die. This is not the way I want to die. Seanan
lifts the knife. The fang-like blade glints in the sunlight, hungry for its moment.

And then Seanan's eyes widen. He drops the weapon. The
man behind me releases his grip and someone lets out a scream
of pure terror. I turn to see a figure clad all in green, fighting
with an athletic skill that marks him out instantly as a Swan
Island man. It's Brocc. My brother. Morrigan's britches, where
did he come from? Behind him is the reason for Seanan's shock:
a huge being who seems hewn from stone. Blows glance off
him. He reaches out and sets his fingers around a man's neck,
and I call out, "Disable, not kill!" The stone man would only
need to squeeze a little and his captive would be done for.

*One more effort, Liobhan. One job to do and you can rest. Do it for
Dau.* Seanan has backed away, but not far. I dive, crashing my
shoulder into his hips, and he topples to the ground. As I suspected, the man is no fighter. Before he can catch his breath I
deliver an open-handed strike to the side of his head. His eyes
roll back; he becomes limp.

Dau. Where's Dau? Heart pounding, I scan the field and find
him kneeling by Corb's body with tears pouring down his face.

He holds Corb's lifeless hand in both of his. His grief is palpable, turning victory into unbearable loss. Yet victory it is—with Brocc and his companion to help us, it's not long before the last of Seanan's men drops his weapon and surrenders.

The coil of rope those men brought with them proves handy. Between them, Brocc and the stone man get all of our opponents, conscious or not, tied securely at wrists and ankles in the same way I was.

Torcan has a knife wound to the shoulder, not deep but untidy. I cut a strip from the shirt of a fallen man and bind up the injury, less neatly than I'd like as my hands won't stop shaking. I'm crying, too, now. Crying and shocked and wondering what in the name of the gods comes next. Then my brother comes over—he and his friend have finished tying knots—and throws his arms around me. It feels good. It feels so good. I hug him back. This is astonishing. And wonderful. How did he know where we were?

"You look terrible," Brocc says. "I wish we'd come sooner, but . . . I didn't get your message straightaway."

I'm dimly aware that the stone creature—I've met him in the Otherworld, in Eirne's realm; his name is . . . True?—has improvised a gag and tied it over Seanan's mouth. Dau hasn't moved.

"Message? What message?" I ask.

"Your hair. Twisted into a little ring. A bird brought it to Eirne. And provided enough information for us to find you."

I know my brother well. There's something he isn't telling me, but that doesn't matter right now. "You saved our lives," I say.

"What's wrong with Dau?"

"Apart from the loss of a dear friend? He's blind, Brocc. Hurt in a bout, back on Swan Island. He was fighting me. A horrible accident."

"Blind, and he can still fight like that? Danu's mercy! Liobhan, tell me quickly what's going on here. That man you just knocked out, the one over there—for a moment I thought he was Dau. His brother?"

With my head swimming, I try to give a concise explanation. Brigid's training in such matters helps. I tell Brocc why we're here, what has happened since we came, last night's and today's events. My brother's expression grows grimmer with every detail.

For the last part, I need Dau. I go over to crouch down beside him. "Dau," I say, and he starts as if struck—he's been miles away. "Brocc is here, with a friend. We need to move Corb and we need to do something about these other men. What's the plan?"

Dau swallows hard. He scrubs his hand over his cheeks, then gets to his feet. He has closed Corb's staring eyes.

"Dau," says Brocc quietly. "I'm sorry about the loss of your friend. Sorry we could not reach you sooner."

"Glad of your assistance," Dau says, straightening his back and squaring his shoulders. "You turned the tide for us, I think. Couldn't do much myself. Things being as they are."

True comes up next to us. "You want us to put these men away somewhere? In that place maybe?" He indicates the building. "Some creatures in there. I had a look. Crow Folk."

Brocc stiffens. When I mentioned I had been captive, I neglected to tell him I was not alone in there.

"Crow Folk? Alive?" he asks.

"Barely alive, I suspect," I tell him. "Go and look if you want. First let me show you this." I hold out my arm, let him see the burn. "Emblem of Lord Scannal's house. A brand. Not just on me, on the other captives as well. That man is out of his mind."

"Morrigan's curse!" exclaims Brocc, glancing again at the

prone and silent Seanan. "You should have finished him off while you had a chance, Liobhan."

"No," Dau says, in a tone that tells me he is once more in charge here. "He will answer for his crimes. Go, look, take note of what he has done. But first . . . Liobhan, we must make quite sure these men can't raise the alarm until we've reached the house and provided an explanation. I want to speak to Master Beanón and Master Naithí. And my father. For now, we need Seanan's crew out of action."

There are so many surprises in that speech I hardly know where to start. "Out of action," I echo. "And you don't mean just tied up and locked up in that place, I take it."

"Since we broke the door down to get you out, no. But you know your herbs and potions. And there's a supply of potent ingredients in there, or so I assume. Can you make a draft that will keep them quiet for long enough?"

Danu save us! What would my mother think? I ponder this briefly and decide she would tell me to get right on with it, but to take care not to kill anyone. I look at my hands. They're still unsteady. I think of Seanan's face as he poured that stuff down my throat. "All right. Needs to be quick, yes? Before someone happens to look in this direction and notice more activity than usual."

"We'll move them down there. That place is shielded by trees, isn't it?"

"Yes. But I can't dose an unconscious man, Dau. We have to wait until they come to." With luck, by the time I manage to throw something together with the limited facilities in the wretched hut, they'll all be able to drink without choking.

"And then what happens?" asks Brocc. "Will you be bringing charges against your brother? Will there be a formal hearing with lawmen present?"

"We'll see," Dau says. "We'll see how many folk are brave

enough to bear witness, now that it has come to this. At least one lawman will be present. If my father wants to keep this quiet, he may see the wisdom in a small, discreet hearing."

"I'll bear witness, Dau," I say quietly.

"I'll speak up, if that will help," says Torcan. "If I lose my position in the household, so be it. We owe it to Corb to tell the full story. He fought bravely."

There's a brief silence. Then Brocc says, "From what you've told me, it seems this Seanan is good at making folk believe his lies. He might say all of you have concocted a story. And you have no independent witness. Nobody who is sufficiently detached from it all to be thought credible." A pause. "Except us. Me and True."

"You would come back with us, Brocc?" Dau sounds astonished. "You, too, would bear witness?"

"I would. I could not stay long. And . . ." He glances at the men lying prone close by; some are groaning and stirring, almost conscious again, but the others lie still. With luck, none of them heard the interchange. "For the purpose of this exercise, I am a wandering storyteller. Unknown to all of you. I happened to be close by when I saw you being attacked and came to your aid. True, you'd best wait for me up in the woods. Your appearance would set the place in an uproar. We'll return home when I've said my piece. Dau, can you make this happen by tomorrow?"

"Yes," says Dau with a leader's confidence. "And thank you. We owe you a great debt."

Torcan and True prepare to move the trussed-up prisoners. Seanan is conscious now; I catch a furious glare as I walk past him, but the gag keeps him mercifully silent. Brocc, Dau, and I carry Corb gently down to the shelter of the willow copse and lay a cloak over him. No time for more.

I get to work at the bench in the old building, going through

Seanan's unlabeled containers and doing my best to identify the contents by smell and appearance. This preparation can't be brewed cold. Thank the gods there is a woodpile, the stuff is dry, and there's a flint by the hearth. I lay the fire, set it burning, return my attentions to the brew. I pray I won't poison anyone.

Brocc is staring into the cages. He seems transfixed by the captive birds.

"Branded, as I was," I say over my shoulder as I chop herbs on the bench. "Maimed, tortured, killed. You see what's hanging there. Before he burned me, Seanan said, *You're next.* Wish I could be more confident that when I relate that story before Lord Scannal's household, someone will believe me."

Brocc doesn't answer. He's still staring into the cage.

"Brocc?"

"Two of them are still alive. They could be saved. Morrigan's britches, this is where they came from."

"Where who came from?" Yes, that really is a chunk of devil's-foot in the jar. I'm treading a very narrow line between healer and assassin. But I'm going to use it. Let Seanan have a taste of his own medicine.

"Crow Folk like these. Marked with the same crude brand. Dead or dying in our part of the forest. I . . . I laid one to rest, and sang for it. Another we rescued and . . . never mind that. Dau, could you call True for me?"

"I'll go," I say.

"I'm capable of staggering out the door and calling in the right direction, Liobhan." So quickly, Dau has lost his composure. I let him go. I don't say sorry. In the back of my mind is the story about the man whose lame leg was mended by clurichaun magic, and Dau's own desperate need to find a cure in the Otherworld. He won't ask Brocc. I know he won't. Corb is lying out there dead and there's a huge problem to be dealt with right here. But I can guess what is in Dau's thoughts alongside all of that. He fought with remarkable bravery and skill, blind man or no. But all the time he would have been cursing the moment fate dealt him that blow. He would have known, as I did, that if he'd been his old self and if I hadn't still been feeling the effects of the draft, we could have accounted for those men without Brocc's help. We could have protected Corb. Dau's allowed a moment of snarling unpleasantness. But only one. If he speaks to me like that again, I'll slap him.

I use Brocc's waterskin to fill the iron pot on the hearth, then hang the pot over the fire. I finish cutting up the herbs. I add dried components from the jars, hoping I've guessed everything right. If I err, it's on the side of not enough rather than too much. While I work, another painful truth comes to me. Dau won't speak to Brocc and True about magical cures, not now and not ever, because they've just saved our lives. Not only that, but Brocc's agreed to stay on and testify. Dau's far too proud to ask for anything more.

True comes in without Dau, who I assume is staying out there with Torcan. Time's passing; it all feels too slow. A murmured conversation is going on behind me.

"True," says Brocc, "we can't leave these creatures to die here. But that one, at least, looks too weak to survive if we simply open the cage. And the other might attack us."

They both fall silent, looking through the wire mesh at the two Crow Folk, one hunched on the perch, staring at them, the other huddled on the floor in a corner. Then True says, "I have something we can try. I do not know if it will help. In truth, I do not know its purpose."

"What do you mean, True?" Brocc sounds taken aback. Whatever this is, it's news to him. I glance across and see the two of them looking at a tiny vial held in the stone man's great hand. Now we're at close quarters, I can see something moving around on True's head, in his moss-like hair. Not the sort of creepy-crawlies that have to be got rid of with oil of rosemary and hard combing. These look like small Otherworld folk. Danu's mercy! What must that fight have been like for them?

"What is that stuff?" I ask.

"It comes from a place of deep magic," says True. "Given to me by my ancestors. I was wounded by the Crow Folk and healed in a waterfall there. The old ones gave me this vial, which holds only a few drops. Its exact purpose, they did not tell me; that is often the way of magic. They said only that I should keep it secret until the right time came, and use it only with an unselfish heart. And that, like all things magical, the use of the contents came with a risk. I do not know if these drops have the same capacity to heal, or whether they will work on the birds. The result might be quite different. But I think now is that time."

It seems True has indeed kept this remarkable thing secret. Brocc is gazing at him in shocked wonder. I'm not thinking of the Crow Folk. I'm thinking of Dau. But the precious substance is not mine to bestow, and I know how tricky magic can be. Anything might happen.

"If Brocc agrees, we should help these poor creatures," the stony man says in his deep voice. Am I really hearing a sort of echo from the tiny folk who ride on him, or am I still feeling the effects of last night's draft?

The idea of getting close enough to the Crow Folk to put drops down their throats or onto their wounds scares me in a way Master Seanan at his worst could not. "Couldn't you sing to keep them calm?" I ask my brother. "To reassure them that you're acting with good intent?"

"I can't," says Brocc. "Another long story." His voice sounds shaky. "But you could."

I stare at him, openmouthed. He can't sing? What does he

mean? He knows I can't sing as he does; he's half-fey, he has magic, and while I am a musician, I'm the offspring of two entirely human parents. Remarkable ones, it's true. But not a whisper of the uncanny in them. "I'll sing, of course," I say, and as I speak my voice cracks. "But it might not be much help."

He offers no further explanations and I don't ask for them. We have work to do. We need our prisoners entirely subdued before we walk away from here. I can hear one of them groaning through his gag, though a sharp word from Dau silences him soon enough.

I finish making the brew. There's only one cup here, the one they used when they poured that stuff down my throat last night. My gown is still damp and sticky from the spillage and my skirt stinks of urine. Gods, I hope someone doesn't throw us in a lockup as soon as we get back. I'd kill for a warm bath and some clean clothes.

True comes out with me, carrying my draft in a jug. With Torcan's help, we dose the men one at a time, leaving the groggiest until last. Seanan flinches away when True moves to untie his gag, but the moment it comes off he starts shouting a tirade of vile insults aimed at me. That's when Dau comes over, kneels down beside his brother, grabs his golden hair, and pulls his head back. Seanan is a little too slow to stop yelling and close his mouth; True's strong fingers hold his jaws apart as I pour the draft in. I'm better at this than Seanan was; I don't spill a drop. When it's all down, True holds Seanan's mouth closed for a while, just to be sure. The gag goes on again. Dau releases his grip and gets up.

"A good job done," he says mildly. "How many still to dose?" He might be talking of administering a mixture to pigs or sheep to rid them of worms.

"Only one, and he's awake now. We'll give him a smaller amount; he's had a hard blow to the head and I won't risk killing him." I think of Corb out there, growing cold under his blanket. A young man who will never marry or father a son; a good son who will never see his parents again. A kind boy, a quick learner, a brave soul. But then, this young man we're dosing was only following orders. Most likely he had no idea what Seanan was harboring in this place of cruelty and shame. He, too, may be a good son. "Half a cup . . . Thank you, True . . . Hold him steady for me."

When the captives have all been given the draft, Brocc calls me into the building. There's some protective clothing there— the two masks, some strong gauntlets—but nothing that would shield the body from a piercing beak or rending claw. Although a monk's habit is made of sturdy cloth, it's hardly armor.

"Will you help me, Liobhan?" Brocc asks. By which he means, *This is risky. You might get hurt. Will you do this for me?*

"Let's get on with it, then," I say. I think it's an ill-conceived plan, but I also see that Brocc wants to help those creatures, wants it with all his heart. Peering in at the two of them, now huddled together on a lower perch and fixing their baleful stare on us, I see how weakened they are. Their eyes are glazed and dull, their feathers droop. But it's less than a full day since one of them was stabbing at me between the bars, and I don't trust them an inch. "What do I do, sing first?"

"Put on a mask and the gloves. Take a stick from the wood basket, but keep it down by your side and don't use it unless you have to."

"I can't sing with this thing on." It's not just that; the touch of the mask brings back the hideous feeling of that gag over my mouth. There's nothing more terrifying than not knowing how long you'll be able to go on breathing. "I'm not wearing it. What next?"

"True, pass me the vial."

True has come in behind us. "Here," he says, handing over the vial with its precious contents. I wish it could bring Corb back to life. But no magic has the power to restore the dead. "One drop each, Brocc. No more. We do not know what it will do to them."

"Leave the way clear to the outside, so they can fly straight out once I've done it." Brocc is next to the main cage entry, a wire hatch like the one I found myself tied to last night. "Your cloak, Liobhan. Put it over my head and spread it out wide. You and True hold it there while you sing, so the wire door is blocked. Keep the cloak up over me while I open the door and lean in; don't take it away until I say so."

Danu's mercy! He may have a mask and gloves on, but there's plenty of him exposed. Beaks and claws will go right through that soft leaf-colored cloth. But he does have a leather jerkin on over his shirt, and he's wearing armguards, too. Of us all, he's the one best dressed for a fight. "Start singing now," he says. "Something calm and soothing. No sudden high notes."

True and I do as we're told with the cloak, lifting it to cover both Brocc and the whole of the wire door. As we do this, I think about the Crow Folk, their fishy stink, their wildness, their moods that are as changeable as a great ocean, and I sing a song about islands, seals, birds flying to roost in the nooks and crannies of a sea stack, storms casting a tangle of shells and seaweed onto a pebbly shore, waves crashing against stark cliffs. It's not calm and soothing, but it feels right. There are no sudden high notes. For the chorus I sing a gentle wordless melody, a calm sea lapping on a sandy beach. True anchors my voice with a single deep tone, and his tiny passengers squeak along, their voices almost too high to be heard.

As we sing Brocc speaks quietly, gently, with great respect. "Drink this, friends. It will heal you. Then you can fly free, away from this place of pain and grief. My people have hurt you; they have tried to destroy you. But you are proud. You are strong. One day you will find your way home. Know that I am a friend and that I will help you if I can. Those who stand beside me are my friends. I ask that you do not harm them." Then he murmurs to me, "One more chorus, then we all step back and duck down with the cloak over us. Sing it now and at the end I'll give you a one, two, three." He opens the wire door and reaches into the cage. My view is obscured; I can't see what he's doing.

Without letting myself think too hard I sing the chorus again, with True and his tiny folk. Another voice joins in from the doorway of the hut, a man's voice, untrained but strong and tuneful. The song ends. I have just long enough to say, "Dau! Get down!" before Brocc counts, "One, two, three," and steps back from the wire, leaving the hatch-like door open. We crouch, pulling the cloak over us, and hear the scratch of claws, the ruffle of feathers as the birds step up onto the edge. Then there's a whirr, a movement of the air above us, and in a moment they are gone. So fast. So final.

We lift the cloak and get to our feet. Dau is beside the main door, crouched down with his hands over his head. "Dagda's bollocks," he remarks in something like his old manner. "Just as well you warned me."

"Are you all right, Liobhan?" Brocc is pale; I see he was less confident of success than he appeared. "True?"

I realize True could not possibly have been fully shielded by the cloak. He's much too big. He has faced this with barely any protection. "I'm fine," I say. "Not that I'd ever want to go through that again. True, are you unhurt? And your little ones?"

"You are a kind soul, Liobhan, like your brother. I am well, yes. Master Dau, did they harm you?"

"Not a scratch. That was . . . remarkable. What exactly were you doing?"

Brocc explains: the vial, given to True by ancients of his own kind; the contents which have just been proven to have remarkable healing power; his own deeply held belief that the Crow Folk, for all their violent and unpredictable actions, are victims rather than aggressors. He describes how he reached over to the perch and how the birds stayed still, opening their fearsome beaks as he administered one drop to each. How, after he withdrew his arm and opened the wire door, in the moment before he ducked down and under the cloak, he glimpsed a new look in their eyes. A look of hope.

44

DAU

A magical cure. The goal I have dreamed of, the prize on which I have fixed my impossible hope. It's there right before me, and I cannot ask for it. Already we owe Brocc and True our lives. For us, they put themselves in peril. And Brocc has said he will come with us to Oakhill to bear witness. How can I ask more of them? Besides, it seems this cure is True's to give, not Brocc's. That makes it even more impossible to ask. Why would True squander the last few drops of so potent a draft for a man he barely knows? So I do not ask, though every part of me is tight with the longing to do so. And Liobhan does not ask, though I can guess what is in her thoughts. Instead, my companions get on with what must be done. They settle the prisoners beside the hut, in a spot where they cannot be seen from further than ten paces away. Liobhan tells the others how to place them so they will not choke or otherwise harm themselves. She says they will be safe for a few hours, long enough for us to return to the house, make our report, and send someone up to fetch them. My mind cannot quite take that in. I must arrange for Seanan, at least, to remain in custody until a hearing takes place. I hope my powers of persuasion are up to it. I hope people will be ready to listen.

Liobhan douses the fire. The dead birds are left where they

lie in the cages; the hanging corpses continue to stir in the draft with macabre semblance of life. I take off my monk's habit and give it to Liobhan. She orders us all out while she removes her soiled and tattered clothing and puts the habit on. Her own garments she makes into a bundle, at my request, to take back to the house. Evidence.

Then there's Corb. It hurts to leave him, even for a short time. True offers to keep vigil, but I say no. True must be safely concealed up in the forest before anyone comes back here. As Brocc, Liobhan, and Torcan perform a last check of everything, I take the stony man aside and thank him again for his help.

"I am glad to be of service," True says. "You are a remarkable man, Master Dau. Strong of heart. Deserving of kindness. I have a gift for you."

I can't speak.

"It does not come without risk," True says. "Like all magic, it is . . . unpredictable. But you are a warrior like my friend Brocc. You are a man of great courage. Will you try it?"

"I . . . I . . ." The word won't come out. My heart feels so full it might burst.

Footsteps approaching; someone else is here. Liobhan. "True is offering you the healing potion, Dau." Her strong voice has been reduced to a thread.

"Two drops left," True says. "One for each eye. They are yours, Master Dau. I cannot promise that they will restore your sight. The magic is not mine, but belongs to my ancient fore-bears. But if you are willing, we can attempt it."

Liobhan makes a little sound, instantly stifled. She's trying not to cry. In that moment she makes the decision for me. "I will try," I say, choking back my own tears. I must act as a man of courage should. "Whether or not it succeeds, this is the most generous of gifts, my friend. Are you sure?"

"I am sure. You are a brave man, and the path before you is

no straight and easy track." There's a pause, as if True is drawing breath. Then he says, "My hands are not delicately made. Liobhan, you have the skill to do this. If I hold Dau still, will you administer the drops?"

Liobhan draws a ragged breath. She sounds overwhelmed. Unsurprising after what she's just been through. But when she speaks, her voice is strong and capable. "Of course. Dau, you should sit on this stool. True will stand behind you and put his hands on either side of your head—that's it, True. We're doing it this way in case the drops sting; it might be hard to keep still. And if it works, it will be a shock to you after so long in the dark." A tiny clink as she withdraws the stopper. "Ready?"

"I'm ready." My heart is going like a galloping horse. My skin is all over cold sweat. Let this not be a dream. It feels unreal. How am I possibly deserving of such a gift? The gods I don't believe in would be justified in smiting me dead the moment the potion touches my eye.

The stuff is cool and refreshing; it falls on one eye then the other. For a moment I see a flash of light and color, impossibly bright. If it were not for True's strong hold, I would jerk my head in shock.

"Shut your eyes and keep them shut," says Liobhan with a healer's assurance. "Give it some time. Breathe slowly, Dau. Make your whole body calm."

"Rest easy, friend." True sounds untroubled. His deep tones are soothing.

Waiting is agony. "How much longer?"

"Count to one hundred."

"No. You should sing. And . . . move closer. Here, beside me."

I feel her kneel down on my right. True keeps his hands on either side of my head, but the strong grip has become more of a gentle, reassuring touch. Liobhan sings. The song is familiar, only there's more of it now.

> *Often he mourned the loss of light*
> *The blaze of sun, the candle bright*
> *Yet there was joy in touch and sound*
> *The wet nose of a loyal hound*
> *Friends' laughter; the song of a lark*
> *Solace and comfort in the dark.*
> *He knew that he would rise once more*
> *Walk forward through the open door*
> *His feet would tread a bright new way*
> *His eyes would look on every day*
> *With constant wonder, hope, and joy.*
> *This gift would heal the wounded boy.*

There's a silence. Then she says shakily, "You can open your eyes now, Dau."

I open them. It is as I long imagined: the first thing I see is Liobhan's face. Her cheeks are wet; tears spill from her lovely eyes. Her bright hair is disheveled, falling in myriad strands over her shoulders and down across the heavy brown cloth of the monk's habit. She has a big bruise on her jaw. As I blink and stare and try to ignore a dizziness that is making everything spin around us, she takes my hand and lifts it, laying my palm against her cheek. The look on her face is . . . remarkable. It is more than I can ever be worthy of, even if I live to be an old, old man.

"You can see," she whispers.

I am wordless. I am flooded with feelings. I am like a pool after a long dry summer, filled to overflowing by fresh autumn rain. "Outside," I say. "I want to go outside."

True helps me stand up; supports me when my head reels. I have imagined him in my mind, but he is bigger and stranger than I pictured him. I wonder what Seanan and his men will say of him, when they report on the fight. I turn and see Brocc in the doorway of the hut. His expression is hard to read. He looks over at True, then turns his gaze away.

"It worked, Brocc!" says Liobhan. "Dau has his sight back!"

"A generous gift," Brocc says. "This was a wise choice, True." Now he's looking at Liobhan, whose face is flushed with delight. She can't stop smiling as she helps me walk toward the door.

Oh, the greens! So many shades, so many layers, the sun on the leaves, the fresh grass, the moss coating the old walls. The colors are a dazzling miracle. I want to stare and stare. But I cannot. We must go. There is work to be done.

"One thing before we leave," I say. "I want to see Corb."

Liobhan is quick to understand. She shows me where he lies, swathed in a cloak. I kneel beside him. It is the strangest, most solemn of moments. Corb was my companion, sometimes my nursemaid. He was my protector. He was my friend. He was my little brother. He lies lifeless here because of that. How odd that I have never seen him until now. His face is long, with prominent cheekbones; his hair is the color of oak bark. He has fine, long-fingered hands. He is so pale. Gray pale. My mind fills with troubling thoughts. If I had not sent him with the dog . . . If I had not asked for volunteers to come up here . . . If I had not expected him to fight . . . But there is no point in that. He is gone. "Farewell, brave friend," I say. I draw the cloak over him again, then rise to my feet.

"He was a good boy," says Liobhan. "A remarkable boy."

I will have to go up to the farm when this is over. I will have to tell his mother and father that their good son is not coming home. I will have to fetch the dog, little Hope. That will be almost worse than fighting blind. But I will do it. This death is on me.

Torcan exclaims with surprise and delight when he discovers I can see. He is quite as I imagined him, handsome and upright with abundant dark hair and a broad smile, though like the rest of us he bears the scars of battle. There's a bandage around his arm and shoulder, with blood seeping through.

"Needs attention as soon as we get back," Liobhan says, seeing me looking. "We'll need Brother Petrán."

The captives are all sleeping heavily now under the influence of Liobhan's potion. We bid True farewell, and I thank him for his kindness, his courage, his generosity. His remarkable gift has changed my future. He tells me I am a fine man, and deserving. Then he heads up to the forest to wait for Brocc. They have supplies; he can camp there overnight.

Walking back to my father's house I want to look at everything, to drink it all in, to rediscover trees and grass and stones and sky, the sheep in the fields, the light and shadow of a fine morning, the faces of my companions. It is so remarkable to have my sight back, though I do feel somewhat unbalanced, like a seafarer stepping off his vessel after a long journey. As we go down the hill we work out our story. Yes, there were two others with us when the skirmish took place—not only the traveling storyteller, but also another man whom he had met on the road, a musician who had some fighting skills. That man could not stay to bear witness, as he was on the way to a family wedding further north. As for my vision, I regained it in much the same fashion as I lost it. At some point toward the end of the fight, I tripped and fell hard. When I rose, I found I could see light and shade with both eyes. By the time we had walked back to my father's gate, all was becoming clear again. A miracle, one might say.

This tale is somewhat flimsy, but we decide a simple explanation will be more plausible than a complicated tale. I hope they believe it, since it will need to cover not only the restoration of my sight but also the anticipated accounts by Seanan and his team of a stony giant appearing and ending the fight. The traveler was no giant; he was simply an unusually tall man. Stone? How could such a thing be? At that point Liobhan will suggest that their memories may be addled by the potion she was obliged to administer. It contained a substance called devil's-foot; the same thing that may be in my father's sleeping drafts. It lingers, Liobhan will say. Makes folk vague; robs them of the ability to think clearly.

As we walk, I'm aware of pain. The potion may have restored my sight, but it's done nothing to help my ankle, and I'm dizzy as well. Still, I use the stick only on the roughest parts of the track. I keep my back straight. I hold my head high. I look down toward my father's domain and rehearse in my mind what must come next.

Liobhan stumbles once or twice. A night's torture and a hard fight have taken their toll even on my strong, brave friend. I reach out a hand to steady her and she glances at me with a grin on her face that is as warm and fine as sun on a winter's day. If I could, I would look only at her. But now is not the time for such things. The smile, the touch of hands, those are enough. Despite what awaits me in my father's house, there is a warmth in my heart such as I have never felt before.

Brocc is very quiet. Something is troubling him. I wonder if he would have wished True's gift to go elsewhere, kindly though he spoke to me at the time. It is not for me to ask him. Perhaps he will talk to Liobhan.

There's no difficulty going in the gate. The guards do give us some surprised looks. There is Brocc, a striking stranger in his unusual clothing; Liobhan, bruised and untidy, in her monk's habit; Torcan similarly dressed, but unhooded; and myself, walking with confidence and meeting their stares full on. The guards ask no questions. Once we have passed, I hear them conducting a rapid conversation in lowered voices. I need to act quickly.

"Straight to the infirmary," I say. "And I'll answer any awkward questions."

The sun is high now and there are plenty of folk around; but although we attract more stares, nobody approaches us. As we enter the herb garden, I see a reception party waiting: three monks standing by the door to the stillroom. Ruarc is nowhere to be seen. A good sign or a bad one?

"Master Dau," says a broad-shouldered fellow with tonsured gray hair. "What has happened?" Then, before I have time to say a word, "Your eyes. Have you . . . are you . . . ?"

"Brother Petrán," murmurs Liobhan. "The infirmarian."

"May we come inside, Brother Petrán? Two of our number are injured and we are all weary. But there are some matters to be dealt with. One in particular is urgent. We need to speak behind closed doors." I glance at the other two monks. "Forgive me. I can see you now, but I do not know your names."

"This is Brother Martán, our apothecary, Master Dau. And this is my assistant, Brother Pól. Please enter. Brother Íobhar has been called away again, sadly."

Liobhan, being a woman, is not permitted to go further than the stillroom. But Brother Petrán is inclined to be helpful. He sends a monk to find Miach, and when she appears, Torcan, Brocc, and Liobhan depart for the bathhouse. The women will stay together, the men will stay together, and I don't need to tell them not to talk. Miach can tend to Liobhan's wounds and Brother Pól to Torcan's. I ask them to come straight back when they're finished. With Seanan and his crew away from the house, this feels safe enough. It does seem that Brother Petrán will be prepared to listen, at least.

Then it's just him and me and Brother Martán sitting together in a corner of the monks' temporary refectory, and it's time to tell them the story. Time to start things moving.

"I suppose you can see that we've been in a fight," I say. "You'll be compensated for the damage to those habits, which we borrowed without permission. If I were to tell you I have a group of bound captives not far from the house and that one of them is Master Seanan, how would you respond?"

45

LIOBHAN

The change in Dau is startling. He's taken charge, not only of our little team but of the most complex and testing situation I could imagine. By the time I've got myself cleaned up and changed into my good clothes, with my wounds salved and my hair washed and plaited, then been escorted back to the infirmary by Miach—she's bursting with questions, but she's being careful not to ask them—Dau has arranged a meeting with not only Brothers Petrán and Martán, but also Father Eláir, the prior from St. Padraig's, as well as Master Beanón, Master Naithí, and master-at-arms Fergal. Even more surprising is that the monks have agreed I can be present. Seems the need to keep this out of the public eye outweighs the rule banning women from this area. Brother Íobhar is absent again, visiting another monastic foundation. I know Dau wanted him to be present; hoped Ruarc would find the courage to support him in any hearing. He told me about the early morning encounter in the stillroom, when his brother's words did not match his actions. I suspect Íobhar has decided to step back from the whole affair. My guess is that he'll stay away until it's all over.

We're in a chamber that must usually be the monks' eating place. I sit between Brocc and Torcan, trying to look unobtrusive. It's perhaps unfortunate that the only clean clothing I had was the russet gown with its embroidered overdress, the outfit I wear to sing. It's on the eye-catching side, but never mind that. It's bliss to be warm, dry, and clean again. Miach was troubled by the bruising on my face, not only from Seanan's blow but from having the gag on for so long. I told her I would explain when I was allowed to.

Dau tells the story calmly, setting out what happened yesterday and today without making any judgments. The faces of his listeners grow graver with every statement. When he gets to the part about Seanan's house of horrors, the herbs and potions and the victims, both avian and human, there's murmuring between Brother Petrán and the prior, as if this confirms something they already suspected. Fergal, too, looks as if this is not entirely surprising to him. Beanón's maintaining a lawman's expression, calm and detached. Naithí fails to conceal his horror.

"One thing I will explain briefly," Dau says, "though it plays no part in what must be done now. You see I am cured of my blindness. It was quite sudden. During the skirmish between my party and my brother's, I tripped and fell flat on the ground. My body was jolted with some violence. As I rose, I found that my sight was returning. First came blurry light and shadow, then colors and shapes, and then increasing clarity. Of all the possible cures I had imagined, something so simple and startling had never occurred to me. But there it is. A miracle, perhaps."

"Praise be to God," murmurs Father Eláir, and the other brethren echo his words. Nobody expresses doubt about this unlikely explanation; the evidence is right before them. How else could Dau have regained full sight so quickly?

Dau refrains from saying that he still does not believe in God. He looks around the circle, meeting each man's eye in turn. It occurs to me that Seanan is not the only accomplished liar in the family. "We have two pressing matters that must be attended to. First, Master Seanan and his party must be retrieved from their current location and brought here. More on that in a moment. Second, my father must be notified of what has happened. You may be aware that he and I are not on the best of terms. Another tale lies behind the one I have just related: the tale of my childhood in this household. It is a dark and difficult story, and this is not the time to tell it, especially as Brother Íobhar, who witnessed those events, is not present today. The enmity between me and Seanan goes back a very long way. My father has always been inclined to believe Seanan's side of a story over mine. My brother can be . . . persuasive. Master Beanón knows, as a man of the law, that a person accused of a crime must be allowed to present his own case, or to have it presented for him. Seanan must be given his chance to speak."

Dau has his audience in thrall; nobody stirs so much as an eyelid.

"But not yet. And he must not be given the opportunity to stir up the household, to spread his opinions into every ear, to influence our father before this matter can be aired in a properly conducted hearing. He and the other men in that group must be confined securely. Held in custody. I am not sure how that might best be done, since Seanan carries such authority in this household."

Beanón clears his throat. "A full legal hearing, with all the required preparation, would take a week or more to organize. But . . . we might conduct an informal hearing similar to the one that was carried out to settle the matter of compensation for your injury. I believe that might be adequate for the purpose. We could hold it tomorrow, meaning only one night's incarceration would be necessary. However, I cannot represent both parties. Master Seanan would be justified in demanding his own lawman. And in requesting sufficient time to discuss the matter with his representative before the hearing."

Does that mean Beanón is choosing to represent Dau? I try to keep the look of astonishment off my face.

"Ah," says Father Eláir. He's a tall, stooped man with neatly tonsured white hair and a scholarly appearance. "I believe I can assist you in this matter. One of our brethren was a man of the law before he joined holy orders. Brother Máedóc would be entirely capable in this role, and I will gladly give him leave to undertake it." He glances at Dau. "He would be impartial. He is a man of conscience."

Hah! If he's truly a man of conscience, how can he possibly represent Seanan? If I were Brother Máedóc I'd be saying I wouldn't touch the job with a barge pole. But then, justice must be seen to be done.

"That sort of hearing would be ideal," Dau says smoothly. "It should be arranged with a minimum of fuss. No grand announcements. The household to continue as usual, as far as that is possible."

"The arrival of these bound captives is hardly going to escape notice," says Fergal. "As soon as someone spots them the whole place will be abuzz. Is there any chance all of this can take place elsewhere? Not only housing them securely, but also the hearing itself? I can supply guards. Carefully chosen men whom I can trust to be discreet."

Brother Petrán and the prior are talking in murmurs, leaning toward each other. Then Petrán says, "They can be housed at St. Padraig's. The monks' cells can be locked and the guards could be posted outside. We can arrange other accommodation for those of our brethren still in residence there. Our refectory would be large enough for the hearing. Father Eláir is prepared to make it available to you."

"However," says the prior, his expression somber, "this

cannot go ahead without Lord Scannal's agreement. He is chieftain; his is the final authority."

Ah. I see the looks that go across the chamber. I want to speak up, but I hold my tongue. It's Brother Petrán who puts my thoughts into words. "That is undoubtedly true, Father. May I suggest . . . If Lord Scannal will not listen to Master Dau, perhaps he will listen to you. And . . . I think he must also listen to me. We've heard some troubling comments on Lord Scannal's failing health. Equally troubling are certain discrepancies in the record of herbal components taken from our supplies. We are concerned that Lord Scannal may have been regularly dosed with a substance harmful to his well-being. It is a very sensitive matter. He should not take his usual sleeping draft tonight. If you agree, I will advise him on that matter."

"What are you suggesting?" Master Naithí sounds appalled.

Seems I do have to speak up. "I was forcibly dosed with what I believe to have been a similar mixture last night," I say. "By Master Seanan and one of his men. I'm prepared to talk about that at the hearing. And about the various preparations we found in that outhouse. It's important that the lawmen concerned go up there and have a look today. And that nobody is given the opportunity to meddle with the evidence. There should probably be guards posted there, too." After a moment I add, "If Lord Scannal's been regularly taking a draft containing devil's-foot, he needs to come off it gradually, not all at once. The side effects of that could be quite severe. Brother Petrán or Brother Martán should make up a weaker version for him to take tonight or he may be unable to attend any sort of gathering tomorrow."

"That is wise counsel," murmurs Brother Petrán. "But it would be Lord Scannal's decision whether to take such a draft or not, once he understands the circumstances."

"I hesitate to say this," puts in Master Beanón, "but if charges may be laid at some future time in relation to this matter, Lord Scannal's response to the sudden withdrawal of the draft would stand as solid proof, one way or the other."

Shit. He's right, of course. But at what cost?

Everyone looks as shocked as I feel. It's Dau who asks the question nobody else is prepared to frame. "Can you describe the likely response, Brother Petrán? How severe might it be? Would my father be incapacitated?"

"A crippling headache, at the very least, sufficient to keep a man to his bed for some while. Tremors. Dizziness. If Lord Scannal did not take the draft tonight, he would be unlikely to sleep. We could offer him something different, not containing devil's-foot. A light sleeping draft. Whether it would help him, I cannot say. Should he choose to cease the old draft straight-away rather than ease off slowly, we should consider delaying the hearing for a few days at least."

More glances around the circle. Everyone knows how important it is to do this as soon as possible. How long can they keep Seanan locked up at St. Padraig's? And what about Brocc, who can stay only one more day? He's the sole independent witness and his statement is crucial.

"We will put the options to Lord Scannal," Beanón says. "He will make his own decision."

There's a moment's somber silence. Then Dau speaks again. "One more thing." For the first time, his voice is unsteady. "I mentioned earlier that one of our number was killed in the attack. We'd all have been dead had not Master Brocc and his companion intervened. The body of Corb, the young man who was my assistant, lies near the building up there. His family lives not far from here. He lost his life in my service. I intended to convey the sad news to his family in person. Perhaps to bring his body home to them . . . But these other matters mean I cannot take the time to do so. Might someone arrange . . . ?"

He looks wretched. I know how badly he wanted to do this himself.

"We'll see it done, Master Dau," Naithí says. "Father Eláir might perhaps permit one of the brethren to accompany the party, so prayers for the departed may be spoken. If I may share this sorrowful news with Iarla, who is always discreet, he and I will make any necessary arrangements." He hesitates for a moment. "Master Dau, may we advise the family that you will pay them a visit in due course? Perhaps within a few days?"

"Thank you, Master Naithí. Yes, do tell them that, please. And offer my heartfelt condolences. To say that Corb was a fine young man is barely adequate."

The room falls quiet again. The enormity of what has happened is sinking in, and with it the dwindling time available to do what must be done.

Father Eláir is the first to speak. "The circumstances dictate that we should act without delay. Along with Master Beanón and Brother Petrán, I will accompany Master Dau to break this unwelcome news to his father. Brother Martán, ask Brother Pól to take charge here for now. Then go over to St. Padraig's and have a discreet word with Brother Máedóc. Provide him with some information about what has occurred; ask him to keep it to himself, but alert him to the fact that he may want to brush up his knowledge of the law as it applies in such matters, and to do so speedily. Master Beanón, when you are free, perhaps you can go across and speak with him also. Answer his questions and prepare him for his conversation with Master Seanan, whenever that might occur."

"I will do so, Father."

"I will ensure one of our brethren is ready to go with the party collecting the young man's body," Father Eláir goes on. "That must be done today. I will send our man to see you, Master Naithí."

"The most urgent thing is assembling the guards," Dau says. "Can you speak to your men straightaway, Fergal? Without raising any alarms?"

"I can and will, Master Dau. You believe the prisoners will still be under the effects of this draft?"

Dau looks at me.

"They should still be deeply asleep," I say. It sounds better than *unconscious*. "Maybe you should take a cart. Bringing what look like corpses slung over the backs of horses can't in any way be made unobtrusive."

"Leave it to me," says Fergal. I get the impression he's almost looking forward to the challenge. That doesn't really surprise me; I couldn't spend time with the men-at-arms and the stable workers without learning how many of them resented Seanan's way of ruling over the household. What does astonish me is that in this gathering of powerful men not one has challenged Dau's account of what just happened. Can it be true? That by speaking out bravely Dau has given every one of them the courage to do the same?

He looks exhausted now. But despite the shadows around them, his eyes are bright with resolve. I wish I could walk over and put my arms around him. Tell him how brave he is. Tell him I understand his pain. Instead I stand respectfully as they all leave the room after agreeing to meet again before supper. As the others move out through the stillroom, Dau lingers to speak with us.

"Liobhan, you should have a word with Iarla about accommodation for Brocc. And Torcan—don't return to the stables. Best if you stay out of sight in case of awkward questions. Go back to our quarters; act as if nothing has changed."

"Iarla's going to be busy," I say. "Brocc can squeeze in with us. I'll ask Miach; she can find us some extra bedding. It's only for one night."

Dau's mouth curves into a crooked smile. "If you say so. I suppose when this is all over, it's hardly going to matter what gossip arises from our sleeping arrangements."

I manage a smile in return, though my face hurts. "Never took much notice of gossip myself. You'd better go. Master Beanón is waiting for you." What if his father refuses to listen? What if Lord Scannal is incapable of understanding? I felt confused enough after taking that draft once, and I'm young, strong, and healthy. What must it do to a man who drinks it night after night? I attempt a calm and confident expression. "Go well, Dau."

"And you." He turns and is gone.

46

BROCC

usk is falling on this day of surprises. When True and I rushed out on our rescue mission, knowing Liobhan needed us, we did not expect to arrive in the middle of a fight. But we came as warriors, and as warriors we helped our friends overcome their enemies. I saw what Dau's brother had done to his captives and shuddered to imagine how it was for the Crow Folk he had held in that place. I saw the brand on my sister's arm and felt a cold fury possess me. But bringing justice to Master Seanan is another man's quest. Even in the grip of such terrible anger I recognized that. My quest lies with the Crow Folk. It was clear they had been tortured there over a long period. How Seanan trapped them, how he brought them in without sustaining injuries himself, why some were left to die out in the forest, is a mystery I hope can be unraveled when he is questioned. I only wish I had known of this sooner. I could have saved more.

So, True's potion gave the survivors back their strength, and the two flew free. The weight in my chest lifted a little with that. I thought I saw some understanding in their eyes, in the moment between healing and flight. I hope I did. I am happy that True chose to use the last drops from his vial to help Dau. I have seen, with some astonishment, a bond between Dau and my sister far deeper than that of comrades. I have seen the startling change in the man we found so arrogant, so difficult, when we trained together on Swan Island. Our mission in Breifne changed Dau for the better. But he is changed again; he is becoming a man of authority and purpose. He was deserving of True's gift. I know this. But I fear how Eirne will respond when we take this story to her. That there was such a cure among us, and that the last of it is gone . . .

Now I am here in Lord Scannal's house, in a quiet chamber with Liobhan and Torcan, eating supper. As the day unfolded, the three of us were called separately to talk to the lawman, Master Beanón. He asked me some questions about what brought me to these parts, and explained how the hearing will be conducted—it is to be tomorrow—and how I should present my account of events when asked. He wanted to know more about the other man who joined the fight, my traveling companion. Among other things, I mentioned that Elouan—I gave True this Armorican name—was an unusually tall and broad man, almost a giant. We'd met at a wayside inn where I'd been telling stories in exchange for a night's lodging. Since we were both heading in the same general direction, we walked on together. No, I was not sure exactly where he was going. To a family wedding, that was all he said.

Beanón had questions to ask about the fight. In particular, he wanted to know if I had seen who delivered the fatal blow to Corb. It was all very well to lie about True; what other option did any of us have? But I would not lie about that. "The biggest of the men," I said. "And yes, I saw it with my own eyes, despite the confusion of the scene. He was following an order from the man I now know to be Master Seanan."

Beanón's tone sharpened, as if, now that I was telling only the truth, he no longer entirely believed me. "Was it not a noisy

scene? Shouts, screams, blows, the clashing of blades? Are you
sure there was an explicit order, Master Brocc?"

"I am. Master Seanan did not fight in this skirmish. He stood
on the sidelines, out of harm's way, watching. I glimpsed him
as he gestured to his man, then pointed to Corb. His meaning
was unmistakable, Master Beanón." I mimed what I had seen.
"I had to fend off another attacker and I could not reach Corb
in time. Master Dau was fighting blind. Liobhan was injured
and slowed by the drug she had been given. And Torcan is not
a trained fighter."

"What about you?" The lawman's gaze was sharp. "A traveling storyteller? I am surprised that this fight ended as it did,
Master Brocc."

"I've had to learn to defend myself on the road," I told him.
"I can't speak for the others."

Beanón allowed himself the slightest of smiles. "Mm," he
said. "You can go now; Iarla will walk you back to your chamber. I don't plan to ask questions tomorrow about the odds of
one side or the other winning the fight. That seems irrelevant.
But your testimony is important—you are the only independent witness to what occurred."

I returned to this chamber. I have tried to rest, as I know I
should. But my thoughts have been on True, up in the forest
on his own. Not that True is ever quite on his own, since his
small passengers go with him everywhere. He and I brought
supplies with us. He will do well enough until tomorrow or
even the next day, should this drag on.

We have seen little of Dau. He came back briefly to check
how we were faring and to tell us the hearing would be going
ahead. The look on his face forbade further questions. I hope
he will tell us more later.

We told Torcan that I am Liobhan's brother. Liobhan trusts

him to be discreet. With all of us confined together until to-morrow, holding back this information would rule out honest talk between us. I think Torcan is aware of the constraint his presence brings, for after we finish the meal, he takes himself out to the antechamber and closes the connecting door. Liobhan and I sit in silence for a while. Only a night and a day, then I will be gone from here. How can I leave her again? Last time nearly broke my heart.

"So tell me," she says, turning that very direct look of hers on me. "How is it, living in that place? Are you content? Is Eirne well?"

"If I answer three questions, you do the same." My voice cracks. I want to weep.

"Oh, Brocc." She draws a long breath, lets it out in a sigh. "This is not a game."

"Where I live now, everything feels like a game or a trick or a tit-for-tat exchange. As a bard reared on tales of the uncanny I should have expected that, I suppose. I lost my singing voice in exchange for safe passage across a certain body of water. A long story. It's all right," I add hastily, seeing her expression. "It is temporary. One year; I bargained the other fellow down. But awkward. More than awkward, dangerous. Eirne was not happy."

"Isn't that a little unfair of her? She must know how these things work."

"She'll be even less happy when she learns about True's healing potion and that it's all been used up. We have no way to help any of the clan who are hurt by the Crow Folk, and my singing was our best means of keeping them at bay."

"And yet you chose to help them. Wanted to do so, badly."

"I believe it's the key. I don't believe they are truly evil. Only lost. Hurt. Broken. Perhaps driven a little crazy by whatever has befallen them. Dau's brother has treated them cruelly, no

doubt of that. But I'm speaking of an event far more cata-
strophic, something that drove them from their true home,
scattered them so widely that they lost their way."

"And you think you can earn their trust?" Liobhan sounds
skeptical. "You're too kind for your own good, Brocc."

"She won't like what we've done. Squandering the last precious drops on *them*."

"Actually, it was Dau who got the last precious drops. I'll
never cease to be grateful for that. Never. And it was True's
choice, not yours. Will Eirne be angry with him?"

I shake my head. "No. Only with me. She . . . sometimes she
is quite cold toward me, Liobhan. And she has been out of sorts.
Not herself . . ." The words start to flow from me; I can't hold
them back. I tell my sister about the clan and about Eirne and
about our struggles with the Crow Folk. Our high times and
our low times, Eirne's sweetness and her fury, her tenderness
and her chilly authority. Her bouts of sickness. The times when
she seems too weary even to speak to me. "She has been much
better of recent times," I say. "Kinder. More ready to listen.
Eating with good appetite, walking out more. But she's always
troubled over the Crow Folk, the danger they pose, the very
limited defenses we have against them. She does not understand my argument, though I have explained in as many ways
as I can find."

Liobhan picks up her cup, takes a sip of her mead. There's a
little frown on her brow. "How long has Eirne been feeling
sick, Brocc? Getting tired, losing her temper more often?"

"Why would you ask that?"

"Just answer the question, will you?"

"Since early spring. Perhaps before that."

She gives me a quizzical look. "There may be a much sim-
pler explanation than you imagine. Isn't it possible your Eirne
may be with child?"

I stare back at her with my mouth hanging open.

"You are husband and wife," my sister says with a smile. "I assume you've been doing the things that husbands and wives do. And you're both young and healthy."

"Oh." This eloquent bard is lost for words. I do not know if I feel shocked or delighted or terrified or just plain stupid.

"You're the son of a healer and you didn't think of this?"

"But why wouldn't she tell me? Why wouldn't anyone tell me?"

"Oh, Brocc. You sound like an infant. Maybe she didn't know either. Maybe she didn't recognize the signs. And it might only just be starting to show. Add her worries about the Crow Folk to her feeling tired and sick, and it's no surprise at all that she's often a bit short with you. Is there a healer in the clan? A midwife?"

I'm thinking hard. Eirne herself was taken from her human foster parents at the age of five. The clan brought her up, more or less; that strangely assorted group of uncanny folk became her family. Moon-Fleet is a healer, yes. But she might know nothing at all of how such matters work for a human woman, or a half-human one. There would have been nobody to teach Eirne such things. "There is a healer. But I'm not sure she would have recognized the signs. And I don't think Eirne knew. Not until . . . not until recently. I was away. Both True and I. When we came back, things were different." Because Eirne suspected this, and she knew what peril the child would face, living in the forest with the Crow Folk all around. Even knowing that, she forgave me. She welcomed me back into her arms and into her bed.

And yet . . . and yet when a bird brought Liobhan's cry for help, Eirne hid the message under her pillow and did not wake me. My wife is kind, and she is cruel. I am a bard. She is of the Otherworld. Why should I find this surprising?

"You're crying," my sister says. "Here." She offers me a handkerchief, then puts her arms around me. "It's a good thing, isn't it? Having a child? I look forward to telling our parents they'll have a grandchild—I can imagine the looks on their faces. And since I'm not likely to produce one for them, and Galen is so close to Prince Aolu he might as well be wedded to the man, it's all up to you."

I cry on her shoulder for a little, feeling grateful that Torcan closed the door. I consider the wonder of a small life growing. I remember how Eirne spoke of how seldom children were born in the clan and how precious each life was. But I think also of those captives flying free from their cage, out into the forest. I remember the one I laid to rest with a song. I recall how the young bird chirruped as I sang, and how it died in my little house while I slept beside it unawares. Is this how it will be when my own child is born? A constant perilous dance with fate, in which each misstep might mean a life taken, each careful move a safe day won, a night of rest?

"I don't think I'm ready to be a father," I say.

47

LIOBHAN

At last Dau comes back to our quarters. He waves away offers of food and drink—we saved some for him, not knowing if he would eat supper elsewhere—and sinks down onto a stool near the fire. "Gods," he says. "What a day."

"Drink the mead, at least." I pour a small measure and put the cup into his hands. He feels cold. "We're full of questions, as you may imagine. But we can wait."

He says nothing. Holds the cup for a little, then sets it down on the hearth without taking so much as a sip. Bends his head and puts his hands over his face.

Brocc and Torcan get up and retreat to the antechamber. It is, in fact, past time for bed. The door closes quietly.

I sit. I wait. I can't tell if Dau is shedding tears; he is very still and quite silent. After a while I don't want to wait anymore. I move to kneel beside him. "I'm here," I say quietly. "I'm here by your side, for as long as you want me. You can talk to me. Or you can tell me to shut up and go away."

There's a long moment, then he brings his hands down from his face and I see his features in the glow of the firelight as he looks at me. He's dropped his mask; this face is full of fear and courage and love. He always was a handsome man. But this face is beautiful. I know in this moment that what is between us now is precious and solemn and lifelong. Perhaps, deep down, I already knew.

"That's better," I murmur, reaching to brush a stray tear from his cheek. My thumb lingers there a little longer than it might. "Can you tell me what happened? With your father?" The news can't be all bad, since we know the hearing is going ahead. But I see that not all is well.

"When I first went in, he thought I was Seanan. 'Oh, Seanan, you're back,' he said, and smiled. Then realized it was me and didn't smile anymore. Sorry I couldn't talk to you just now. I was trying not to scream and throw things."

I pick up the cup and put it back in his hands. "Drink. Please. You've got another day of this to get through tomorrow. You need to keep up your strength."

He drinks, shudders, wipes his mouth. Sets the cup back down. "We told him the story. He insisted on ceasing the draft immediately. No compromise, even when the likely consequences were spelled out for him. He wouldn't believe Seanan might be responsible for doctoring the contents. That needs further investigation. Iarla has been told what's going on. He and Brother Petrán will look at who might be involved, though it doesn't help that Seanan dismissed his body servant, Ardgan, yesterday morning and the man's already left Oakhill."

"Morrigan's britches," I murmur. "It's even more of a tangled web than I thought."

"Father didn't want to believe any of it. But the facts of what happened are undeniable, and I was backed up by the others. Liobhan . . . I found out why Seanan chose yesterday morning to execute his unpleasant plan for you. Naithí said a message came from Lord Ross this morning, calling off the betrothal. My father commented that it was disappointing and that the reasons were a mystery to him. But Naithí said Seanan was furious long before that, as soon as he heard the visitors were leaving early. My guess is that someone had seen me talking to Cormac and passed that information on to him. He'd have guessed the truth straightaway. I'm sorry, Liobhan. I'm so sorry you had to go through that."

"It certainly wasn't the most pleasant of experiences. But it wasn't your fault." My arm has been poulticed and bandaged. It still throbs. Worse than the pain is the thought that I'll be spending the rest of my life with Master Seanan's brand on me, as if I were a prize cow. "It's a pity your brother has never learned to settle his differences by negotiation. Thank the gods that girl isn't marrying the man."

"Liobhan."

"Mm?"

"I don't know how it will go tomorrow. Maybe we should have waited. Given Father more time, so his mind would be clearer. He kept asking where Seanan was, though we'd explained that he and his men were in custody. He didn't want to decide anything without Seanan present. It took some time for him to understand that if he didn't approve this informal council, his heir would face a formal hearing presided over by someone of higher standing than a local chieftain, with the charges including abduction, unlawful imprisonment, and torture. Beanón had to point out the inevitability of that news spreading far and wide before Father would agree to the plan. So it goes ahead. Seanan will lie. He'll do what he's always done, twist the facts so I'm the instigator of everything. He'll probably mention your unhealthy influence over me, or how going blind addled my wits. His men will back him up. Nobody will care about a few crows stuck in cages and experimented on. Everyone else will be afraid to speak out against him. And Father will believe exactly what he wants to believe, no more, no less. That's if going straight off the draft doesn't render him unfit to understand any of it."

"How long since you had anything to eat?" With an effort I keep my tone light.

"What?"

"You're talking as if disaster is inevitable, Dau. But it's within your power to prevent that. Right now, you need to look after yourself and build up your strength, so you'll face this like the warrior you are. So eat. And drink the rest of that. Pity I can't brew up relentless hope for you. I know you feel sick with worry. I know your mind is spinning. If it helps, imagine I'm Archu and do as I say without question. Eat. Drink. Rest."

He stares at me for a long moment, then his face relaxes into a smile. "What are you offering?"

"A slice of chicken pie with a dish of vegetables. It'll be cold by now, but ours was quite tasty. There's some fruit, too. Everything's on the table, there, under the cover. I might make chamomile tea. I have everything I need in here. Don't want to disturb the others."

He sits at the table and, seeing my eyes on him, starts to eat. But his mind is not on the meal. "It was odd that Brocc turned up just when he was most needed. With his strange friend."

"The mysterious Elouan. I've seen him before, on a certain memorable day when I coerced you into singing."

"You've coerced me into quite a few things. Didn't we dance together three times?"

"You enjoyed that as much as I did." I scoop out dried chamomile flowers from my little jar and drop them into the jug I keep for the purpose. I set the kettle on the fire. I remember dancing with Dau in the royal household of Breifne. And I remember dancing with him in the forest, perhaps that same forest out of which Brocc and True appeared today, a miraculous rescue party. "It wasn't odd that Brocc turned up. When I was in that place, tied up and helpless, a little bird came in, not one of the Crow Folk but a tiny thing no bigger than a wren.

They're uncanny creatures. Messengers between worlds." I
have Dau's full attention now. He would once have scoffed at
such an idea and accused me of making up fanciful tales. But
he's known me long enough now to understand that this is no
wild flight of imagination. "It unpicked the knots binding my
wrists up to the wire. Just as well, because it had been set up so
that if I passed out or fell asleep the cage would open and the
Crow Folk could get at me. Before the little bird flew off it
plucked out some of my hair. I was dizzy and confused, and I
couldn't think why it would do that. But it flew back to Eirne's
realm, to where Brocc was, and showed him the hair, and the
bird told Eirne where to find me."

"Told her? How? Do these birds have human speech?"

"No, but Eirne can understand them. Brocc knew it was a call
for help. He came as quickly as he could. Not as fast as a bird
can fly, but perhaps quicker than most human folk can walk."

"What was Seanan going to do, just before Brocc and his
friend came into the fight? What was he threatening?"

I hesitate, thinking how it must have been for Dau, blind in
the conflict, doing his best, hearing his brother's voice utter
those chilling words.

"What was he going to do, Liobhan?"

Something in the way he speaks makes me suddenly cold. I
look at him and for a moment I see Seanan's eyes looking back
at me. My heart is suddenly hammering. "Save that voice for
tomorrow. Save it for your brother." I turn abruptly away and
busy myself with the kettle.

There's a silence. Then I hear Dau say, "I'm sorry. I'm sorry,
Liobhan."

"It's all right. Just don't speak to me like that again. The
answer to your question is, he got out a knife—Ultán was holding me, restraining me—and . . . Seanan was going to do something to my face. Cut me, mark me. Put out my eyes. One or

all of those." Everything comes flooding back. Not just that part but the night before, and Corb, and the whole sequence of horrors. Tomorrow I'll have to tell it all over again, tell it and answer questions, perhaps from Seanan himself. Perhaps from Lord Scannal. "Shit!" I exclaim as I spill hot water onto my hand.

Then he's beside me, kneeling before the fire, and he takes kettle and cup from me and sets them aside, then wraps his arms around me and holds me close. "Hush, hush," he whispers, though I am not saying a word.

48

LIOBHAN

This is the day. I hear Brocc and Torcan go out the main door, no doubt heading for the bathhouse and privy. Dau is still asleep. I roll up my bedding and stow it in a corner. I take off my night-robe and put on my clothes. I'll have to wake him. But not quite yet. Let him sleep as long as he can before he must face what awaits him. For Dau, the hearing will be a battle more daunting than any fight with swords or knives or bare fists. This is brother against brother, and the weapons are words, gestures, arguments. The ability to influence hearts and minds.

When Dau suggested we share the bed last night so we could both get a good sleep, I rolled my eyes at him.

"Isn't there a story about a pair of lovers who slept with a naked sword between them?" he said. "I suppose we could do something similar. Though maybe not; this bed is on the narrow side."

"A Swan Island warrior is trained to exercise restraint and strength of will and so on," I said, while my body was busy telling me how much I wanted to lie down with him and hold him and do all sorts of other things, tired and bruised as I was. "But I know and you know that we wouldn't be able to keep our hands off each other. And this is the wrong time and place for that."

"You're saying there will be a right time and place?" Something in Dau's voice made my heart turn over.

"How could you imagine otherwise? But not under this roof. Not until we're gone from here." I took a careful breath. We had just made a momentous decision. Maybe that was why my heart was suddenly racing.

"And not on Swan Island?"

I glanced over at him. Now there was the hint of a smile on his face.

"That's a challenge that remains to be faced. A puzzle that's still to be worked out. Sleep well, Dau. Think of good things."

He didn't sleep well, but at least in the end he did sleep. I tossed and turned, plagued by unanswerable questions. They're still going around and around in my mind this morning. The fact that Dau has his sight back doesn't necessarily mean I'm free of my debt bondage. That decision will be up to Lord Scannal. What if Dau is allowed to leave and I'm not?

Nothing for it now but to face the day and do my best. I gather my wits and my strength and promise myself I will answer questions with calm and clarity and give Dau all the support I can. Then I gently wake him.

The hearing is to be in the afternoon. We've been told Master Beanón and the other lawman need this morning to talk to everyone who will be called to speak, and to take statements from some others. And the monks have to get everything set up at St. Padraig's.

After a quick breakfast Dau is gone. I think of him out there going from place to place and person to person, acting like the chieftain's son he is, making sure the plan is as perfect as he can make it, with all its components in place. Meanwhile Brocc,

Torcan, and I try to keep one another entertained. Brocc tells stories. I sing songs. Torcan teaches us a complicated game using different-colored pebbles. We tidy and clean our sleeping quarters. People bring us food and drink and, later in the morning, Miach comes with fresh clothing for me to wear at the hearing. She's found me a sedate-looking gown in dove gray, with a shawl in dark blue. The gown almost fits; it's just a little too short. She brushes my hair for me and plaits it into what would be a demure style on some other woman. I don't need a mirror to know I could never look demure in a thousand years, but I thank her for the effort. I aim to draw as little attention to myself as possible.

As I'm thinking how difficult that could be, Miach says, "I'll come with you if you want. Master Beanón said I didn't have to, because I've already told him what I know about the stillroom and writing in the book and so on. But I thought you might like some female company. I asked Iarla and he said I could go. Who knows, the monks might think it's more proper to have two women there rather than only one."

"I'd like that. Thank you, Miach. Can't say I'm looking forward to any of it, but at least by the end of today it will all be over."

Brocc declines the offer of a blue tunic, preferring his unusual green outfit. As a traveling storyteller, he can get away with looking somewhat eccentric. He leaves off the leather jerkin and substitutes a short cloak of Dau's, plain brown in color. Torcan's soberly clad in a clean tunic of the household blue, without the family emblem, and gray breeches. We wait, and wait some more, and finally Iarla himself comes to fetch us. It's not far to St. Padraig's; we'll walk.

Of course it was never going to be possible to keep this quiet from the household at large. Folk will have noted Seanan's absence from last night's supper and today's breakfast. They will

have seen the worried faces, noted the consultations behind
closed doors, observed the fact that influential members of the
household were suddenly much occupied with something that
was not their usual business. There will have been a lot of coming and going between here and St. Padraig's, far more than on
a regular day. Not to speak of the trips to and from Master
Seanan's torture chamber.

Iarla leads us through the house and out a back door, past
the infirmary where we are joined by Brothers Petrán and
Martán. Dau, we're told, is already at the monastery. It makes
me shiver to think of him there. There was such hatred in Seanan's voice as he menaced me with that knife, a hatred that was
not for me—that man cares nothing about me—but all for his
brother. What did Dau ever do to him? What fault is it of a newborn babe if his mother loses her life in the birthing? What if
every such child were made an object of lifelong loathing? That
would set a blight over every town, every village, every small
settlement. I imagine Dau's mother in the afterlife, looking
down on her sons and weeping. Today, I hope the youngest will
make her proud.

St. Padraig's is a sad-looking place. The part that was burned
is still a ruin, though there are signs of preparation for rebuilding: a neat stack of blackened stones; a wide patch of newly
raked ground; debris heaped at the edges of the monastery
land, as if nobody was quite sure what to do with it. Strong old
yews stand guard, scorched but living. The main monastery
building still stands, though it now has a temporary entry, and
today guards are standing outside it. My heart starts to race. I
make myself breathe in a pattern. Today of all days I must be
mindful of my Swan Island training.

The two monks head our small procession. Miach walks
beside me, Brocc and Torcan behind. It does my heart good
to have my brother here. I'm glad of all the people who have

befriended us and stood by us, not only Torcan and Miach and poor Corb, but all the others who have remained calm and practical and honest despite the poison Seanan has spread through this household. There are words I could use for Master Seanan. Vile. Loathsome. Cruel. Deranged. But he's not going to show that side of himself in this hearing. He may be a hideous specimen of mankind, but he's no fool. He'll be all calm control, all tricky words, everything aimed to convince his father that he's right and everyone else is wrong. Whose will be the final decision? At that other hearing, where I put my hand up for a year's debt bondage, things were settled by mutual agreement. I'm not sure that can happen here. It might be up to Lord Scannal. Circumstances being what they are, I don't find that reassuring.

The refectory is a long room with a row of windows to the east and a hearth on the other side. There's a lectern in a corner—perhaps it's usual for a monk to read from scripture at mealtimes—and a hatch-like opening to a kitchen. At the far end there are two doors, both closed. Today the place has been set up with benches in rows at one end, facing three long tables set around an open area. There's also a small side table at which a monk is already seated with pen, ink, and parchment sheets before him. I imagine Master Beanón has insisted on there being a written record of everything, despite the unofficial nature of the proceedings. Guards are posted at every entry, with more stationed behind the benches where we are ushered to sit. Miach and I are the only women present. Near us on the benches are various members of Lord Scannal's household who may be called upon to speak, Fergal and Iarla among them.

We don't have to wait long. A guard opens one of the doors at the far end and Father Eláir comes in, followed by a gray-haired monk whom I guess to be the former lawman, Brother Máedóc. Now here is Dau, with Master Beanón. Dau's choice of clothing carries a message: a plain linen shirt, an unadorned gray tunic over it, a good leather belt around his waist. Dark trousers, practical boots. His hair swept back from his face. His expression is a masterpiece of control. That is a Swan Island man if ever I saw one. Our eyes meet, then we look away.

I'm waiting for the moment when Seanan appears. Waiting and wishing it didn't need to happen; waiting and hoping the bastard gets everything he deserves. Thinking of the poison draft. Remembering the hot iron and the hungry knife. Thinking of Corb.

But Seanan's not here yet. The prior remains at the table facing us. The others have moved to the side tables and are standing there, waiting.

Lord Scannal comes in. He's using a stick for support, but making a visible effort to hold himself straight. I know him to be of middle years, but he looks old and frail; his eyes are deeply shadowed. Master Naithí is beside him. They, too, move into place, and I see how this will work. Lord Scannal is at that top table, looking directly at us, with Naithí on one side and Father Eláir on the other. At the right-hand table sit Dau and Master Beanón. At the left-hand table is Brother Máedóc. Beside him is an empty seat.

The prior speaks. "We welcome you, Lord Scannal, to this house of prayer. May the Lord God send us all his wisdom on this testing day. Please be seated."

Lord Scannal sits; the rest of us do the same.

"My lord," Father Eláir says, "it is some while since you have honored us with a visit. I regret that this one could not occur under happier circumstances. However, I have opened our doors for reasons of some urgency. This is not a formal hearing; it has been agreed that the proceedings will be informal and private. Certain matters will be set out before you, arguments considered on all sides, and an agreement reached between the parties concerned before the end of the day. If these proceedings fail in that objective we will move, with your lordship's consent, to refer the matters to a formal hearing. That would be costly in both time and resources. And what has occurred would become public knowledge, not only here in Oakhill but far more widely. It would become the subject of gossip and unrest. That is to be avoided."

The prior looks around the room. He includes everyone in his gaze, even the guards. *There are one or two monks here whom I don't recognize, including the scribe. I don't see Brother Íobhar. Seems he won't be back in time. It's all too easy to equate his absence with cowardice.*

"What takes place here today is confidential," Father Eláir says. "While the overall result of the hearing is likely to become known quite quickly, the details of who attended, what was said, how a conclusion was reached, are not for sharing beyond the walls of this chamber. Is that understood?"

There's a general murmuring indicating that it is. *I hope someone has explained this to Seanan and his men, since they are not yet with us. It's not for me to stand up and point that out.*

"Very well," says Father Eláir. "I will explain my own role in this. Since Lord Scannal does not wish to preside, and since Master Beanón will be assisting Master Dau and Brother Máedóc doing the same for Master Seanan, I have Lord Scannal's approval to conduct the hearing. I will ensure that things remain orderly and that time is not wasted. We have no desire for this to stretch to a second day." He pauses. Dau has whispered something to Beanón, who raises his hand. "Yes, Master Beanón?"

"Might it not be appropriate for Master Seanan to be present for this clarification, Father?"

"This has been explained to Master Seanan and has his approval. But yes, it is time he joined us." The prior glances over at one of the guards and the man goes out a side door. I know him—it's Canagan, one of the brawniest of the men-at-arms and a regular attendee at our after-supper gatherings in the stables.

I know how capable Seanan is, in his singularly twisted way. All the same, I've wondered if he might have lost his composure after being trussed up, dosed with a sleeping draft, and locked in a cell. But no; when they bring him in he is neatly dressed, blue tunic with the wretched symbol on it in silver, fair hair neatly brushed, shoulders square and chin up. The only sign that anything is awry, apart from the two guards escorting him, is the fact that his wrists are bound in front of him. That shocks me. What do they think he'll do, dive across the chamber and seize his brother by the throat in front of everyone?

Seanan's eyes are immediately on Dau. It's as if nobody else is in the room. He doesn't scowl or sneer or raise his brows. There's no need for that. I can feel the loathing in him, the resentment, the longing to destroy. It's deep in every part of the man, eating him up.

"Be seated, Master Seanan."

Seanan sits where directed, alongside Brother Máedóc. Canagan and another guard take up stations a discreet three paces behind these two.

"Very well," says the prior. "We're all here. Brother Máedóc, I will ask you to confirm that the man you are representing understands the purpose of this hearing and has been advised as to how it will be conducted, including the limitations on when and how he may speak?"

"He understands and has been so advised, Father."

Dau confers with Beanón, and Beanón raises his hand again. When the prior nods assent, he asks, "Is it deemed necessary for the safety of those present that Master Seanan wears restraints on his wrists? We are concerned for his comfort."

Now Seanan raises his brows at Dau. Dau stares into space, impassive.

"When it is his turn to speak, we will remove the ties. Until that time it's considered unwise to do so. Lord Scannal, do you differ?"

Lord Scannal starts. He's been staring at Seanan and is caught off guard. "Ah—no, not at all, Father," he says, perhaps unsure of what was just asked. He lifts a hand to his face. I can see it shaking with some violence. He lowers it to the concealment of the table. He adjusts his expression; squares his shoulders. I see something of Dau's strength of will in his father and am startled by it. To be here at all, under the circumstances, is remarkable.

"Master Beanón, you will speak first. Please proceed."

Beanón's good. I thought so at that other hearing, even though I ended up with a year's debt bondage because of it. He sets out the astonishing train of events that led to the skirmish in which Corb was killed and Seanan and his men were captured. There's no mention of Lord Ross and his daughter, which is fair enough since we can't prove that Dau's interference in that matter was the spark that set Seanan off. Beanón says nothing about the long-standing enmity between Dau and Seanan. His summary starts with Dau realizing I'd gone missing while walking the dog, and ends with Seanan and his men being locked up in the monastery cells. It includes my incarceration in the outhouse, the fact that I was drugged, gagged, and bound, then beaten, branded, and threatened with a knife.

I stand strong against a tide of dark memories. I hear how incredible the whole tale sounds, even when told in such a calm and level manner. Beanón deals quickly with the part where Brocc and his traveling companion appeared from nowhere to rescue us. I'm trusting that Brocc will deal with any questions capably. When the measured statement of facts is complete,

Beanón says, "Were these acts of cruelty and violence aired in a formal court, I have little doubt they would lead to very serious charges, Lord Scannal. Many charges, some of which would attract penalties such as periods of debt bondage, incarceration, or banishment, not to speak of substantial reparation to be made. We must hope today's proceedings result in matters being settled by mutual agreement."

The more I think about that the less likely it seems. How are Seanan and Dau ever going to agree about anything? Unless there's some plan afoot that I don't know about.

It's decided between the two lawmen that Dau will make a statement, Seanan will respond, then various other parties will be called by one or the other lawman, or by Father Eláir, to testify or to answer questions. Lord Scannal is saying nothing, but there's no doubt he is listening now. Seems to me that through sheer force of will he is keeping himself upright and attentive. I may not think much of the man but at this moment I admire his strength.

Dau rises to his feet. He's using the techniques we learned on Swan Island to keep his posture upright, his breathing even, his voice controlled. His hands are by his sides and perfectly relaxed. "Thank you for that clear outline of events, Master Beanón. I can confirm that it was correct. I will not squander precious time by going over the whole story again. I will say only that when it was decided Liobhan should enter this household to serve a period of debt bondage in partial compensation for the accident that robbed me of my sight, my brother Seanan agreed that her safety would be assured while she stayed here. Master Beanón was present. Indeed, he negotiated very capably on Lord Scannal's behalf at that hearing. I'm sure he is as shocked as I am that the promise of safety has been broken, and in so violent a way. Liobhan has worked hard in this household. She took on the thankless task of nursing me in my sickness, when it became apparent that no better provision was to be made for me. She performed that job with kindness and competence at all times. To see her treated so ill by my brother and his men is nothing short of sickening. For a man who would be chieftain to act as Seanan has done is outrageous. It must, at the very least, call his moral principles into question. Since Liobhan entered this household she has done nothing but good. And yet, he set his brand on her with hot iron. He left her to the mercy of wild creatures. He held a knife to her face and made vile threats. A future chieftain of Oakhill? I think not."

The chamber is silent. I feel my cheeks flush; I can't look at Dau, though I want to. That this would be his first statement astonishes me. It humbles me. I turn my gaze down to the floor.

"My brother has been under this woman's influence since long before she blinded him and called it an accident." Seanan has his voice under control, but he's riled by Dau's words, there's no doubt of that. "Every action he takes, every choice he makes is hers. It's a weak man indeed who lets a woman rule him. That's not going to change now he has his sight back. He sees only what she wants him to see."

"Master Seanan." Father Eláir speaks with quiet authority. "Please, no interruptions. You will be given your opportunity to respond. Master Dau, continue."

"Later, I will wish to question Seanan's man, Ultán, about his role in what occurred, and what orders he was directed to carry out. He may also wish to provide information about that outhouse with its squalid contents. We have not spoken much of that. But it seems to me strongly indicative of my brother's violent and erratic tendencies." Dau waits a little; it's a studied pause. "I understand we have a record of statements from the other men who went to that place yesterday under Master Seanan's leadership. Am I right in thinking those men will not appear for questioning in this hearing?"

I didn't know this. If Dau's been told, then Seanan must have been advised, too. Perhaps he didn't understand what it might mean. He looks mightily displeased. "Correct," says the prior. "I consulted Lord Scannal and was granted permission to obtain their evidence in that way, with each man questioned separately. Ultán's case is different, as he is more directly implicated in Master Dau's account of what happened. We have a written record of the statements, which can be read out later. Meanwhile, the men will remain in custody."

I see Seanan open his mouth then close it again; seems he understands the wisdom of keeping things as simple as possible. But I understand something more: that if those men were questioned in here, with him watching on, they would say exactly what he wanted them to say. He has them well trained to obey.

Dau goes on. "I will mention, in passing, that the outhouse contained a significant stock of herbs and other components such as are kept in the stillroom of my father's house, along with equipment for brewing drafts of one kind or another. Also many tools, which might be used for a variety of purposes. The condition of the creatures my brother held caged there made it absolutely clear that those tools had been used as instruments of torture. When Liobhan speaks, she can tell you more of this. Master Beanón and Brother Máedóc have seen that place. We left it more or less as it was. There were two more of the creatures there, in a sad condition but possibly still able to survive. We did not wish to leave them in the cages, so they were set free."

"To fly out and wreak havoc on local farms and villages." Seanan interrupts again. "Have you not heard of these creatures before, brother? You use such words as *cruel* and *vile* against me, your own kin. These things are pure evil! They are spawn of the devil, rending and tearing and menacing man and beast alike—"

Brother Máedóc lays a hand on Seanan's arm. Seanan jerks away, then collects himself and falls silent.

"We know of them, yes." Dau is calm. "No creature, however fierce and wild, deserves a lingering and painful death such as these endured. That is all I need say concerning the Crow Folk. To return to the matter of stillroom material found in the outhouse: one of the items was a fungus known as devil's-foot. I'm advised that this is a particularly dangerous substance when ingested, though it is also highly effective in sleeping drafts. On the night after her abduction, Liobhan was forcibly dosed with a draft she believes contained a significant amount of devil's-foot. She fought against it, but was obliged to swallow or die. The following day, after the fight, we used a similar mixture, with a far smaller amount of the fungus in it, to render our prisoners immobile while we made our way back to Lord Scannal's house and fetched the help we desperately needed. I regret that this was necessary."

Regret? Hardly. But the lie is smoothly told. I suppose he's explaining this now so he can't later be accused of trying to withhold the information.

"I remind you all that when Master Seanan and his five men-at-arms ambushed and attacked us, our own group consisted of a blind man, a woman who had endured a night of torture, a kitchen boy just fourteen years old, and a stable hand. Had not Master Brocc and Master Elouan happened to be passing, we would all have been killed. As it is, Corb lost his life. His death weighs heavily on me, as it should on Master Seanan and indeed on Lord Scannal." For just a moment, he turns to meet his father's eye. I see something pass over Lord Scannal's features—a shadow, a memory.

"Corb came to Lord Scannal's house to work in the kitchens, in order to assist his family on their nearby smallholding. Perhaps he told them, with pride, how he had been given the duty of helping look after the blind son of the household. Perhaps he said how hard it was at first, with no training and nobody to ask for help, and a patient who went crazy with pain. I hope he had the chance to tell them how he grew to perform the job with grace and strength and patience. How he proved what a fine young man he was. How he repaid my shortness of temper, my impatience, my frustration, with kindness and consideration. That such promise was lost to a pointless act of violence sickens me. It fills me with sorrow. That attack took place under Master Seanan's direction. Yes, I was blind then. But I did not need to see Corb fall on the field to know what had been squandered there. Something precious. Something irreplaceable. A fine young life. A son. A brother. A comrade. Lost, not for a fine and noble cause, but to satisfy one man's desire to watch others suffer. His will to dominate. His drive to quash all who would challenge him. There must be no more of it. It is time for my brother to pay the price for what he has done." Dau inclines his head toward the prior and Lord Scannal, a gesture of respect, then sits down.

"If I may," says Beanón before anyone else can speak, "I will suggest that we call our witnesses to testify briefly now rather than wait until Master Seanan has spoken. If Brother Máedóc and Master Seanan have questions, they might address them to the witnesses as we go along. I believe that will be more efficient."

"Brother Máedóc?" asks the prior.

Máedóc and Seanan hold a murmured consultation that goes on for some time. Eventually the lawman straightens up and says, "We have no objection, Father." Perhaps he thinks Seanan needs a little longer to compose himself.

"Thank you," says Beanón smoothly. "Mistress Liobhan, will you step forward?"

I'm glad of the gray dress, the tidy plait, the shawl. But I can't help walking like a warrior, shoulders square, head high, and no doubt the light of battle in my eyes. I move to stand in that empty space between the tables, unsure of which way to face, since inevitably I will have my back to someone. I do what seems most appropriate—I drop a small curtsy to Lord Scannal and the prior, then turn so I'm looking at Beanón and Dau, but on an angle so I can still see Seanan out of the corner of my eye. I don't trust the man an inch.

"Shall I speak now, Master Beanón?"

"Please do. A brief version of events, starting when you were in the garden with the dog. Wherever you can verify the information that Master Dau has provided, please do so. We are particularly interested in hearing your account of those times when Master Dau and other members of his group were not present. I know this may be hard for you. Please take your time."

It is hard. But I've been well trained and I get through it. I can't tell them anything about how I was abducted, because I can't remember that part at all. I start from when I came to in the outhouse, in the dark. I tell about the torture, the branding, the draft forced down my throat. I draw their attention to the bruising on my face. I roll up my sleeve, strip off Miach's neat dressing, and show them the mark on my arm. I explain about the wire door to the cage and how if I had fainted or lost consciousness for a moment, the thing would have fallen open and let the desperate birds out. I can't tell them about the tiny messenger who flew in to help me. And nobody would believe I managed to stay awake all night after being drugged with devil's-foot. Besides, Master Beanón has already said I was unconscious on the floor when Torcan found me. But I've had time to prepare a lie. "I was there for hours. The birds were pecking at the mesh, trying to escape. They broke some of the wires, and there were sharp ends sticking out. I rubbed my wrist bonds against those until the cloth came apart. But I couldn't undo the gag or the leg ropes—I was near fainting from the devil's-foot draft by then. I passed out as soon as I hit the floor. I knew nothing more until my rescuers brought me back to consciousness."

"An unlikely story," says Seanan, turning a particular look on me, the one that's intended to make folk quake in their shoes. I stare right back at him. I will not let that man scare me.

I go straight on, filling in more detail about what was in the wretched outhouse, including the stillroom supplies and equipment, dropping in a comment about the meticulous record-keeping that is now done by the monks with regard to the removal of such materials from their place of work. I back up Dau's account of the fight and its aftermath, adding things I saw that he couldn't. I name Ultán as the man who killed Corb. I name him as the man who held me while Seanan poured that stuff down my throat. I name him as the man who restrained me when Seanan brandished his knife before my eyes. "But it was Master Seanan who ordered these things done," I say. "It was plain to me at every point that he was the one giving the orders. He stood back from the fight until that moment when he taunted his brother and held his knife up to my face."

"Amusing," says Seanan. "You speak with disgust of a draft administered to you, yet you seem to have no trouble with a similar potion administered by your party to mine, of sufficient strength to render us unconscious for the best part of the day and leave us with splitting headaches. That is a curious way to look at guilt and innocence."

"I am confident in my ability to judge quantities accurately and wisely, Master Seanan. If you doubt that, you might ask Brother Petrán for his opinion. Your skill in that area is less reliable, I fear. Were I not a person of robust build I could have died from the dose you gave me. I saw the condition of your captives in that place. I saw the decaying corpses left in cages still holding the living. I saw the wounds inflicted on them, the horrific burns. I deduce that your judgment is as flawed as your apothecary skills. I wonder at your choice of the family emblem as the brand you set upon your victims, myself included. Do you care so little for your position as Lord Scannal's heir that you are prepared to spread that proof of your crimes abroad for all to see? But then, you weren't planning to set me free after I'd had my punishment, were you? If Dau hadn't come to rescue me, I'd have been finished off and dumped in a hole somewhere."

"Keep to the facts, if you will, Mistress Liobhan." Brother Máedóc is courtesy itself.

"My apologies, Brother Máedóc. I don't have much more to tell. We found ourselves fighting for our lives. Dau fell heavily at one point; he told us later that his sight began to return at that moment. We were saved by the intervention of Master Brocc and Master Elouan, but it was too late for Corb. I prepared the draft for our prisoners while the men bound them. The draft was necessary so we could safely leave that place to seek help. Master Elouan had to move on. The rest of us made our way back to the gates, and the rest you know."

"It is a strange story," comments Brother Máedóc.

"Passing strange," says Father Eláir. "Like something from an ancient tale of heroes and monsters."

I decide to let this interesting remark rest in the silence that follows. It's clear to me who the monster is in this story.

"Anything further, Mistress Liobhan?"

"I believe I'm finished, Father Eláir."

Seanan has questions. Of course he does. He rattles them off at me, probing for anything he can think of that might paint me as unreliable. First it's the drafts, not only the one we made him take, but every remedy I've prepared for Dau, every component I've taken from the stillroom. He brings Miach into it and she answers with remarkable poise, perhaps secure in the knowledge that she has adhered scrupulously to Brother Petrán's rules. He goads me with salacious suggestions about my relationship with Dau. He doesn't know I've endured hours of training for this kind of interrogation. Not that I enjoy it. But I stand tall, speak calmly, make sure I maintain concentration. I stick to facts, except when a lie is essential. When I think the question is irrelevant, I ask Master Beanón to rule on whether I should answer. What's obvious but cannot be said aloud is that the whole performance has one purpose only: to make Dau lose his composure, to turn him into the crazy, frustrated individual he was at the peak of his illness, a poor soul who shouted and screamed and struck out at those who would help him. A man who would have leaped off a cliff or cut his own throat, if I had not extracted a promise that he would live. I breathe. I stay strong. And so does Dau.

It goes on awhile. It goes on too long, and eventually Father Eláir puts a stop to it and calls Torcan to make a statement. Torcan is nervous, but he does well, backing up my version of events and Dau's. Father Eláir calls Brocc.

My brother strolls to the open area, the borrowed cloak flipped artfully back over one shoulder. His dark curls are glossy, his eyes bright. He looks less like the man who charged in to fight for us yesterday and more like the musician whose voice has charmed even a queen of the Fair Folk and whose deft fingers can draw magic from the harp. He's both, of course; warrior and bard.

"Master Brocc," says Father Eláir. "We are grateful that you could stay to assist us. Please give us your account of yesterday's events."

"We had been walking since early morning, my companion and I." Brocc cannot give testimony without making it sound like a story. "Master Elouan is a musician, skilled on the Armorican small-pipes. He was heading for a family wedding; his talent as an entertainer is no doubt highly valued at such events. I am a storyteller. As you may imagine, we had a great deal in common. We met at a wayside inn and walked on together."

His voice is so beguiling, his manner so engaging that nobody tells him to hurry up and get on with it. I'm back in my seat beside Miach. Despite my churning gut I'm enjoying every word.

"After a peaceful start to the day, we emerged from a tract of forest and saw before us a fierce and most uneven skirmish. It seemed that a body of well-armed men had set upon a group of innocent travelers, among them a woman and a young lad. The woman—Mistress Liobhan here—screamed, 'Help!' Then I saw this man"—he indicates Seanan with a dip of the head—"take out a knife and hold it to Mistress Liobhan's face, while the largest of his underlings held her pinned against him. Truth to tell, I had no idea if Master Elouan was a fighter. But most of us who travel the roads alone know how to defend ourselves. And I would not stand back and see a woman hurt if I could help her. The two of us ran forward and entered the fray. Events then proceeded as both Master Dau and Mistress Liobhan have told you. We defeated the attackers. We subdued Master Seanan's group without employing our knives. We helped to bind them. Later we assisted with administering the sleeping draft. And I helped release the captive birds. I have some knowledge of such creatures and was able to let them go without anyone being hurt." He falls silent.

"Have you more to add, Master Brocc?" asks Father Eláir after a few moments.

"For now, no," Brocc says. "Master Dau's account of what happened after that was perfectly accurate. Master Elouan went on his way. We returned to Lord Scannal's house. Master

Dau sought out various people to advise them of what had occurred. I was offered excellent hospitality, thanks to Master Iarla and his assistants. And here we are."

"Any questions, Brother Máedóc? Master Beanón?"

Beanón has none. I'm wondering if Seanan will mention Master Elouan's unusual appearance. But Brother Máedóc, after a quick consultation, also says he has no questions. At this point I don't see how Seanan can make a plausible argument in his own defense. But he will, no doubt. I glance at Lord Scannal, who hasn't said a word since this began. No questions. No comments. Does he think it's all a pack of lies, even after Brocc's account? Or is he trying and failing to make the unsavory pieces of this puzzle fit together? His favorite son a murderer, a torturer, a liar. If he accepts that, he must accept that he has wronged Dau grievously. Lord Scannal's a chieftain. Someone folk look up to. Someone they trust. Yes, he's been weakened by the poison Seanan's been feeding him. Not only the sleeping draft, but also the lies whispered in his ears, day after day, year after year, since Dau was a child. But much of the household remains loyal to its chieftain, I think. There are many honest faces around me. It seems to me there is a turning of the tide in this household, driven by Dau's courage and the enormity of Seanan's actions. But we haven't heard Seanan's statement yet. And the only person he has to convince is his father.

Behind me, one of the brethren is seized by a violent fit of coughing. I half rise, turning to see if I should offer help, but the man's all right, Brother Martán is murmuring to him and someone is offering water in a cup. I turn back, making my expression calm. That's not easy, because in that moment I spotted a monk sitting in the shadows at the back of the room, behind the benches. A tall, handsome monk with tonsured red hair. Brother Íobhar is here. He must have slipped in after the proceedings began, and done so very quietly. I may be the only one who knows he's among us. My heart is thumping hard now.

"Very well," says the prior. "We'll hear from you, Master Seanan."

Fergal comes forward and, with a little knife, severs the ties around Seanan's wrists. Seanan gives him a look as sharp as any blade. If he's exonerated, if he steps back into his old role, Fergal will be losing his position in the household very soon, along with anyone else who might have been seen to help Dau. Fergal organized the party to go up and retrieve the captives. He chose the guards who are on duty here today.

Seanan rises to his feet. Moves to the center. Turns to look at his father, and speaks as if they are the only two people in the room. "My lord. Father. You must know that this is a pack of lies, a warped and twisted version of events as fantastic as any story Master Brocc there might invent to entertain a crowd. It is nothing short of preposterous. You must know where the blame lies for these damaging falsehoods. With my brother. With your youngest son, sitting there with a smug expression on his face, barely able to control his amusement at the trouble he has caused your house and your people, the shame he will bring down on us if this ever becomes public knowledge. You know him. He's been a liar since he spoke his first word."

He pauses for dramatic effect, and Father Eláir takes the opportunity to say, "Master Seanan, as time is limited, it will be most helpful if you can give us your own version of yesterday's events. You might begin with Mistress Liobhan going missing from the household—it would seem you have a different explanation for that."

I can't see Seanan's face very well—it appears that he plans to address his whole statement to Lord Scannal. Dau is sitting quite still, very upright, with his gaze straight ahead toward the table where Brother Máedóc sits. I breathe in a pattern, hoping he's managing to calm himself the same way.

"I know nothing of how Mistress Liobhan made her way to the outhouse. One of my men reported seeing smoke rising from the chimney. As I reserve that place for my own private use, I was disturbed enough to ride up there and check. Ultán came with me; he will back up my version of events. We found the woman inside the building, tampering with my belongings. She's always got her nose into someone's business, whether it's my brother's supposed maladies or the work of the stillroom or the personal lives of her betters. She cast a blight on this house from the moment she stepped in the door—"

"Master Seanan." Brother Máedóc speaks courteously, but his tone has the authority of the lawman he once was. When Seanan turns, his face no longer calm, the monk beckons him over and murmurs something, perhaps about the wisdom of keeping to the point.

"I don't need your advice!" Seanan snarls. "I didn't ask for a legal representative! I can speak for myself!"

There's a moment's hush, then Father Eláir asks quietly, "Are you sure, Master Seanan?"

"Would I say so if I were not sure?"

"Very well." The prior is a picture of composure. "Brother Máedóc, stay where you are, please. We'll still need your assistance with related matters. Go on, Master Seanan. As I advised others, it is best to keep to the facts."

I wonder if Seanan is about to lash out at him, too, but he draws breath and resumes his statement. "I won't deny I was angry to find the woman in a forbidden place, meddling with what did not concern her. We tied her up to teach her a lesson. We gave her a sleeping draft to keep her quiet. Under the circumstances, it was entirely appropriate. She had committed an offense. More than one offense. I had the authority to punish her for that, and I did so."

"Master Seanan." The equable voice of Beanón is welcome after Seanan's poisonous lies. "Mistress Liobhan was missing from midmorning until Master Dau's party found her just after dawn the next day. To be tied up for, I presume, most of that very long time seems rather a severe punishment for trespass. And would it not have been appropriate, if you considered she had committed an offense, to bring her back to Lord Scannal's house so the matter could be dealt with by him?"

"I act for my father. Everyone knows that."

I feel it then. A chill. A change in the air. It's as if a trapdoor has been opened on a deep dark place.

"With respect, I doubt very much that Lord Scannal would have dealt with the matter in the way you say you did, Master Seanan. We've heard that the draft you gave Liobhan could have killed her. And what about the mark on her arm? The burn?"

I hold my breath, shocked at Beanón's directness. I can't bring myself to look at Lord Scannal.

"An accident," Seanan says smoothly. "She's a strong girl. She fought against us as we tried to restrain her. She fell against the hearth. Anything else she says is complete falsehood."

Brocc rises to his feet. "Might I speak, Father Eláir? I have something pertinent to add at this point."

"Keep it brief, Master Brocc."

"I mentioned earlier that I have encountered those large crow-like birds before, in a different part of the forest. Several of Master Seanan's caged birds had suffered burns, and some had knife wounds as well. Most of these were done in a particular shape. It is the same shape you have seen branded on Liobhan's arm. It is the same shape you see marked out in silver on Master Seanan's tunic: a sword and dagger crossed. Lord

Scannal's family emblem." There's a gasp of shock from the people sitting around me. Brocc goes on. "Some time ago I found one of these birds lying dead in the forest, with just such a mark carved into its breast. I have seen others wounded, dying. I understand Master Seanan sets traps for the creatures. I believe he may have been torturing his captives for some time. Setting his brand on them. Not so much a sign of ownership as a symbol of power. But then, if he is telling the truth about acting as chieftain in these parts, perhaps he can do anything he pleases." My brother sits down.

"Why do you imagine I take this action?" Seanan snaps. "I imprison them solely as a deterrent! The purpose of inflicting wounds, of killing a selected few, should be obvious—it frightens the others away from these parts. You should be grateful that I am protecting the people of Oakhill! What would you have me do, invite the vile creatures onto our farms to feed on our livestock? Open the doors of our homes to them, so they can rip our children to death?"

Lord Scannal is as pale as chalk. Father Eláir shuts his eyes for a few moments, simply breathing. Then the prior says, "For now, go on with your account, please, Master Seanan. You entered the hut, you found Liobhan there, you drugged and restrained her. You left. What was your intention then?"

"We'd have returned and released her, of course. Once she'd learned her lesson."

"You left her alone there." Dau speaks. For the first time, his voice is not quite steady. He mustn't let his anger overwhelm him. *Breathe, Dau. Count up to ten.* He's standing. He can see me. For just a moment I put my hand over my heart, fist clenched: a warrior's sign of respect. That sign means, *I trust you.* It means, *I am your comrade.* It means, *You can do this.* "And when you went back, you brought five armed men with you," Dau goes on. "For what purpose? Does it take six of you to apprehend a young woman who has been bound, tortured, and drugged? Or was I the one you feared, *brother?*"

Seanan bursts into mocking laughter. The sound rings out across the quiet room, strident and shocking. "You! The little brother who would hide away in a dark corner rather than own up to his misdeeds? The child who would creep out to cause mayhem, then retreat into sullen silence? The boy who was so full of lies nobody could ever trust him? You think I could ever be frightened of you?"

One . . . two . . . three . . . four . . . five. "Oh, yes," says Dau. "I think you are afraid now. I think you greatly fear the truth. And I come here armed with truth, Seanan. It is the most powerful weapon of all."

49

BROCC

Dau continues to astonish me. On our mission to Breifne
he proved himself able as a fighter and outstanding as
a spy. But the man I knew was often arrogant, supercilious, all
too ready to put others down with a well-aimed insult. The
Dau I see today is a leader of men. That is in every part of his
body. It is in every word he speaks. It shines from his face. As
for the way my sister and Dau look at each other when they
think they are unobserved, that I can scarcely believe. Each of
them is destined for life as an elite warrior, a member of the
Swan Island band. I do not think there is any room for tenderness in such a life. I do not believe there is any room for love,
not the kind of love I enjoy with Eirne. When we were training
on the island we spoke of it once or twice. How a bond of affection, whether between brother and sister or between lovers,
would interfere with the execution of a mission. Of all those
who trained with us, Liobhan and Dau were the most driven,
the most competitive, the most dedicated to the task. Perhaps
I misinterpret those looks. Perhaps I deduce too much from
their sharing a bedchamber. She did nurse him through his
illness. I could have asked her last evening, while we waited for
Dau to return. But my mind was full of my own woes, and I
did not ask.

I knew Dau was a chieftain's son. I imagined a life of privilege before he came to Swan Island, and perhaps it was so then. But the situation now is poisonous. The eldest brother has usurped his father's authority and set his own stamp on all. Somehow, despite the presence of a number of very capable folk within the household, Master Seanan has managed to wrest control from Lord Scannal and career off on his own warped and wayward path. Now here we sit in the quiet surrounds of the priory, and with each word the man speaks, the more appalled I become. How has he done this? And why does Lord Scannal not speak up? He seems frozen, whether with horror or disbelief I cannot tell.

"Truth?" Seanan's tone is mocking. "You wouldn't understand the meaning of that word, *brother*. You're a disgrace to the family name."

"You would have me prove my worthiness by carving my father's emblem into innocent flesh? By branding it on a woman's body with hot iron? If that is your notion of honor, Seanan, then I walked away from this place not a moment too soon."

The prior speaks. "Master Seanan, may we return to the earlier question, regarding the skirmish that resulted in the death of the boy, Corb? With what purpose did you take a party of five armed men with you when you returned to that place? If you went there to free Mistress Liobhan from her bonds, surely you and your man would have done the job quite capably."

Seanan is caught unprepared; he takes his time in forming an answer. "I knew my brother was looking for the woman. Searching widely. Others were assisting him. It occurred to me that he might have gone up to that place. Perhaps with a group. Since Dau is known to be erratic in his behavior, and since he has trained as a fighter, I thought it best to be prepared for trouble."

"Erratic?" echoes Dau's lawman. "Master Dau seems anything but erratic to me. What do you mean, Master Seanan?"
His tone is soft and courteous. I think of the subtlest of traps,
closing so quietly the victim does not know it is there.

"Master Beanón, you were present at that hearing when we
negotiated the terms of Dau's return home and the penalty for
the woman's attack on him," Seanan says. "You heard the evidence about his bouts of anger, how he would curse and shout
and hurl objects, how he would try to hurt himself and others.
How lack of sleep drove him out of his wits. How he could
not cope with the loss of his sight. Everyone knows he exhib-
ited that kind of behavior after his return here. Why else did
he require two personal attendants? Now it seems he's been
miraculously cured. Dau can see again. That does not mean
he is cured of his . . . instability. It does not mean he has suddenly learned to tell the truth. Father"—he turns to Lord
Scannal—"you know he's always had a streak of cruelty. Remember what happened to that dog, what was its name? Rose?
Remember—"

"Snow." Dau's voice is cold and clear. "Her name was Snow.
Let me tell you what happened to her. Let me tell you what
happened to me. And then you may judge, all of you, which
brother is telling the truth."

"Is this tale pertinent to the matter in question, Master
Dau?" The question comes from Brother Máedóc. Seanan may
have more or less dismissed him as his own representative, but
the monk has not forgotten his duty as a lawman.

"Most pertinent, Brother. This goes right to the heart of it."

"Indeed," puts in Beanón. "My lord, Father Eláir, I'm aware
of the matter to which Master Dau refers. We spoke of it in
private, this morning. It is deeply personal. I advised Master
Dau that it was entirely up to him whether to include it. I can
confirm that the tale is relevant. In my opinion it should be

heard, especially as it seems Master Seanan would use his own version to discredit his brother."

"Very well," says the prior. "Proceed, Master Dau."

He begins. The merciless killing of the dog he loved, the dog he had trained for three whole years when he was a boy. One brother holding him back, the other torturing the animal while he was forced to look on. Then being hauled before his father, and Seanan telling lies, saying Dau killed the dog himself when she would not obey an order. Dau's hands and face and clothing dyed scarlet with the blood shed by Snow as, cradled in his arms, she took her last labored breaths. Every person in the room is motionless and silent.

He goes on, calm and composed, only his eyes telling of a pain that still lies deep within him. Cruel acts, from as long ago as he can remember. When he was four. When he was seven. His brothers dropping him down a dark hole; leaving him stranded in a bog; making him climb to the highest, most perilous branches of a tree, then abandoning him there. Shutting him in an oak chest and leaving him for hours. Throwing him from one to the other until he soiled himself in terror. Each time, every single time, when their father called the boys to account, Seanan would have a well-prepared explanation of how Dau had done it himself, brought it on himself, disobeying sensible instructions, breaking rules, causing mayhem. In private, Seanan would threaten to harm those Dau loved if he told the truth. Their father always believed Seanan anyway. After a while young Dau became silent under questioning. He endured his punishment without a word.

Sometimes he would make a friend. Sometimes a newcomer to the household would be kind to him. A tutor, a stable hand, a gardener. Each time, as soon as the bond became known, that person would be dismissed and sent away. Now, there are few in this household who remember Dau as a child.

His account is not emotive. He does not wring pathos and heartbreak from this tale, as a bard might. There is no need for that. The plain, stark facts are enough to make a man weep.

"After Snow died," he says, "I tried to make an end of myself. Garalt, who worked in the stables, found me in time and stopped me. He helped me to leave my father's house. We went . . . elsewhere. To a friendly household far from here. Garalt taught me to defend myself. He taught me to be brave. He taught me that a man should always stand up for truth. That is all I have to say."

I can hardly breathe. I, a bard who could recount a hundred tragic tales of waste and sacrifice and shame. I see Dau standing there, tall and quiet, dignified and strong, and I realize this is a tale of triumph. He is a survivor. He is a good man, despite everything. He has come through the fire and emerged burnished bright: a sword of truth.

"Utter nonsense," says Seanan. "Complete rubbish. I told the truth then, and I tell the truth today. He can do nothing but lie. You know that, Father. Dau ran away; he did not want to be here. He was no loyal son, he was . . . he is an aberration, born of our mother's sacrifice. I have stayed by you. I have supported you. I believe in you. I am your son, your heir. Do not doubt me!"

Lord Scannal rises to his feet. He looks on the point of collapse. He's a ghost of a man. His hands tremble constantly, and there's something deeply troubling in his eyes. Into the quiet following Seanan's outburst, he speaks.

"My family is riven in two, and I do not know what to believe," he says. This is not the quavering, uncertain voice I expected, but a tone both quiet and authoritative, despite the note of pain that underlies it. It is the voice of a chieftain. "The events of the last two days trouble me deeply. At the very least, it appears I have been negligent in my care of this household and of my community. The events of the distant past may seem irrelevant to some. My sons were children. I was mourning the loss of my wife. It was long ago, and to revisit that time opens old wounds anew. But since Seanan has used each son's account of those events as the measure of honesty, we must look at them again. Two brothers face each other here, each purporting to tell the truth. I know which I believed back then. I know which sounded the more truthful. Seanan speaks with passion. He loves this community and works every day to sustain it. Dau speaks with eloquence. But he chose to walk away, and he has become a stranger. How can I weigh this?"

My heart turns cold. Liobhan reaches out a hand and the woman beside her clasps it. Dau stands still as stone. Then a voice speaks from the back of the chamber, behind us.

"You can add the testimony of an eyewitness, Father. I believe that will tip the scales clearly, one way or the other. When you made judgment, when you decreed punishment for those childhood misdemeanors, I was there, as I was when the events themselves occurred. For long years I have held my tongue on these matters. Now I believe it is time for me to speak. With your permission, Father Eláir."

Brother Íobhar. The man who was once called Ruarc. Because, of course, there are three brothers. He comes forward at a measured pace. He is like the others, a handsome, well-made man. His tonsured hair is red, not fair like that of his brothers. He stands in the open space between the tables. Now the three of them are on their feet, close together. The space between them is full of tension; this is like the moment before the roll of thunder, the bright spike of lightning.

"Master Seanan. Master Dau. Please be seated while we hear Brother Íobhar's statement," says the prior.

I've thought how easily this whole hearing could descend into chaos, despite the presence of guards. Seanan is no longer bound. He and Dau obviously loathe each other. Dau is an expert fighter. But we are in a monastery. I'm starting to believe that whatever happens, this cannot have a good ending. There is no way father and sons will agree on anything. There is no way they can reach a solution acceptable to all.

Íobhar does not speak with the anger and arrogance of his older brother. He does not speak with the devastating simplicity of his younger brother. He speaks like a man who has held something back too long and must now let it out though it hurts him greatly to do so.

"I give this account with humility. I give it with shame. I give it in the knowledge that those gathered here may judge me, but also knowing the final judgment rests with our heavenly Father alone. I say again that I was present during all the events Dau described from our childhood. I saw them all. I was party to many, under my brother Seanan's instruction." A great gasp goes around the chamber. Father Eláir makes an economical gesture, and we fall silent. Seanan's hands are tight fists on the table before him.

"I was present, too, for the aftermath of those episodes, when our father interrogated us, wanting explanations. Sometimes Dau was found in a place he could not have reached on his own—the dark hole, the high treetop, the tiny island of safety in the bog, the locked chest. Sometimes he was soaking wet, or muddy from head to toe and shivering, or wearing soiled clothing. He had cuts, bruises, hair shaven off, all manner of things that would have given a parent pause. But Seanan was quick with a story every time. Even with the dog, when nobody had ever seen Dau show the creature the least unkindness. Seanan knew how to be plausible, even when his explanation was little short of ridiculous. Dau soon gave up trying to explain. If you are not believed when you tell the truth, why even attempt to do so? He was younger, smaller, weaker. So when Father quizzed him, he said nothing. He took his beatings; he had come to expect hurt.

"And I? I did not plan those cruel escapades, those attacks, those calculated nightmares. That was all Seanan. But what Seanan told me to do, I did. I aided him in his tormenting of our little brother. I held Dau back while Seanan killed the dog. And when Father asked questions, I answered as Seanan had bid me answer. I lied to save myself from a life of terror. Because of my fear, I did great wrong. A lifetime of repentance cannot free me from the stain of that. Daily, hourly, I pray for God's forgiveness. I must strive to live in truth, and pray that the light of salvation will enter my heart and cleanse my tainted spirit." Íobhar draws a shaky breath. "You might ask why I did not speak out earlier; why I did not do better for Dau when I first discovered he had been offered such inadequate care, blind and distressed as he was. I would have done so. I wished to do so. But I was called away suddenly to the monastic establishment at Inishmacsaint. Only later did I discover that Master Seanan had arranged that very call for his own purposes. I will provide documentary evidence of his meddling in due course, Father Eláir. A request has been sent to the brethren at Inishmacsaint; I know such a record exists. My presence in his household was inconvenient for Seanan at that time, as indeed it was more recently during the visit of Lord Ross, when I found myself once again required urgently elsewhere. Seanan knew I would no longer countenance his cruel treatment of our brother. He knew I had suspicions about the cause of our father's continuing ill health. He knew, perhaps, that I might move to thwart certain plans he had in mind. He needed me out of the way and used his influence to make it happen. But I am here now, and I have laid before you the whole truth. If I must pay a penalty under the law for my misdeeds, so be it."

Dau's eyes are wide with wonder as he looks at his monkish brother. Seanan jumps to his feet. "Call my witness!" he shouts. "Call Ultán! What is this, an attempt to declare my entire life a crime? I demand that my witness be heard!"

There's a brief silence. Then Beanón says, "What Master Seanan requests is reasonable, even if his manner of doing so is not. Master Dau's witnesses were heard." He glances at the prior.

"Bring Ultán in, please," says the prior, but his voice is almost drowned by shouting from outside, and the sound of running feet. Two of our guards go out, followed by Fergal. The shouting dies down, but none of them comes back in.

"We will take a brief adjournment," says Father Eláir. "Master Seanan, if your witness is available we will give him the opportunity to speak. I appreciate the importance of doing so, especially as he will most likely face charges in due course. For now, Lord Scannal needs some private time to consider the statements. Master Beanón, Brother Máedóc, we will attend him in the small room next door, along with Master Naithí. Master Seanan, you are still in custody; you will be escorted elsewhere until my lord needs you again. Master Dau, you may wait here or out in the courtyard if you prefer. Stay close, everyone; we may need to question some of you again. When it's time to return we'll ring the bell."

Doors open. Folk move to their designated areas. Two guards take the protesting Seanan away. Dau comes over to Brother Íobhar and puts his hands on the monk's shoulders. The meaning of this gesture is clear. *You told the truth. That was brave.* Brother Íobhar wipes away tears. The two of them retire to a corner, sit down together, and converse in lowered voices. I see no sign of triumph on Dau's face. He will not gloat over this victory; he's not that kind of man. Besides, there is too much sorrow wrapped up in it. A tangle of past misdeeds to be unraveled with delicate fingers. Or maybe left alone. I wish I knew what they were saying to each other.

I can't be honest with my sister. I can't give her a big hug as I want to. Here in this hall I am a wandering storyteller and I hardly know these people. Instead I go outside with Torcan. We stretch our legs, walking past the burned area, looking at the work just begun. It seems startling that out here the sun is shining, the birds are caroling, and the ancient yews watch on unperturbed, their lives too long and deep to be greatly touched by the follies of humankind. For a while we sit side by side on a low wall, not saying much. At one point I see a pair of brown-robed brethren moving faster than might be thought appropriate for monks, and then consulting with Fergal and a guard at the far end of the building. For all Father Eláir's caution, I think it will be hard to keep this tale from becoming public. Unless Lord Scannal chooses to believe Seanan despite such overwhelming evidence against the man. That would be easier for him. He'd keep his heir. He'd keep things the way they've been for years. But he'd lose the trust of many good folk in his household. Perhaps Seanan would send them all away. But he couldn't get rid of the prior. And what about the monks who raised the suspicions of a poisoned sleeping draft? What about Brother Íobhar?

"I wonder if they'll kick him out," Torcan muses. "The brother, the one who spoke up. Can he keep on being a monk after that?"

"I don't know the way of such institutions. He's told the truth, even though it took him a long time. He sounded penitent. Perhaps Father Eláir will set him to digging the garden or emptying the privy for a while."

"I can't quite picture it," Torcan says with a grin. "But there could be worse fates."

I wonder how long it will take Lord Scannal to make a decision. I'm torn between the need to get back to the forest, where True is waiting alone, and the wish to stay here longer, to be with Liobhan longer and to be certain of her safety. She'd be unimpressed if I told her this. She'd say she's a Swan Island warrior and can look after herself. That's true enough, but these circumstances are exceptional. Extraordinary. Bizarre. If Seanan keeps his position in the house and she is forced to remain here, I hate to think what might happen.

The bell rings, clear and bright. We rise and walk back to the refectory.

When we are seated as before, the prior addresses us. He's looking grim. "Lord Scannal has reached a decision and will address you shortly. Before he does so, I have some sad news for you. A man has taken his own life within the walls of this house of God. One of the men accommodated in our cells, Master Seanan's man Ultán. He is in God's hands now, and at peace."

Seanan is on his feet. "Where were the guards? I suspect foul play! He was my witness! Why was his statement delayed?"

"Master Seanan, calm yourself. I have answered your questions already; I have no more to add. But for the benefit of those present, I point out that the guards cannot watch every man for every moment of the day. We will, of course, assist Lord Scannal with this matter in any way we can. This tragic sequence of events has now cost two lives. We will pray for both men. But for now, we must move on. Be seated, Master Seanan."

He obeys, glowering. Not saddened by the death of his man or the nature of Ultán's passing, only furious because he's lost the one person he was sure would support him.

"I will proceed, then," says the prior. "We have passed the matter of those men-at-arms who were involved in the skirmish to Master Fergal to deal with, since as master-at-arms he has the authority to do so. He spoke to each man in the company of a scribe this morning. The written record reveals that each man stated he was acting under Master Seanan's orders, and that each man believed that if he did not obey, he would lose his place in Lord Scannal's service. Master Fergal will make arrangements for those men to return to Lord Scannal's household, where they will be under strict supervision for a period."

It surprises me that Seanan does not leap to his feet and challenge this. Instead he sits silent with arms folded.

Father Eláir sits down; Lord Scannal stands. I understand he is close to my own father's age, but he looks years older. The tremor in his hands has increased.

"I have considered all the statements," he says, and his voice is uneven now, his breathing labored. "I have weighed the evidence. As chieftain of Oakhill, I bear responsibility for ills that occur within my household and my community. As the father of three sons who were brought up without their mother's presence, I bear responsibility for ills that occur within my family. We are not here today to consider events of the distant past. We are not here to weigh guilt or innocence in the matter of my eldest son's treatment of his young brother years ago, nor the choice of the middle brother to stand back and let certain things happen. We are not here to pass judgment on lies that were told at that time, nor on my own failure to open my eyes and ears to the unpalatable truth.

"We are, however, bound to give those events some weight in determining responsibility for what has happened now those boys are men. I remind myself that when Dau was ten years old his eldest brother was no child, but a young man of fifteen. When the episode with the dog occurred, Dau was thirteen years old. His brother, five years older, was a man by all standards. At that time, I chose to believe the story he told, not least because Ruarc—Brother Íobhar, as he is now—backed it up. It was the same with earlier incidents. I was deaf to the truth. I heard what I wanted to hear. Anything else was too hard. I was weak. I will not be weak again."

It is so quiet in the chamber, a person could hear the footsteps of a beetle in the wall, the subtle movement of a spider in a web high above. It is so quiet, I might hear my own heart beating.

"Seanan. You were my right-hand man. You were my heir. I took pride in your abilities. I saw a bright future for you. Your acts of pointless cruelty, then and now, your choice to control others by fear, your senseless hatred for your brother, all these render you unfit to hold any position of authority. You are unfit to be chieftain of Oakhill, and you will not inherit that title from me. As penalty for your misdeeds, I banish you from Oakhill forever. Should you set foot within my territory again, or cause others to enter this place with ill intent, you will be taken into custody and these matters will be dealt with in a formal hearing. You will be gone from this place by nightfall, and you will be beyond my borders by morning. Is this understood?"

Seanan is silent. I am not sure he has taken in the import of this.

"Is this understood?" Lord Scannal asks again. "I might point out to you that there is a matter of a sleeping draft still to be investigated. Should that become a formal charge, you might find yourself facing a far graver penalty."

"You wrong me," Seanan says, tight-jawed. "You wrong me grievously. How can you rule here without me? For years I have done everything for you, everything! How will you—?"

"Enough," says Lord Scannal. "You will be escorted from this place and given time to gather your possessions. You will not ride alone to the border. Guards will accompany you. Guards chosen by Master Fergal. You may leave us now."

And Master Seanan does, head still held high, blue eyes glaring baleful challenge to anyone who dares look at him. Just as well he'll be guarded until he is away from here. He looks capable of anything.

The door is closed behind him and his escort.

"I thank you for your attendance and for your tolerance," Lord Scannal says. His voice is fading; I think he is fighting tears. "I thank the community of St. Padraig's, and Father Eláir in particular, for their assistance on this most difficult of days. I have just one more thing to say, and I must say it before this company. Dau. My son. I am sorry. But no apology, no payment in silver, nothing can compensate for what was done to you in this house. I will regret that for the rest of my days. You stood up today and showed yourself to be a fine young man. A son of whom I could be truly proud. A future leader." He's about to say something more and I can guess what it may be. So, it seems, can Dau, for he speaks quickly, before his father can go on.

"I believe justice has been done today, Father. I also thank those who made it possible. I do not wish for any compensation. I wanted only that the truth should come out, and that my brother's ill deeds should be recognized. I am satisfied with the way that has occurred. I thank Master Beanón for his expert help. I thank Brother Íobhar for his courage in speaking out at last. It is not easy to acknowledge past faults. I hope his honesty does not put his future among the brethren in jeopardy. I am glad that he has found a right path, and I wish to make it plain that I forgive him." He bows his head in his brother's direction, and Íobhar returns the gesture. In my mind a grand song is writing itself, a song I cannot sing for nearly a year, about the bonds of brotherhood.

"As for the future," Dau goes on, "we might discuss that privately, Father. But I must make it known that I have no desire to remain here in Oakhill as part of this household, in whatever capacity." Thus he neatly avoids any discussion of who might become Lord Scannal's heir with the departure of Seanan. "I wish to leave Oakhill within a few days. I need your sworn promise that since my vision is now fully restored, you will free Liobhan from her debt bondage immediately so she may return home with me. We are comrades. We work together. We live in the same community. Her freedom is the only compensation I require. I want your promise on this issue before we leave this hall."

Oh, gods! The look on Lord Scannal's face is terrible to behold. He gazes at Dau and sees the strong, courageous, honorable chieftain that might have been, the son who, because of those past ills, will turn his back on Oakhill and make his own life on his own terms. Seanan will not be chieftain. Ruarc cannot be chieftain. There is no other. "I give my word," Lord Scannal says. "Consider the debt bondage acquitted in full. You are free to go, you and your friend. Fergal, Iarla, you will attend to the arrangements." He draws a shaky breath. "Dau. I would be pleased if we could meet later, privately. If you wish, Master Beanón could be present."

Dau nods in assent. I think he, too, is fighting back tears.

And just like that, the proceedings are over. Father Eláir thanks everyone again and we disperse. I stand outside with Liobhan, waiting for Dau. He is slow to follow; he is in some kind of discussion with the monks. The afternoon shadows are growing longer. I know what I must do, and it hurts.

"I should go straight back," I tell my sister. "No need to

return to the house; I have everything with me. And True will be waiting. If I walk straight to the forest we'll have enough time to be home before dark."

Liobhan gives me a penetrating look. She looks tired beyond belief. Her eyes are rimmed by blue-gray shadows. There's a crease of pain on her brow. "That's quite a distance," she says, summoning a ghost of a smile. She knows, of course, that in the Otherworld time and space play all sorts of tricks.

"True knows the secret ways better than I do. But it is far, yes, so the sooner we're off the better." I gaze on her, wanting to remember the way she looks now, her dauntless courage shining through despite everything. "Make sure you get a fresh dressing on that burn," I say. "That's your sword arm."

"Don't remind me. I can just see myself arriving on Swan Island and being told I'm not fit enough to have my old place back."

"Liobhan . . ." I glance around to make sure nobody is close enough to overhear. "About that. Going back, I mean. You and Dau . . . ?"

"Me and Dau what?" There's a combative note in her voice now. I take that as a good sign.

"I could hardly fail to notice that there's something more than comradeship between you now. Won't that create difficulties for you on the island? I don't imagine the rules have changed since I left the place."

Liobhan grimaces. "Isn't Swan Island all about making the impossible happen? We'll work something out."

"Good luck with that."

"I'm told certain of the elders may have bent the rules a little in the past. Anyway, it might amount to nothing. Don't read too much into our sharing a bedchamber. A lot of the time that was Dau having nightmares and me trying to calm him down. I slept on the floor."

"He owes you a lot. Makes me wonder if you came here willingly, despite the debt-bondage arrangement."

"He would have made an end of himself. I couldn't have that."

We are quiet a moment, the news of Ultán fresh in our minds. Did he finally feel the weight of his misdeeds? Did he recognize the cost of loyalty to an evil master? He will carry the answers to his grave.

Almost before I know it, it is time for me to go. Dau extricates himself from those who want to talk with him—there is a small crowd—and comes over to us. "You're leaving already?" he asks me.

"I can't stay any longer. Folk are waiting for me." True will be wondering if I have fallen into more strife; perhaps considering coming after me. I cannot let that happen. And Eirne will be waiting. Eirne who is carrying our unborn child. Conscience requires that I tell her about the healing drops and how we used them. "I'm sorry," I say. Oh, more sorry than they can know.

"You saved our lives," Dau says. "We are indebted to both of you. Please convey my thanks to your friend. His generosity has transformed the future for me."

"No debt," I say. "We're Swan Island men still and we help one another. I will pass your message on to True. Now I must go. You have many things to do, and I have many miles to walk. Farewell, friend." I give Dau a quick, hard embrace. "Liobhan. Keep singing, will you? I may not hear you from that other realm, but I'll know."

Now she's really crying, and so am I. We hug for a long moment, then step away.

"Safe journey," my sister says.

"And you, dear one. Farewell." As I walk away, I hear birds

singing in the ancient yews. From a distance come the voices of monks, chanting. The melody is in the mode druids call willow, which is suitable for this occasion: not sad, exactly, but contemplative and solemn. It sounds entirely right. "Be happy, the two of you."

I head up the rise and away from Lord Scannal's domain. True is waiting: my comrade, my brother. Soon I will reach the forest and set my steps for home.

50

DAU

All I want is to sit in our quarters with Liobhan, share a cup or two of mead, and make plans for leaving this place as soon as we can. But everyone wants to talk to me and I cannot deny them the opportunity. I cannot refuse to have supper in the hall with the household, or to talk with my brother before he returns to the infirmary. He was brave today. I had hoped he might speak out, but I did not expect it. He laid his sins bare, not only for the prior and his fellow monks, but for a far wider audience. I understand how much that cost him and I honor him for it, despite everything. It seems his faith in God is a true faith, and although I do not share it, I respect him for it.

With supper over, my father calls me to talk in private with only Beanón and Naithí present. I would like Liobhan to be with us, but I do not request it. My father asks the question I did not allow him before. Will I consider staying? Since I am now heir to the chieftaincy, will I not take up that responsibility instead of pursuing my life as a mercenary fighter?

I do not offer an explanation of what we do on Swan Island, which is so much more than he believes. Our work is secret and must remain that way. I thank him for the offer and explain, as best I can, that I am unsuited to be chieftain, and that the damage done during my childhood cannot be erased so quickly. I feel no tie with this place. I am sorry I cannot learn to know Ruarc anew. I am sorry Seanan's wickedness has broken the family in pieces. But there are many good people here. With their support, my father can mend this community. He still has time.

There is no bond of affection between us, and I do not think there can ever be. It is too late for that. For now, we make an effort to speak civilly to each other, to stay calm, to ask Beanón or Naithí for an opinion when we cannot agree. Thus we make some arrangements and agree to certain provisions. Liobhan and I will depart in two days' time. Tomorrow we have a job to do.

At last I am free to return to our quarters. Torcan is there with Liobhan—I asked him to stay so she would not be alone. He settles in the antechamber and I sit down before the fire. Gods, I'm weary. Now that we are on our own at last, I feel the weight of what's happened in every part of my body.

Liobhan puts a cup of mead in my hand. She's in her night-robe with a shawl on top, and her hair falls loose over her shoulders, warm gold in the firelight. "Tell me, if you want," she says. "Or just sit awhile. You must be exhausted."

"Did you have that burn tended to?"

She rolls up her sleeve, shows me a neat new dressing. "Miach did it for me."

"Liobhan?"

She looks at me, brows lifted. "What? Don't tell me you've agreed to be chieftain of Oakhill after all?"

"You know me better than that. I have a favor to ask. Will you come with me to visit Corb's family tomorrow? Just the two of us? They've been given the news. They've received his body. But I need to go there in person and talk to them. I thought we could leave the following day. Arrangements will be made for that."

Liobhan smiles. "Of course I'll come. If only to help you with the dog. I hope you've worked out how we're going to get her back here. She's a bit young to run alongside the horses."

Mongan finds me a basket arrangement that is sometimes used when a rider needs to transport a small child. We ride to Corb's family farm, giving Seanan's place of torture a wide berth. Corb's father, red-eyed but composed, receives us with courtesy; if he is angry, as well he might be, he gives no sign of it. Corb's mother has no words. She stays in her chair, and on her knee is the little dog, Hope. As we sit with them, and as I explain that my father will pay a substantial sum in compensation since their son died in my service, her hand moves gently against the dog's back, and the dog stretches up to lick away her tears. Sometimes she holds Hope close to her as if she were a human baby, and I want to weep myself for such a loss.

Corb's father is faultlessly gracious. I tell him how much I valued his son's service, his friendship, his kind nature. Liobhan tells how Corb was thrown into the job of nursing me through the worst of my illness, and how he kept on going even when he was exhausted and downhearted, and how, in the end, he proved the very best helper and companion I could have. She tells how brave he was and how ready to take on every new challenge. I say I am sorry. I am sorrier than I can ever put into words.

When there is no more to be said, we rise and make our farewells. And for the first time Corb's mother speaks. "You'll be wanting to take her. Little Honey." A sob breaks from her as she stands up and lifts the dog as if to pass her to me. I understand in that moment that I must leave Hope behind.

"She seems very content here," I say. "Perhaps it would be best if she stayed with you. We have a long journey ahead of us, too much for such a little one. Would you be prepared to keep her? She's from good stock. In time, she'll be useful around the farm."

Corb's mother enfolds the dog in her arms and shuts her eyes. It is answer enough.

Her husband sees us out. "Thank you," he says, rendering me instantly wordless.

"Farewell," says Liobhan. "Corb was a good son; you brought him up well. He was brave, wise, thoughtful, and kind. And he loved you; he spoke of you fondly."

"Farewell." Right now, that choked word is all I can manage.

We ride away, and though there are things Liobhan could say, she stays quiet. Thus we come back, for the last time, to my father's house. And though when night falls I long for the comfort of her arms, and I see an answering look in Liobhan's eyes, she sleeps in her bedroll before the fire, and I in the bed. Torcan has returned to his duties in the stables and will reclaim his pallet in the men's quarters. Slowly, the whole household will become used to the new way of being, a way without Master Seanan.

51

LIOBHAN

We leave Oakhill with three good horses, two to ride and one to carry our belongings. They were chosen by Mongan as part of Dau's negotiations with his father, and we'll be taking them all the way. That means traveling in short stages, with several overnight stops—a plan that would have accommodated the needs of a young dog as well as the horses. I know Dau is upset by what happened with the little one. I remember how she slept on his bed, close to him, and how peaceful he looked then. He made the right decision. But it has cost him.

As well as our possessions, which are few, we're carrying rather a lot of silver. The fee paid for Dau's future upkeep, determined on the basis that he would be dependent for the rest of his life, was seven hundred and forty-one silver pieces. He pointed out to his father that since he was now restored to full health and would be departing immediately, the better part of that fee should be refunded to the Swan Island community. Naithí performed a calculation, taking into consideration the quality of the horses. The pouches hidden in various parts of our baggage contain a total of seven hundred and twenty-nine silver pieces. It's just as well both of us are Swan Island warriors and that we've been provided with some weapons, thanks to our friends among Lord Scannal's men-at-arms. Canagan took me aside at the stables and told me all of them were greatly relieved by Master Seanan's departure.

I've considered what Seanan will do, where he will go, whether he will be eaten up with resentment. I've imagined him following us with ill intent. Part of me wishes Dau had asked that his brother be held in custody until we had time to get home. But we're strong, we're trained for that sort of thing, we can look after ourselves. And each other.

Our first night is spent at a hostelry that provides communal sleeping areas, one for men and one for women. No private quarters. It does have good stables. We settle the horses, eat supper, avail ourselves of the bathing facilities, then bid each other a polite good night. Some time later I'm woken from a sound sleep by shouting from outside and a terrible wrenching shriek. I throw on some clothes and grab my knife. One of the other women in the sleeping area mutters, "Oh, gods, not this again," and puts her pillow over her head. The rest of them are either still asleep or doing a good job of pretending.

Moonlight fills the courtyard with deceptive shadows. A man is yelling a string of foul curses, and he's hitting someone, or something, hard with a stick. It's not a woman screaming, it's a dog. Is the man trying to break up a dogfight? Stop an attack? I stride toward them, but Dau is there before me, charging out of his sleeping quarters, seizing the man's upraised arm and wrenching the stick from his grasp.

"Stop that!" His voice is like a scourge. "What are you doing?"

"What business is that of yours? Who do you think you are?"

I'm beside them now, ready to help if Dau needs me. The moonlight glints in the dog's terrified eyes. It's a big brindled thing, widemouthed, chained up and cowering. Violent tremors run through its body. The screaming has dwindled to a thready whimpering. One ear is half-gone, one eye is swollen and reddened. There are welts and scratches all over its body.

Fate is full of surprises.

"Let me go!" yells the man. "You're breaking my arm!"

An audience is gathering now; faces between window shutters, figures in doorways.

"I think not." Dau is cold and calm. Perhaps only I realize how angry he is. "No creature deserves this kind of treatment. What offense could possibly warrant it?"

"My dog, my business. Barking at nothing. Keeping folk awake. Refusing good food. Trying to run away. It's a good-for-nothing piece of shit." The man aims a kick in the dog's direction. Dau applies pressure on the arm and the fellow spits out another curse. "Let me go!"

"Your dog, is it? *A good-for-nothing piece of shit*, I think that was your eloquent description." Dau applies further pressure, and the man squeals in pain. "Not worth much, then? What'll you take for the animal? Two coppers? That's a fair price for such a worthless creature, surely."

The change is instant. "Two coppers? You're joking! This boy's young and fit. He's a fighter. He'd earn you more than that in one night. Keep him hungry, keep him wound up, he'll beat the toughest dog anyone can put up against him."

There's a pause. I imagine Dau counting to five. I'm inclined to do the same.

"Hold this person for me, will you?" Dau says casually, letting go. I move in, pushing the man to his knees, grabbing his wrists, pulling his arms up behind his back. Dau crouches down. He's not trying to touch the dog, only looking. Taking in the bites, the scratches, the lank coat, the haunted eyes. "It's all right," he murmurs. "You're safe now. That life is over.

There, now. Good boy." When he gets up, he does it slowly, so as not to startle. When he speaks to the dog's owner, he keeps his voice quiet. "Three coppers," he says. "You want him off your hands, don't you?"

"Ten coppers. A bargain at that."

I pull the man's arms up a little higher, knowing what pain that will send through his shoulders. Interesting; none of the folk looking on has a word to say.

"Five."

Just as well this person doesn't know we have a king's ransom in silver with us. We're not looking like wealthy folk right now. I've thrown on my tunic over my night-robe. Dau is in plain trousers and shirt, and barefoot. But he talks like a nobleman.

When the fellow doesn't counterbid, Dau says, "That is my final offer. Take it or leave it."

There's no way he'll let this man take the dog with him. I know that, but the man doesn't. "You get the chain thrown in," he says, his voice tight with pain. "That's worth a bit. Ow! That hurts!"

"Do you not understand the words *final offer*? I don't want your poxy chain. Five coppers and you walk out of here without your arms broken. Someone find me a length of light rope, will you?" This is addressed to the silent onlookers; I see a man head over to the stables.

"All right. Five. Robbery, that is. Let me go, will you?"

I glance at Dau; he shakes his head. "If you want your five coppers, you stay right there until I fetch them," he tells the captive.

I hold the fellow while Dau goes for the coins. We've supplied ourselves with smaller currency to pay our way; nothing invites thieves more than the bright gleam of silver. While we wait, the man who went to the stables brings back not a length of rope, but a leather collar and lead, worn but serviceable. When he edges close, the dog lets out a subterranean growl, showing its teeth. The man steps back.

"Just leave it there," I tell him. "My friend will put it on. And thank you."

"Good fighting dog, that," mumbles my captive. "Worth twice what he's paying."

"Shut your mouth." I want to give the fellow a kick. He's not only cruel, he's stupid with it. Since it would probably frighten the dog even more, I don't do it. While I wait, I ponder the immediate future. It's getting more complicated by the day.

Dau returns. I release my grip on the man. Dau holds out five coppers and the man snatches them as if they might vanish. Then, with slow, deliberate movements, Dau crouches down and inches toward the growling, shivering dog. He talks in a murmur—"Good boy. It's all right," and so on—and after a long, long time he is close enough to put the collar on. "Good boy. Bravest of boys."

The chain is harder. It's been around the dog's neck awhile and it's been digging into the flesh. The man from the stables comes in beside Dau, provoking another bout of growling. They take their time, Dau holding the dog and murmuring reassurance while the stable hand uses a tool to prize a chain link open. When they finally work the thing off—without being bitten—there's muted applause from those who have stayed to watch. I realize suddenly how cold it is and how bone weary I am, not only from the day's riding but from everything.

The dog's owner has disappeared. The master of this hostelry has come out in his nightshirt and stockings, with a blanket over his shoulders, and is talking to Dau. The dog hasn't moved; Dau holds the lead quite casually and stands two paces from the creature, looking as if nothing is amiss. I note that he is still speaking very quietly and moving very slowly. Every single thing is calculated. Every single thing is a tiny step on this wretched creature's journey to a better life. I have never been prouder of my friend, not even when he stood up and spoke truth to his father.

I decide to take myself quietly back to bed. I know Dau won't let that creature out of his sight all night, which may well mean sleeping on a pile of straw in the stables. My admiration for him does not stretch as far as volunteering to keep the two of them company. I murmur, "Good night," and retreat to my bed. I don't think we'll be riding on tomorrow. Maybe I can sleep late for once.

By the time I drag myself out of bed the next morning, it's become clear that Dau will need a while to work with the dog before it can possibly come with us. The animal is terrified of its own shadow. It cowers and cringes and bares its teeth if anyone comes close. I was right about the stables; Dau and the dog slept there last night and will do so again, in the quiet company of horses belonging to various travelers. Only two men work there. Fortunately, they're inclined to be helpful.

I can't help. I like dogs well enough, but I don't have the special magic that lets a person win a dog's trust even when it's half-mad with fear. Dau has that. Where a damaged creature is concerned, it seems he has infinite patience. I leave them to it. To stop myself from dwelling on the probability that Dau and I will not share a bed before we get to Swan Island, which might mean it never happens at all, I find a secluded spot not far from the inn and run through the daily exercises I've been neglecting. But even as I work my body into a sweat, my thoughts return over and over to the same dilemmas. We'll have some explaining to do when we reach the island. Some negotiating. There's a no-dogs rule on Swan Island. How Dau is going to get around that I have no idea. And there's the other issue, the rule that doesn't exactly forbid members of the fighting group from forming relationships, but which spells out all the reasons why such liaisons are not considered a wise choice. I thought we'd talk about it while we were on the road and work out a plan. I thought we'd have time together, alone, to act on our feelings. Now I'm picturing us lying on opposite sides of the bed with the dog in the middle, baring its teeth at me if I so much as move a finger.

I go through the exercises twice. I'll do them again in the afternoon. I climb a tree and look out northwest, trying to see Swan Island. But it's too far; I can't even glimpse the sea.

Days pass. I exercise, I walk, I ride, I make myself useful about the place. I fill my time with activity. Dau and his dog work with more cautious steps. On the third day I see them walking together, the dog on a loose lead. The animal is letting him close; it is staying by him. When others come too near, it still shrinks down, shaking. If a traveler brings a dog, this one turns crazy. Its voice becomes a death shriek; it seems uncertain whether to bolt in terror, charge forward to attack, or just possibly make friends. I observe this once or twice and recognize how frightening folk might find it, for the dog is big and solidly built.

On the fourth day Dau comes to find me, without the dog. He's left the creature in the safe confinement of a stall, overseen by the stable workers. I hardly know what to say to my friend. He's doing something good. He needs to take this slowly. And he can't leave the dog on its own for long. I wish I didn't feel the way I do, as if suddenly what's between him and me is not important anymore.

"Will you come out for a walk with us?" he asks. "He needs to learn that you're a friend. That he can trust you."

"If you want." I know it sounds ungracious.

Dau frowns. "Something wrong?"

I'm seriously tempted to smack him in the face. And I hate myself for it. I look at him, he looks back, and suddenly I can say it. "I think I might be a little bit jealous."

After a startled moment, Dau grins. "Help me now and we'll be away from here sooner. Remember Hawthorn House? I'm hoping they may let us stay there a bit. Just us, I mean."

Hawthorn House. The place that seems like an inn but is really something more. It's where I was given my penalty of debt bondage and newly blind Dau encountered his brother Seanan for the first time in years. It did have plenty of rooms; plenty of privacy. Silent serving folk who prepared meals and retreated. Ample stabling for horses. But all of that surely isn't for the benefit of a pair of thwarted lovers who just happen to be Swan Island warriors.

"And the dog?"

"I'll work something out. Rules should be flexible. I'll train him to herd the sheep."

Anything less like a sheepdog I couldn't imagine. But this is Dau. If he says he can do it, he probably can.

The days pass. Dau names the dog Justice. It seems a good choice. I become part of the training, so Justice has two people to trust. He learns basic commands: *sit*, *stay*, *down*. Indeed, he is so quick at this that Dau guesses he once had a kind owner but fell upon hard times. Justice learns to be close to the horses in the stables, and then to be close while they are moving around the courtyard. He learns to come to Dau or me when called. He learns to walk beside us without a lead. On a triumphant day, when the sun is high and I can feel home beckoning, Justice runs alongside while we ride. A short ride, true, but we can soon be on our way.

With love and consistency and good feeding, Justice becomes

handsome. His eyes are bright; his brindled coat is developing a glossy sheen. He'll always have scars, not only the visible ones but the hurts inside. There will be times when he remembers the past and is overtaken by fear. But his courage warms my heart.

At last we move on. Our pace is still gradual; we cannot expect too much of our new companion. So an overnight stop, and another, and then we come to Hawthorn House, the long, low building with its lovely trees to either side of the entry. Little birds are everywhere, hunting insects or seeking ripening berries. We ride up to the house and dismount. Dau calls Justice in close and attaches the lead. The door opens and out comes a familiar figure. It's Illann from Swan Island, a friend from the mission to Breifne.

"You're here!" he exclaims, not sounding particularly surprised. "Welcome!"

"You were expecting us?" I ask, dismounting. "How did you know?"

"A message by pigeon, from Lord Scannal to the elders, which came by way of the Dalriadan court. Dau, we heard you were cured. That has delighted everyone."

"Who else is here?" Dau asks. "We'd been hoping for a couple of nights' rest before the last part of the journey. As you see, we have a dog with us. Justice. He's been ill-treated in the past and I don't want to push him too hard."

"Just me and a few other fellows. They're heading out on a mission in the morning, and I'm here to greet you and ride back with you. There's a local couple cooking for us and tending to the horses, though I've been helping with that to keep myself busy. Thought you might be quicker. And now I see these very fine mounts you've brought with you, I'm even more surprised."

"Long story," Dau says. "We'll tell you later." His voice is tight. Illann is a good friend and we're glad to see him. But we had so hoped to be on our own here.

A man comes to lead the horses to the stables at the back of Hawthorn House, which in almost every respect resembles a wayside inn of good quality. Justice pads into the house by Dau's side, and Illann makes no comment.

I remember something important. "Our baggage, the stuff on the packhorse—there are some rather valuable items in it. Can it be brought straight in here?" I glance around the big chamber that serves as a dining room; there's not a soul in sight. "Repayment of a significant part of the compensation. From Lord Scannal."

"Morrigan's britches," murmurs Illann. "I'll see to it right away. Make yourselves comfortable."

"I'll come with you." Dau passes Justice's lead to me. "I'll help you get the horses settled."

I wait, easing my aching back and hoping Illann's not expecting us to ride on in the morning. I imagine trying to explain our situation to him. Justice sighs, then lies down with his head on my foot. I wish life was a little less complicated. I wish matters of the heart could be settled quickly and decisively. I almost wish Dau and I were still no more than good friends. But when he comes back in a bit later, I remember a wisewoman calling him a handsome prince. I catch a little smile on his lips, and I know I don't wish anything of the kind. Justice is instantly awake and on his feet. I realize he has neither barked at Illann nor cringed with fear before him. Perhaps Illann has the right smell; perhaps he smells of the stables. He is both Swan Island fighter and trained farrier, and he often works in the landward settlement that is an extension of the island community. An idea comes to me, still half-formed but definitely promising.

It becomes plain, without anyone saying so, that Illann and Dau have had a conversation that wasn't about our baggage or our horses or the earlier part of our journey. Illann points us toward the room where Dau rested during our last, somewhat fraught visit to Hawthorn House—a generously sized chamber with a comfortable bed and its own anteroom. He shows us the privy and an outhouse with facilities to heat water and to bathe. He advises us that the folk who look after the house will provide supper. And it seems an agreement has been reached that Dau and I, with Justice, will stay on here for three more nights after the other Swan Island warriors in residence have left on their mission. "I'll still be about the place," Illann adds. "If only to help you protect all that silver. I've got my own place to sleep, next to the stables. I'll be out of your way." He pauses, a quizzical expression on his features. "You know I divide my time between the island and the mainland settlement," he says. "Looking after the horses doesn't stop me from undertaking a mission when I'm called upon. Some might say doing both means you can't do either properly. I see it differently. Knowing animals makes me more useful when we ride out on island business. And after the extremes of a mission, I have a new appreciation of what the animals go through in support of our work. Makes it still more important to look after them well, keep them in good health, keep them happy. So I do that work better, too. At least I hope I do."

Dau and I exchange a glance. One of our earliest conversations on the island, when we were trainees and bitter rivals, was about just this subject, though neither of us approached it with Illann's wisdom.

"You might give it some thought," Illann adds now. "With the dog and all. I don't suppose Cionnaola will be keen to have him on the island, even on his best behavior. I believe there's a vacant cottage in the mainland settlement."

I feel a little queasy. My own idea was something along those lines, minus the cottage. But I do not like the image that springs to mind, which is of myself outside that humble abode hanging garments on a line, with a clutch of squalling children at my skirts, watching Dau head off on a mission. That is not my future. I've never wanted it and I don't now. I'm a warrior. If I weren't, I'd be back in Winterfalls singing at village hand-fastings.

We stow our gear and settle in. We bathe and change our clothes and eat supper in the big room, the three of us at one end and the party of Swan Island men at the other. There's no idle chat. They're on a mission and we don't get told about it. But I note with interest that one of them is familiar, not from the island but from our mission to Breifne. A sturdily built man meets my eye, gives a nod, then looks away. It's Garbh, once bodyguard to an unpleasant individual who was then prince of that kingdom. Garbh lost his position because he stood up to dance with me even though I was in trouble with the prince. I know Archu was hoping to help him in some way, and it seems he's done just that. Garbh will be an asset to the Swan Island team. I'll ask Archu about it when I see him. After one of the quietest meals I've ever had, Dau and I bid Illann good night and return to our quarters with Justice following in our steps.

The other party is still in the house, but once we're in our own quarters we're shut off from everything. We close the ante-room door behind us. I could sleep in there, with Dau in the main chamber. But I want to share that big bed and watch the flickering light from the hearth playing across his skin and glinting on his bright hair, and I want to feel his hands on my body and his mouth on mine and . . . My mother gave me instructions when I left home, the sort of instructions a wise woman gives her adventurous daughter, and I can't forget

them. I've seen too many women destroyed by childbearing.
I've seen too many brought low by men's careless use of them
and men's ignorance of the true cost. A babe a year until you
die of it. Too bad if a woman wants something else. Too bad if
she has something different to give. Courage, strength, a bright
sword. A voice for justice.

"Maybe I should sleep in there," I hear myself say as I glance
back toward the anteroom.

"Don't," says Dau. "Please." In his voice is an echo of the
Dau who waited in this very chamber, blind and in pain, to be
told he had no choice but to return to the home he loathed and
the family he feared. Just possibly, the man who once struck
me as arrogance personified is not sure he's worthy of love.
When I don't say anything, he spreads out his cloak in a corner
and encourages Justice to settle down on it. Lays an old blanket
over the dog. Makes sure someone has left the dish of water he
asked for earlier. Then turns and looks at me in the lamplight.
There's no mask on his face, no trace of pretense. He trusts me.
He wants me. He loves me.

"I'll stay." I clear my throat and go on. "Only . . . you need
to understand, I have no intention of . . . of settling down. I'd
be a terrible mother. And I have other things to do."

I see that Dau is shocked. Has he not considered that certain
activities often lead to the birth of children? Do I really have to
explain this to him?

"Come here, Liobhan," he says, reaching out a hand. I move
forward despite myself and feel his arms around me, warm and
strong. "There are lots of ways we can give each other pleasure
without that risk. You think I'd expect any woman to want me
as the father of her children? With a family like mine?"

"Oh, but I didn't mean—that wasn't at all what I—" I make
myself breathe slowly, which is not easy with his hands moving

against my body. "Dau, you're talking nonsense. What about your patience and kindness with Justice? You would make an excellent father. Just the kind of father you needed yourself when you were young." My treacherous mind shows me an image of the handsome children Dau and I might produce together. I will it away.

"Like your father," Dau says against my hair.

"Nobody's like my father. You'd be different, but just as good."

It's quiet for a while then, as we touch and kiss and fail to keep our breathing steady. Then Dau says, "Shall we try, then? The pleasure without the risk? Might take a little of the Swan Island warrior's self-restraint. But I think we can do it."

"Mm." Some other time I will tell Dau what my mother taught me about the moon-cycle and at what times one might be less likely to conceive a child. That method is not exactly foolproof and nor are some other possibilities she shared with me. I have a feeling they will come in useful, all the same. But not now, while we remove each other's clothing and lie down together and use hands and lips and tongues to give each other the most excellent pleasure, all the better for the long wait. It's not possible to stay silent, and at one point Justice lifts his head and whines. Dau gasps, "Good boy, Justice," and the dog settles back onto the cloak.

When we're done—for now—we lie in each other's arms, listening to the dog's slow breathing.

"I'm not sure if I want to laugh or cry," I murmur. My hand is warm over Dau's heart, which beats steadily if somewhat more quickly than usual. "What will we do when we get there? Pretend everything's as it was before we left? Meet in dark corners when nobody's around? Or make a grand announcement? Illann will probably tell them anyway."

"They'll know the moment they see us," says Dau, brushing my hair back from my brow with gentle fingers. "Let's not plan now. Let's just lie here and go to sleep. And when we get there we'll make the impossible happen. Isn't that what Swan Island warriors do?"

52

BROCC

I'm afraid," Eirne says. "Afraid of bearing a child, afraid of raising a child. How can one person be a mother and a queen, and do both well?"

My heart turns over. "We will help you," I say quietly, stroking my wife's silken hair as we lie in each other's arms, in the shelter of her retreat. It is dark of the moon, and outside all is hushed. Eirne's strange lamp spreads a golden glow across the leafy chamber. "All of us. I will do my share. A child has two parents."

"I had two, briefly. They taught me nothing at all. Most certainly nothing of love."

"Your people love you, Eirne. I love you." I wish Liobhan was here. If anyone can convey a message of hope, it is my sister. But she is probably the last person Eirne would want to advise her.

"It's not enough."

There is such sadness in her voice. I fear for her. I fear for our unborn child, whose movements can now be felt within Eirne's belly—what magic, our babe is already learning to dance! When we came back from Oakhill, when we told Eirne what had happened there—to Liobhan, to Dau, to True and me—she showed no anger. But as she listened a profound stillness came over her. It was as if she withdrew deep inside herself. Even when True spoke of the healing drops and how he had chosen to use them, she held that disturbing calm. And when she gave me the news of our child—no news to me, since Liobhan had guessed it—she did so with quiet detachment, as if none of it really mattered. Tonight is different. Now she's telling me the truth.

"You fear the Crow Folk. We will do our best to protect you, to protect the child, to keep the whole community safe. Trust me, Eirne, please. I am learning more about them. We will find a solution."

There's a long silence then. Eirne stares up at the ceiling, but I think she sees something quite different, something that darkens her eyes and tightens her jaw.

"What if I don't love the baby?" she asks. "What if I can't feed it? What if birthing it kills me?"

It's as well she is not looking at me. I cannot mask my unease. It's a struggle to keep my voice bright and confident. "You're young and healthy. Surely all will be well. Why not talk to Mistress Juniper? As a wisewoman, she will have answers to all your questions. She must have helped birth many babes."

"How can you know that, Brocc?"

"My mother is a wisewoman. I could not grow up in her house without learning such things. I'm sure there's nothing to worry about." I do not speak of the times when my mother returned home red-eyed and exhausted from a childbed that had gone awry. I do not tell Eirne that I, too, have my fears, not only of the birth itself but of the years to follow. Hard as it is to admit, even to myself, I am not sure I want our child to be raised in the Otherworld. That child will be as much human as I am. As Eirne is. It will bear equal parts of human and fey blood. As such, it might be brought up in either world. Each

world holds its share of risks, its share of opportunities. I was
brought to the human world as an infant, too young to remember anything but the safe, loving household in which I was
raised. In bringing me to Winterfalls, Conmael did me a great
service. Eirne was snatched from the human world as a small
girl and left in the Otherworld with fey folk entirely strange to
her. It is no wonder she now has such fears. What our child
needs is to be born into love, raised in love, taught hope and
wisdom and strength. It needs the sort of upbringing I had. I
am my mother's son. I am my father's son. I must ensure this
happens. "We can do this, Eirne," I say. "Remember how Gentle-
Foot was with her little one when it was newly born? That
sweetness, that tenderness? That fierce wish to protect? The
moment you set eyes on our child you will feel the same."

Eirne sighs. "You sound so sure, Brocc. I am full of doubt.
Full of fear. Surely a queen should not doubt herself."

"I don't doubt you, Eirne. You will be a fine mother. But . . ."

She sits up abruptly, shaking off my arm. "But what?"

"It's all right to feel sad sometimes," I tell her. "It's all right
to weep. It's all right to worry. If you can, just let it pass. The
sun will rise again tomorrow. You will still be surrounded by
love and hope and music, my queen. We will share your bur-
dens. We will tread the path with you, whatever it brings. You
won't be left on your own. I promise."

Eirne lies down again, her head on my shoulder, her arm
across my chest. She presses close against me, like a child seeking warmth. Gradually her breathing slows, her eyelids close,
and she is asleep.

I am wide awake. I hear my own words in my mind, confident, sure, strong. I wish that was all I felt. I wish I was like
Liobhan, whose strength and hope are always with her, even
in the darkest times. It is just as well I have been robbed of my
singing voice until after the child is born. Every bright tune

would be underlain with darkness; every sweet song would have its shadows. Every comic ditty would bear a sting in the tail. Deep down within me, there is doubt. There is fear—for my wife, for my child, for my clan. And something more, something I could not confess to anyone. Seeing Liobhan again opened my eyes. And my heart is riven, torn between that world and this. Between that family and this.

I lay my hand gently against Eirne's belly, where the small swell of our unborn child is now quite visible. *Little one. My son. My daughter. What path will you tread? All around are thorns, monsters, shadows. Oh, how can I keep you safe?*

I draw a deep breath and whisper into the stillness of the lamplit chamber. "I will be the father you need. I will be strong, wise, and good like the father who raised me. This I swear with heart and spirit, forever and always."

ACKNOWLEDGMENTS

This book could not have come to fruition without the assistance of many people along the way. Heartfelt thanks to the team at Pan Macmillan Australia: Claire Craig for continuing to support my work through the ups and downs, Brianne Collins for her insightful editing, and Julia Stiles for the meticulous copyedit. A big thank-you also to the US team at Penguin Random House: Anne Sowards, Miranda Hill, and the copyediting staff, for a thorough and thoughtful job.

To my agent, Russell Galen, and the team at Scovil Galen Ghosh Literary Agency, thank you for your excellent work on my behalf and your ongoing support. Gratitude to Mélanie Delon for another amazing cover.

Special thanks to friend and fellow writer Aiki Flinthart, author of *Fight Like a Girl*, for her invaluable assistance with fight scenes.

Photo by Sean Middleton

Juliet Marillier was born and educated in Dunedin, New Zealand, a town with strong Scottish roots. She has had a varied career that includes teaching and performing music. Juliet now lives in a historic cottage in Perth, Western Australia, where she writes full-time. She is a member of the druid order OBOD. When not writing, Juliet looks after her small crew of rescue dogs. She is the author of the Blackthorn & Grim novels, including *Den of Wolves* and *Tower of Thorns*, and the Sevenwaters series. Juliet's historical fantasy novels and short stories are published internationally and have won numerous awards.

CONNECT ONLINE

JulietMarillier.com
 Juliet.Marillier

Ready to find
your next great read?

Let us help.

Visit prh.com/nextread

Penguin
Random
House